"I want to possess ye, *Leannán*"

He murmured against her lips . . . "I want to make ye mine as no other man will ever be able to do."

Annora's head was spinning. The dreams and fantasies had come to this, and she did not stop to wonder at the right or wrong of it. Her body quivered . . .

CRITICAL ACCLAIM FOR NANCY RICHARDS-AKERS

The Heart and the Heather

"Storytelling is an art and Ms. A̶̶̶̶̶̶̶̶̶̶̶̶̶̶̶̶̶̶̶̶̶̶̶̶̶̶̶̶s exceptional ̶̶̶̶̶̶̶̶̶̶̶̶̶̶̶̶̶̶̶̶̶"

The H̶̶̶̶

"The book sings ̶̶̶̶̶̶̶̶̶̶̶̶̶̶̶̶̶̶̶̶̶̶̶̶̶̶̶̶̶."

̶̶̶̶̶̶A̶̶̶̶

"Soul-stirring"
Romantic Times

The Heart and the Holly

"Spectacular characters, searing sensuality, and alluring history"
Rendezvous

"A shimmering story that will live and breathe within your heart."
Romantic Times

Other **AVON ROMANCES**

WILD IRISH SKIES

NANCY RICHARDS-AKERS

AVON BOOKS ◆ NEW YORK

AVON BOOKS
A division of
The Hearst Corporation
1350 Avenue of the Americas
New York, New York 10019

Copyright © 1997 by Nancy Richards-Akers
Inside cover author photo by Tom Wolff
Published by arrangement with the author
Visit our website at **http://AvonBooks.com**
Library of Congress Catalog Card Number: 96-95490
ISBN: 0-380-78948-5

First Avon Books Printing: June 1997

AVON TRADEMARK REG. U.S. PAT. OFF. AND IN OTHER COUNTRIES, MARCA REGISTRADA, HECHO EN U.S.A.

Printed in the U.S.A.

WCD   10 9 8 7 6 5 4 3 2 1

To all who would seek the truth, and strive to make it heard, for they will be as angels, and the fluttering of many wings will not be ignored.

Ceol na naingeal, tugamoid no tugan aire do.
The music of the angels, let us give heed to it.

Acknowledgments

"To conceal the Truth of History is the blackest of infamies."

Irish, Unattributed

Once again, I am indebted to the archaeological, historical, and scholarly materials contained in *Wicklow: History and Society,* Editors, Ken Hannigan and William Nolan, Geography Publications, Templeogue, Dublin, 1994.

I wish to extend my gratitude to James Lydon, Professor Emeritus, Department of Medieval History, Trinity College; William Nolan, Lecturer in Geography, University College Dublin; Mary Kelly Quinn, Department of Botany, University College, Dublin; Professor Alfred P. Smyth, Master, Keynes College, University of Kent at Canterbury; and to the staff of the Irish Book Store in New York City, especially Denise.

To every scholar, librarian, historian, lecturer, professor, and archivist who graciously and generously offered me advice, leads, theories, and all manner of assistance in my quest to uncover the historical record of what happened in the Wicklow Mountains in the summer of 1399.

And lastly, posthumous recognition is due Jean Creton, a Frenchman who accompanied Richard II to Ireland in 1399, and whose chronicles and color illustrations of that campaign preserve the only known eyewitness account of a drama nearly forgotten by history; and to Thomas D'Arcy M'Gee, author of *A*

Memoir of A. M. MacMurrough (James Duffey and Sons, Dublin, 1886), who wrote the following on English historians:

" . . . of whom it is hard to say which is the most ignorant of the facts, or the most illiberal in their judgment. Ignorance of the actions of men, even remotely connected with their subject is censurable in historians; but when, unknowing facts, they dogmatically lay down suppositions in their place, making up in assurance what they fall short of in research, there is no condemnation too heavy for their offense. History is only valuable for its truth, its equity, and its retributions."

Author's Note

For readers of *The Heart and the Holly,* I beg your indulgence regarding the repetition of these notes.

The geographic boundaries of County Wicklow, Ireland did not exist in the fourteenth century. Wicklow was not shired until 1606, and until then was administered as a part of Dublin. In medieval Ireland, Wicklow and its mountains were—as they had been for more than a thousand years—part of the province of Leinster, and what one called Wicklow depended in part upon one's race.

If one was Anglo-Norman/English, and living in Dublin with a view of the shadowy peaks to the south, one might have called them the Dublin Hills. The native Irish, on the other hand, did not have a common name for the glens, blanket bogs, and granite peaks, and it is believed they referred only to specific mountains or vales, streams, woodlands, or lakes by name.

Herein I exercise an author's prerogative and use the term *Wicklow* because it is a point of reference readers can locate on modern maps.

As for my use of Irish—a remarkably sensual and lilting tongue despite the spelling—it may seem archaic to those familiar with the language spoken in Ireland today. Owing to the historical context of this story, I relied upon *Introduction to the Irish Language,* Reverend William Neilson, P. Wogan, Dublin, 1808; *The Metrical Dindshenchas: Text, Translation and Commentary, Vols. 1–5*, Edward Gwynn, Royal Irish Academy, Dublin, 1903; and *Early Irish Lyrics, Eight to Twelfth Century, Translation, Notes and Glossary*, Gerard Murphy, Oxford University Press, London, 1956.

Prologue

Dublin Castle
May's end, 1399

Rian O'Byrne was a condemned man. There had been no trial. No one had been called in his defense, only English witnesses had gone before the king's priest, who had passed the sentence. The prisoner was Irish and within the walls of English Dublin. That alone was sufficient evidence to be declared both murderer and spy, and by this time on the morrow, his head would be mounted on a pike above Nicholas Gate.

The chamber in which he waited was dank and fetid, and more hole than chamber. A narrow vein of light seeped through a chink in the masonry, and staring into the blackness above him, Rian watched that thin silver line fade to nothingness. His last day, indeed, his last sunset were finished ere they'd begun. This was not the spectacular blaze he'd imagined would herald his closing hours. As a young warrior, it had amused him to picture death as a magnificent golden chariot racing out of the heavens amidst a brilliant flash of lightning and the blare of horns; in reality, death would be an Englishman reeking of sour ale, bloated with indigestion and wielding an ax.

1

Death didn't affright Rian O'Byrne. He believed in neither heaven nor hell and had no dread of the afterlife, if there truly was such a realm. He'd been a rogue who'd cared for no one and nothing. He had been neither good nor heroic. Indeed, he'd never done anything if there hadn't been some pleasure or amusement for him, yet that did not stop him from fancying that when it was time to shed his mortal bonds he would journey in that chariot over the waves to Tir na n-Og.

The door opened. Rian heard booted footfall but could not turn fast enough to see who entered.

"Irish cur," a soldier cursed. His foot made contact with Rian's chest. Someone laughed.

"Is mairge a dheanadh subhachas ri duchachas fir eile!" Rian growled. *Woe be to him who makes mirth of another man's woe.* He had a little energy, and too much boldness. "May yer death be long and painful, and where ever ye fall *air an leadairt le geur-lainn, luidh an sín gus an grod thú,"* he condemned him to hell on earth. *Mangled with sharp swords, may ye be lying there till ye rot.*

A hand grabbed a length of Rian's hair and gave a violent jerk.

"On your feet, you murdering bastard."

There were two soldiers, each took one of Rian's arms to yank him upright.

Rian staggered. There was a spasm in his side, and a sensation of pressure where they had pummeled his ribs. His back was afire with the pain of their floggings, yet in spite of this abuse, despite the manacles at his wrists and leg irons at his ankles, Rian maintained his balance. Even slightly hunched, Rian towered over his gaolers, and when he stood as straight as he might, he didn't miss the alarm in their eyes. It brought a momentary smile to his face, and giving his manacles a shake, he emitted a low, feral snarl.

The soldiers shrank back, and fearing to touch the prisoner, they used their daggers to prod him out of the musty hole. The Irishman was a giant. A beast that needed to be broken. To look at him—filthy hair hanging below massive shoulders, features contorted into a grotesque inhuman mask, and still standing after the beatings and floggings they'd dealt him—was certain evidence this creature was no mere mortal but a minion of evil, mayhap of Satan himself.

"Through the door. Out you go," one of the soldiers ordered, taking care not to look into the Irishman's eyes, nor to get close enough that the savage's breath might touch him, lest he fall under some dark spell that might cause his pryvete-parts to shrivel and cease working.

Rian went outside and did not wonder at their purpose. His thoughts were elsewhere as they had been much of this day. In the dark, close fastness of his mind, there was an angel with blue eyes and hair that spun like a halo round a pretty face, and when that specter passed he bethought himself of the worldly delights he might miss come death. Would there be wilderness abounding with stag and blackbird, fox, stoat, and boar after the executioner was done? Would there be feasting and fighting, and fleet horses for him ever again? Speckled salmon the size of otter? The music of the wind in the great greenery of oaks? Honey, whortleberries, and heathpease? And what of wine, swiftly served, fair-haired maidens and wanton women, slowly taken? Again he saw that pretty face, that halo bright.

The soldiers delivered Rian to one of the gate towers, where an officer escorted him up narrow winding stairs. As they ascended, Rian kept his gaze down. He watched his bare feet moving at the end of blood-streaked legs. The timeworn stone was cool, smooth. Those feet didn't look like they belonged to him. He heard a knock, the sound of a door opening.

"You have the prisoner?" this from a man with an older voice, who spoke as if he held some position of authority.

"Aye, my lord, the Irish spy is here."

Rian entered the chamber.

"Raise your head, man," said the authority. "You, prisoner! Raise your head, if you please. Can you not hear me?"

Rian complied, and saw a man of perhaps five or six decades, dressed as a knight at his leisure. Indeed, the Englishman was known to Rian. He was Sir Thomas Picot, the Lord High Justiciar's liege man, and commander of Dublin Castle, and while Rian recognized Sir Thomas, he was not surprised the older man gave no hint of ever having set eyes upon him. It had been many years since Rian had feasted at the English king's high table, and he bore no resemblance to the fine warrior of long ago. No doubt he already had the appearance of a corpse. His hair was matted with grime, his body was swollen and bruised, and the smell of him had to be worse than a dung heap.

"You have been brought here in order that I—" The man's voice caught, and he stared at Rian. Palms planted upon the table, he leaned forward and stared. His features revealed nothing of his thoughts. At length, he addressed the officer, "That will be all for now. You need not stay. I shall call for an escort when I'm done questioning this man."

The officer left. A latch settling in place was the loudest noise in the chamber as Sir Thomas came toward Rian and spoke in a voice that was no more than a whisper.

"It looks to me as if you should sit down, O'Byrne. Please, won't you come over this way . . ." He pointed to a bench near one of the windows.

Rian heard Sir Thomas call him by name, and for the space of a heartbeat, he imagined endless wilderness and fleet horses, the great greenery of oaks, plentiful wine, and fair maidens. For an instant, he imagined something beyond tomorrow dawn, and the executioner's block. "I was not certain whether ye knew who I was, sir. It's been many years."

"Not so long that I've forgotten such a fine traveling companion as yourself, nor could I ever forget the man who saved my niece's life." Sir Thomas slipped a hand beneath Rian's arm as if to guide him to the bench. "They've been harsh with you?"

"Not bad for a condemned man." The bench was before an open window, and once seated, Rian shut his eyes. The evening breeze soothed his battered flesh in bittersweet solace. He must not get too comfortable.

"I may be able to change that." Sir Thomas set a drinking horn between Rian's manacled hands. "This need not be your final night."

Rian's eyes opened. His regard narrowed to skeptical as he sipped from the drinking horn, and then in a voice muted to match Sir Thomas's whisper, he said, "Why do I think 'tis not as easy as ye make it sound?"

"Nothing ever is. Verily, to dare speak of this poses a great risk to the parties involved. Should I go on?"

Rian understood. He nodded for Sir Thomas to continue. No one would ever know of this conversation from his lips.

"You, of course, remember my niece."

"Aye." That, too, had been in a time before, yet Rian remembered. So long ago that she must surely be wed by now, a mother several times over, and certainly owning little, if any, remembrance of him.

"Once before you saved her life," said Sir Thomas, although Rian did not have to be reminded of that. "Now I ask that you do the same again. She must needs leave Dublin this very night, and while I could not adequately repay you before, this time I can offer your life in exchange for taking her out of danger's way."

The prospect of cheating death ignited a thrumming sensation through Rian's body. "Ye'll be releasing me to escort yer niece out of town?"

"Nay, I cannot release you, but I can allow your escape, following which you must kidnap her, or at least create the appearance that she was taken against her will, and that she was injured, mayhap fatally, in the process."

"That is all?"

"My niece must be on the other side of the town wall by midnight, out of the fringes by dawn and at Wicklow harbor within four days."

Rian responded with a low whistle of disbelief at this nearly impossible task that Sir Thomas spoke of as if it were no more daunting than churning butter into cheese. Inside him, the thrumming intensified. It was energetic, positive, and stronger than the pain. He would accept any proposition if it offered the possibility of keeping his head affixed to his shoulders beyond tomorrow. "And if she's not there in four days?"

"The entire exercise will have been for naught. If you fail, you'll be hunted down, and upon your apprehension, I'll deny any knowledge of this discussion. Get my niece to Wicklow, and your freedom is guaranteed. Plus there will be silver for you at the harbor."

"Why do ye do this?"

"It is as I told you, my niece faces grave jeopardy. I had intended this night to find a man desperate enough to do my bidding, and it would appear Fate and Fortune look down upon the both of us with Favor. It is nothing less than a miracle that the moon and stars would align to cross our paths at this particular moment in time. As for the unusual, if not drastic, measures I employ, if there were any other solution, it would already have been pursued. This, however, is the only way to save my niece."

And the only way for me. Rian drained the wine from the horn vessel. "I will do it, Sir Thomas, and 'tis a pledge on my very life I give to ye that I'll be seeing yer niece safely to her journey's end.''

''Very well said, Rian O'Byrne. Very well said. 'Tis an unholy bargain we strike this night, but you must know it is a good and right thing you do. Tomorrow was not meant to be your judgment, but when that day comes, there will be a place in heaven for you. Of that I'm certain.''

Two or three days ago such earnest sentiments would have prompted Rian to laugh in Sir Thomas's face. Now he said nothing. Mayhap it was true, and he was being given much more than a reprieve from the executioner.

Mayhap Rian O'Byrne the condemned, the forsaken, was being given a second chance.

Part One

Chapter 1

Five years before
Year's end, 1394

"Come, my honeyed-lassie, spread yer boughs a-wide for me."

Someone had been overgenerous with his ale this night, for the voice that rose in song was slurred, and it echoed along a deserted Dublin quay, magnified by the midnight black waters of the Liffey.

"Laddie-cock's a-waiting long for thee, long for thee. With a down derrie derrie, and a rose-red mouth, and a hey-nonny-nonny nonnie."

A dog began to bark. Another howled. Up the steep hill that was Fishamble Street, a man yelled for silence. A spew of curses followed, and in a tower high above the tangle of narrow lanes, Annora Picot tossed and turned beneath a mound of fox and marten pelts.

It was a nasty dream. *Laddie-cock,* indeed. Annora buried her head beneath a plump pillow in an effort to banish the vulgar lyrics. Although, sooth to say, it came as no surprise that her mind might wander along the way of twenty devils to conjure up something so carnal. Much better to focus upon the Epiphany Eve feast to be held eight days henceforth. What was wrong with her that she

11

was not hearing the monks singing the *Alleluia Psallat* or, at the very least, banqueters joining in the refrain of a more frolicsome melody? A seamstress was coming on the morrow to fit her gown for the feast, and she should dream of that, her drowsy conscience scolded.

"We are invited to attend King Richard's banquet," her mother had informed Annora on Christmas morn. Along with an invitation bearing the royal seal, Catherine had given her daughter a small oblong package wrapped in silk and tied with a length of velvet cord. Inside had been an eye mask of deep blue velvet with a celestial design of stars and moons stitched with gold and silver threads; seed pearls were sewn to the center of each tiny star. As was tradition, guests would wear eye masks on Epiphany Eve, and Catherine was determined that her daughter would be the most notable woman at the king's high table.

The widow Picot and her daughter were prominent citizens of Dublin, the widow being one of Ireland's most prosperous wool merchants, and no expense would be spared on their gowns and headdresses. Catherine had suggested to her daughter that this feast was the perfect opportunity for Annora to find a suitable husband among the earls and barons who had accompanied his majesty to Ireland.

Before it is too late, Catherine had added for emphasis, worrying aloud as she often did about her daughter's future.

At six-and-twenty, Annora remained unwed. This was not, however, for lack of suitors. It was her choice, having rejected proposals from the most eligible Anglo-Norman earls as well as an assortment of knights, merchants, and foreign dignitaries. Annora was not unhappy. In faith, she was quite content. Her life was a good one; exceptional, in truth, and envied by many. Sooth, there were those who whispered Annora Picot had been blessed by the faeries. How else could it be that a widow's only child enjoyed such a charmed life? Annora was beautiful of face and form but without a shred of vanity; she was financially independent but kind of heart, gentle of soul, clever, and generous; and residing like a princess royal in one of the more impressive towers situated along the wall that enclosed Dublin town. As her name, derived from the Latin *honor,* implied, Annora Picot was a paragon of reputation and beauty, of whom never an unfavorable word had been uttered.

Faeries or not, there was nothing Annora desired or needed that any suitor of her experience could offer. Verily, the prospect of marriage was unthinkable. Annora would rather perish before surrendering her wealth to some man, who would never appreciate the toil from whence that fortune had flourished. She could imagine no enticement that might make her abandon her mother to move away from Dublin to some remote and desolate fortress. There was nothing that could convince her to give up her role in their business. All in all, Annora liked the comforts of her tower, the companionship of her mother, and the challenges of their wool exporting enterprise.

There was naught to gain in wedding herself to any man, especially one who bored her to tears. Her friends from her youth, now wed, with children of their own, often gossiped of romance and its attendant pleasures of the flesh, but Annora knew nothing of such things. William Piers, Knight, had reeked of the stable yard; Alexander de Bickner had made no secret of his need for money to repair his castle; likewise the alderman, Thomas Ware, of yellow teeth and breath like the mouth of Hell, had been preoccupied with her profits, and demonstrated no romantic sensibilities; and as for Sir Henry de Hay, a gentleman of passable good looks and commendable cleanliness, he had demeaned himself in her eyes by talking of little but his diplomatic aspirations. The roll of clumsy, sweaty-palmed, and offensive suitors was endless, and in Annora's opinion, the gentlemen in the king's entourage could not be any better.

Still she would attend the feast, and the reason why, she had told her mother, was an entirely straightforward one. Simply, she liked to dance and appreciated fine entertainment, and this feast was certainly to be the finest she would ever experience. Richard of Bordeaux, the first English monarch to visit Ireland in more than 150 years, was a lavish host, and the Epiphany feast would be his most spectacular event since landing at Waterford in early October. Indeed, the extravagance of this young king preceded him. Everyone who was anyone in Anglo-Norman Ireland would be there, eager to enjoy the minstrelsy and dancing, the abundance of food, the mummers and jongleurs, and most especially the gifts that his majesty would—as was his generous practice—dispense.

There was, however, something more that intrigued Annora. Something that was not simple to explain to her mother. Indeed, it was something quite unspeakable, for it went contrary to the laws of Parliament. Something about which no one would imagine the dutiful, obedient, and poised Annora Picot would daydream.

Her mind was teeming with visions of the natives who lived in the mountains to the south of Dublin. It was rumored that some of the Irish chieftains had been invited to the feast, and while Annora breathed not a word of these privy thoughts to a soul, she couldn't dispel her fascination at the prospect of seeing the warriors, perhaps even sitting beside one of them. *She was waiting for that. For the wild Irish.* And she had been dreaming of bare chests, muscled arms and thighs, and a tangle of unruly hair that flowed over battle-scarred shoulders.

No wonder her mind had summoned up such a vile ditty. She buried her head deeper beneath the pillow. If her mother ever knew what a depraved creature she was at heart, Catherine would be disappointed, not only in

Annora, but in herself for having failed to rear a re-
strained and chaste child. Not to mention her mother's
certain apprehension because her daughter's fantasies
involved Irish warriors. Annora could not bear to cause
her mother a moment's self-doubt. She would never allow
such a thing, and must needs strive to overcome this
weakness. She must needs banish every impure thought
from her mind.

*"Hey nonny nonny nonnie, spread yer boughs a-wide
for me. Laddie-cock's a-waiting long for thee, long for
thee."*

Another loud, off-key voice joined the first. A woman
joined in for a few phrases, then broke off to laugh, low
and sultry.

Annora opened her eyes and poked her head out from
beneath the pillow. The night air in her chamber was
frigid. This was no dream. Perchance her soul was not
wicked after all.

The drunken wassailers must be some of the thousands
of English soldiers who were passing this winter in
Dublin. Indeed, by the increasing racket it could very
well be an entire squadron making merry beneath her
window. It was long past curfew hour, and if the offensive
noise had roused her, it was sure to disturb her frail
mother, who slept in the chamber above hers. She must
put a stop to it forthwith.

Parting the bed-curtains, Annora slid from beneath the
covers, and dragging one of the larger furs about her
shoulders, she padded across a floor strewn not with
rushes, as was the usual practice in most households, but
with more pelts. It was richly endowed with worldly
goods, this bedchamber belonging to the charmed Annora
Picot, for there were only a handful of others in all of
Ireland who could boast of having more than one fireplace
set into their lodging walls, not to mention tapestries
from Paris to keep out the wind, mattresses plump with
eiderdown, sachets of bergamot and cloves stitched to the

bed-curtains to sweeten the air, an excess of our lady's bedstraw beneath the mattress to ward off fleas, plus reflecting mirrors from Venice, and massive furnishings suited for the Holy Roman Emperor, carved with whimsical winged beasts and polished with sandalwood oil.

Upon reaching the window recess, Annora first opened the frame in which small rounds of pale green glass had been secured with lead, then she unlatched the wooden shutter and pushed the casement outward. The wind off the Liffey was sharp and damp, blowing loops of pale golden hair about her face. She caught her breath, then exhaled, a trail of clouds forming a second halo about her head, and resting her palms on the ledge, Annora bent forward to get a better look below.

There were four persons, three men and a woman standing within the arc of torchlight at the base of the tower. Two of the men were English soldiers. She could tell by the way they wore their hair, cropped bluntly along the jaw, and by their plain garb that was seen about Dublin these days, coarse colorless tunics over leggings sorely in need of mending, and no more than a thin blanket for protection from the elements. While King Richard's army, a host nearly twice as great as Richard the Crusader had led on the plains of Vevelay, was impressive in its size—30,000 foot, plus 4,000 mounted soldiers was the precise count—there was nothing to commend its conduct or appearance. The English soldiers were inadequately outfitted, poorly fed, meanly housed, and when they were not embarked upon military expeditions outside Dublin, they passed their time whoring and drinking with such abandon that the city was, at times, all to naught, being little more than one large brothel.

The third man, whose arm was wrapped around the woman, was taller than the others. Indeed, he was a giant of a man, everything about him being imposing. And he was no English soldier. A patchwork of furs hung across one shoulder, his legs were bare under a baggy, knee-length tunic, clumsy-looking boots were laced to his calves, and beneath the torchlight, his long hair held the sheen of burnished wheat in a summer field. Annora's breath caught. He was a fascinating sight, and she leaned out as far she might but still could not see his face. She imagined his features. They would be rugged and sharply defined. He would have high cheekbones, deep-set, probing eyes, a full, sensual mouth that could ravage a woman, and there would be a scar. Assuredly, there would be a scar upon those savage features, she fancied. Aye, as surely as he was *one of them*, one of *the wild Irish*, there would be a puckered line cutting across his brow—perhaps lying at a slant beneath one eye, or mayhap at the corner of that hungry mouth.

As the men sang, they passed a leather bottle between them, and after they had each imbibed long and deep, the woman went into that man's embrace for a kiss. But it was no ordinary kiss, no quick embrace. There were groping hands, rucked skirts, entwined limbs, swaying, melded torsos, and throaty noises that Annora could hear all the way at her tower perch. Annora stared. She had never seen such a kiss, and certainly, she had never experienced such a kiss as that. But her overactive imagination had evoked such things, and she closed her eyes, entertaining visions of a bare chest, a sensual yet masculine mouth, and hair that flowed over battle-scarred shoulders. Her lips parted, one fingertip rose to touch them, and hearing the woman laugh, she raised her eyelids.

The tawny-haired giant was looking at her, a knowing, lopsided grin turning up at the edges of a mouth that was full and wide. Her heart lurched in her chest. A small whispered, "Ooh," escaped her, and her hand fell away from her mouth. She returned his stare. The woman and soldiers were moving on, but the large man beneath Annora's window didn't follow. Instead he swept her an improbable bow, low and courtly, perhaps mocking, although she was not certain until he began to sing.

"Hey-nonny-nonny nonnie, spread yer boughs a-wide for me. Laddie-cock's a-waiting long for thee, long for thee."

With a jerk Annora flung herself away from the window. She flattened her back to the interior wall of the tower, breathing hard at the audacity of the man who would sing such words to her, and flushed with awareness of the enticing rasp in his voice. Angling her head to one side, her flaming cheeks cooled against the stone, but there was no cure for the pounding of her heart. She clutched the fur about her, took several deep breaths, and listened. There was no more noise. Not a sound. No rasping voice raised in song, no laughter, and when, at last, she dared to peer outside once more, the lane was empty.

He was gone, but not her wayward thoughts. They lingered. As the old year waned and December turned to January, Annora's dreams were haunted by imaginings of a dark glen in the distant mountains. Every night thereafter, her sleep was troubled by the memory of an Irishman, tall, smiling boldly, and by the sensation of lying down in a field of wheat to feel the summer wind upon her bare skin.

Chapter 2

"It would be wisest, I think, to wait until one of the apprentices can escort you, daughter," Catherine said.

Annora had come to bid farewell to her mother ere she hastened on an errand. Catherine was sitting by a window, reading. The sunshine was bright this day in early January, and her chamber was warm despite the newfallen snow that had drifted against the window in the night.

Catherine set the small leather-bound collection of verses upon her lap. "I would much rather you did not venture outside the town walls alone."

"'Tis many times I have made the trip to the convent on my own. The distance is not far, the weather is fine this day, and I promise to be back before dusk." Annora gave a reassuring smile. She leaned down to kiss her mother on the brow, then straightened to secure the hood of her cloak.

Every fortnight she visited the Convent of Our Lady of Victory, which was located outside the walled town on a parcel of land overlooking the sea. Annora was the convent's most substantial benefactress, making Our Lady of Victory an uncommon haven from hardship and misfortune. But it was not gifts alone that accounted for the security and comfort of the women who resided

within the confines of the holy house. The community of
Our Lady of Victory was comprised not only of holy
sisters and novices, but an assortment of orphans, widows, abandoned wives, the infirm, disfigured and simple-
minded, and even an occasional harlot or other female
who had sinned. Women, born into diffcrent lives, who
were now an odd sort of extended family that toiled to a
single purpose. Trained by the nuns as spinners, carders,
washers, bleachers, and dyers, they transformed the raw
wool supplied by Annora into yarn that boasted a range of
colors more spectacular than any rainbow. This Irish yarn
was prized by the finest tapestry weavers in Europe, and
Annora sold the colored lengths of wool to merchants
from places such as Mainz and Genoa, Bruges and
Florence. The profits were split between Annora and the
convent.

"You should not worry, Mother. I will enjoy the walk.
Besides, are you not anxious to see how the migonette
and bilberry dyes have worked when combined with fresh
moss?" For several months they had been trying to
brighten the tone of their purple yarns, and at last,
Annora hoped they'd blended a dye to achieve the color
that was in high demand, which no other merchant had
been able to offer.

"As always, I am eager to learn the results of your
endeavors, and as always, I am certain it will be a
success. But are you not being impatient, Annora? There
is no particular need to go this day."

"Nor is there any need to put off until the morrow what
I can do now. Abbess Thomasin will be expecting me,
and I cannot tarry any longer if I intend to return before
nightfall. You must needs put a stop to your worrying."
Annora tried to maintain a smile. She did not like to
naysay her mother, nor did she like the grayish tinge upon
Catherine's complexion. Her mother had always been a
delicate woman, but this latest illness that had come upon
her shortly before All Hallow's was different than before.

No decoction of eyewort, nor infusion of angelica or hindberry mixed with wine had been able to restore the color to her cheeks; no tempting minted lamb with peppermint rice, no elderberry funnel cakes, nor Swithin cream had been able to increase her appetite and halt the withering of flesh upon her bones. Once Catherine Picot had been a beautiful woman, now she was small and gray and moved with a slowness that was visibly painful. Annora pushed a brazier as close to her mother as safety would allow. "Remember what I told you. Worrying is a fruitless waste of energy. You must rest so that you will be well enough to attend the Epiphany feast on the morrow."

"But the soldiers . . ." Catherine began to protest anew. "How can I not be anxious?"

"What about them?" Annora tucked a fur about her mother's legs. Although the chamber walls were curtained against drafts, Catherine could easily catch a chill.

"There are so many of them. And so unruly. So unpredictable."

"And their business is theirs, and mine is mine. Pray tell, how could English soldiers interfere with my visit to the convent? I am not a child to be misled."

"That is precisely my concern. You are no child, but a woman."

"I have always been safe." It did not need to be said that she had the protection of her uncle. Sir Thomas Picot was a knight by occupation, and having sworn fealty to the Lord High Justiciar, he had been assigned the command of Dublin Castle for many years. He was a powerful man, both respected and feared by friend as well as by foe. He was also the closest to a father Annora had ever known, her own father—Thomas's elder brother—having perished the summer she was born. As for Thomas, having no family of his own, Annora was as dear to the unwed knight as a child of his own flesh and blood could ever have been. When he'd been a young captain, Sir Thomas had proudly shown her off to the mayor and archbishop; he had held her before him on his saddle for many a ceremonial occasion; and since taking her first steps, Annora had been watched after by every soldier under his command. The streets of Dublin had always been safe for Sir Thomas Picot's niece.

"The town is different these days," said Catherine.

"And what might happen?"

"Oh, Annora, have I sheltered you too well?" Catherine raised pale hands in query. She glanced upward as if in search of heavenly response to her query. "Did I go too far in making certain no harm would ever come to you? My debt was profound, my intent only honorable. But did I go too far? Marry, how is it that you could ask such a question?"

Catherine often spoke as if she were the keeper of some secret. When Annora had been young, she had noticed this from time to time, and as the years had passed, she heard the tone more and more. It was in Catherine's voice this afternoon when she spoke of a debt, and as she had as a girl, Annora did not ask her mother what any of this meant. As always, she did not want to displease her mother, did not want to pry or upset her, and whenever Catherine spoke in this way, there was always the hint of distress. Long ago, Annora had resigned herself to never understanding.

"Nothing out of the ordinary will come to pass." Annora slipped her hands into woolen mittens. They were soft and dyed to match her blue cloak. It was one of the convent's special dyes called *Annora Blue*, for it matched the vibrant color of her eyes. "Upon my return I will bring you some fresh currant buns from Mistress Waddington. You would like that, would you not?"

Catherine gazed at her daughter with a smile of devotion before speaking. "You are too kind, my dear. You spoil me these days."

"As rightly I should. You have indulged me since the cradle, Mother, made me the envy of all Dublin, and now it is my turn to do the spoiling." At the chamber threshold, Annora blew a farewell kiss to her mother, then she was on her way.

Outside, the air was pungent with woodsmoke. There had not been a hard freeze on the Liffey this winter, and vessels clogged the river. The clang of riggings mingled with the cries of gulls, the jingle of harnesses, and the creaking of carts over icy cobbles. A fishmonger hawked a supply of salted herring, and church bells tolled the noon hour. The lanes were crowded with the usual assortment of well-dressed merchants, heavy purses hanging from their belts, servants attending to household errands, children chasing piglets, dogs chasing children, geese squawking, and ladies strolling in sedate pairs toward St. Michael and John's Church for Sext prayers. There were beggars lurking, soldiers loitering, lepers huddling in the shadows. Criers shouted out the news of a birth, a marriage, a house for sale.

"Good afternoon, Mistress Annora." A portly gentlemen garbed in a brilliant red houppeland bowed.

"Sir William"—Annora returned the greeting as Sir William de Geneval fell into step beside her—"Good afternoon."

"How is Mistress Catherine? She is recovering, I trust."

"My mother is better. I thank you, sir, for asking."

"Ah, full good. Full good. It would be a shame if Mistress Catherine were to miss the feast. I am told you are invited to the king's table."

"That is true. We have been so honored." Annora felt a slight flush rising upon her cheeks at this evidence that she and her mother had been the subject of some previous conversation. While she knew gossip was as common as it was unavoidable, she still did not like it. "I am off to

Our Lady of Victory, and regret that I must hurry. Good day, sir,'' she said, and then doubled her pace to put a good distance between herself and Sir William.

Beggars stepped aside. They did not extend a palm to Mistress Annora, for they knew there was always a crust of bread or an offering of porridge for those who knocked upon the Picot garden gate.

Annora smiled at one and all, but could not prevent a tiny frown at the unfamiliar faces. English soldiers were everywhere, more of them seeming to arrive each day. She held her cloak close and angled her face into the hood as she hurried past a group of men standing around an open fire. Normally, in this town of mostly wicker and timber buildings that burnt regularly, ordinances prohibiting open fires were strictly enforced. But who would dare to tell these hungry, poorly clothed men that they could not try to warm their hands any way they might?

Quickening her steps, Annora turned into Dame Street. The Church of St. Mary de Dam was within sight. She had almost reached the gate in the town's eastern wall when the door to one of Dublin's less reputable taverns was flung open, and enraged voices burst forth.

"Out with you!" a man roared. "My girls don't share their talents with savages."

"Picky whores, is it now?" came a second man's cocky reply, his accented voice giving way to a rumble of laughter. "Can it be they prefer louse-infested invaders?"

"Watch your tongue, you native scum!"

This was followed by something Annora couldn't discern. It sounded like an Irish curse. There was a low, feral bellow, and the thudding impact of a fist against flesh. Annora had heard enough fights on the quay to recognize what was happening. In the next instant a large man came hurtling through the door.

She tried to get out of the way, but couldn't move fast enough. The man slammed into her, and she cried out.

Annora was thrown against the wicker wall of the inn, her hood fell back, and her hair tumbled free from the tidy coils at her ears. Somehow she managed to maintain her balance while he collapsed in the ice and mud at her feet. She would have moved away, if she'd been able to do so, but the great hulk of a man lay upon her feet, and when he rolled onto one side, she watched in dismay as his hands gripped fast to her kirtle hem. There was a streak of blood across one knuckle. Clearly this was the man who had done the punching. She tried to pull her kirtle free, but he held tight to a fistful of fabric.

"Loose my gown, sir," she said with what she hoped was sufficient dignity and authority.

"'Tis my honeyed-lassie," the man in the mud drawled in accented English. There was a rough, male quality in his voice. "And she speaks to me. But why so harsh a tone?"

Annora's gaze darted from the large hand clutching her kirtle to his face, and her heart raced. It was the blond giant from beneath her window. Sorcery was at work. This Irishman was an almost exact replica of the rugged, angular vision of her imagination. This was no refined lordling, no pampered courtier, but a man who lived and fought hard. His features were uncompromising, with cheekbones that were high and as angular as was the line of his jaw. His mouth was full, slightly irreverent, definitely sensual. And his eyes. Oh, his eyes. Annora stared into the bluest eyes she had ever seen. They were the color of the sea with a touch of green, and she could not dispel a troubling vision of drowning—verily, of willingly surrendering to the water and letting the waves pull her down.

"*Come, my honey-lassie, spread yer—*" he started to sing.

"Silence. Have you no shame?" she admonished as she sent up a silent prayer that Sir William was not observing this scene. If anyone were to carry this tale to her mother, it might have a disastrous affect on her health. She must get away. "Look at you. If you could only see yourself. Tossed out in such a disgraceful manner from a—" She hesitated. "From a—a—"

His laughter cut her off. "And ye. Will ye not be looking at yerself now?"

"What about me?" Annora demanded, indignant. She was mad at him, mad at herself. What, pray tell, was she doing talking with him at all? She tugged at the kirtle hem, but he didn't seem to notice her efforts.

"What of yerself, the angel asks? Why, will ye not be looking at yerself and wondering at such a scowl of displeasure upon such a heavenly face? The face of an angel, 'twas what I was thinking when I saw ye in that tower window. But I've no recollection of an angel that glowers."

She yanked again at the kirtle, still to no avail.

"Aye, I'm remembering what I saw in the night. Indeed, fair lady, how could I be forgetting such a beautiful specter as yerself? An angel, ye were, with flaxen hair blowing in soft curls about yer pretty face. But now look at ye. All scowls and stern lines and not a shred of understanding for a man in need. Tell me, have ye never gone head over heels for love, fair lady?"

There was no doubt about it. He was brash. And wild. Everything that she dreamed of, all that was wayward in her mind. Everything she must needs deny. Her frown deepened, and she pursed her lips even tighter.

"Och, and ye'll be running me through to the bone with such looks, I'm thinking. Tell me, fair lady, is it murder ye're contemplating upon this poor body or merely permanent disfigurement?" His query held a teasing note.

There was that same lopsided grin she had seen staring up at her from beneath the torchlight. The knowing look wasn't there. But the wicked glint of amusement in those deep blue eyes was just as alarming. Mayhap, in all likelihood more. Her heart was beating far too fast.

"Cat got yer tongue?" His smile deepened.

"Please, sir, if you would be so kind, let go of my gown." She couldn't prevent a sudden frantic edge from making her voice sound higher than normal.

"A proper lady, are ye? Divinely beautiful, full-grown by the looks of it, and totally innocent, I'm thinking." He pulled on her gown, winding the hem about his wrist as if he were bringing in a large salmon, and although she tried to resist, he forced her to bend down to him. He brought her closer to those eyes, that mouth, that smile. And when he was so near that she bethought herself the sensation of his breath touched her cheek, he murmured, "Would ye like me to warm ye, fair lady? Melt ye? Would ye let me be the first one to teach ye the joys of love?"

She gasped, yanked once more at the kirtle hem, and this time, he let go. "How dare you mock me? Insult me?"

"Nay, ye're mistaken. There is no mockery in my offer. I did not mean to insult ye. It would be a pleasure and an honor to teach ye the delights of passion. *Croidheag, in rega lim i tír n-ingnad hi fil rind?*" he whispered.

Annora's meager familiarity with the Irish tongue was not enough for her to understand what he'd said. It was forbidden for Anglo-Normans to speak Irish, and the natives living in Dublin were required to speak English. Still the soft words made her tremble, and she dared not ask for a translation, nor look into his eyes to see if the gentle, seductive tone was reflected in those sea blue depths. Swiftly she hiked her skirt above her boots to hasten away. She started to run, but could not go fast enough to escape his final words.

Shameless, and resonating with accents of the wild Irish hills, they chased her through Dame's Gate.

"The Dublin winter is long, *leannán,* and ye must not

be forgetting that I know where it is ye live. There's time yet to teach and learn, and keep each other warm. I intend to show ye a thousand pleasures, *sweetheart*. That I promise."

Chapter 3

❝**T**here will be Irish at the king's table, niece," Sir Thomas warned Annora as they walked up Winetavern Street. He was holding her elbow to guide her over a patch of ice. "I trust you will not be offended."

"Nay, sir, I will take no offense." Annora infused her reply with the proper dose of maidenly sincerity, knowing, at the same time, a twinge of penitence. She was as bewitched as ever by the prospect of feasting with the Irish. Not even the incident outside the tavern had dampened her lurid fantasies. Her soul must, of a certainty, be depraved, for yesternight she had dreamed of the tawny-haired giant calling after her as she dashed through Dame's Gate.

"They are a proud race, these men who live in the wilderness of the high hills," Sir Thomas continued. "And ofttimes their warriors adhere to ways that are different from ours. They are stubborn—like hounds with a juicy bone. Nothing more."

"You speak in defense of them, uncle, even though it is generally your practice to meet them in battle rather than in a banquet hall."

"It is possible for a man to appreciate his enemy,

especially if that enemy is valiant and hardy, swift of foot, and strong of hand."

"Only if that man is as equitable and wise as yourself," Annora amended. She gave him an impulsive hug.

It was mid-afternoon. Annora and Sir Thomas were bound for the Epiphany feast. Catherine was not with them. A light snow had been falling since the Matins bells, and as there was no predicting what the weather would be when the feast concluded after midnight, Catherine had not ventured out. Her cough had returned but not her energy, and even in better weather the walk to Hoggin Green, where a residence had been prepared for the king on nearly the same ground upon which Henry II's wickerwork palace had stood in the winter of 1172, would have been overwhelming.

Servants were sweeping snow from the footpath. Straw had been spread to prevent slipping upon ice, and planks had been laid across puddles and the usual layer of slime and dung that coated the ground. Sir Thomas and Annora reached Hoggin Green without any noticeable harm to their finery. Annora's new gown was protected by a great fur cloak; she had managed to keep her walking boots dry, while carrying blue leather slippers; and beneath a loose hood her headdress, a metal wreath crafted of stars enameled in gold and silver, remained secure.

A bonfire blazed on the open land before the king's residence. A guard acknowledged Sir Thomas, the doors to an inner yard were opened, and Annora shook the snow from her outer wrap. There was a matter that required Sir Thomas's presence, and he proceeded to the armory, while Annora was escorted to a small antechamber reserved for those guests invited to sit at the high table. Although others were already being admitted to the feasting hall, his majesty's honored guests would be led in by the king himself, and thus it was that they were waiting for the formal procession to commence.

Annora had removed her walking boots and was

securing the decorative latchets of her blue leather slippers when a horn blared. Squires rushed through the chamber, arranging everyone in the order of how they would be seated. Annora reached into the deep pocket of her gown, grabbed two cumin seeds and popped them in her mouth to sweeten her breath, then hurried to her position in the line.

A full fanfare of trumpets echoed through the corridors. Richard of Bordeaux, King of England and France, and Lord of Ireland, had arrived upon the threshold to the feasting hall. He was a handsome man with a straight, strong figure, being tall and well-limbed, and a suitably noble king with the fair-haired glow of the Plantagenets, and a fondness for fashionable raiments. The fanfare continued as the young king led the procession to the raised dais. The other guests rose in deference to his majesty, who, upon reaching a massive chair situated under a gold canopy embroidered with lioncels and fleur-de-lis, waited until each honored guest stood before their place, whereupon he waved a hand indicating that everyone should resume their seats. The fanfare was replaced by benches grating on the floor, skirts rustling, dogs growling, and the murmur of voices.

The king's table was nearly as long as the raised dais upon which it was situated, and perpendicular to each end, there was a shorter table extending toward the center of the hall. Richard's earls, his dukes, barons, his priest and advisors sat with his majesty at the main segment as did Sir Thomas, the mayor, and the archbishop, plus the chieftains with their long hair, pointed beards, and wind-seared faces, who unlike the English were not wearing eye masks. Most notable among the Irish was Art Mac-Murrough, King of Leinster, a fierce warrior of powerful frame, and an able politician to whom the English parliament in Ireland paid annual tributes. The Black Rent it was called, and so great was MacMurrough's power that whereas King Edward had once derived

30,000 mares out of Ireland each year, the cost to King Richard was almost the same to retain a foothold in it.

Annora sat on a bench constructed for two persons at the end of one of the shorter tables. While this implied she was of lesser rank, and while there was no chieftain near to her, it was an excellent seat with a far better vantage point from which to observe the king as well as the entertainment that would take place between each course. The space beside her was empty, reminding Annora of her promise to give her mother a detailed account of the evening. Now she began to survey her surroundings, taking note of every aspect no matter how small.

The trestles were covered, not with lengths of wool, but with burgundy velvet, the borders being embroidered with young lions and flowers de luce, the symbols of Richard's own, newly adopted standard. She ran her fingers along tiny stitches, marveling at the artistry and skill. Next she touched the rim of the mazer set before her; it was a goblet, crafted not of wood or horn, or silver as were the archbishop's and some of Catherine's, but of gold. There was such a goblet before each place, and Annora could hardly credit the notion that Richard, who had come to wage war, must have transported them all the way from England.

There was a gallery opposite for the musicians, each musician being dressed in the same colors as the canopy above the king's chair. Pennants displaying the royal colors were flying from the rafters.

Dublin gossips had made much talk of the improvements ordered at Hoggin Green, and this banqueting hall was confirmation that while Richard's army had fought its way north from Waterford, artisans had been preparing a fitting residence for his majesty. The walls, plastered and whitewashed, had been painted with red lines to represent masonry blocks, and each block was decorated with a remarkable likeness of an animal native to Ireland.

There were wolves snarling, foxes peering from a den, stoats protecting their young, stags bounding, rooks nesting, salmon leaping, and curlews darting in and out of crashing waves. It was a magnificent extravagance, leaving no doubt to the rumor that his majesty's fondness for lavish lodgings and entertainment had already dissipated the treasury he'd brought for the purpose of war.

There was another fanfare, drawing Annora's attention to the entrance, where the surveyor of ceremonies was beginning to cross the hall.

"Welcome, welcome. Good cheer, dear friends," the Surveyor sang to the music of a single lute and host of tambourines.

As he passed through the middle of the hall, Annora noticed a scattering of men, who—like the chieftains at the king's table—were not wearing masks. A few were seated, others were standing. *Irish.* They were not dressed in the English style; no velvet, silver tissue, or brocade; no jewels or bobbed hair nor parrot-colored hose in orange or purple, blue or scarlet. They wore tunics and leggings of the finest saffron-dyed wool. Their short fringed jackets were lined with fur, and so, too, was their footwear designed for the winter weather. No ornamented pointed shoes for these warriors, but boots of leather lined with fur and secured to the knee. Several of them wore formidable battle swords at their waist, or had thrust great daggers with looped handles into belts, which was a breach of etiquette that hadn't gone unnoticed by the tollkeeper's wife, whose expression made Annora think the woman had failed to dodge the contents of a chamber pot being emptied into the street. The forstraught woman looked as if she had been holding her breath for some time, and Annora could not prevent a tiny smile. In the next instant, however, her heart skipped a beat. That smile vanished, and a sudden thrill rushed through her, followed by a ripple of alarm.

There, standing against a wall, arms crossed at his

chest, was the Irishman from below her window. Like the
other Irish he wore no eye mask, and his thick, golden
brown hair was free and long, a practice despised by the
English, who favored a tidier, chin-length bob. His
clothes were simple and traditional, his woolen *leine*
being the same saffron color worn by the others of his
kind. The nasty patchwork of furs was gone. He was
sober, it would appear, and even among his own, he was
the tallest, most imposing man Annora had ever seen. His
fringed jacket hugged wide shoulders, and the open neck
of his *leine* gave a glimpse of muscled chest. He was a
bold display of strength and confidence. Even in his
enemy's hall, here was a man who knew little of fear,
even less of convention. Here was a man wont to getting
what he desired. A man who did not obey the laws of a
foreign king. No wonder he had dared to be brash with
her. This Irishman, no doubt, enjoyed everything in life
to its fullest. The notion tantalized Annora; the man took
her breath away.

As if he'd sensed her gaze, he glimpsed in her
direction. As if he'd recognized her despite the blue
velvet mask, he smiled that knowing grin. As if he were
coming to greet her, he pushed away from the wall.

Annora turned and forced herself to focus upon the
Surveyor. His song ended with, "May the Good Lord
send each and all a Happy New Year." He stood before
his majesty for the presentation of the salt, the ceremonial
confirmation that Richard held the highest rank. But
Annora was not watching. Unable to restrain herself, her
glance darted back to the Irish giant. He was the
unknown, the forbidden, the wind in the summer, and
she could not resist a peek.

By all the company of heaven, she almost cried aloud.

He was cutting across the hall and coming straight
toward her. And by the look of it, his grin was deepening
with each long stride. In seconds, he reached the dais.
She looked straight ahead but that didn't stop him. In

another second, she sensed his huge person hovering over her, saw a vague outline reflected in her goblet. She did what she must, and turned far enough around to whisper and be heard.

"Go away," Annora ordered, fully expecting to see the shadow upon the goblet retreat. "Hence!" The shadow moved but didn't leave. Instead the Irish giant put a leg over the bench to sit down, but he did not do so properly. To her horror, he straddled the bench and faced her as a flourish of chimes and horns resonated from the musicians' gallery.

The laverers were entering. With fringed towels draped about their necks, these servants, whose task it was to help guests wash their hands, carried pitchers of warm, spiced and herbed water. One of them poured some water into a single bowl set between Annora and the Irishman.

"Go away," she repeated, then swished her hands about the bowl with an air of preoccupation. The mingled scents of orange and cloves encircled her. But they did not obscure her awareness of him.

"And why should I be doing such a thing as that?" he drawled in that low, rasping voice. " 'Tis a place of honor, I am assured, with a fine view, and finer company."

"That seat is reserved for a special guest of the king," she managed to say with much the same dignity and authority she'd used outside the tavern.

"And that special guest would be me. This is my seat." He slipped his fingers into the bowl alongside hers.

"I don't believe you," said Annora. She had to swallow twice before saying this, and even then, her mouth was dry and her voice cracked. He had not touched her, but there was something intimate about seeing his hands in the bowl with hers. This was disturbing. Alarming. Annora had shared a laver with other men, but she had never been aware of those men as she was of this man, nor of the irresistible energy that seemed to be emanating from him. She stopped swishing and held her hands motionless, but that did nothing to abate the invisible pull. She stared at his large hands, more than twice the size of hers. They were rough and scarred, yet to gaze upon his long fingers stirred something within her, and Annora heard an inner voice taunting her with the suggestion to let her fingers entwine with his. *It isn't a mortal sin; the sun will still rise on the morrow; dragons will not swim up the Liffey to devour Dublin; let it happen*, the voice whispered.

Blessed Holy Mother, how could it be that this man brought out the worst in her? How could it be that her mind sheltered visions, ideas, images, temptations that were both unholy and illegal?

"Look up there," he was saying, and she did. "Two seats from the king. That is my uncle. This is my place."

He pointed at one of the chieftains, a great bear of a man, and with a skeptical eye, Annora looked from this bear to the Irishman beside her. The only possible family resemblance was their size, for the chieftain's hair and eyebrows were black as midnight, his features were fleshy, and his mouth was twisted into a permanent frown. He was not the intriguing, wild warrior of a young woman's fancy, but the menacing savage that haunted every naughty lad who had been warned that next time he misbehaved, he would be sold to the Irish. And didn't every child know what the *wild Irishry* did? Why, they ate little Anglo-Norman children to break their fast.

As if he knew what she was thinking, Annora's Irishman regarded her with his striking grin. But he did not speak of dire threats to naughty lads. "Perhaps now that I've explained myself, ye'll be telling what it is ye're doing here. How do I know that is yer rightful seat?"

Annora glared at him. It made no difference that he was obviously teasing her. She pursed her lips into a tight, angry line, and having no intention of answering, held out her hands to be dried. That done, the laverer removed the bowl, and Annora watched the fiddlers getting into place on the gallery.

"Och, now, but ye're a fair sight to behold when ye're riled. Like a little yellow cat, ye are, with yer back arched and claws drawn. Ye're breathtaking even with that chilling disapproval in yer eyes and the stern set of yer pretty mouth."

The archbishop stood to give the blessing.

"Hush." Annora bowed her head to pray but could not stop herself from wondering if he was still smiling. She closed her eyes to stop herself from peeking.

"'Twas a splendid treat to encounter ye outside that tavern, fair lady," he continued to whisper as if he had not heard her entreaty.

Squeezing her lids tighter, Annora tried to concentrate on the blessing.

"Oh, King of Stars, hear our prayers," the archbishop intoned. "Be with us at the breaking of bread. Be with our earthly monarch, Richard, your son. Extend to him your most holy—"

"What a sight ye were, provoked into righteous indignation," were the Irishman's quiet words, uttered in the same cadence as the archbishop's invocation. "'Twas a memorable mishap, wasn't it now?"

She opened her eyes and scowled. He was smiling.

"Amen," said the archbishop. The guests replied the same while the Irishman whispered to Annora, "I did not damage yer kirtle, did I?"

"How did you recognize me?" she wondered aloud, one hand rising to make certain her velvet mask was in place. She never heard his query about the kirtle.

"How indeed? Who else in all of Ireland would have such glorious hair? 'Tis bright as sunshine. And that mask doesn't hide yer mouth—full and ripe for kissing—nor does it hide the vivid color of yer changeable eyes. Och, if only ye could see how they're doing it now just as they did yesterday, going from a pretty blue to a hue as vivid as the petals of the wild clarie in midsummer. Such eyes, I've never seen. Eyes alive with challenge. Eyes that . . ." He leaned forward, and because he was straddling the bench, one of his knees grazed against hers, while the other brushed against her backside where it met the edge of the bench. "Wild clarie eyes that are alive with passion," came his whisper.

Annora tried not to fidget at his provocative words. It was said that the seeds of wild clarie mixed with wine excited bodily lust. As he leaned even closer, she felt sure his large body was going to envelope her.

"Nor does that mask hide yer womanly form," he murmured.

Annora started to speak, but a fanfare of horns and drums and bells cut her off. The fiddlers began playing, and another line of servants paraded through the hall bearing platters of food. This night, there would be more than thirty courses, and it was customary to display the dishes in this fashion at the outset. A pair of swans passed Annora. Next came a boar's head surrounded by polished apples.

"You've never seen my womanly form." She spoke without moving a muscle. Her lips hardly parted.

"Och, but I was imagining it in my daydreams, and I saw ye in my sleep. And now that I'm seeing ye, 'tis a delight, it is. Indeed, ye're as perfect to feast my eyes upon as I'd fancied."

Annora felt a fierce blush upon her cheeks. *Feast his eyes, indeed.*

From all around her came exclamations of "ooh" and "aah." A peacock, its plucked tail arranged in a fan, was being presented. No one was noticing Annora. Thank goodness, for the Irishman came even closer to her until his warm breath fell upon her neck. Beneath the table his leg pressed firmly against hers. No one knew what was happening, no one but Annora. She tried not to tremble, tried to shut out his words, to ignore the sensation of his muscled leg against her thigh.

His husky whisper continued, "Aye, yers is a perfect female form, I'm thinking. All soft curves and pearly-fair skin that beckons to be caressed by a lover, and it's looking forward to being that man, I am."

She gasped, sharp and quick. In nervous reaction, she grabbed her goblet and took a sip.

"That was not shock now, was it? Don't be telling me ye've forgotten how I made ye a promise. Och, did I forget to tell ye about myself? I always keep my promises, my angel. Always."

"I'm not your angel." She took this opportunity to edge away, but the bench was too small to put more than a few inches between them. At least, they were no longer touching. That was much better. And so was the wine. It was piment, its strength disguised by honey and spices. She had another sip.

"Och, but you're breaking my heart." He gave her an overly dramatic look of dismay.

Annora laughed. It would have been impossible not to, any more than she could have stopped the tiny smile edging up at the corners of her mouth. She set the goblet down. "As if someone such as yourself had a heart. You're plaguesome, and should learn to behave. Here comes my uncle, and he is more protective than any father could be."

"The Lord Justiciar's liege man?"

"Aye, that is my uncle," Annora said with a touch of pride. She was not surprised that an Irishman would know of Sir Thomas, the knight, but she was surprised when he stood to greet her uncle, who in turn spoke to the Irishman as if he were known to him. How could that be possible?

"Rian O'Byrne, I am pleased to see that you decided to join us after all," said Sir Thomas. "Can I hope that my advice was heeded? Or perchance you are not as uncivilized and forsaken as they say. Has town life improved your ways, O'Byrne?''

The man her uncle called Rian O'Byrne tossed back his head in robust laughter. There was a twinkle in his eyes, and he looked not at Sir Thomas but at Annora, when he said, ''I know of at least one who would say I am boorish and beyond redemption.''

Sir Thomas studied the two young people. ''Everything is all right, is it not, niece?''

Annora gave the only possible reply, ''Aye, uncle.''

The two men fell into conversation, but Annora was too absorbed with the thoughts spinning round her head to hear anything. She had gotten her wish and was sitting beside one of the wild Irish. But she had not wished for this precise one. She had not reckoned with sharing a bench with the man who had in effect volunteered, nay, pledged to take her chastity. Furthermore, it had only been a wish, a fantasy that was safe, because such things never came to pass. Or did they? She stared at the Irishman.

O'Byrne. The name was as familiar to Annora as it was to every resident of Dublin, who lived in fear of Irish barbarians and spoke of the Cullenswood Slaughter as if it had occurred only last week. O'Byrne. O'Toole. Mac-Murrough. O'Connor. These were the clans that dominated the hostile mountains and dense woodland beyond the vale of Dublin. *Terra guerre* was what the English called the territory controlled by the Irish. *Land of war*. While the settled lowlands under dwindling English control were *terra pacis*. *Land of peace,* wherein English law, speech, custom, and allegiance held fast against many enemies. King Richard was not pleased with this shrinking *terra pacis,* nor with the disloyal English whom he called degenerate.

Richard had come to Ireland to reassert English ascendancy over the island. He intended to win back the loyalty of the degenerate English, those Anglo-Normans whose parents or grandparents had married Irish and were themselves more native than English; further he intended to consolidate the shrinking English lands and to secure the *terra guerre* for English colonists. To accomplish this, Richard needed the submission of the chieftains, and he would induce that submission by means charming and flattering, as well as by bribery, guile, bloodshed, and force. This feast was the charm and flattery. There had already been several months of fighting, and it was said the Leinster chieftains would soon swear fealty to Richard; they would promise to lead their people out of the province, including the mountains in the region referred to as Wicklow by the English and *Uí Bríuin Cualann* by the Irishry, who still told the sagas of Cellach Cualann, the last king of the heroic age of the Leinstermen.

Annora looked at the O'Byrne chieftain and saw a fierce warrior who was old but not defeated; the kind of man who would fain stand and die before making easy agreements with an enemy. As for the cocksure and brash Irishman, whom her uncle called Rian O'Byrne, it seemed improbable that he would swear fealty to any invader, especially one who wore purple leggings. If the other Irish warriors were like these O'Byrnes, and if their race was as stubborn as her uncle claimed, Annora doubted the king's plan would be accomplished. At least not for many years to come.

"The first course arrives," remarked Sir Thomas, drawing Annora from her contemplation.

Fruit in pastry tarts was being served. Sir Thomas returned to his seat, and the Irishman sat down beside Annora. Properly, this time.

Chapter 4

"Aye, ye're as fair of face and form as Sir Thomas boasted, and I've seen for myself the fiery spirit of which he spoke." Rian O'Byrne grinned at the exquisite woman beside him.

She was staring at her fruit pastry, and while he could not see those clarie blue eyes, he enjoyed the sight of thick lashes resting against flawless skin, of moist, plum-colored lips, of a delicate chin and slender neck, and of the visible swelling of opulent breasts, high and round beneath the bodice of her velvet gown. There was a stirring in his loins at the prospect of having her in his arms, of feeling her flesh against his, of fondling those bounteous breasts, and inhaling her musky female scent. Soon she would be his to pleasure and teach, his to make warm on a long Dublin night.

His promise—though declared while sprawled in the mud—was no jest. For all her elegant poise, costly clothes, and refined English manner, there was something exciting about her that went beyond physical beauty. He'd sensed it when he'd seen her in the tower and outside the tavern. There was something about her that hinted of a hidden sensuality and passion that, once released, would be wild, seething, maybe unquenchable. The prospect enthralled him, enticed him, made him want her. And what Rian O'Byrne wanted—especially when it came to women—Rian O'Byrne went after. Her seduction would be his winter's sport, his diversion from the politics his family wished he would take more seriously. He had not thought to encounter her again so soon, nor to discover that she was quite so susceptible to him.

"My uncle spoke to you about me?" It was not so much a question as a horrified exclamation.

"To be sure. Though he did not mention this disagreeable side ye insist upon showing me."

Annora was aghast, but she managed to retort, "You have me at a disadvantage. Beyond your name, I know nothing of you except your fondness for ale, vulgar songs, disreputable taverns, and the company of immodest women."

"I'll not be denying any of it, though ye wound me with such unflattering barbs. Of course, 'tis pleasing to have proof of that quick wit of which yer uncle boasted. Och, a beautiful woman who's clever and honest. What's a poor man to be doing now?" His grin faded to a smoldering look of the sort that set maidens swooning. His voice softened. "I believe I love ye, lass."

"Be serious," Annora admonished. Her cheeks must be scarlet, and to keep herself from touching her face, Annora picked up a bite-sized fruit pastry.

"Och, but I am being serious." He took her hand, and before she could guess what he intended, his lips slipped over her fingers to take the pastry into his mouth. "'Tis a sweet plum," he drawled, licking twice about the end of her finger. "Like the ripe color of yer lips. Will they taste this sweet, I wonder?"

Her hand was trembling.

"Aye, I love ye, and have done so for weeks. It was late November when I met yer uncle near a burned village called Clonegall, and we rode together—odd pair that we were—both being bound for Dublin. During that journey, Sir Thomas often talked of his beautiful, clever niece, and as we crossed the Aughrim to make our way up the coast, I found myself falling in love with this Annora Picot, although I never thought to meet her. And then in Dublin, I fell in love with a haughty angel with a flaxen halo. That those two women are one and the same is a miracle, and that ye're here beside me this night is one as well. Now, will ye be telling me, what else could that be excepting love?''

She snatched back her hand and thrust it safely out of his reach. ''You're an impenitent rogue. Boorish and beyond redemption,'' she said, while she could not help wondering what it would be like if a man such as Rian O'Byrne loved her. What would it be like to be held against that chest? To have those lips touch hers? Such thoughts were beyond redemption. It was dangerous to sit beside him, and she would do well to avoid conversation with him unless it was absolutely necessary.

''Nay, I speak the truth,'' he protested, but said no more.

The remaining fruit pastries were taken away, a juggler came out to perform, and Annora and Rian did not talk to each other through the next six courses and alternating entertainments, conversing instead with others at the table. The silence between them ceased, however, when the seventh course was set before them. It was a hedgehog sculpted out of some kind of chopped meat, and Annora, who had been sipping more of the honeyed wine, began to giggle.

Rian leaned to the side until his shoulder rested against hers. ''Ye're right,'' he whispered. '' 'Tis a frightful creature.''

She covered her mouth to control the laughter. ''I am not usually so ill-mannered.''

''Nay, 'tis not ill-mannered, but honest.'' He motioned about the hall. ''What a disgrace it is to witness their foolishness; every one of them acting as if that little beast set before them is something to be admired. I wonder how many good wives of Dublin will try to shape such a delectable in the year to come. Can ye not see all the little hedgehogs being served come Eastertide?''

Annora's giggles started anew. She must not have any more of the piment.

"Laughter is a good thing, Annora." He used her name, and she did not object. "Yer uncle told me that he does not see ye laugh as much as ye used to. Why is that?"

"I am not a child anymore."

"Not a child, yet a maiden still," he observed, and was pleased to see a blush coloring her cheeks. This was going to be a foolishly easy seduction. "Although yer uncle told me many things, there is still something I do not understand."

"I ween you're going to ask," she said.

And he did. "Why aren't ye wed?"

Annora did not expect this, and she picked the currant eyes off the hedgehog, then popped them in her mouth as she considered what to say. The currants were dry from old age. She washed them down with more piment, then asked a question of her own, "What did my uncle say?"

"That ye're overly fond of yer money."

Another ripple of laughter escaped her.

"Sooth? Do ye prefer yer money to a husband?"

"Nay, but it seems most men prefer money to love," she spoke with unexpected candor. It must be the wine. Why else would she confide in this impertinent Irishman? Certainly she did not trust him. "Perhaps you will not comprehend this—for my own mother does not—but I have no husband because I have never been courted by a man who preferred me more than my money."

"Och, but I do understand," Rian said. He rested the backside of his hand against her cheek at the edge of the velvet mask. This was not the seducer giving a calculated caress. This was genuine, impulsive, and tender, and tentatively, the pad of his thumb stroked her cheek even though he knew that he should not allow it. "I'm seeing before me a woman possessing beauty, intellect, and integrity, and I know those qualities should be appreciated. But what I will never accept are the Anglo-Norman men who dared to court a woman such as yerself, but failed to treasure ye. They were fools, and ye were right to refuse them. Coins are cold, lifeless, but ye're alive with spirit and wit, and there's a passionate soul, I'm thinking, hidden beneath that poise and veneer. 'Tis not the money to be admired and coveted, but the woman who could amass a fortune."

The sting of tears made Annora blink. There was nothing that could have touched her more deeply. Such sentiments were the single thing above all else she had yearned to hear. Indeed, if any one of those gentlemen— even the pungent William Piers—had managed to utter anything remotely similar, she would be wed to that man.

"Come and dance with me." Rian reached for her hand, then pushed the bench away from the table and stood. He'd seen a momentary shimmer of tears in her eyes and was beset by a sudden acute awareness of how lonely she must be, and why it was she did not smile. He'd never felt that way before, had never seen inside another soul before. It was almost as if he'd acquired a conscience, and he didn't like it. He had to shake off this unusual feeling. "Come. Dance with me. Let's be setting some of that passion free this night."

Annora could not refuse. She loved to dance. Besides how could she deny the man who had spoken the words she had given up any hope of hearing? How could she naysay the man who understood when her own mother did not?

The music was lively. Drums and horns and cymbals

set a brisk tempo that inspired Annora's feet to tap out a matching rhythm. She stood and allowed Rian to wrap an arm about her waist as they joined other couples in a large circle. The dance steps followed a pattern that began with the gentlemen bowing to their ladies, after which the couples joined arms to circle first in one direction and then in the other before one couple raised their joined hands for the others to go beneath.

" 'Tis Mistress Annora in the blue gown and mask of stars. Do you see her?"

"Aye. Dublin's Beauty is dancing with the Irishman."

Annora overheard these remarks as the large circle reformed and they danced past a table at the lower end of the hall. She glanced up at Rian, and he smiled as if he knew what she was thinking, as if he were saying, *"Aye, I heard, too. Do we really care what they think? These folk who would admire hedgehogs."*

The large circle split into two, one forming within the other. Annora and Rian remained on the outer circle as the couples faced each other to begin another pattern that ended when the circles rejoined into one, and indeed, as they danced past onlookers there was more for Annora and Rian to hear.

"Mayhap Mistress Annora will tame the savage beast," a lady with a bluish gray complexion remarked in a loud voice. "Teach him proper English ways." She was ancient, in her eighth or ninth decade to be sure, for the wimple swathed about her head and beneath her chin had not been in style since the previous century.

" 'Tis said she is blessed by faeries," said her companion, a slender young man with a lisp.

"Then anything is possible."

On they danced. Rian mused, "Blessed by faeries, it is now?"

" 'Tis what they say."

"Are ye Irish then?" At this point, the line of dancers broke apart, and partners faced each other, linking arms to spin in circles. "Being Irish would account for that fiery passion ye struggle so hard to conceal."

"You are mistaken. I am no more Irish than do I struggle to conceal anything."

"Och, Annora, ye must not be telling me lies. 'Tis pointless, ye know, to hide from me. I saw the truth when ye leaned out the tower window. I know what ye were thinking when ye looked down and saw our merrymaking. And I've seen hints of it this very night. There are things ye're wanting to do, Annora. Forbidden things that ye struggle to control. Besides, Sir Thomas told me about the time ye fancied yerself in love with a prince from Novgorod and disguised yerself as a lad to get on a vessel bound for Russia. Does that not speak for itself?"

"My uncle spoke to you about that!" Annora's heart was racing.

The couples were forming a circle again, and as Rian slipped his arm about her waist, they fell into step with the others. "Aye, he did. Why do ye think I fell in love with ye?"

"But I was only eleven years old!"

"Eleven years, yet free and laughing. And I know how to make ye as happy as ye were then." He held her close as the couples looped and turned their way back toward the dais. "I'll make ye laugh. Let me show ye that passion is not a wicked thing, and that ye should not be hiding from it as ye do. I'll set ye free."

A sudden languor settled upon Annora. It must be the dancing in circles that had caused this weakness. She was tired, nothing more, and perhaps had emptied her goblet once too often. That was why she had to rest her head against him. Praise be, the musicians had stopped playing, and the dancers were returning to their seats for the next course. Soon she would be sitting again. Soon the hall would cease its spinning, and she would be revived.

"Ye're mine, ye know," said Rian. They were back at

their places, and a platter of roasted pheasant wings was set before them.

"I know nothing of the sort," she replied. It was not a prickly retort, but a soft, almost breathless assertion.

"Then ye must be listening mindful to what I have to say. *Croidheag, in rega lim i tír n-ingnad hi fil rind?*"

"You said that to me once before."

"Aye, outside the tavern."

"What does it mean?"

With the tip of one finger he tilted her chin upward until he stared straight into her eyes. Only then did he speak. *"Mistress of my desires, will ye go with me to a wondrous land where there are stars?"*

Annora's heart leapt. Those ocean blue eyes were probing, intense. Again she experienced the awful sensation, nay, it was no mere sensation, but a *desire* to surrender to the waves. She trembled, and tearing her gaze from his, stared blindly into her lap. The hall had stopped spinning, but she did not feel at all like herself.

"Rop tú mo baile, rop tussu m'airer."

He was speaking most softly, as if to persuade her to look up. Annora did not understand, for he spoke Irish, but it sounded like poetry, and she enjoyed the beguiling rise and fall of the words, the husky timbre of his voice. He switched to English.

" 'Tis time to open up yer wings, *leannán*. 'Tis time to fly and soar. Stay with me this night, *sweetheart*, and when ye open up those wings, let me in. *Be ye my vision, be ye my delight.* Let me fulfill my promise."

There it was said, and there could be no doubt what he meant. Annora continued to stare at her lap. It was safe and harmless to dream of feasting with the *wild Irishry*, even to dream of bare chests and muscled thighs. There had been little peril in laughing with him as she had this night, of dancing and flirting with him, for flirting was, indeed, what she had been doing with Rian O'Byrne. But anything more, anything beyond this time and place, would be dangerous. Verily, it was forbidden.

He repeated, "Be with me this night."

"I am going home, sir, to my mother's home."

"But ye forget. I know where ye live."

"Please." She raised her face to him. "Please, don't go there."

"What are ye afraid of?" Rian scrutinized her as if searching for an answer upon her face, in her eyes. "It is me? Or yerself?"

"Fear has nothing to do with it." Annora's gaze did not waver beneath his regard. "It is my mother. She is not well, and I would not want her to be disturbed in any way."

"Yer uncle shared his concern about his brother's widow," Rian said in sympathy. He did not look quite so feral, nor as aggressive as he had a moment before. "I am sorry about yer mother. Instead of tonight, say ye'll spend time with me tomorrow. I know ye'll be walking to the convent, let me go with ye."

Annora hesitated. He had been right. She was afraid to be alone with him, afraid of that little voice taunting her, *Dragons will not set fire to Dublin if you talk with him, if you spend time with him, if you let him kiss you.* Only several hours in his company, and she was more wicked than ever; there was much to fear in being alone with him, for she was no longer wishing to feast with an Irishman, but to kiss one. But even more than that, she was worried for her mother; she was afraid that if she said no, he would come to the tower tonight, and to distress her mother would be worse than setting Dublin aflame. "Aye, you can walk with me."

"Ye'll be departing at midday?"

She nodded.

"I will be there, and will do nothing to cause an ill woman a moment's anxiety. Ye have my promise." He smiled at her, slow and knowing, with a twinkle in his ocean blue eyes that beckoned her to come closer. ''And I never break a promise.''

Chapter 5

It was well past midnight when Sir Thomas escorted Annora home. A maid unbolted the tower door, and once Annora was safely within, her uncle returned to his lodgings at Dublin Castle.

"Your mother is awake, Mistress Annora," said the maidservant. She took the blue leather shoes Annora carried, then helped her out of the cloak and set it aside for a good brushing in the morning.

"Pray, Devasse, why does she not sleep at this late hour?"

"All is well," she assured her young mistress. "She is merely eager to have you home, mistress, and to hear about the feast. Your dear mam is like a child, bless her. Mistress Catherine hasn't slept a wink, and with the ears of a fox, she's been sending me down to check the door every time someone passed in the lane."

"Thank you for sitting with her, Devasse. I will go up directly." She accepted a beeswax taper to guide her way.

"Will you be needing me, mistress?"

"Not tonight. I'll manage on my own. Good night to you."

Annora climbed to the landing outside her mother's chamber. There was a sliver of golden light glowing beneath the door. Catherine would be in her curtained tester bed, nestled against a mound of pillows, surrounded by favorite possessions. Her books were always nigh hand, alongside her Holland lute, a small likeness of Annora on her sixth birth celebration, and the illuminated Psalter she had received on her wedding day twenty-seven years before. A dish of dates and almonds in sugar would be within easy reach. The chamber had become her entire universe these past weeks. No more visits to Our Lady of Victory on the cliff above the sea, no strolls on the common land, no browsing at the ribbon stalls on market day, or dinners with Uncle Thomas at the castle. Not even an afternoon in her beloved walled garden. Catherine had not left the tower since Christmas. Even the priest came to hear her confession and give holy communion.

The light from beneath the door gave Annora pause. Her thoughts took to wandering, two images melding into a single memory: the summer sky at sunset and picking cherries in the archbishop's orchard at Shankill. Granted it was an odd association, but it was vivid, and one that Annora would never forget. The widow Picot and her small daughter had had an open invitation to visit the archbishop's manor and avail themselves of the bounty in his orchard. There were cherries in summer, quince and apples in autumn, and Annora's earliest memories were of those outings to pick cherries.

Even now in the dead of winter, she could close her eyes and hear the buzz of bees, feel the sun, smell the grass, taste cherry juice upon her fingers, and see the red stain upon her mother's lips. It had been a full day's adventure that included seeing the archbishop's newest foals, fishing, and playing hide-and-seek with the tenant children. At dusk, they would ride back to town, mother and daughter singing French rounds to the amusement of their escort, and always Annora turned westward to watch the golden light of sunset streak the sky.

At the age of not more than four or five years, she had believed that it must be a different sun in a different sky, for it was never so splendidly observed from their tower. Verily, she had wondered if the people who lived in the mountains saw yet another sun, and being even farther from Dublin would that sun be an even better one?

"Mama," a young Annora had asked. She was already big enough to ride her own pony, and had trotted alongside Catherine, perched upon her little English sidesaddle in imitation of her mother. "Do the Irish have their own sun?"

"Whatever do you mean?"

But Annora's young mind had already bounded on to something else, and she did not focus on suns but chattered instead of the Irish air, deciding that the people who lived in those mountains must have their own air, their own sun, all of which must, sooth to say, be superior, for why else would the English wish to take their land from them?

"Do you know any Irish, Mama?"

"Conall is Irish," Catherine had replied, speaking of the man who helped in the garden. "And so is Sister Brigit. As are the men who bring their currachs up to the quay to sell herring."

"I mean *real Irish*. The ones who live in the mountains," she had clarified. The Irish Annora envisioned painted their faces blue with intricate designs that spread downward and across bare chests; they screamed like avenging angels and were stronger, braver, and more ferocious than even the boldest English knight. Such had been her thoughts even at a young age, yet Annora had never revealed them to her mother. Aloud she had merely asked, "Do you know any of *those Irish*?"

"Once, full long ago, I did. They were hostages when your uncle was provost at the castle. That was how I came to know them."

"Can we go into the wilderness and meet them?"

"I would not know where to find them. In good faith, I do not even know if they survived beyond the night they made their escape." Catherine had paused. A momentary sorrow had shadowed her expression. It was almost as if she had not liked giving that answer. In the next instant, all trace of grief vanished. She'd smiled that distant, contented expression of one who safeguards a precious secret. "I do not know what happened after that night. But I do know what came before, and someday I will tell you the most remarkable story of a miracle, and how a great tempest surged out of the sea to change many a life."

As the years passed, Catherine had often mentioned that tempest and its miracle, but she had yet to relate the story, and whenever Annora asked, she was advised the time was not right. For Annora, that untold story became more than a secret. It was a mystery of great power, prompting her to weave and concoct her own explanations, including one in which her father had not really been an elderly merchant named Geoffrey Picot but an Irish hostage. Annora shocked herself with such imaginings; therein lay the source of her wicked soul, she decided. Indeed, Annora came to believe that her fascination with the Irish would not have persisted, nor have taken such a lurid turn, if only her mother had recounted the story of the tempest.

"Annora, is that you?" Catherine asked from the other side of the door, her voice pulling Annora back to the moment at hand.

"Aye, 'tis me." She stepped into the warm chamber. The air was heavy with the orange essence of bergamot oil, one of Devasse's housekeeping tricks to mask the odors from tallow dips and burning braziers. Annora went to her mother's bed and sat upon the edge, noticing as she did that the dates and comfit had not been touched. She kissed her mother's cheek, then commenced an animated recounting of the feast.

"Lastly, there was your favorite," Annora said, having described the musicians, jugglers, and mimes, the swans and peacock, and what the sundry ladies of Catherine's acquaintance had worn.

"Almond spice cake?" asked Catherine. "The tiny ones?"

"The tiny ones, aye. And I brought you one." Annora withdrew her hand from the deep pleats of her gown, where a small round cake wrapped in a bit of cloth had been hidden. She presented the little cake to her mother.

"How pretty, and with powdered sugar as I prefer. I will save it for the morrow," Catherine demurred. "Please, set it on the chest."

Annora had heard this before, and knew that in the morning, it would be forgotten, and that Catherine would be paler and weaker than the night before. "I will not tell you about the Epiphany star unless you eat it now. And all of it."

"You are too cruel." There was a flicker of mirth in Catherine's tired eyes. "When did you become such a domineering daughter? I cannot recall ever having been so overbearing with you."

"In truth, we both know you spoil me most terribly. Now have a bite, and I will go on."

Catherine nibbled at the little cake. Annora smiled.

"It was after the play of *The Good St. George*. All the torches and candles were extinguished, and the hall fell into darkness—as black as the Liffey on a moonless night—and then high above the rafters, the most brilliant star appeared. By the glory of the angels, I have never seen such brightness, such a glistening of hope and faith," marveled Annora. "If I did not know better I would have believed we were gazing up at the very star that led the three kings to Bethlehem. Uncle said it was a taper set between several pieces of Venetian mirror, and 'twas moved across the ceiling by pulleys as are used on the quays to load the ships. Another bite,'' she encouraged her mother to finish the cake. '''Tis good, is it not?''

''Delicious. But what of the gentlemen? The English lords who came with his majesty?'' Catherine wanted to know. ''I have heard about pastries and jugglers and hedgehogs, but you have said naught of the king's men. Was Thomas Mowbray, the earl of Nottingham, in attendance? And the heir, Roger, earl of March?''

''They were at the high table.''

''And?''

''Presentations were made,'' Annora replied, knowing there was much more than simple curiosity behind that *And?* Her query was laden with the unfailing hope that her aspirations for her daughter might one day become reality. But it was no longer enough that her mother wished her to find a husband; Catherine had, of late, decided that an English husband with a peerage in Ireland would be best. Catherine, herself, had been a Talbot; her mother, a Warrene; and hers before, a Montfort, descended from Plantagenets, and thus Annora offered not only the Picot wealth but a noble lineage, which when matched with one of Richard's earls, would guarantee her daughter a future both secure and prosperous.

''And?'' prompted Catherine once more.

''When the musicians played a country dance, I was partnered with the earl of March,'' came Annora's reluctant reply. ''But you must needs not attach any importance to it. He danced with many women.''

''None as beautiful as you, I am certain. Nor as wealthy. He is a fair young gentleman?''

''English earls are much the same as Irish earls, Mother, in both appearance and conduct,'' Annora said. She did not wish to be ill-mannered or to disappoint her mother, but this issue of selecting a husband was the single way in which Annora felt she had failed her mother. She wished it could be otherwise, and had tried to explain herself, but had failed in that as well. Catherine Talbot had been wed at the age of sixteen to a man older than her father, and it had never occurred to her to naysay her parents and refuse Geoffrey Picot, who wanted her only for her family's political connections and the lands that comprised her dowry. Marriage was like negotiating an exporting contract, she had often told Annora; one looked for the most advantageous arrangement to benefit all parties, and money was, naturally, part and parcel of that. Faith, what judicious man would want an impoverished bride?

"There was no one who interested you?" asked Catherine on a sad little yawn. Exhaustion was overtaking her. She appeared to be sinking into her nest of pillows.

There was no choice for Annora except to tell her mother a falsehood. "There was no one."

She could not say a word about Rian O'Byrne. Her mother wished her to find a husband, not to be flirting with one of the wild Irish, such behavior being nothing more than a frivolous, indecent waste. The Statute of Kilkenny—intended to abolish contact between the English and Irish, and to force the degenerate English to abandon their Irish ways—had, among other things, outlawed marriage between the races. Although the statute was no longer as formidable as it had been twenty-six years before, Catherine, ever-cautious and determined to obey the letter of the law, would be far more troubled by the truth than was her disappointment at Annora's well-intentioned lie.

Catherine closed her eyes. "Nonetheless, daughter, you enjoyed yourself, did you not?"

"Of a certainty. It was a most memorable evening. One that I will not soon forget," she said, reaching out to smooth a stray hair from her mother's brow. Annora began to sing, "*I had a little daughter, they called her Peep-Peep. She waded the waters so deep, deep, deep. She*

*had a flock of lambies to guard while in sleep. A flock of
lambies in safety to keep, keep, keep.''*

It was the nursery song Annora had always asked for
when she awoke from a bad dream; and her mother would
sit with her, singing until she fell back to sleep. Catherine
had learned the fanciful lyrics and melodious tune from
her grandmother, who had grown up in England, and it
was the first song she had taught Annora.

*"I had a little daughter, they called her Peep-Peep,
And with that flock of lambies she crossed that water deep;
Pray, what did she find on the other side?
Alas, 'twas no meadow, full-flowering sweet,
    but a rocky hillside steep, steep, steep.
So my little daughter, she climbed up the mountain high;
Oh, the poor little thing, wishing little girls
    could fly, fly, fly!"*

There were three stanzas, and before Annora finished
the last, her mother had drifted to sleep. She kissed her,
left a candle in a wall mount, and departed.

In her chamber, Annora removed her star headdress
and slipped off the walking boots. She reached back to
begin the task of unlacing her gown when there came a
noise at one of the windows. A bat trapped between the
shutters, mayhap. She paused to listen, and heard it
again. If not a bat, had the weather turned to sleet? She
went closer to the window overlooking the walled garden.
It was neither sleet nor a bat, but someone throwing small
objects against the shutters.

Curious, she threw open the shutters, and peered out to
see Rian O'Byrne in the snow-shrouded garden. He
looked every bit the savage native wearing that patchwork
of furs across his broad chest, with too much golden
brown hair hanging below his shoulders. He had come
over the wall by the chestnut tree. Annora saw his
footprints in the snow, and he was standing where

Catherine's rose bushes from Windsor bloomed in summer, his exceptional height and powerful body dwarfing the latticework frame through which crimson and white blooms had entwined to make a bower.

"What are you doing here?" Annora asked, breathless and worried, and thrilled.

"Fear not. I've merely come to wish ye sweet dreams. I did not bid ye farewell at the feast," he spoke in the sort of controlled whisper as was used by mummers when they wished to be heard at the back of a hall. *"Beannact De leat."* His voice floated upward on a white cloud.

"What does that mean?"

"God's blessing with ye."

Annora whispered in response, *"Beannact De leat,"* bungling the unfamiliar words.

He smiled up at her. "Even if ye can't speak Irish, I'll still love ye forever."

She returned his smile. *"Beannact De leat,"* she tried again, and it did not sound half as clumsy as the first attempt. "I may surprise you yet."

"That would be most pleasing." Rian lifted a hand, set fingertips to his mouth, and blew a kiss. "Until tomorrow, then." He retraced his footsteps across the garden.

Without a sound he vaulted over the wall and into the night.

Chapter 6

❦

But Rian O'Byrne did not return on the morrow.

Nor did he come the following day, not even to offer an apology, and this bothered Annora more than she would have liked. There was no reason for such a reaction, yet with each passing hour, Annora seemed to be thinking more about Rian O'Byrne instead of less. She did not even hear Devasse when the maid returned from the butcher and announced that half of the English army had gone in the night.

The church bells were ringing for Nones when Annora set out for Holy Trinity to fetch the priest. It was not Catherine's usual day for confession, but something was troubling her, and she had asked for Father Anselm. Annora had been happy to run the errand in Devasse's stead; anything to keep her mind off Rian O'Byrne.

It was late afternoon, and being winter, dusk was already upon Dublin. Ordinarily this was when the bustling quays and narrow lanes began to empty, but today they remained swarming and noisy. Rumors were spreading up and down the alleys with the speed of cinders on a dry August day. Everyone, it seemed, had heard something, but no one knew what to believe, and people had been pouring out of doors to hear more. There must be someone who knew why the English soldiers had departed their encampment outside the town wall.

" 'Tis the Lord's very own truth, my Andrew swears to it," declared a laundress. Her Andrew was a hay dealer, and spent much time beyond the fringes. "The king and his earls rode out of Dublin at the head of the army."

Annora stopped to listen.

"They were headed south, did you say?" a man called from the throng.

Several folk affirmed this in one voice. Everyone had something to say about this, but it was Peter Bellew, spice merchant, who spoke loud enough to be heard above the others.

"Aye, they rode south to meet with the Leinster chieftains in a field near Tullow," said the spice merchant. "I have heard the chieftains will attest to oaths of indenture."

"Art MacMurrough will do this?" someone asked, incredulous.

"Aye, MacMurrough and Gerald O'Byrne both. They have agreed to quit the whole of Leinster."

Annora wondered if she had heard correctly. Was it possible that the king had accomplished his goal in exchange for a few roasted swans, some almond spice cake, a night of entertainment, and the promise of eighty marks a year to each chieftain along with the right to call themselves *Knights of England's King?* The crowd believed this must be true, for there was an outburst of cheers followed by much embracing between persons both high born and low, rag and tag, cut and long-tail. Barber surgeons, waxworkers, and lawyers, butchers, fishmongers, beguines, and shoemakers began to dance. A well-dressed youth, son of the castle cuirass maker, linked his arm through Annora's to spin her in a circle.

Above the frenzied jubilation, Peter Bellew declared, "Our good King Richard succeeds! The *terra pacis* is restored, and it will be safe to dwell beyond the fringes of Dublin.''

Annora disengaged her arm from the well-dressed son and forced her way onward to Holy Trinity.

Later, when she returned with the priest the gathering had not dispersed, having instead swollen to twice its original size. The tavern keepers were dispensing aqua vitae in the lanes, and the cheering, kissing, singing, dancing hordes did not cease this jollification until late into the cold winter night. There was much celebrating, especially by the remaining English soldiers, who would soon be able to go home.

The achievement was commendable. By February 28, the first Sunday in Lent, MacMurrough and O'Byrne would quit the whole land of Leinster, between Dublin and Wexford, including the granite peaks and blanket bogs of Wicklow, with their warriors and families. The future boded well, for having succeeded in Leinster, King Richard would accomplish the same in Munster and Connaught.

But with the gray light of dawn came the first whisperings of doubt. It had been too easy. Much too easy.

"Something is not right," Catherine remarked.

The words made Annora shiver.

Still there was more celebrating that night. The brisk, thin humming of fiddles rose and fell over the open land beyond the town walls, where soldiers reveled around bonfires, and at the castle, barons, knights and earls feasted, while the residents of Dublin kept to their dwellings. Although they were English in the eyes of the law and their monarch, those lawyers and butchers, wax makers, clerics and merchants of Dublin did not view the world as did their cousins in England. These laborers, these shopkeepers, these ladies and gentlemen were English by blood, but not by birth. They had been born and raised in Ireland, many had daily contact with Irish, some even had kin among the natives, and no matter what their king wished, no matter what their ancestry, they had in many ways become more Irish than English.

They had an understanding—albeit imperfect—of how the Irish thought. They knew how the Irish clung to their own saints, their own language, and how theirs was an ancient society of warriors, ferocious, daring, and resolute. They knew the depth of the Irish hatred for the invaders, who had been trying to conquer their island for more than two hundred years, and they knew the chieftains had used artifice against their enemies in the past and would not hesitate to do so again.

King Richard appreciated none of this, and accepted what had come to pass in that field near Tullow as a praiseworthy affirmation of his superior authority, and the sovereignty of England. Indeed, it was whispered that the king was depending on this success in Ireland to effect his election as Holy Roman Emperor.

The people of Dublin, to the contrary, were not certain of Richard's success. Verily, they had started to suspect something was not right. Not surprising, there were no eager settlers stepping forth and asking to be granted lands in *terra guerre*. That was Irish territory, and only an English monarch could be so arrogant to believe that the chieftains would abandon their lands to make way for an English Ireland.

A fortnight passed. The feast days of the saints Prisca, Agnes, Vincent, and Hilary came and went, and it was time again for Annora to visit Abbess Thomasin. The new purple dye was working well, and they were now trying to perfect a distinctive yellow tint. Most shades of yellow contained too much brown or tended toward orange, but the Our Lady of Victory yellow would be as bright and clear as sunshine. The nuns had been using rhubarb root and sundew, but it was still not quite right; and today, Annora was bringing a jug of freshly distilled spirit of hartshorn. This infusion, made from animal horns, had both medicinal and cleansing properties. It was especially effective for lightening dingy bed linens and, mayhap, would enrich the yellow dye.

Annora made her way through the remnants of the English encampment. In the past sennight, the soldiers had dispersed north and west, and only a few thousand remained in Dublin. The open field was a mire of mud and litter. Stray dogs along with a few pigs were nosing about for something to eat, and Dublin's lepers moved like ghosts in search of anything to wear or barter. A few fires still burned about which soldiers huddled, yelling curses at dogs and lepers. Annora did not dally. Soon the camp was behind her, and the road was much the same as before the king had come to Ireland. She passed a group of children pulling a cart laden with turf bricks. Two friars walked past and nodded in greeting. A woman she knew to be a midwife rode by on a stocky pony.

The convent was over the next rise. She had been this way a thousand times before, and it was not landmarks so much as the sound of the sea that told her she was near. From behind came the thud of hooves, the tinkle of a bell. A horse was approaching. She moved to the side of the road and glimpsed a great black stallion advancing at a gallop. The rider wore a black mantle, the hood pulled over his head. She could not see a face, but knew the rider was no gentleman by the way he rode at full speed, straight for her. Her mother's every warning about coming this way alone surfaced in her mind.

Annora continued walking. The horse slowed, then it was right beside her, and she had a sudden acute awareness of the leather pouch beneath her kirtle. Apprehension coiled within her belly. She stared ahead, forcing her feet to move ever quicker, hoping that nothing in her gait proclaimed the presence of the leather pouch thumping against her hip.

"Let me take ye the rest of the way," the rider said.

She would know that deep rasping voice anywhere. This was no outlaw, and her first instinct was to reproach him for frightening her.

"There's no reason to walk." Rian O'Byrne extended a hand to help her mount behind him. "Come up here. I'll not be biting ye now."

"I like walking." She did not stop. "Go away."

"Is that how ye always greet yer acquaintances?" His horse ambled alongside her. He bent low in the saddle to talk with her. "I've come to accompany ye to the convent."

"Some sixteen days too late," she remarked over her shoulder. There was more than one reason to be angry with him.

"But I'm here nonetheless." He swung off the horse, pushed back his hood, and stood in front of her. He gave her no choice but to stop. "Had ye given up hope of ever seeing me again?"

"I had."

"Och, ye're breaking my heart, and here I was thinking ye were worrying yerself sick for me. Are ye not going to ask what kept me away?"

"Nay, I will not ask, for I have no interest in your affairs." But she did wonder, and hoped she had not betrayed herself.

"It was on account of my uncle," he explained, anyway.

"I have heard what happened at Tullow."

"I was not there. My uncle does not trust yer king, and while he was at Tullow, I was in the forest guarding the way to his fortress. There were sixteen of us, and we formed an ambuscade should the English attempt any treachery."

"But it was not necessary."

"Not yet, anyway."

"You do not trust Richard?"

"I do not concern myself one way or the other. It makes no difference to my thinking. Yer Richard can be as honorable or dishonorable as he pleases, for in the end nothing will change. I have no use for politics; they are a distraction and a waste."

Tiny lines knit across her brow. His voice had changed. It was overbearing, almost contentious, and it occurred to Annora that he was wont to argue about this. She frowned. "What do you care about then?"

"Pleasure," was Rian's simple answer. He smiled that lopsided, wicked grin. "I care about living every moment to its fullest whether 'tis in a pitched battle or between the blankets. And if there is danger and risk involved, then 'tis all the better for it. But mostly, I enjoy ladies, lovely and lively. I do not know if yer king is honorable, nor whether the foreigners will be leaving our land, nor if the English will one day become Irish, nor the Irish become English. There is only one thing of which I'm certain: there is no guarantee of tomorrow, and I would hate to die knowing I had squandered my final hours. To become embroiled in politics would be a miserable waste of this mortal life and its pleasures."

"And you are still boorish and beyond redemption," she retorted, wondering if the flush she felt rising upon her cheeks was as bright as it was hot.

"Och, ye must not be treating me with such harshness. Be kind, for I'm still in love with ye," he murmured. Purposefully, he infused his voice with an intimacy that was suggestive. He was running out of time. Given the speed and manner in which the political situation was developing, it did not appear his winter in Dublin was going to be as long as he'd anticipated. If he intended to seduce Annora, Rian would have to be accomplishing it sooner, and faster, than he would have preferred. Part of the pleasure was in setting the sensual snare. There was much titillation in the slow, deliberate process of making a woman want him with such intensity that when it was time, she did not resist. This particular technique had never failed Rian, and it excited him to think of Annora overwhelmed with desire. "If ye will not ride, at least, don't be turning me away now. May I walk with ye the rest of the way?"

The right and proper thing would be to tell him no, but Annora was still fascinated by Rian O'Byrne, this breathing, powerful vision of all she had fancied Irish and wild. In truth, what he said about pleasure and life heightened her fascination. She was more beguiled than ever, especially when it came to kissing.

Perhaps that was what she needed to put an end to this unholy preoccupation. Perhaps if she kissed him just once, then she would be able to tell him to go away with conviction. Maybe this was like the Lady Mary's Day Fair, when she had begged Catherine for a Columcille cookie. Annora had never had one of the Irish biscuits shaped into a letter of the alphabet, but surely they must be the most delicious treat. She had never smelled such a richness of honey and hazelnut, and did not want to share with her mother; she wanted the big letter "A" all for herself. But once she had the cookie, she discovered it was so sweet she could not have more than a few little bites, and she fed the remainder to the gulls.

Perhaps Rian O'Byrne's kiss was what she needed to stop thinking about the wild Irish, and about Rian O'Byrne, in particular. Perchance it would not be as extraordinary as she imagined. Possibly what she had witnessed from the tower was neither pleasurable nor gratifying. Mayhap, after one kiss, she would never yearn for another. "Aye, you may accompany me to the convent, Rian O'Byrne."

Annora resumed walking in the direction of Our Lady of Victory. Rian fell into step beside her. His horse followed.

"How is yer mother?"

"She is no better, but, praise God, she is no worse."

Rian frowned, not at this news but because he had once again experienced the novel sensation of knowing how lonely she must be. It was a waste for a woman such as Annora Picot to remain unwed. He wondered aloud, "Ye've confided one reason why it is ye're not wed, but is there another?"

"I'm not certain I understand."

"Could yer mother be another reason? While such devotion as yers is noble, surely yer own mother does not want ye to be wasting away yer life with her?" It was a blunt question, and when Rian angled his head to measure Annora's reaction, he was surprised to see the trace of a smile upon her face.

"Is it not every mother's greatest wish to see their daughter wed? Mine is no different." There was no bitterness in her voice. Her smile deepened at the thought that no man—be he Irish or English—could ever understand an unwed daughter's dilemma, especially if she had attained her twenty-sixth year as Annora had. "Devotion to my mother is no waste. Everything she has ever done was for me, and if it was not for the best, she did not do it. In fact, I believe the reason she never remarried was because of me. She must have feared how a second husband might treat a stepdaughter. Oh, how the disapproving crones clucked at the worldly riches she gave me. *Sinful for a widow on her own to live like a queen,* I heard more than once. *Dangerous to spoil a female child with such excess. She'll grow up to naught.* They were jealous, and they were wrong; the green before their eyes blinded them to the abundance of the love and tenderness she bestowed upon me.

"I am not sure how Irish children are raised, but the English do not have much of a childhood. The poor must begin work at a tender age, and it is not uncommon for children to be sold or newborn babes to be abandoned in the hope that the kindness of strangers will prevail. As for the children of wealthy or titled parents, they are first fostered out, sometimes hundreds of miles distant from their mother's gentle love, then they are bartered in marriage, pawns in territorial disputes and military alliances.''

Annora paused. All around them, the frozen winter countryside was quiet. There were no birds or insects, no rustling of leaves, no distant bleating of lambs, no bubbling of water in a nearby stream. The only sounds were their dull, uneven footsteps, the rhythmic clip-clop of hooves, the jingle of a tiny bell affixed to the bridle, and the distant crash of waves rolling in from the sea. Rian said nothing, but the look upon his face indicated he was listening. Annora went on:

''It is not without value or purpose to remain with the woman who not only gave me life but has given me happiness and comfort; the woman who, by example, taught me forbearance, generosity, courage, and forgiveness, as well as Latin and French, scribing and calculating; and above all, the woman who defied the priests and even my Uncle Thomas to allow me to become myself and employ the skills and attributes she had imparted to me. It would, however, be a terrible waste to consign myself to the wardship of someone who is little more than a stranger; a terrible waste to go away with a man, and to pledge my obedience when I did not know what he would give me in return. That would not only be a waste but exceedingly foolish.''

Rian grinned. ''Ye're not only a beautiful woman, but a wise one. What a singular wonder, ye are, Annora Picot, and I can think of none other, Irish or English, to compare with ye.'' *Bless me Sweet Jesus, 'tis the God's truth,* Rian swore to himself, threading his fingers through his hair, unsettled by this fleeting inner candor. In the next instant, the thought came to him that if his seduction of Annora succeeded, and if she gave herself to him, there would be something rare in that giving. The possibility fascinated Rian. It made Annora's seduction even more alluring. This woman valued herself highly. She had not squandered her beauty or passion, and what a blissful, heavenly reward it would be if she made him worthy of that which she had guarded so well and so long.

"Tá se an-gheal: ceol na naingeal, ceileabar ná eanlaith, dúil na ndeag-ban. Do geall tú damsa e," he recited in Irish. *"Confegsat fathi is druthi. Na dean dearmud. Rop tú nom-thocba i n-áentaid n-aingeal."*

"What does it mean?" she asked, spellbound by his lilting voice.

"'Tis very bright: the music of angels, the warbling of birds, the hopes of all ladies. Ye promised it to me. Diviners and druids beheld it. Do not forget. Mayest ye raise me up to the company of the angels."

"It is beautiful, but . . ." she hesitated.

"Go on. What is it?"

"I cannot explain why, but it seems to be filled with loneliness."

Like you, Annora Picot, came his silent reply. Aloud, he added, "There is more. Listen now: *Ni hiarram iomaduig: Cuir leaba glas luacra fum, co raib inad for nim nar, corop tú mo dilesea, co ndernar do retir. Na dean dearmud."* He translated, *"I do not ask too much: Put a bed of green rushes under me, that there may be a place in high heaven, that ye mayst be my love, that I may do yer will. Do not forget."*

"It is an ancient lyric?"

Rian gave her that lopsided grin. Usually he spun some tale about forbidden love between a Red Branch warrior and a faerie woman of the *sidhe,* part-angel, part-human, who had fallen to earth to torment mortals. Instead, he said, "Nay, 'tis not old at all." Most inexplicably, he told the truth, "I wrote it."

Annora stopped and pivoted to look at him in a kind of astonished wonder. "Perhaps you are not quite as boorish as I thought, Rian O'Byrne."

"Offering me compliments are ye now? What am I to

be thinking next?'' he asked, full of charm. He looked down into her eyes. His regard was bold and penetrating, as if he could perceive the secrets of her soul, and he was rewarded by the sight of a pretty rose flush upon her cheeks. *What more will ye offer me, sweet Annora? What more?*

Annora was holding her breath. She could not tear her gaze away from those ocean blue eyes, and there was that wicked glint like sunlight on the crest of a wave, welcoming her, nay, encouraging her to fling herself into the water. It was a look that made her think of kisses. He held her in his gaze, probing, intense, and her lips parted as if he had her within his thrall. Her mouth was dry, and her tongue flicked out to moisten her lips.

His regard shifted downward to her mouth. She trembled. There was a long, loaded moment as he moistened his lips in the precise manner as she was doing, and when he looked again into her eyes, it seemed to Annora the world went still. For the space of a heartbeat, they shared the same domain in the universe. Then it passed, and she dared to breathe again.

"Did time just stand still?" she whispered, incredulous and innocent.

"Och, now, *leannán,* time has been known to do that once or twice," came Rian's reply. He called her *sweetheart,* and reached out to take her hand in his.

In response, she buried her mittened hand within the folds of her cloak.

"What is it ye're afraid of?" he asked softly.

"I'm not afraid," Annora insisted. Sooth, she was terrified. Men had tried to take her hand before, and she had been repulsed by their attentions. But this was different. She was glad Rian O'Byrne wanted her hand. She was thrilled by the wicked, beckoning glint in his eyes, and that lurid little spirit within her made Annora think—nay, it caused her to *hope*—that if Rian O'Byrne wanted to hold her hand, mayhap, he might want to kiss her as well.

"Aye, ye're not afraid of me," he said, speculative, thoughtful. "But there's fear nonetheless about ye, and I'm thinking 'tis yerself ye're fearing." He was not flirting with her but speaking low and gentle. Something was happening to Annora Picot, but Rian didn't know what it was, and he was worried it would thwart his plans for her. He had to do something, and he had to do it before the promise of this moment was gone altogether.

Rian stepped closer. He saw her surprise, and cupped his hands beneath her elbows. Before she might stop him, he pulled her toward his chest.

Chapter 7

"**W**hat are you doing?" Annora brought her hands between herself and Rian to push him away. It was an instinctive reaction. On occasions too numerous to count, men had pulled her into quiet corners, into sheltered doorways, or beneath the branches of an oak in full summer. Those times, however, she had been in command of her body and soul. Those times, she had not sensed the man's power; she had not heard the pounding of her heart. This was different. This time, enlivening sensations were rippling through her, and she was finding that she quite liked them.

Rian was right.

Annora was afraid of herself.

Despite a pious upbringing, her thoughts were impure. She was *enjoying* the pounding of her heart and the potent heat emanating from Rian, when she should have instead been heeding the many discourses she'd heard on chaste behavior, when she should have been considering her mother's reaction, if Annora were to become the subject of unsavory gossip. But she wasn't thinking of chastity or her mother.

Restraint had fled her. In its stead, something inside Annora taunted her to wind her hands about his neck, to stand up on tip-toe, and raise her mouth to his. *Fire-*

breathing dragons will not swim up the Liffey to devour Dublin. Mortified, terrified that some part of her was capable of following through on such a brazen suggestion, she looked down at the toes of her boots poking from beneath her kirtle and waited for him to step away.

"Och, *leannán,* do not be pushing me away now. 'Tis my intention to show ye there's naught to fear," Rian said. He set a finger aside her chin to tilt her head upward. Her mouth lifted toward his. "I'll not hurt ye." His voice was tender and full of promise.

Annora stared at him, mesmerized. He was so close she felt the airy caress of his words. Her lips parted in anticipation, her hands fell to her sides, and there was nothing between them when he wrapped an arm about her waist to pull her against him. His other hand trailed from her chin along her jaw to the nape of her neck. Annora trembled at his featherlight touch. *To think such large hands could be so tender.* To be near him was impressive. His already remarkable height seemed immense, for the top of her head barely reached his shoulder; and even through layers of clothes, she was aware of his strength. There was an unaccustomed scent about him. It was a distinct, salty essence, and she drew a deep breath, liking the way it seemed to soak into her.

"Close yer eyes." Rian whispered the alluring command, and she obeyed. He brushed a kiss across her mouth. Her lips softened to his. He had not imagined she would be so responsive, nor so sweet. There was the taste of honey and cumin as he had never savored before; attar of roses wafted from her hair and skin. To kiss her made him think of the velvet promise of what could come later, and he wanted more, much more. Rian had a vision of undressing her, deliberately, leisurely, and of unpinning her golden hair to watch it loop about her naked shoulders. He considered lying atop her, and how it would feel at that highly sensuous moment when his bare chest made contact with her full breasts. These images caused a tightening in his groin, but Rian knew he must not frighten her. For now he must needs be satisfied with a kiss.

So this is kissing, Annora sighed. It had happened. Rian O'Byrne was kissing her, and it was everything she'd imagined and more. It was most enjoyable. It made her lips throb, her skin tingle, and her toes curl. She dared to move her lips against his. But it was not only her lips that wished to press against him. Her whole body was seized with unfamiliar need, and she leaned into his chest. She didn't think one kiss would be enough, and at this precise moment, the thought didn't disturb her.

Rian felt her relaxing against him, sensed that first little surrender, that first little success, and he knew this had been enough for now. He lifted his mouth to gaze down at her. He saw the high color of erotic excitement upon her cheeks and brow, and a bright luminescence in her eyes. They had changed hue, darkening to the vivid sapphire of wild clarie. These were the manifestations of freshly awakened passion, not fear. Uncertainty perhaps. Astonishment. Mayhap even pleasure. But not fear, and this was a mighty stimulus to a man of Rian's appetites. From years of experience, Rian knew he should stop, but he couldn't. Not quite yet. He had to kiss her again. He wanted one more taste of those sweet lips, and he brought his mouth to hers once more.

This time, his kiss was different. Delicately, his tongue ran along the seam of her lips. Once, twice, then he exerted a slight pressure to enter within. His tongue traced about the inner edge of her lips, smoothly, slowly. Almost immediately she opened to him.

Annora's senses were reeling. This kiss was even better than the first one. She'd never imagined tongues were part of kissing, and it was a wonderful thing that they were. Faith, she was right to think that one kiss would never be enough. A greedy little need was unfolding within her, and on an inward sigh, a small husky sound escaped her.

Her little moan pleased Rian. He knew it was spontaneous, just as he knew that her body would soon be reacting to his touch in other, equally spontaneous ways. Quick, hot desire filled the length of him, and if she had been anyone else, he would have had her skirts about her waist, no matter the time of year or place. His big frame and powerful legs had supported many a woman in the throes of passion, but that would not do with Annora Picot. He didn't want to repel this woman, and not only because he didn't wish to jeopardize his ultimate goal. He had begun to envision their eventual joining would entail unforgettable ecstasy, especially for her, and that every aspect of their joining would be so breathtaking, so perfect, it would imprint itself upon her for all time. It was an intriguing conceit.

He stopped his probing kiss, and straightened. "Does that frighten ye now?" Rian asked.

It was impossible to catch her breath to speak. Annora gave a tiny negative nod.

"Good."

This time, when Rian reached for her hand, she didn't pull away. He took off the woolen blue mitten, raised her hand, and kissed it, briefly, lightly. "I do not want ye to be afraid. Not ever. And especially not of me," he said, while putting her hand back into the mitten. When this was done, he linked her arm through his, keeping her close by his side. He covered her mittened hand, where it rested up his forearm, with his, and cast a quick glance toward the sky. Clouds were gathering. The wind had changed direction, gusting out of the northeast. "The weather is turning. It'll be snow any time now, I shouldn't wonder. We should not tarry."

They walked the rest of the way in silence, and upon

reaching the convent, Annora showed Rian to the stable, where an old man, wrinkled and gray and twisted from an ailment in his joints, greeted them. Despite his advancing years and slow gait, the old man had charge of the horses and farm, and as he always did, he expressed profound gratitude to Annora. The old man had been the convent's first foundling following the Great Pestilence nearly fifty years before, and in repayment, he had pledged his life in service to the nuns who had taken him in when others had barred their doors to a weary, starving child, who knew not from whence he had come or how long he had been roaming the countryside. The child had not even known by what name his parents had called him, and together the good sisters had agreed to call him Nicholas, after the saint.

It pleased Nicholas to witness the improvements Mistress Annora had brought to the only home he had known. Our Lady of Victory had become prosperous and independent, imbuing it with a certain shield from the greed and political caprice of the outside world. Of equal importance to Nicholas, Annora's generosity meant the nuns seldom had to turn away those in need as had too often been the case when he was younger.

After stabling Rian's horse, Nicholas offered the younger man the hospitality of his modest quarters, a seat by an open fire and a warming drink. Annora went in search of Abbess Thomasin, passing the great Celtic cross that marked the center of the yard. Our Lady of Victory was remarkable in many ways, especially for the substantial stone construction of the diverse buildings within its protective wall. In addition to the stable, there was a chapel and cloister, the abbess's lodge, a steep-pitched, stone-roofed dormitory cum refectory, a kitchen compound, a school, an infirmary, and a long edifice, wherein the production and dying of yarns was accomplished.

Some of these buildings were ancient, a holy house

having occupied this site for many hundreds of years. Originally it had been a monastic community of scribes who meticulously copied and illuminated ecclesiastical manuscripts as well as ancient Irish epics. *Gabriel's work*, it was called. The name of the monastery, however, had long since been forgotten, while the origin of Our Lady of Victory was a tale well known. In 914, Ostmen—those bloodthirsty pirates who came out of the north in dragon-prowed, long boats—prowled the coast. Terrified peasants, fleeing before the advancing invaders, sought shelter in the holy house, and there, with the scribes and a meager handful of warriors, they prayed to the Virgin Mother, reciting in one voice their Ave Marias followed by Paternosters, beseeching Mother Mary's intercession.

The battle had been swift and fierce, the outcome nothing less than a miracle, for the Ostmen suffered heavy losses when a fierce wind swept many of their number off the cliff and into the sea. The holy house, having been saved by the grace of Mary, the Blessed Virgin, was henceforth known as Our Lady of Victory.

It was common knowledge that fishermen, when casting their nets into the ocean, often saw angels hovering above this stretch of coast. For generations it had been told that Divine beings watched over this fragment of the mortal realm; they were messengers of the Lord, radiating the light of goodness and wisdom, of conscience and grace. It was said—and believed by many—that those angels warded off evil, and anyone who promised themselves to the convent was, in turn, granted eternal protection. Since the Ostmen, Our Lady of Victory had endured the Bruce invasion, four plagues, periodic raids by English bandits as well as by native Irish, not to mention numerous violent storms from the sea, but it had survived, and with the blessing of the eight brightest angels from the City of Grace, it would continue to do so for another century, at least.

This afternoon, Annora's visit was not to be as lengthy as usual. Ordinarily she toured the yarn works; often she visited the school; and always, she had currant cake and sweet wine with Abbess Thomasin while they deliberated a host of business details. Were the supplies of raw wool adequate? Was the quality acceptable? How hieful could a particular order be filled? Did Armagh wool absorb the dyes better than that from the sheep of Kilkenny?

Snow began to fall as Annora was crossing the yard, and upon finding the abbess in her lodge, she delivered the hartshorn, plus the pouch of sterling pennies from beneath her kirtle. In return, she accepted a packet with samples of green yarn for her consideration, green being the next color they intended to improve once yellow had been perfected. She enjoyed a small piece of cake and, when finished, agreed to take the rest for her mother. Catherine had a special fondness for currant cake, especially if it had been baked by Sister Fidelma as it had been this day.

"Mayhap you should not be so quick to depart with the weather such as it is," Abbess Thomasin suggested. She rang a bell. A novice entered to wrap the cake in butterbur leaves. "Would you not rather remain with us this night? You are always welcomed."

"I must return to town, else my mother will be consumed with worry."

Abbess Thomasin smiled, serene, accepting. "I did not expect you to say otherwise. Mistress Catherine is no better?"

"I fear not." There was a pocket in the lining of her cloak, and it was there that Annora secured the cake.

"Daily we pray that your mother will be restored to her former self," the abbess said. She made the sign of the cross, invoked a prayer in Latin for healing and mercy, and when done, signed herself again, saying, "In the name of the Father, the Son, and the Holy Spirit.

Amen.'' Her eyes were sad with compassion. She had been a wife and mother before taking her vows, and had not forgotten the despair of the world beyond the convent walls. ''We will pray for the both of you at Vespers, and each morning, the children will light a candle to your mother as will Nicholas, I am certain, for he has always been her devoted servant. If you will not stay, mayhap one of the women should walk back with you.''

''I did not come alone this day. I had an escort. An Irish warrior.'' Quickly Annora added, ''He is known to my uncle.''

''Ah, that is very wise these days.'' The abbess rose to give Annora a fond embrace. Her own daughter had perished in a fire thirty years ago, and over the years, Annora had become as dear to her as the child she'd lost. She had watched another woman's daughter grow from an energetic toddler with a halo of bouncing yellow curls to a curious girl, adventuresome, playful, and clever; from a radiant young woman eager to master her lessons and read every book in the convent library to a benefactress, bountiful and self-confident. Like Catherine, the abbess had hoped Annora would make a fine marriage, and she had not yet abandoned that hope, for despite her years, Annora did not look a day over nineteen.

The abbess understood a woman's need to achieve a sense of accomplishment, to be independent, and to devote one's mind and skills to some purpose beyond basic survival. There had been no way for Thomasin de Barie to attain that except by entering the convent. As for Annora, it was a miracle that she had a choice; a rare and wonderful thing for a woman. There was time yet for Annora to make other choices about matters such as marriage. The Good Lord would not neglect a woman such as Annora Picot. She would be a remarkable wife, devoted and loving, compassionate, and generous. Of a certainty, Annora was the kind of woman who would change a man. Mayhap, the abbess speculated, God was saving Annora for some particular soul in need of transformation.

The abbess went with Annora to the stable and watched the Irishman lift her onto his horse. "You will see that Mistress Annora is safely delivered to her mother?"

"Aye, lady abbess," Rian assured. There was an old blessing he'd been taught to invoke each time he left Aghavannagh, and although many years had passed since he'd spoken the words aloud, they came to him. In Irish, he said, "Bless to me, O God, glorious Lord of angels, the path whereon I go. Father, be thou ever present to guard me, and at my journey's close."

Abbess Thomasin gave an approving nod. The Irish might be considered uncivilized by some, but she knew their devotion to Christ and the Virgin was as absolute as it was steadfast. Annora could wish for no better escort than this warrior. She gave her blessing to the both of them.

Rian swung up behind Annora, who clasped the abbess's hand a final time. He pulled up the hood of his mantle, wheeled the mount round, and they went into the yard.

Nicholas and Abbess Thomasin stood at the arched gateway to watch their departure, and when the great black horse had disappeared over the first rise, the abbess returned to her study. Nicholas secured the gate for the night.

Chapter 8

A thick curtain of snow made it impossible to see more than a few paces in any direction.

There was nothing by which to keep one's bearing, the landmarks used by travelers to guide their way having been obscured from sight. Not even a vague shadow that might have been a bare tree or the line of a low stone wall was to be seen. Nothing but white, and a strange silence. Even the sound of the sea had been somehow muffled.

"We should find shelter," said Rian.

"It can't be much farther." Annora was sitting sideways before him, and when she turned her head away from the protective shelter of his chest, great heavy flakes landed upon her eyelashes. She blinked them away, then peered into the storm, but saw not a thing. "Surely the fires in the encampment should be visible by now."

" 'Tis the snow playing tricks on ye. We're not so close as ye'd like to think."

"Perhaps it would be best if we returned to the convent."

"If I thought we could retrace our course along this winding road, I'd say 'twas the best idea, but I fear we've already missed more than one turn and have strayed some distance from the road." It was impossible to discern the

83

sides of the byway, or in which direction to angle or turn each time they crested another rise. The danger of getting confused was real. Indeed, it could prove fatal. To one side of the king's road, the land came to an abrupt halt above the sea; in the other direction were the dense forests of *terra guerre* in which to get lost. " 'Tis wisest, I'm thinking, to dismount and continue on foot. Hopefully it will be easier to heed any hazards." He slid off the horse, then reached for Annora and set her on the ground. "Besides, moving about will keep us warmer."

The snow on the ground was already high enough to cover Annora's wooden pattens, sobering proof that this storm, like most aspects of the natural world, could easily defeat mortals. She had heard of winter storms in which people vanished, in which entire herds of cattle had been frozen in place and buried until spring, and of such cold that men and women had lost toes and fingers, even an ear, if too long exposed to the elements. Annora had never been outside in such a snow. Always she had watched through the green glass of the tower windows, and always it had seemed beautiful, magical. Snow was something in which to make merry, something that, at worst, might inconvenience everyday transactions on the quay, but it had never been a dread. They had always been warm and secure in the tower, always had enough wood or turf, always enough to eat.

Now that magical snow was something vastly different, and wishing for reassurance, Annora reached for Rian's hand. It was impossible to be brave without this contact to affirm she wasn't alone. Her mittened hand clasped his.

Rian almost stumbled when Annora grabbed his hand. Her apprehension was palpable, and he experienced an actual sensation in the region of his chest upon realization that her need was focused upon him. It was an unsettling, unfamiliar sensation, but never so awful as the memory it aroused.

Through the windows of Rian's mind flashed long

neglected images of his wife. He saw her bloodless face as if she were before him, heard her begging for his help as if she were beside him, and he remembered how he'd failed her. He had not been able to prevent Muiríol's death; indeed, there were many who blamed him for it. Verily, he had never wanted to be responsible for another human life, and he did not intend to be in such a position again. Rian never wanted to care enough one way or the other about anyone or anything.

That Annora Picot had caused him to think of Muiríol was staggering. No two women could be more dissimilar, and yet somehow Annora had stirred up the past. Something inside Rian that he'd believed deadened had been reawakened, and he didn't like it. Mayhap this matter of seduction had gotten out of control. Perhaps his plan should be abandoned, and once he'd seen Annora safely to her mother, he should return to the mountains never to encounter her again.

"How far do you think we've actually come?" asked Annora.

"In all likelihood not yet half the distance," he replied, forcibly clearing his mind of anything beyond the present. "Is there any shelter hereabout?"

" 'Tis mostly gardens tended by Dublin folk who live within the walls, but among the plots are scattered an occasional cottage for summer nights when the town is too hot."

Rian asked how many of those cottages there might be, and Annora told him no more than a dozen. He pondered their options.

"Since it is bound to be a shorter distance to a cottage than to the town gates, we must take a chance and pray we soon stumble upon one."

They turned westward, away from the sea, and shortly found themselves going down a steep incline.

"There is a stream hereabouts?" he asked.

"Aye, a brook winds through the allotments."

"We'll not go any farther then, for we don't wish to be getting our feet wet."

They trudged back up the incline and cautiously continued along the ridge of the embankment, where it was possible to follow the curling path of what was surely a stream. They had not gone far when, out of the blinding whiteness, a flint cottage loomed before them, appearing so suddenly that if they'd been going any faster they would have collided with it.

"We are blessed," said Annora upon finding the door unlocked.

They entered with the horse.

On one side of the single room was a byre separated by a slatted railing from the area intended for human occupation. There was a heavy table against one wall, a bench beside the door, and a neat stack of turf in a corner. The rushes upon the tamped dirt floor were old, but clean; the roof appeared to be holding; the walls were secure; and a pyre of kindling and turf was arranged in a fire pit. Nature had not yet taken back this room. There was naught but a faint rustling of tiny creatures in one corner, no odor of rodent infestation.

"We'll be fine now," said Rian. He took off his cloak, shook off the snow, then draped it over the railing. Annora followed his example as Rian reached for the flint in the pouch at his waist. Crouching beside the fire pit, he unsheathed his dagger, set its point in the middle of the pyre, and struck the flint against the blade. Sparks flew, a wisp of smoke rose from the dry leaves and twigs. Rian withdrew the dagger, leaned forward and blew. The kindling ignited. The little blaze popped and crackled, and after a few minutes, Rian arranged additional turf into the best position to create a slow-burning fire.

Annora crouched beside him. A ring of stones circled the fire pit, and she held her hands a mere breath above one of them, massaging her fingers and hands until the stiffness began to leave her extremities. Next she sat back to work on her legs and feet and toes. Rian did the same, and for a while neither of them said a word. At length, she sighed, and he glanced sideways at her. There were faint smudges beneath her eyes, and her pretty features were twisted into a little frown as she kneaded her lower leg. In sympathy, he spoke, " 'Tis hard work, is it not, to trek through such cumbersome snows?"

"I did not know it could be like that."

"Aye, we are fortunate it was no worse. We should rest now," Rian said. He stood and began to push the floor rushes into a single pile a safe distance from the fire. After fashioning this makeshift pallet, he pulled the table away from the wall, and set it on its side so that the top served as a wall to hold the fire's heat on the one side, while keeping the colder air on the other side. "If the snow continues through the night, it could be knee high by the time the clouds break. The trip back to town will be even more arduous. We will be needing every dram of our energies." He sat upon the pallet with his back against the tabletop, his long legs extended before him. " 'Tis not bad," he remarked at his handiwork, and grinned, satisfied and optimistic. "Ye should not be shy now. *Suid go dluit le mo taob.* Join me. *Sit close by my side.*"

Gratified, Annora sat beside him, and when Rian lifted the patchwork of furs in invitation for her to come closer, she went beneath, knowing that she would never criticize the garment again. It did not reek of onions or sour ale as she had imagined, and it provided much needed warmth as did his gigantic body.

Rian looked down at her. The firelight cast a golden glow upon her delicate features, heightening her soft beauty, enhancing her infinite femininity, inviting his attention. The coil of hair had come undone and bright curls tumbled about her neck, over one shoulder; soft wisps framed her face. His gaze moved to her lips, which seemed to him as plump and ripe as a plum that should be eaten else it might spoil. Annora Picot was an exquisite, desirable female, and they were alone with a long, cold night ahead of them. Rian brought her up against his torso. Her head was resting upon his chest, and after he wrapped the fur across the both of them, he slipped his hands back beneath the fur and entwined them about her.

"Thank you," she whispered. Rian O'Byrne covered her as thoroughly as if he were a blanket. It was almost as if he'd swallowed her up.

"Och, 'tis nothing."

"Nay, you have saved my life."

Rian swallowed the denial he wished to utter. *He did not wish to be responsible for her. He could not be responsible for her.* "Sleep now," he said. "Fair dreams be with ye this night."

"Fair dreams," Annora replied. Her eyelids closed, but it was not sleep that settled upon her. Rather it was awareness of Rian O'Byrne's body. She smelled the tangy aroma, through the coarse tunic she sensed his body heat, and when he spoke or moved, she felt his muscles rippling, flexing, she even heard his heartbeat. But it was not the same awareness as when he had kissed her. It was different. This was somehow safe and reassuring, and she drifted to sleep, knowing that for tonight she was secure with this man.

But Rian did not sleep as easily. He was thinking again of Muiríol. It had been a long time since he'd thought of her. In those first months after her death, he hadn't been able to escape the memories. Now he hardly remembered her at all.

He had been nineteen and Muiríol only fourteen when they had wed. Seven months later she'd celebrated her fifteenth spring, and three weeks after that she'd been dead, still nothing more than a child. Rian could not conceive of what manner of woman Muiríol might have become over the past six years, for she had never expressed any opinions or desires, had never spoken of dreams or aspirations, had never revealed any singular qualities that might have distinguished her from any other wife. Muiríol had followed him about like a kitten on padded paws, waiting to do his bidding, never making demands or voicing complaints. She had been sweet-tempered and passing pretty, and she had endeared herself to Rian because he knew she loved him and depended upon him.

Then he had failed. He had failed to honor that love. He had failed to protect her.

Rising above the howl of the wind, Rian heard Muiríol's young voice, and this time, it was not cries of agony he heard, nor the pleas for help that used to haunt him. It was the rare laughter, and her wispy little-girl voice when she asked if he wanted another helping of cheese soup or if he liked the fringed jacket she had embroidered for him.

Long into the night, Rian stared at the glowing fire, and when he finally succumbed to sleep, his mind was not host to the demons he had too often seen since his wife died, the devils that grabbed at him, bayed at him to forsake God, to deny virtue and faith, and turn away from family and friends. It was not the devils who had advised him to pursue wickedness he heard that night. Instead Muiríol continued to whisper to him, warning him, urging him to be careful with Annora Picot.

"Yer heart is good, *deg-oclach*," Muiríol assured. She called him *brave warrior*. "Ye know I've believed that always, and have never abandoned ye, never doubted ye. Be cautious with Annora Picot," she counseled. Her little-girl voice was far too wise. "She holds the key, indeed she does, and ye must do naught to prevent her from unlocking the coffer chest that holds yer heart. Ye must be keeping her near and dear, *deg-oclach*. Never let her go."

Chapter 9

A shrill wind roused Annora. It moaned round the cottage, battered at the roof. She shuddered and sat up, leaning forward to warm her hands above the stones around the fire pit. A faint glow illuminated the space beside her. Rian was gone from the pallet. Annora twisted around to peek over the edge of the table. The rest of the cottage was in shadows. It took awhile for her eyes to adjust. First, she saw the sparkle of icicles streaking the wall, then the outlines of a horse and man. Rian was whispering to the beast as he rubbed its flanks.

"Hello," Annora said.

Rian gave the horse a final pat, and moved toward the fire.

"What time of day might it be?"

"Mid-morning, I would be guessing, for the fire has nearly burnt out. Soon it will be naught but embers."

"And the storm?" She looked up at him. He stood in the arc of light, looming so tall that his face remained obscured.

"The snow has stopped, but not the wind. We cannot be traveling, for 'tis a fierce wind that blows, and 'tis white as lamb's fleece on the other side of the door. We would not be able to see our way any better than before." He hunkered down. "Are ye hungry, now?"

"Only a little. 'Tis not my custom to break my night's fast with anything more than a bit of bread, and some water or cider to quench my thirst."

"Will dried cherries suffice instead of bread?" Rian produced a small leather pouch, and when Annora's reply was positive, he next revealed a wineskin. "As for this, 'tis neither water nor cider, but the finest hazelnut wine in the hills from Imail to Clara."

Annora smiled.

"Och, yer expression brightens. Do not be telling me ye've got an excessive fondness for drink." He frowned. "Alas, I was thinking ye were just about the most perfect female I'd ever known."

"Nay, 'tis not *excessive fondness* that makes me smile. It pleases me to think how your wine is the perfect accompaniment for fresh currant cake."

"Currant cake, is it, now, and fresh, ye say?"

"Baked only yesterday."

"Ye would not be trifling with a hungry man, would ye?"

"I would never do such a thing. 'Tis from the convent. I was bringing it to my mother from Abbess Thomasin. Pass me my mantle, if you please."

Rian reached back for the cloak. He handed it to her and watched her reach inside the garment.

"Here it is. The very best currant cake in all the Vale of Dublin," Annora said in an amicable rephrasing of Rian's praise for the hazelnut wine. She unwrapped the cake, split in two, and handed the larger one to Rian. He, in turn, divided the dried cherries. They passed the wineskin between them.

"You boast with righteousness. The wine is commendable," Annora said. It was sweet and potent. She must needs be mindful not to drink too much else she might become giddy and talk about things of which she ought not to speak. Annora had already behaved in a manner quite unlike herself with this man. She did not need to do anything else that might encourage that tendency again.

"Commendable," he scoffed as if her praise were an insult. "But is it not the *finest* hazelnut wine ye've ever imbibed? What say ye now?"

"I cannot say," she said. "I've never had it before."

"Never?" Rian did not conceal his astonishment.

"Never," Annora affirmed. It was with prudence that she chose her words, "I have lived my entire life under the rule of Parliament as it was enacted at Kilkenny before I was born." Intended to abolish all connections between Anglo-Normans and native Irish, the Kilkenny Statute of 1367 dictated almost every aspect of English life in Ireland. The English language must be spoken; English fashion maintained; English food, law, and even saddles were required; the use of Irish names was forbidden. Regarded with equal loathing by Anglo-Normans and Irish alike, the statute had been flaunted from the moment it had been declared the law of the land. It had never achieved its purpose. Verily, its failure was in great part responsible for the recent arrival of King Richard.

Despite the statute's lack of success, there were some English in Ireland who dared not defy a single chapter, no matter how absurd, petty, unjust, cruel, or inconvenient. Catherine Picot had been one such individual, and she had raised her daughter to obey its every requirement. To any observer, Annora Picot was as obedient a citizen as her mother. Annora's behavior was faultless. What took place in her mind was, however, most disgraceful. There were no warders to monitor her dreams, no informers to eavesdrop upon a young woman's fantasies, and when all else was said and done, mayhap it was the enforced, outward denial of all things Irish that had made Rian O'Byrne and his kind enticing to Annora. Her cheeks grew warmer. She stared at the fire.

"While there is much about my life that may be thought unusual, much that has caused the gossips to whisper behind their hands, there is one thing about which my mother has always been most conventional. She has never challenged the statute in any way. We have never bought wool from Irish shepherds even though it is often finer and more reasonably priced, never hired any Irish workers unless they spoke perfect English and agreed to abide by the law. There was no other choice for my mother, for as a widow granted the right to run her husband's business, there was far too much to be put at risk."

Annora paused. Rian was watching her, listening intently, and she bethought herself how strange it was that she had spoken more of herself to him than to anyone else.

"As a child, I did not comprehend such complex matters as the statute, or the notion of choices and the risks against which a woman must guard her person and property. But later, when my mother allowed me to apprentice with her, I, too, had certain choices taken from me, and then I understood. As women, even women of wealth, everything we have—be it our livelihood or the roof over our head—is at the sufferance of others, in particular male others, who are more often than not covetous and scheming. My mother has lived with the persistent belief that those jealous ones were waiting for her to make the merest slip, waiting for any excuse to demand punishment and the confiscation of our assets, eviction from the tower, and revocation of our rights as merchants. Without fail we have observed English custom and dress, and faithfully avoided anything Irish, even something as simple as this wine."

Rian was struck by the waste of what she described. It confirmed his distaste for politics. "What ye say makes this a very costly drink. Rare. And alarming." His deep whisper was alluring, his movements were deliberate. He held up the wine skin, and poured a single drop onto the tip of his finger, and as his gaze held hers, he rubbed that moistened finger along her lower lip. "Och, how could I be forgetting yer life is fettered by a fortune? And such a fortune it is, having the power to blind foolish Englishmen to yer beauty and wit."

"Are you flirting with me?" Annora asked. Of course he was. In thought, word and *deed*. Her lips were tingling where he touched them, and her tongue licked away the intoxicating moisture. Her head was spinning from the wine, or mayhap it was the way his rasping, low tone skirled up her spine. This was dangerous. The wine was dangerous. Rian O'Byrne was dangerous.

"Och, *bé find*, what am I to be telling ye? I find myself in a secluded cottage on a long winter's day with a *fair lady* and an excellent wine, and ye ask if I'm flirting with ye. Does the bee not always know his way to the sweetest nectar?" He gave her a bawdy wink. "Ye did not think I was such a fool as yer Englishmen now, did ye? There is no fortune on earth that would blind this Irishman to yer qualities."

Annora smiled, although she ought to be chastising him instead. Rian O'Byrne was captivating and handsome, and irresistible, but she could not have stopped herself from smiling. Truth to tell, being with him in this intimate manner pleased her. He was everything which her lewd, wayward imagination had fancied. She had thought it safe to dream about rugged features, honed muscles, and a hungry mouth, because fantasies, especially those involving *wild Irishry*, did not become reality in Annora Picot's world. He spoke of fools, but she was the fool, not him. The fool for allowing herself to smile, allowing herself to enjoy sitting close and flirting. "Nay, I would never think you're a fool, Rian O'Byrne. A scoundrel mayhap, but no fool," she said, breathless, enthralled.

He returned her smile. Her expression was soft, yielding. There was a certain ripeness in the sleepy-lidded look of her eyes that he had seen in countless other women. There was something else, too. Something he'd never seen before, and it made him uneasy, made him wish that he could walk out the door and never look back. Of course, it wasn't possible to leave, but he could create distance between them, and without saying another word, Rian rose to fetch more turf. He busied himself with building a fresh pyre, then rebuilding, rearranging, stirring the ashes, and reconfiguring the turf. Only when it was impossible to prolong the task another minute did he look back to the pallet.

Annora was sitting with her knees to her chest. She had tucked the mantle about her legs, her hands were hooked about her knees. He watched her stiffen as if to prevent herself from shivering, but she shook despite her efforts, and it occurred to Rian that he had caught her in an unguarded moment. She was not as brave as she wanted him to believe. The exterior poise and veneer of confidence were not the outward grace of some inner serenity, but a manifestation of isolation, and Rian could not shake the notion that this must be how it was for her much of the time. Annora Picot was beautiful, blessed, admired, and generous, yet alone, and in a constant struggle to pretend it was not so.

Something jolted inside Rian. She was awakening something in him even though he knew it was best not to care whether she were brave or alone, or if she were truly serene or actually trying to create a facade of composure. He didn't want to care, nor to allow himself a moment's compassion for her, but he couldn't stop himself from sitting beside her, couldn't stop himself from putting an arm about her shoulder and pulling her to him as he'd done the night before. In silence, Rian cursed himself. Women were good for one thing, he must remember that; one thing and nothing more. That was why his arm was wrapped about her shoulder. Sex and seduction. There was no other reason to pull her close.

"Is that better now?" he asked.

"It seems your promise to keep me warm becomes reality." Annora angled her head to look at him. That knowing, lopsided grin was edging up at the corners of his full mouth. A predatory look came to his eyes. What had possessed her to speak in such a bold manner? No doubt, he was remembering the rest of that promise. He was remembering how he had offered to teach her the joys of love, how he had promised to show her a thousand pleasures.

Annora swallowed. Her eyelashes fluttered down, modest, uncertain. Warmth was rising on her cheeks. His gaze was moving over her, and she held her breath while through her mind seeped the image of waves tugging at her toes, lapping at her ankles, splashing at her calves. It was overtaking her once again, the way of twenty devils. The water was warm. *Come in,* a devil called. *Dragons will not swim up the Liffey.*

Slowly she exhaled, and wondering if Rian grinned still, Annora could not stop herself from peeking.

Rian heard her gasp. He observed her confusion, saw the evidence of her failed effort to resist looking at. His loins tightened, blood coursed through him, and in the space of a single second, every noble intention he'd considered yesternight fled.

This was it. The time had come. There would be no returning this woman to Dublin as chaste as she had been upon her departure. Rian smiled much as he had when he'd seen her framed in the tower window, much as he had when they'd collided outside the tavern. Aye, the time had come, Rian decided, staring into her upturned face. He was going to consummate his seduction of Annora Picot, here and now.

"Nách cúala, maidid cridi cech duni día seirc is día

inmuni?'' whispered Rian. He translated the lilting Irish on a hush so subdued Annora had to lean closer to catch the words, *''Have ye not heard, the hearts of all break with longing and love for her?''*

From the fire came the pop and crackle of dry twigs catching flame. From the other side of the cottage drifted the even breathing of the horse, from the shadows came the scurry of mice. Annora heard none of this as she stared at Rian, well and truly enchanted. This was no fantasy. Rian O'Byrne was real. He was flesh and blood and muscle, and he could transform from dream to reality every unrestrained imagining of her mind. She knew this as certainly as she knew this moment would never come again.

Rian watched her eyes deepening to a vibrant blue. He murmured, ''Wild clarie. Do ye know what they say about the seeds of the clarie flower?''

She nodded. *Aye.* A wee shiver splashed like a wave at the back of her neck. There was no Englishman, no Norseman, no Venetian, Parisian, or Florentine who was as adept as Rian O'Byrne was with words. His was the magical tongue of a libertine versifier. It would be next to impossible for a woman to resist a man such as Rian O'Byrne. Impossible for Annora, who had a sudden vision of being on a strand as the tide turned; water was surrounding her, the waves were getting larger, coming closer together.

If Rian O'Byrne asked, Annora would surrender to his beckoning ocean eyes.

''But ye've no need of such a drink now, do ye? There's wild clarie in yer blood, I'm thinking,'' he drawled, hoping that he was right about her, that there was passion hidden beneath her perfect facade, and that an unquenchable fire was starting to seethe within her. ''Do ye know what I've been wanting to do since I saw ye with yer hair spinning round yer face like a halo?'' He didn't expect an answer, and raising a hand to the coil that remained intact, he went on, "I've been wanting to run my fingers through that glorious abundance."

Quickly, deftly, Rian freed the last of her hair. A profusion of flaxen tresses tumbled to her shoulders, blending with the hair that had been loose since the night before. He took a ragged breath, part wonderment, part anticipation, and spreading wide the fingers of both hands, he threaded them through her hair. Starting at the nape of her neck, Rian worked upward, raising those long locks off her back and shoulders, moving higher until the ends sifted between his fingers. Again he lifted the luxuriant mantle, but this time, he used only one hand, not two, and instead of letting the hair slip away, he entwined it about his fingers.

"Och, to wrap myself in its silken softness. I've been waiting for this, wanting this. Just as I've been wanting to caress yer pearly fair skin, *leannán*." He called her *sweetheart*, and with his other hand, he ran one long finger down her cheek to her chin. He rubbed the pad of his thumb across her lips. Instantly they parted to his touch, and very clearly, he whispered, "And from the first time I saw ye, I've been wanting to kiss ye. And ye must not be reminding me of what passed between us on the road yesterday, for delightful as it was, I'm finding those kisses were not enough. Not enough by far," he whispered as he lowered his mouth to her lips.

Annora's breath caught, and in the next heartbeat, his mouth claimed hers. Lightly he feathered, nipped, and brushed at her lips. He rained kisses over her face, her neck, behind her ear, and she returned them with an eagerness that matched his fervor. She heard him groan. His hold about her tightened, and he rose to kneel before her, pulling her to face him in a similar kneeling stance. He drew her to him, holding her chest against his torso to kiss her thoroughly.

Her mouth opened to his probing tongue. Her body

was melting into his. She swayed against him as his hands slid from her waist, over her hips, and down to her buttocks. His large hands cupped her backside and squeezed. A wave crashed over her. In another moment, the water would pull her out to sea. Heat rippled through Annora. No one had ever touched her like this before. His hands were massaging her bottom in a slow, circular motion, and she sighed in amazement as the whole of her seemed to be awakening to this fondling. Her skin tingled, her breasts grew taut, and a tide of desire swirled about her. Soon she would not be able to stand against the force of it.

His lips rose from hers. She opened her eyes. He was staring at her with blatant desire. A flush of exhilaration flared upon her face. Her heart was thudding in her throat, and as his scorching gaze held hers, his hands continued their gentle, circular pressure against her backside. What huge hands they were, and such long fingers, pressing and kneading along the roundness of her bottom. Those lovely, long fingers dipped into the valley of her backside, they skimmed downward, and delving between her legs, it seemed his fingers nearly reached the other side of her. All the while he kept kissing her, hard and demanding. There was an unfamiliar contraction at the secret apex of her, and it did not stop, but instead intensified. He had not actually touched that private place, yet the sweet presence of his fingers near such sensitive flesh made the throbbing undeniable, insistent.

Kissing was wonderful, but this other sensation was unimaginable. She knew men touched a woman's female parts, but she had not imagined a woman could throb in this way. It was not pain, but a yearning that weakened her legs and made her tremble. The needs of her body were stronger than any conscious thought she'd ever had.

"Ye're not afraid are ye, *leannán?*" He felt her trembling.

"Nay, I am not afraid of you. You have shown me

there is naught to fear from you.'' It was barely a whisper as her head fell back, hair trailing on the ground behind her. The ache between her legs was increasing, and she did what her body demanded. There was an emptiness that needed to be filled, and she arched upward, searching for a remedy.

Rian saw the rapid little pulse at the base of her throat as her head fell back. He was reminded of butterfly wings. *Pulse. Pulse. Pulse.* He could almost hear the thrum of blood as she tilted her hips to him. Lust charged through him with the speed of an arrow flying from a bolt. His loins clenched tight, his gut contracted, and his thigh muscles tensed as his shaft became engorged with desire. She would soon be his, soon he would be inside her, and the prospect of such heavenly release made him reckless.

''Ye inflame me.'' Rian took her hand. He guided it to the swollen length of his sex. ''Feel what ye do to me. The power ye wield over me.''

''I never dreamed,'' she whispered, breathless. His phallus was larger than her hand, and very hard. Even through his leggings, she sensed an almost impalpable vibrating beneath her fingers. It was as if it were a breathing, living thing.

Rian groaned in an agony of desire. Her quietly spoken astonishment confirmed her innocence; it confirmed that he would be the first. Another pulse of desire shot through him, making him even firmer, thicker. Her small hand was trembling, and the promise of the pleasure when there would be no barriers between them was a mighty erotic force. His voice was raw with desire. ''That part of me wants ye. Aches for ye. Grows for ye.''

Reluctantly he removed her hand and placed it about his neck. He held her hips to position his straining erection against the female cradle of her. He rocked into her, gently at first. ''Do ye know what I want to do to ye?'' he murmured against her lips. He rocked again, exerting a little more pressure. "Do ye know what it is I'm going to do to ye?"

She nodded. She knew.

"Let me hear ye say it."

"You . . . you want to . . ." She could scarcely speak, focused as she was upon the bulge between his legs that fit so perfectly to her. Shocking warmth was seeping through her. "You want to have me."

"Och, there is more to it than that, and I want to hear ye say it." He rotated into her, exerting more pressure. Both his hands gripped her bottom, those fingers reaching, probing.

"You want to"—Annora had never said the word before—"You want to . . . to diddle me."

Rian laughed not in mockery or unkindness. It was a remarkably tender sound, and on impulse, he kissed the end of her nose. But when he spoke his expression was entirely roguish. "Diddling is for skinny English boys. I want to possess ye, *leannán,* to lie between yer milky white thighs, and ride ye, love ye, make ye mine as no other man will ever be able to do. *A ben, día rís mo niamh tind, is barr óir bias fort chind,*" he said. *"O woman, if ye come to my firm lust, a crown of gold will be on yer head.* Are ye ready for me do ye think?"

Annora's head was spinning. The dreams and fantasies had come to this, and she did not stop to wonder at the right or wrong of it. Her body quivered. She wanted this even though he did not love her, even though there could be no future between them, even though it could destroy her mother, even though it was against the laws of God and man. Her private parts molded to the maleness of him, and she savored the myriad pleasures sweeping through her. Annora wanted this because she knew this time would never come again. "I will not stop you."

"But are ye ready for me?" Rian reached under her kirtle to caress her leg. He moved up the woolen over-the-knee stockings, past the leather garters that held them in place. Soon there was naught but bare skin. The flesh of her inner thigh quivered beneath his fingertips, and as he skimmed higher, she relaxed, parting her legs to his touch. Higher, higher he went until he could go no further. There was no barrier at the top, where the skin was warm and smooth, and his seeking fingers brushed across the downy nest between her legs. She gasped, jolted. "Nay, do not move away. I must check that ye're ready," he said as he sought her female source. Easily he inserted one finger between the damp netherlips. She was hot and dewy, and a groan rumbled from deep in his throat at this evidence of her readiness. He stroked his finger in and out of her. In and out, in and out. She was tight, mayhap, too tight to accommodate him, and cautiously, he slid a second finger inside, then a third, manipulating, stretching.

A series of throaty little whimpers escaped Annora. She had no more control over the sounds she was making than the way her body was reacting to his touch. Never in her most carnal imaginings had she thought there could be such bliss as this, and she clasped her hands about his neck, unashamed by the moisture between her legs and the abandon with which she opened to him. She was in the ocean now, deep and wild and stormy, and very soon the waves would close over her head, but she was not frightened, and she moved on his probing, tormenting fingers.

"Och, ye're a natural, ye are, lovely Annora," Rian said. He had been right about the hidden passion; she wanted more, and he knew this was only the beginning. Most mortals would never experience such earthly delight. He helped her recline upon the pallet, bent her legs at the knees, parted her thighs, and knelt between them, still stroking her. With his other hand, he pulled the leather cord from his leggings, and parted the fabric to release himself.

Annora's breathing was shallow, rapid, and when his

man's instrument sprang free her heart skipped a beat at the sight of it. It jutted between the overlapping front of his tunic, standing upright to reveal the potency of its arousal. It made her think of a great siege engine, a massive, battering weapon of distended, vibrating flesh, and she could not believe it would be as pleasant as his long fingers. Still she was not frightened. She trusted him not to hurt her, and glanced to his face for assurance. But he was not looking at her. She saw in amazement that he was looking downward, his gaze fixed between her legs, watching his fingers stroke her.

Rian knew that he must needs take charge not to hurt her. He must prepare her for his entry, and he knew exactly what to do. With one hand, he spread open her female lips. In the firelight, she glistened, tantalizing, almost ready, and with his other hand, he held the head of his erect yard against that abundant dew.

She shuddered as the broad male tip skimmed up her parted sex, then down, gently pressing as it moved over her, but never entering, and after several such exquisite caresses, he leaned closer to place his full length against her. This pressure was more than Annora could stand. The ache inside her was excruciating, and moaning, she writhed against him, reveling in the friction she created by rubbing her exposed parts along his swollen flesh.

"Och, ye're an eager one, ye are, my lovely Annora. Now, don't ye be worrying. Don't ye be getting anxious. I mercly want to make certain this first time does not pain ye any more than is necessary." Deliberately, he continued to rub at her outer folds drawing out the plentiful female juices. This not only lubricated him, but she was getting wetter than any woman he'd ever been with before. The poised Annora Picot was making little noises of need, her hips were moving frantically, and she was squirming against him as she spread her legs wider, rubbed against him harder, faster.

It was time. She wanted him inside her, and Rian was

more than happy to oblige. He pulled back a few inches to guide the helmeted tip to her. Easily, it entered. Indeed, it seemed she swallowed him as those lips compressed about the rim. The velvety flesh of her sheath was hot, slick, and her body welcomed him, her inner muscles contracting in reaction to his invasion. He wanted nothing more than to plunge into her, but neither did he wish to alarm her, and using every ounce of control he might muster, he held himself still in deference to her inexperience. This honest intent was, however, shattered in the next second when he sensed a quivering within her. Annora's body arched upward, she cried out, and there was no time to discern whether she cried from a virgin's discomfort or sensual need. The sudden movement pushed him deeper. He was half-way in, and he was past any vestige of self-control.

"Now," he growled. " 'Tis time."

He breached her maidenhood with a single powerful thrust, roaring with savage pleasure as he buried himself to the hilt. Her inner flesh tightened about him in a clasp that would have been painful were it not for the astonishing moisture that continued to flow over him, and he emitted another feral growl as those inner muscles accommodated him, indeed, they coaxed him deeper. He leaned forward to her chest, but did not rest his weight upon her. Instead, he lifted her upper body off the pallet and held her at this angle, allowing for enhanced penetration. He began to move, each thrust long and slow, each time pulling himself out to the very tip, so that when he reentered her, it was even more delicious than before.

Annora grasped his shoulders, her fingernails digging into him. She registered every aspect of this sensual motion. At the beginning of each thrust, she was aware of the enormous tip of his manhood as this thickest part of him opened her to his shaft; each time, she was aware of the exact moment when the rim of that tip slipped into her; with each penetration she moaned as inch by inch of his massive, pulsing shaft entered her, and each time, when he had filled her, she met his body with eager movements of her own.

"Follamnaig mo chridesea," Rian cried. It was a harsh, raw, almost desperate outburst, followed by another, *"Corop tú mo dilesea."*

Neither of these utterances did Annora comprehend, but when his movements quickened she understood.

Without inhibition, without guilt, without any regard for the future, Annora writhed beneath him in eager response, matching his movements, and urging him on with her sighs, her hands. He bucked into her, his burnished brown hair swinging against her face, his torso pumping faster, and the small dark cottage reverberated with primal groans, the impact of pounding flesh.

Annora was in the middle of the ocean, caught in a whirlpool, the forces of nature spinning her out of control. She cried out frantic, held tight to Rian, heard him bellow, sensed him jerk, tighten, and for a second, she was frightened. For a second it seemed she could not breathe. Then a great wave pulled her from that vortex, lifting her, where she might breathe again, and carried her in gentle, undulating fulfillment back to land.

In the end time stood still.

They were the only two people in the world, and this was the moment that mattered.

This moment was beginning. And end.

Muiríol, the betrayed child bride, was long gone from Rian's thoughts, and Annora bethought herself at ease with what had come to pass.

INTERLUDE FIRST

Interlude

As soon as the winds had diminished, Sir Thomas had led a search party for Annora, and while half the men had searched the road to the convent, Sir Thomas had taken the others to inspect the cottages among the garden plots. In the first, they had found an elderly couple crushed beneath a portion of collapsed roof; in another cottage huddled a band of lepers, several of their number having perished, for they possessed not a flint among them. The storm had been sudden and brutal, and Sir Thomas had accepted that even if Annora had found shelter, she might not have survived. The knight had been sorely discouraged. He had faced numerous enemies, and had marched valiant into many a battle, but he did not think he had sufficient courage to return to Catherine with such wretched news as the death of her only child.

Thus it was that Sir Thomas never questioned how Rian O'Byrne came to be with Annora, nor what could have transpired in that lonely cottage. His only consideration was gratitude that there had been someone to help his niece survive.

That winter, Rian came to Dublin often, and each time, he visited Annora. Three times, he escorted her with the blessing of Catherine and Sir Thomas to the convent, and on each of those occasions, they passed several hours in the flint cottage by the stream.

Through February and into March, King Richard continued to receive oaths of homage from the Irish. Chieftain after chieftain set aside his girdle and skein, and fell down upon his knees at Richard's feet. These humilities satisfied the young monarch, who believed his conquest of Ireland to be near at hand, and failed to comprehend that this land and its people could not be so easily vanquished.

The first Sunday in Lent, the day MacMurrough and O'Byrne had pledged to quit Leinster, passed as if it were any other day. The Irish did not move. Still the king was not deterred.

On Lady Day, March 25, the Feast of the Annunciation, Richard knighted at Christ Church cathedral four Irish chieftains, among them two Leinstermen, Mac-Murrough and O'Connor. But this strategy miscarried when MacMurrough and three other chieftains, O'Byrne, O'Moore, and O'Mullain, were arrested and detained at the castle on charges of plotting against the English. After several days, MacMurrough was set at liberty, shortly thereafter the others escaped.

None among the Irish would forget this English perfidy.

Within hours, they rode out of Dublin steadfast in their belief in English treachery, the course of their hatred for these foreigners deeper and darker than ever. Rian went with them. It was not safe in *terra pacis* for an Irishman, especially a warrior from the hills of Leinster.

Annora did not cry when Rian bid her farewell. She had known there was no future for her with one of the wild Irish, nothing beyond this moment, yet she hadn't been ready for it to end that spring afternoon.

They were visiting in the garden, and Rian had strolled alongside Annora as she cut the earliest flowers from the rose arbor, but it had been too chilly to linger over long on the path. Although winter had left Dublin, the wind off the Liffey was as incessant and damp as always, and having filled the basket with crimson and white blooms, they stood in the recessed entryway that led from the workroom, where the scribes kept their accounts, to Catherine's walled garden. The entryway offered an intimate shelter from the wind as well as from the curious eyes of anyone who might be glancing out a window. Rian could drape his arm about Annora, and she could nestle against him. They could abandon their pretense of friendship and be lovers exchanging heated gazes, sweet kisses, caresses, and fervent promises of what it was they would do when they could be truly alone. There, they could speak in voices that no one inside the workroom could hear above an incessant clicking as the scribes rapidly moved bits of bone back and forth on polished tally sticks.

Something was different this afternoon. There was a strange quality in the way Rian looked at Annora, and she suspected what was going to be said. She had heard about the arrests, MacMurrough's release, and that the chieftains and their warriors were leaving Dublin. She knew what was to come. It was inevitable.

"Ye won't be forgetting me now will ye?" asked Rian. He threaded both his hands through the thick burnished hair that made him appear so wild. It was a movement that was somehow boyish, almost vulnerable. "I have to be going, and I won't be coming back. Do ye understand?"

"Aye," she said, softly, sadly. This time would never come again, and her heart began to ache. It was well and truly over.

"Ye won't be forgetting that ye're mine for all time?"

"How can you say such a thing?" Annora imagined her expression must be brittle. There was a momentary tremor in her chin she could not control, and in an effort to conceal her misery, she pressed her lips together in a thin, taut line.

" 'Twas the fire between us, *leannán*. I knew from the first kiss that ye would be different from any other. Ye're mine forever, *sweetheart*. Mine. *A ben, bennacht fort. Ropo mían dom menmainse aitreab ríchid réil. O woman, a blessing on thee. It were my mind's desire to dwell in bright paradise,*" he translated to English, one sentence flowing into the other. "That is what ye've done these weeks. Allowed me to dwell in bright paradise, and for that ye're mine forever. For always. *Is fírithir ad-fíadar.*" His head went to one side, surveying her with unnerving closeness, his eyes flickering over her face and form as if he were chronicling, memorizing. His grin was dangerous, unforgettable.

She would always remember.

"*Is fírithir ad-fíadar,*" he whispered, and took a bright red rose from the basket on her arm. He touched the rose to her lips, then kissed the flower, and again touched her lips with it. "*This is as true as anything told.*"

"I won't forget."

"Let me hear ye say it then. Say it for me. What is it ye won't be forgetting?"

"I'm yours for all time."

Grinning, he tucked the rose behind his ear. Then he was gone from her side, not even taking a moment for a last kiss. He strode across the greening garden and went over the wall as he had done before.

Rian O'Byrne walked away from Annora, and he never looked back.

Annora exhaled a great breath and the basket fell, roses scattering in the doorway and down the steps to the path. Her chest heaved as if she'd just reined in a headstrong horse after a hard gallop along the headland above Dublin Bay. She closed her eyes. Not wanting to see the empty space beside her and the spilled roses, she set her cheek against the cold stone of the tower wall. Several minutes passed before she had sufficiently braced herself to go inside and pretend everything was the same when, in truth, it wasn't, and never would be again.

This was not a matter of love. Annora didn't love Rian O'Byrne.

It was, nonetheless, a matter of her heart.

Annora had given a piece of her heart—not to mention the whole of her chastity—to a man she would never see again, and for that reason she was, indeed, his forever. For that reason Rian O'Byrne would always be in her heart.

Every winter she would think of him; certainly, every time it snowed, or an Epiphany star was suspended above a banquet hall; and whenever she glanced to the south, where the dark, wild mountains reached toward the sky, she would remember their stolen hours in the flint cottage, and nothing would ever be the same.

From that afternoon onward, for all the remaining days of her life, Annora Picot had a secret never to be told.

Part Two

Chapter 10

⌒⌒⌒⌒

Four years later

"A goddam pirate, that's what you are!" The angry voice rose above the din of Essex Quay. Dublin was restless. It was May's end *anno* 1399, the three and twentieth year of King Richard's reign, and the man's irate assertion was only one among scores of provoked, anxious declarations that day. "A goddam pirate."

"A pirate, is it?" drawled the object of this vehemence. He was a stocky, balding man, whose haphazard manner of dress gave no hint as to his race. His reply dripped with mockery. Not a single utterance from the other man had moved him in the least. "It may well be I'm a bleeding bandit, but there are many others who would be willing to accept my offer. If you wish passage for your family on my vessel, then you must pay my price."

On a loading platform several feet above the quay, Annora stood with James Buttevant, her steward, and the most senior and trusted of the Picot employees. They were overseeing the loading of her latest cargo, and despite their own problems, Annora could not ignore the dispute below her. At the mention of a family she glanced

117

beyond the two men to a slight young woman. She was pale and disheveled, and clutched a squalling babe in her arms, while two other children, wide-eyed and silent, barely knee high, clung to their mother's skirts.

The waterfront had not been this busy since silting in the Liffey had reduced available moorings. Most merchants used the port at Dalkey, but this day was reminiscent of those when Annora became her mother's apprentice almost fourteen years before. The tide was high, and the river was clogged with vessels from the farthest end of Merchant's Quay at the northwest corner of the town wall to the mouth of Dublin Bay. The wharves at Oxmantown were occupied and, up the river past the Dominican school on Usher's Island, a host of currachs dotted the water like so many gulls at rest on a smooth sea.

The mood was tense, and Annora was as anxious as everyone else. Tomorrow at sunset the celebration of Saint Petronilla the Virgin would begin, and of late, Dublin's laboring class never missed a feast day, for it meant they didn't have to work. This, in part, accounted for the eagerness along the quays to transfer goods from ship to shore, load on new cargo, and return to the sea with all possible celerity. There was, however, more than the prospect of idle workers on a feast day to concern the people of Dublin.

There were rumors; and with the chiming of each canonical hour, there had been more particulars to be told, with each recounting the story became worse.

This morning, a cog out of Arklow had arrived on the incoming tide, and the word went forth that as many vessels as time could permit would sail this day. Almost immediately, the taverns and inns had emptied of sailors, and a crush of townspeople had descended on the quays along with mates and cabin boys and boatmen of every rank. Added to that were the dock workers and merchants, an assortment of city officials, and soldiers from the castle. There were probably Irish spies wandering the waterfront as well as agents in the employ of the Lord Lieutenant and archbishop, plus ordinary thieves and felons mixing with folk such as the husband who was looking for a way north for his family and the balding man who sought to profit by this latest turn of events.

Below Annora, the husband cast a despairing look at his young wife and children. He pointed a condemning finger at the profiteer, and spat in disgust. "Down to hell with you."

"I've no intention of that, sirrah," came the arrogant reply. "But it may well be that you and yours shall be communing with the prince of demons himself, if you don't take my offer."

Annora could remain silent no longer. She turned to her steward. "Master Buttevant, have we room for any additional passengers?"

"There's always room." James Buttevant gave a knowing grin. He didn't have to be told what Mistress Annora was thinking, or what she was going to say next. Over the years, he had taught her much about this business, and in turn, he had learned about benevolence from the clever young woman who gave so much of herself to others. In anticipation of what she intended, he moved from the platform to offer the husband passage on one of Mistress Picot's ships.

The offer was accepted. At Annora's insistence, no payment was accepted. The family was directed toward a gangplank, whereupon the stocky pirate searched for someone else to bilk. Annora resumed her earlier conversation with Master Buttevant.

"While you have always been insistent in the practice that a ship must never sail until it is full, do you not agree an exception might be made this day, Master Buttevant? I do not think we should wait for the final delivery of raw wool."

"Aye, an exception is in order. There is no telling

when John Ware will arrive. If he comes before dusk, then you'll not forfeit your place in the order of ships departing on the next tide. But if 'tis later, then there is much to risk. If there is any truth to the rumors, you would be wise to retain that place and be among the first to have your cargo—even less than full—out of Ireland and bound for the Continent.''

"We are agreed then. That is good." The wind blew a stray curl across Annora's forehead. Her hair, gathered into a cream-colored net at the nape of neck, was as lustrous and golden as ever, making her seem far younger than she was, and not in the least bit like a woman wont to making weighty decisions. She stuffed the loose strand of hair into the bag of netting. "If you will, sir, direct the master of the *Hermes* to sail directly to Lubbeck; only the *Hera* is to follow its customary itinerary, and make certain the ship's master understands not to port at Wicklow if there is any sign of trouble.''

Hera and *Hermes* were two of the ocean-going vessels Annora had acquired in the past four years as her involvement in the business had increased. When she was not occupied at Our Lady of Victory, Annora spent her days at the quay overseeing the purchasing and exporting operations, inspecting the warehouse inventory for quality, and reviewing a variety of contracts and investments with Master Buttevant. This active participation did not stem from lack of trust, for Annora's employees were steadfast and hardworking, rather it owed to Annora's singular talent for solving problems. Her quick mind was always devising a more efficient means to accomplish a task. Bold and inquisitive in her approach to commerce, she was an endless source of ideas for projects that would consolidate resources or maximize profits. Annora enjoyed the challenges presented by an expanding enterprise; most of all, she found satisfaction in seeing her ideas flourish.

The profits had been significant, and much of them had

been invested in real estate. Annora owned warehouses in St. Malo, Antwerp, and Lubbeck, where her agents dispersed both raw and finished products through the Hansa towns to Russia, and at Bourgneuf Bay, where her agents traded Irish woolens in exchange for salt. Two summers past, she had entered into a lucrative partnership with the Friscobaldi family in Lucca, securing virtually the whole of the Italian market.

The dye works at Our Lady of Victory had expanded. There was a new building for looms, and another dormitory had been constructed to accommodate an additional thirty-five women trained in weaving and embroidery. Now Annora exported frieze, worsted, and serge, plus finished mantles lined with fabulously colored fabrics known as Irish silk. In Naples, Our Lady of Victory serge was used to trim the robes of the king and queen; at Visegrad, the Hungarian queen owned fifteen mantles woven and embroidered by the women of the famed Irish convent; and Our Lady of Victory yarns had been used for the needlework gracing the great cathedral at Chartres, and in the myriad palaces of the Holy Roman Empire at Mainz, Prague, and Salzburg.

This evening, after leaving Dublin, the *Hermes* would sail south. On a routine voyage, her vessels would call upon several coastal towns to take on additional raw wool and deliver passengers as well as goods from Dublin before heading to the open sea. This time, Wicklow would be the only stop, and it would be brief. Any farther south than Wicklow, and there could be trouble.

"Mistress Picot! Mistress Picot!" a lad called up and down the quay. "Where is Mistress Picot?"

"What business have you with the wool merchant?" One of Annora's apprentices stepped forward. His posture was custodial as he stood before the lad, legs spread and arms akimbo.

The lad said something to the apprentice, who, in turn, had further questions.

Annora was watching the mechanical crane hoist a massive bundle of unwashed wool off the quay. She had heard *"Mistress Picot,"* but it had not registered in her mind that someone was calling her, and she hadn't looked away from the swaying bundle. While it had been four years since her mother's death, there were moments when Annora forgot that *"Mistress Picot"* referred to herself, not to her mother. Sometimes four years was an eternity, and at other times, it seemed not more than a fortnight or two had passed since her mother's final days. Her memories drifted back to that last week in April, when Catherine had asked to be taken out of Dublin.

"I do not want my last breath to be oppressed with the decaying odors of town life," Catherine had said with the serenity of one who knows the end is near, and Annora, ever hopeful for a miracle, had taken her mother to the convent. Perhaps a change of residence was what she needed. Mayhap a few weeks away from the noise and stench of the waterfront would restore her health.

Each morning, Catherine had been carried to a pallet in the convent orchard. The air had been scented by moist earth, woodbind, and fresh-baked currant cake, and there on the fourth day in the light and warmth of the sun, within the sound of the sea, within sight of whorls of blue bugles and rows of purple betony swaying in the wind, her illuminated Psalter and Holland lute nearby, Catherine Picot had departed this earth surrounded by friends, her daughter at her side, and a choir of children singing the *Nunc Dimittus*.

"Mistress Picot! Mistress Picot."

The apprentice let the lad pass. He scurried up the wooden steps and stopped when he was close enough to tug on Annora's skirt. She glanced at the grime-blackened face of one of Dublin's hundred or more street urchins.

"Yer uncle is come to see ye, mistress. Sir Thomas, himself, it is who gave me the message, and asks ye to be returning to yer tower at once.'' He swiped a runny nose on his bare arm.

"My uncle is at the tower?"

"Aye," the boy replied, earnest and with more than a touch of self-importance that he had served as a messenger between two such notable personages.

"What is your name?" Annora assessed the skinny child. He could not be much older than five or six years at best.

"They call me Bean Pole, if ye please, mistress."

Annora opened the metallic mesh purse hanging from her waist and withdrew a coin, knowing in her heart that *they* were not a mother and father, nor a grandparent or other relative, but the other waifs who roamed the alleys and quays. "This is for you, Bean Pole." She pressed the coin into his palm, and closed his small, dirty fingers over it. "You would not let anyone take it from you, would you?"

He stared at his toes and did not answer.

It was more than likely an older boy was crouched behind a nearby barrel, watching and waiting to snatch it from him. The lad would not utter a word, fearing the wrath of someone stronger and bigger as much as he feared that the beautiful lady might take back the precious coin.

"I suggest you spend it straightway. The pastry cook in the passage behind Page's Court makes excellent funnel cakes. Do you know the shop?"

"I do, mistress."

"That is good, and I will send Edmund with you, for he has not eaten anything this day." She waved to the apprentice, then added, "You must tell them Mistress Picot sends you, and the good wife will make certain to put an extra dollop of honey on top."

"Thank you," said Bean Pole, and when the young apprentice named Edmund arrived, the lad skipped off by his side.

Annora went to the other end of the platform where a plank led onto the *Hermes*. James Buttevant approached to speak with her at the ship's rail. "Master Buttevant, I must return to the tower. My uncle awaits me."

"Off with you then, and send Sir Thomas my regards, if you would." A frown crossed James Buttevant's brow, but his voice was pleasant enough. "There's no need to hurry back. Do not worry yourself about our progress here. There will be no more delays."

Annora nodded, knowing that Master Buttevant could be relied upon, but when she lifted her kirtle to descend to the quay, she frowned. She had seen Master Buttevant's expression, and could well imagine what he'd been thinking. It was not often her uncle came to the tower. Ordinarily she went to his lodgings at Dublin Castle, where they dined together every fourth night. But then nothing was ordinary about this day.

It was the rumor brought on the ship out of Arklow that had thrown everything and everyone into such a state of disorder. The Arklow crew claimed King Richard had returned to Ireland. He'd landed at Waterford not to seek peace with the chieftains, it was said, but to wreak vengeance.

Such intelligence was not received with the slightest rejoicing by the English of Dublin. It was viewed as entirely unfavorable. The arrival of the king and his army could not bode well. Apprehension swept the quays. Too fresh was the memory of Richard's previous visit, when he'd left behind a mountain of unpaid bills. This time, it was rumored, the profligate monarch would not bother with the pretense of keeping accounts to be settled at a later date; this time, he would merely take what he needed for himself and his army.

As if economic misfortune was not a serious enough cause for trepidation, alarm had been roused in the general populace by the specter of pestilence. The weather was warming, and with the arrival of summer came the likelihood of plague, a peril that would be increased considerably if the town and its resources were overwhelmed by thousands of soldiers.

But there was more.

The rumors assumed an even more menacing character when the people heard his majesty was filled with naught but rage. Unlike his first campaign, Richard did not speak of peace or conciliation, and given that upon his departure four years before, the security of Dublin had been as tenuous as ever, it seemed certain that whatever came to pass in the next few weeks could only make matters worse.

King Richard had failed in his previous mission. The glorious oaths of fealty by the chieftains had not increased the boundaries of *terra pacis*, nor had the winter of 1395 wrought any measure of peace to Ireland. No sooner had Richard returned to England than the Irish had set aside their masks of humility and renounced their allegiance. War had continued as before, Art MacMurrough and the Leinster clans having sworn never to rest as long as a hostile power existed on the shores of Innisfail. The last great battle had been at Kellistown on Saint Margaret's Day of the previous year; and while it had ended in victory for the Irish, it had also been a disaster, for the Leinster clans under MacMurrough and O'Byrne had slain Roger Mortimer, earl of March, the king's lieutenant in Ireland and heir to the English throne. King Richard had come to avenge Mortimer, and to vindicate his royal majesty against the *wild Irishry*.

"It will amount to nothing," Annora tried to persuade herself, referring as much to why her uncle wished to see her as to the consequences of Richard's arrival. *Nothing,* she repeated silently, but it hadn't been nothing the last time the king was in Dublin. The news this day was a stark reminder of everything she'd struggled but failed to forget. Annora didn't want to remember the Irishman with unruly, burnished hair, ocean blue eyes, and knowing smile, but she did. Perhaps she had tricked him into believing she didn't care there had been no future for them, that her heart had not been shattered when he'd left without looking back. But she hadn't tricked herself.

It hadn't been a matter of love, she'd tried to convince herself, but she'd never been good at lying, and across the days and months and years, across the miles of bogland, hills and forest, her heart ached to be reunited with the piece she'd given to a man who could never be a part of her life.

At Christmastide, the memories returned. Whenever it snowed, Annora's mind filled with Rian O'Byrne. She remembered how it was when he'd kissed her, how he'd caressed her lower lip with his thumb, and how he'd whispered to her Irish things that she never understood, but which sounded too lovely to resist. Sometimes in the middle of a long winter night, a startling vision of the bloodshed between the English and Irish would chill her heart, and she would whisper an Ave Maria for Rian O'Byrne and every soul who lived beyond the vale.

Annora had kept her secret well. And oh, how she wished that it might have been as easy to forget as to conceal.

Mayhap if she toiled with greater diligence, or if she devoted more of her energies to good works in behalf of others, she would forget. She must continue to seek penance. Since that winter, Dublin had benefited from Annora's acts of atonement. There was the cistern at St. Patrick's Cathedral, the leper window at St. Michael and St. John's Church, and the orphans house in Oxmantown, not to mention the streets that had been paved at her expense, and the time she rebuilt the spire at St. Mary's after it had been blown down in a violent tempest. Everyone assumed these generous gifts were in memory of Catherine Picot, for no daughter was ever as devoted to her mother as Annora. There was no reason to suppose they were contrition for a secret never to be told.

Not a soul suspected what she'd done with one of the wild Irish; and as had happened many times before, the thought of what could have come to pass that winter made Annora shudder. It was no less than a miracle that her folly had not taken seed, or that her mother had never suffered humiliation stemming from her daughter's indiscretion. Annora sent up a silent prayer of thanksgiving. She made the sign of the cross.

In the name of the Father, the Son, and the Holy Spirit. Amen. As she did with each memory of that winter, she gave profound thanks. She vowed never again to behave in such a foolhardy, wanton manner. There would never be another man to caress or hold Annora. Such joy would never be hers again. Her heart had been hardened. There was nothing to risk a second time.

Chapter 11

❦

Sir Thomas was in the garden. He sat in the shade of a chestnut tree, and at Annora's approach he stood. He embraced her in greeting when she reached his side, and asked her to be seated. Devasse appeared and set out refreshments. There were cool drinks, a small wheel of imported cheese, and a basket of strawberries.

"Something is amiss, uncle?" She popped a strawberry in her mouth.

"I could never hide a thing from you, could I?"

"There never was a time." Another strawberry was devoured.

"While you, on the other hand, could all too easily pull the wool over my eyes." He gave a fond chuckle.

Annora sliced off two pieces of cheese, offered one to her uncle, and ate the other. "What brings you to my residence? You must tell me, and without another moment's delay."

He held up a scroll of vellum that Annora had not noticed until this moment. It was secured by a braid of golden ribbons. The seal was large, the wax bright red. "It is from the king, and was delivered to me at the castle shortly before midday."

She waited for the rest, but he said nothing more. A strange, vast silence stretched between them, magnifying the little sounds of the garden when his voice did not fill the void with further explanation. A magpie chattered in the uppermost branches of a tree, a line of doves cooed on the wall, and bees hummed at the arbor where the early roses were opening their petals. There was the rustle of leaves and the snap of pennants flying from the tower rampart.

"Aye, go on," Annora said. "What is it, uncle? What does the king write?"

"His majesty is soon to make his way toward Dublin."

"You did not come here to tell me what has been on the tongue of every living soul since the Tierce bells."

Sir Thomas purposely unrolled the vellum. He held the missive at arms length to read in silence, his lips mouthing each word as if checking to make certain he had not misconstrued its contents, that they were the same as when he'd first read it.

Annora heard nothing more than an occasional mumble, and could make no sense of anything except the official royal ending, *"Teste* ourself, Richard Plantagenet, King of England and France, and Lord of Ireland, at Waterford in the three and twentieth year of our reign."

Sir Thomas sighed and raised his head.

A chill shot up Annora's spine. *Sweet Holy Mother.* There were tears in her uncle's eyes. What could it be to elicit such a reaction in this man who had not cried at Catherine Picot's death? Sir Thomas was a knight. He had witnessed the worst that humankind could inflict upon its own, and while not a heartless man, there was little that could shock him, or so she'd thought. "You must tell me what it says," came her plea. "Nothing can be as bad as not knowing what it is that affects you so profoundly."

"How right you are. I am sorry, niece. Forgive me."

"There is naught to forgive."

"Ah, that is yet to be decided," he said. The tears

were gone, but there was a weariness about him she had never seen before. His careful tone conveyed the impression this speech had been rehearsed. "I am midway into my sixth decade and can testify that honor has been at the foundation of my every action and decision. Since my tenth year, when I joined the Lord Justiciar's household as a page, honor has been my strongest virtue. Always I have respected and fulfilled the oaths to which I have pledged myself, first as a page, then as a squire, and later having made my vigil and sworn my knightly vows, as a knight and an official of the crown. Always my loyalty has been unwavering, my faith in that fealty constant. Never would I have thought myself capable of cowardice or treachery, but this very day, I find myself entertaining deeds of both nature."

Anguish was evident in the brittle quality of Sir Thomas's voice. He whispered, mayhap because it was difficult to speak these words aloud, or because he did not want anyone other than Annora to hear. She rested a hand on his forearm. "Perhaps this is not something you should discuss with me."

"Nay, niece, you are the precise one in whom I must confide," he said, his countenance reflecting the love and concern he'd always held for his niece, and never more since Catherine's death. Sir Thomas worried that Annora would never marry, that she spent too much time at the quay, that she gave away too much of herself, her time, her kindness of spirit, and material possessions. It saddened him to gaze upon this unique woman, ever beautiful, still radiant. Too rapidly, the years were passing. He did not like to think that she would never know the joy of a lover, nor the closeness of destined hearts. Annora had always been different. Disapproving gossips had called her contrary; others, somewhat more sympathetic, had said she was special.

Now it mattered not what they might call her, and Sir Thomas must accept that he had failed her; that it had been wrong to encourage her independence of spirit, to let her follow such an unconventional course. Mayhap it was inevitable, for Annora had been different since the moment of her arrival, and only Sir Thomas and Catherine had understood why. The knight had always assumed that before Catherine died she would tell Annora about the tempest, but she hadn't, and now he wondered if the time had come for him to speak the truth. He ran a tired hand across his eyes, and sighed as if gathering the necessary energy to speak again.

"Can it not wait, dear uncle? Mayhap you should come in and rest anon."

"Nay." He patted her comforting hand where it rested upon his forearm. He must speak, and before it was too late. "The king informs me of what he intends upon his arrival in Dublin. Among other things, his majesty asks that the archbishop administer a solemnization of matrimony; he further directs me to attain a suitable gown for the bride, and to prepare the great hall at the castle for a celebration. His majesty, of course, reminds me of his fondness for minstrelsy and lavish entertainments, and advises that I must spare no expense with the arrangements."

"The archbishop? A solemnization of matrimony?" Annora's expression was as puzzled as her voice. "The king plans a wedding? What of his child wife? This makes no sense."

"You must see for yourself." Sir Thomas handed the scroll to his niece.

Annora glanced downward. Another chill darted up her back. Her shock was absolute, rendering her speechless as the words swam before her, two words in particular, *Annora Picot,* coming in and out of focus. Her hands trembled. A bitter taste rose in her throat as she scanned the text. It was the third paragraph that concerned Annora:

*Know that we, fully trusting in the fidelity and
service of Thomas Picot, Knight and commander of
our fortress at Dublin, have given him power to
admit to our wishes.*

*Item, whereas for certain urgent reasons concern-
ing us and our land of Ireland, we have thought fit to
join in holy matrimony our cousin, Harry of Monmouth, and Annora Picot, our subject, and a
woman of noble lineage residing in Dublin.*

*Item, we enjoin upon you in the faith and homage
which you owe us to inform the archbishop of our
plans.*

*Item, the bride is to be garbed appropriately, and
is to be delivered to our presence within six hours of
our arrival at Dublin.*

*Item, exchange of vows between Harry of Mon-
mouth and Annora Picot before our witness in
accordance with the laws of church and state
will . . .*

Annora could read no more. "Surely he is not serious?
This cannot be legitimate. Perhaps 'tis someone's notion
of a jest, and a cruel and exceedingly poor one at that."

" 'Tis no jest. The missive was brought here by the
priest, Richard Maudelyn, who once again accompanies
the king to Ireland. Maudelyn put it in my hands himself,
having come ashore at Dalkey with a small company of
men-at-arms. I have no doubt it is from his majesty."

"But a marriage between myself and Harry of Monmouth. Is he not a mere boy?"

"Twelve or thirteen, and soon to be knighted, I am
assured."

A rush of nervous laughter escaped Annora. "And this
young knight-to-be would agree to such an arrangement?
I am old enough to be his mother, not to mention that a
cousin of the king would surely prefer an alliance with a

bride whose recommendation is more auspicious than that of wool merchant.''

"Monmouth has no more choice than you in the matter. He is a hostage.''

"A hostage?''

"Aye, as the eldest son of Bolingbroke, the king holds young Harry for the obedience of his father. His majesty also holds the only son of Thomas of Woodstock.''

"That is the only thing in all of this that makes any sense," she said. Being familiar with the stories of court intrigue, she knew how Richard had arrested his uncles Arundel, and Woodstock, and had exiled his cousin, Henry of Bolingbroke, duke of Hereford, revoking his patents and confiscating his holdings. Arundel had been executed, Woodstock, too, was dead, mayhap murdered under his majesty's guard in Calais; and Bolingbroke's hatred for Richard was said to be deep and smoldering. He was in Paris, and it was widely accepted that whether or not he had ever been a threat to Richard did not signify, since the king, by his own actions, had most certainly transformed the popular Bolingbroke into a real danger. "It is no wonder he holds Monmouth hostage. The king is wise not to trust Bolingbroke, considering the unjust treatment he has exacted upon him. But it explains not the motive for this wedding. What is there to be gained?''

"I can only surmise 'tis money," Sir Thomas said mildly. He knew this would provoke his niece. "The exchequer is bankrupt, I am told.''

Nausea seeped through Annora. She pushed away the strawberries and cheese. A quick image of the gentlemen she had refused before and after her mother's death flashed across her mind's eye. How right Catherine had been to worry about the jealous ones, to warn Annora that her security was in constant jeopardy, that it could be easily wrecked at the caprice of a powerful man. Now it appeared the thing that had afforded her so much was about to be her undoing. She gripped the edge of the table and took several deep breaths to banish the wambling from her stomach. It mattered not to Annora that this was the king's will; she refused to accept there was no alternative. There must be any number of other ways to replenish the royal coffers, if only she could think of them. Her mind began to churn.

"If Richard needs money, he need only levy a tax against my ships," she suggested. "I would fain pay any amount."

"Aye, and having been collected, that would be the end of it, but wed to young Harry, Richard will have access to your money and control of your interests, here and abroad, for many years to come. It may also be the king's strategy to leave Bolingbroke's son in Ireland when he departs."

"I won't do it."

"It would be treason to refuse."

"And I would rather die upon the executioner's block than wed any man forced upon me."

Sir Thomas frowned. " 'Tis a most alarming proclamation ye voice, niece, for I can well imagine such a scene."

"You know then 'tis not idle talk. There is no threat dire enough to force me to wed."

"Have you never owned any desire to marry?"

"Of a certainty, it has crossed my mind," she said. "My heart is not hewn of granite, uncle, and I confess to having looked with envy upon many a girlhood friend with children at her side. In truth, there have been times when I have known loneliness. Times when there was no one by my side, no one with whom to share this tower, my life, my secrets; when there was no one to turn for affection or comfort, a moment of companionship or advice."

"There was not a single gentleman among your suitors to qualify?"

"Not a one," she lied, while seeing blue eyes and a bold grin. Her heart contracted with familiar pain.

"Mayhap—"

"Do not!" Annora cautioned her uncle to silence. "Can it be you would dare suggest there is something favorable in the king's proposal? You must know I would rather die than accept a husband of an age to call son."

"Pray, then what manner of gentleman would suit if the king's nephew is not favorable enough?"

"First, he must be a man, not some stripling. He would be near to my age. A man who has known adversity and survival, and who appreciates the notion of independence. If I were to marry, I would not wish to feel superior to my husband, nor would I wish to find myself in charge of someone not yet formed of his attitudes. I would want an equal. Someone with whom I might exchange contemplative discourse, and someone who might help me, if need be, not the other way round. And I would want that man to have the willingness and strength to stand by me despite all else. I would want that man to be willing, if need be, to abandon all for me. And though 'tis nonsensical to own such an ambition, I would want that man to love me before we are wed. I want no man for husband whose greatest desire is for my possessions and not myself. Which brings us full circle to the issue at hand: I would rather die than surrender a single shilling to the whim of a profligate, whether that man be monarch, commoner, or the pope, I care not."

"Shush, niece, you must not speak like that," Sir Thomas admonished. "There is nothing for you except to obey."

"I refuse. Just as I refuse to accept that there is no solution for me."

"You must not speak in this manner." Sir Thomas cast

a nervous glance over each shoulder. He scanned the corners of the garden, and along the top of the wall. "At least, you must lower your voice. If I cannot stop you from speaking in such a manner, at least, do not allow the world to hear your blasphemy."

Annora lowered her voice. "In honesty, uncle, do you sit before me and expect me to believe that you came here to force my obedience?" Her voice fell even lower. "You yourself said you'd pondered treason this day. Is it truly your intention to graciously deliver me unto the king's avaricious purpose?"

In spite of it all, Sir Thomas had to smile. "And why do I think there must be some scheme already bubbling about that fertile cauldron you call brain?" It was a question that needed no answer.

"How long before the king arrives?" asked Annora.

"No earlier than Saint Alban's Day. He marches for Kilkenny, and from thence to Kildaire and Dublin. If he meets with resistance from the Irish, his arrival could be delayed until July. Richard has sworn to see Art Mac-Murrough dead, and should the opportunity arise, his majesty would certainly pursue the Irishman. Mayhap even into the mountains."

The mention of those mountains sent a fleeting vision of a handsome face with a wicked smile across the canvas of Annora's mind. She remembered how quickly, how easily she had been drawn to him. It was one of those rare things a woman perceived in an instant, and it was that same sort of instinct that told her what had to be done now. "Would you help me, uncle, if there was a way I might escape this?"

"I would never naysay you."

"Without your aid, this is the end of my life as surely as if I'd been condemned to the faggots for a witch."

Sir Thomas accepted the verity of this. What Richard asked would be the death of Annora, and he could not bear to witness her suffering. Sooth, it would be easier to flaunt honor and disobey his king. It was a blessing Catherine did not live to see this. Annora stood and started to walk around the garden along a path of iridescent crushed seashells. He had seen this before. It was her thinking mode.

Four times she traced the path that hugged the garden's perimeter. Halfway round the fifth time, she cut back to the chestnut tree, set her palms atop the table, and leaned close to whisper, "That is precisely what I shall do, uncle. I shall die."

"You must explain yourself."

"I must disappear. I can only escape this if I am dead or, at least, presumed to be. I must create the illusion of my death. Will you help me?"

"I've already said I would."

"But you did not know what I intended."

He shrugged. "I know it will not be moderate, infallible, or lacking in peril. Am I right?"

"Aye. 'Tis dangerous, uncertain, and extreme. So, too, is it simple." *If all the pieces fall into their exact places in a sequence of events that are for the most part beyond the realm of mortal control,* Annora thought, but did not say aloud. Even to breathe the word *if* implied a lack of confidence, and she didn't want her uncle to think she was anything but positive. She didn't want him to try to talk her out of this. "My problem is how to get out of Dublin without being seen, while leaving enough evidence to suggest I have suffered at the hands of foul play. There is a method for this madness, I ween."

She explained the plan as she envisioned it from start to finish, detailing what it was she needed Sir Thomas to do in her behalf. "If you agree, uncle, it must be set into motion immediately. There's not a moment to spare."

"As you say, 'tis fraught with danger and totally uncertain." But Sir Thomas had no better solution to offer.

"Nonetheless I must risk it."

"And there is every possibility that it can succeed. In good faith, I trow it will. For who would have thought merchants would pay such prices for yarn, or that you could have convinced the Hansa towns to grant your cargo safe passage, or that kings and queens would wait months for a single mantle woven by widows and strumpets?"

She smiled at his indirect assent, and kissed his cheek. "I will miss you."

"You must not contemplate such a sorrow. I have always wanted to sail across the sea to places such as Lubbeck."

"You will visit me?" she asked, wondering if this had been her destiny from the start. Perhaps she had never been meant to find happiness in Dublin. Mayhap leaving was what she should have done four years before, instead of staying and pretending as if nothing had changed, instead of hoping and dreaming that one day Ireland might be a different place, and he might return to her.

"Of course, I will visit. Of course. But first I must go to Master Buttevant and make certain the *Hera* is delayed until tomorrow night. Then I will return to the castle to inspect the prisoners. You must pray there is someone who will fit your need, and who will agree to the terms of your service. Else I will not be visiting you anywhere except in your husband's home."

Chapter 12

"**H**e's mine," declared a brunette. She put hands to hips and threw back her shoulders to show off large breasts. Her tunic was short, offering a provocative view of thigh.

Two whores were arguing, loud and furious, each claiming a right to the only customer who had entered the bordel house since the Tierce bells. Usually at this time of the day, Drake's was as crowded as it was on any evening, patrons packed into the common room, cheek to jowl, drinking ale and mead, singing bawdy tunes, and waiting for a turn with one of the girls. The Widow Drake's whores were known for their accommodating ways. No one was turned away, not even Persians or the occasional Numidian from one of the merchant vessels. This afternoon, however, the house was deserted, and with the day half gone, the girls were anxious to earn their keep. It did not matter that business would be brisk on the morrow during the Feast of St. Petronilla; the widow expected a daily allowance from her girls, else she might turn them out.

"Yours, you say, and by what right might that be?" the other whore demanded. She was a redhead, tall, and on the thin side, but clean. The Widow Drake made her girls wash every morning and every night.

" 'Tis only fair. You got the last one!'' The brunette wanted the customer who sat at a table, a tankard of ale and platter of oysters before him. He was a big man, handsome and strong with a pleasing masculine face boasting liquid blue eyes, and a sensual mouth. The dark-haired harlot was used to men who were either too skinny or too fat, and whose breath was stale, skin was spotty, and teeth were rotting; anguished men whose wives were frigid and had been long without any carnal comforts, rough men who, having been at sea, took their satisfaction with a woman as if she were a man, and soulless men who could not perform unless elaborate charades were enacted or frightful pain inflicted. She had experienced many men, and it wasn't often she spent time with one such as this. He exuded an uncommon raw energy, and she wanted him.

"Aw, Nellie, fair you say? 'Twas I who opened the door to him, making him mine. And stop poking out your titties,'' snapped the redhead. "I was the one who showed him to the table, brought him the oysters, and he spoke to me first. Called me *maith an cailín,* he did.''

"You always get the pleasing ones,'' sulked the brunette, knowing that he must be from the hills. *Maith an cailín* was Irish, and if this man was anything like the others of his race, he would be a worthy partner for an afternoon of bawdy play with a *good girl.* It would be nice to enjoy her work for once, but that wasn't something she dared say aloud, so she pursed her lips and pouted.

"There's no need to be squabbling,'' the man drawled. He had finished eating, and placing the empty tankard atop the platter, pushed them to the middle of the table. His grin was amused, lustful. He was still hungry. "There's no need to be arguing. I'll be wanting the both of ye.''

"Both of us?'' Nellie gasped with delight. "Oooh, I like that. So does Breeda. Don't you?''

The redheaded Breeda smiled. "Oh, I do like it. That I do. Has it been such a long time?" she purred at the man, inviting, suggestive.

"Aye, that it has." He stood up and grinned at how the one called Nellie displayed her breasts. He liked what he saw. Both of the whores were young, not more than sixteen summers, and they still had their looks, firm bodies, and good health. Even better, they were both eager. He hadn't been with a woman in months. The last time had been in Carlow sometime between All Souls and Christmas. He couldn't recall exactly when, and barely recalled that the woman had been the wife of a knight, half-Irish, and lonely for her father's people, she'd told him. He'd only spent a few hours with her, which was ever the way of it these days. He hadn't been with any woman more than once in many years.

It had been a long time since he'd wanted anything more from a woman beyond his satisfaction, many years since he'd experienced a rush of bliss that went beyond mere physical pleasure, and it seemed like a lifetime since he'd even enjoyed the game of seduction. He hadn't been in Dublin in many years. In the past, he'd often come for the easy pleasures to be found in a brothel such as Drake's, or sometimes for the heightened enjoyment of a seduction; more often than not it had been for the simple excitement derived from the risk of being Irish in the English stronghold. For most of his adult life, he'd been in and out of Dublin every few months, but that had changed after the chieftains left four springs past. He hadn't been back since, and he'd surprised no one as much as himself when he'd agreed to make this journey.

Art MacMurrough had summoned the Leinster chieftains to Idrone, and it was his chieftain's task to bring information of what was happening in the vale to that gathering. Were the English of Dublin preparing for war? Would an attack come from the north as well as from the south? The Irish knew what had come to pass in the harbor at Waterford. They knew the English king was returned to Ireland with another vast army, and *éasch-laghs* had been dispatched through the hills and glens. It had taken less than two days time for these *female couriers* to carry this intelligence from a village in the hills above the English town of New Ross into the farthest bogs of the Leinster plain, and across the highest peaks to the foothills of *Uí Briúin Cualann*.

Compelled by the urge to immerse himself in peril, the Irishman had agreed to act for his chieftain. He had returned to Dublin. The town was a dangerous place this day. He liked it this way, and was looking forward to uncovering what he might about the English king and his plans, but first he needed a good lay. He grinned at the dark-haired whore with the big breasts as she sashayed toward him.

"A long time, you say." Nellie tilted her head to look up at the big man. She stepped close to his towering frame, and lightly, temptingly, brushed one hand across his lower torso. "Do you think you still know how to use it?"

"If there's anything I've forgotten, I'm sure ye'll be teaching me." He caught her passing hand and held it to his groin. Her fingers wrapped around his manhood, and she stood on tiptoe as if to kiss him.

"Hey, you'll be doing none of that now," admonished the Widow Drake. "Nothing until he's paid. You've been here long enough to know the rules, Nellie. Same as with the food and drink." The Widow Drake lounged across the ledge from behind which she served up ale, and watched over the goings-on in her establishment. She extended an open palm.

The man tossed several coins; they skittered across the wooden surface. It was more than enough for two whores. He hoped it was enough for the woman to overlook the fact that he was Irish.

"Show him a nice time, girls." The widow gave a nod. He'd paid with silver, not with the tokens accepted by Dublin's inns and taverns. He could have four girls if he wanted. Quickly she swept the coins off the counter. "A full, nice time."

The whores laughed. They knew exactly what to do, and each curling an arm about his waist, they led him down a dim corridor where worn, uneven curtains were tacked across a series of doorways. Halfway down the corridor, the girls pushed aside a length of fabric to enter a small windowless room. Light filtered through gaps in the wicker walls. The only furnishing was a sort of platform raised several feet off the ground and wedged into one corner. As soon as the curtain fell back in place, the whores began to move around the man in a tight circle, smiling and cooing, prancing and preening, their hands stroking him, their thighs and buttocks rubbing against the bulge of his erection as they lifted and let fall their tunics, each time raising the hem a little higher until he had a glimpse at their private parts, felt the warmth of flesh, smelled their female musk. He grinned, and answered in the affirmative when the brunette asked if he liked what he saw.

"And would you like to see more?" she countered.

"Aye."

She slipped the tunic off her shoulders. The flimsy garment fell past her legs, pooled about her feet. She took his hands, molded them to her breasts. "Come on now. Come with me." She moved backward until they reached the platform upon which she stood so that her breasts were almost level with his face. "Come, have a taste," she said, and presented a puckered nipple to his mouth while the flame-haired Breeda knelt on the ground before him.

Eagerly the Irishman nipped at the offered breast. Somewhere in the back of his mind, he was aware of the redhead kneeling before him, and he angled his torso to her reach. He knew what she intended, and widened his stance as she rolled his tunic out of the way.

"Sweet mercy," the redhead exclaimed at the sight of his penis. "Will you look at the size of this tool. 'Tis as enormous as the rest of him. A big handsome boy, it is." She stroked the engorged flesh, then rolled it between her palms.

The whore named Nellie peeked around the man's shoulder. "Oooh, a treasure to pleasure," she giggled and watched Breeda's lips close over the swollen head. The man reacted with a jolt, suckling harder on her breast, his teeth grazing her nipple. The brunette closed her eyes, and ran her hands across his shoulders, down his back. Oh, it was nice to be able to enjoy her work.

"And what have we here?"

A voice intruded on the brunette whore's pleasure. There was a man peering between the curtains. He had the look of an English soldier but not one from the castle, rather the sort that came off the ships from Bristol. "Go away," she said.

He stepped into the room. "Not while you're in need of another cock."

"We don't need anything," she said. The Irishman still suckled at her breast, his eyes were closed, his torso was pumping, and a quick downward glance showed the length of him sliding in and out of Breeda's mouth. Neither of them had heard any of this. "He's paid for the both of us."

"Has he now?" the English soldier asked as he mounted the platform. His tone and manner were argumentative, almost defiant, and standing behind the brunette, he grabbed hold of her waist to grind himself against her naked backside.

"Stop that," she cried.

The Irishman raised his head. He stared at the soldier. "I'd be backing off, if I were ye."

"Oh, would you now? She's a strumpet, ain't she?"

He tossed a token on the floor. "And I'm paying for her."

"Keep yer money. She's already paid for," the Irishman answered. The soldier's face was flushed, he reeked of ale, and the whore stared at the Irishman, her features contorting as the drunk drove himself a second time against her buttocks. "She's not available. Now back off, and leave the room."

"Seems to me you've only got one cock, and it ain't available right now." He tried to raise his tunic with one hand while the other hand slid from its grip at the brunette's waist down her thigh to delve between her legs.

"Back off, I'm telling ye."

"What's that accent I hear? You ain't one of those damned wild Irish, are you? I don't take orders from savages, you know." The soldier swayed forward, and in a slurred voice, he whispered to the brunette, "Tell your friend on the floor there to get up and give service to this animal while you pleasure me."

"They're both with me. Leave now before—"

"Before what?" he challenged with a menacing laugh.

The redhead pulled away from the Irishman.

The two men glared at each other. One stood on the floor, the other on the platform. The naked whore was between them. Agitated breathing filled the room. Time slowed as if they were becalmed on a smooth sea, and then like a sudden summer squall, everything happened at once. The English soldier lurched to one side. He pushed the dark-haired whore off the platform and drew forth a dagger from the belt at his waist.

"Ye may be an idiot, but I'm hoping ye're not a fool," said the Irishman, evenly. He didn't take his eyes off the poised weapon. "Sheath yer dagger."

Raising his arm higher, the soldier aimed the blade for the Irishman's chest and lunged. The Irishman caught the soldier's wrist in one large hand and squeezed as if to make him drop the weapon. The soldier struggled, the two men moved as one, forward then backward. They stumbled and careened against a wall. The Irishman lost his grip on the other man's wrist, and in that instant, the soldier punched him squarely in the jaw. The Irishman reeled, swung a punch of his own, made contact with bone, and then the two men began to fall. Someone screamed. There was a horrible gurgling, the crack of a skull.

Both men were motionless on the ground.

Several minutes passed before the Irishman realized he was neither awake nor asleep. There was a buzzing in his ears, a throbbing between his eyes. Voices swirled about him like the fingers of a cold fog. Flashes of silver streaked across closed eyelids as he tried to lift his head. In an instant, his mind fled the present, racing backward to a time past, to another brothel in this town, to another fight.

It had been much the same. It always was for an Irishman in Ireland, where even a strumpet was too good for the likes of a native warrior. He remembered landing on his backside in the icy street, and he remembered staring into the face of an angel. Some things, however, did change, for this time when he managed to look there was no angel. No clarie blue eyes, no halo of gold hair. This time, there were two English soldiers, their sallow, spare faces contorted with hostility.

"Irish cur," one of them sneered.

The Irishman didn't hear. He was listening to another voice in the depths of his mind. It was an angel, whispering from the past. *Loose my gown, sir*. It had been a long time since he'd remembered. *I'm not your angel*.

"Do you think he's a spy?" the second soldier asked.

"A spy? A shepherd? It matters not. Pruitt is dead. He's Irish and a murderer."

These words jerked the Irishman back to the present. *Pruitt is dead*. He rolled his head to see this fellow called

Pruitt who had started the fight and was lying on the floor beside him. The Irishman stared into blank eyes, saw a trickle of blood at the corner of Pruitt's mouth. It would do no good to explain that it was Pruitt who had caused the trouble.

"Then the Irishman dies, too."

"Such a barbarian head will be a fine trophy mounted above the castle wall. His majesty will appreciate the decor upon his arrival."

As they hauled him to his feet, the Irishman knew his fate was sealed this day. The English had always had a fondness for decorating the castle walls with the heads of their Irish enemies; in 1316, when his grandmother had been a wee child, some 400 heads had been procured in Wicklow for this purpose, among them those of his grandmother's father, her uncles, and brothers, including a lad of only ten summers. Aye, his destiny was grim. He was in Dublin with no one but himself, his wits and bare hands, and there was only one chance for him.

Swiftly his mind replayed how he had entered the bordel house, how to retrace his way through the cony-warren of lanes to the river. *Downhill,* he reminded himself, *head north and downhill,* and giving forth a feral roar, he thrust his arms upward and outward with such unexpected intensity that he freed himself, causing one of the soldiers to stumble to his knees. Emitting another bellow, he charged the second soldier, and using the entire force of his body, propelled the stunned man against the wicker wall.

It was a valiant effort, and he might have succeeded, had there not been more English in Drake's, who having heard the ruckus came to their comrades aid. Five against one. The odds had turned. Yet even when they backed him into a corner, he didn't surrender, but faced them, knees slightly bent, and clenched fists raised as he taunted them, alternately in Irish and English.

Five English soldiers rushed one Irishman, and showing no mercy, two English held the one man while the other three beat him.

This was it. The end of the fight, the end of his chance to escape, the end of his temporal journey.

He had never denied he was going to die as surely as any other man. The prospect of death didn't frighten him. Still he experienced an overwhelming rush of misery.

The end was at hand, and he had naught to show for the past thirty years except a few scars and some pleasant memories. It had been his choice not to care about anyone or anything, his choice to pursue pleasure and avoid entanglements. He'd believed it was a good life, and he'd thought his heart was inured beyond emotion. Yet in this final moment he didn't like what he saw, didn't like what he felt.

It required no effort to imagine what would happen when word reached the hills that his rotting head was impaled above the town wall, where once the head of his great-grandfather had been displayed. His death would probably be dismissed with a shrug. He could almost hear his own dear mam saying, *'Tis no surprise, his coming to such an end. I was never expecting anything more.* Indeed, it would be only a matter of months, perhaps a sennight or two, before he was forgotten, and as he slipped into unconsciousness, one awful truth pierced his heart. No one was going to cry for him. There would be no lament for Rian O'Byrne.

Chapter 13

"**T**ell me, Sir Thomas, how did your niece greet the news of her betrothal?" inquired Richard Maudelyn, priest of the royal chapel. It was late afternoon of Maudelyn's second day in Dublin, and he was dining with Sir Thomas in his host's castle lodgings.

"Mistress Picot is flattered," was Sir Thomas's cautious reply. It was the sort of thing he imagined Maudelyn would expect to hear.

"I remember your niece from his majesty's previous visit," commented the priest. "A remarkable young woman, whose favorable appearance and singular conduct were much noted. As I recollect, she was much admired, although there were some who spoke of independent ways. Does she remain engaged in matters of commerce?"

"She does. Verily, since her mother's death such activities have occupied most of her attention." Sir Thomas did not like Maudelyn's condescending tone, nor the impression that the priest already knew the answer. On Annora's behalf he added, "She is meticulous, thrifty, and efficient. Every one of those qualities, I am assured, bodes well for excellence in a wife." Sir Thomas motioned to a servant for more wine. This was not the time for a leisurely meal, rather he should be finalizing

149

Annora's plan. Perhaps if he could not bore Maudelyn into retiring to his guest quarters, he might bring on a wine-induced exhaustion. It was a choice Rhenish wine, the best Sir Thomas had to offer, and Maudelyn did not refuse when the servant refilled his goblet to the brim.

"And is there verity to the stories that she has turned down many offers of marriage?" quizzed Maudelyn.

"Aye, 'tis all true." Sir Thomas was already considering what he should say next. He must needs do nothing to cast doubt on Annora's state of mind. There must be no reason for anyone to suspect her disappearance from Dublin—when it occurred—was anything other than against her will. Praise be, upon his departure from her residence yesterday, his niece had thought to send her maid to the dressmaker to request an appointment. It was a brilliant touch, lending credence to the impression that she had gone to bed yesternight to dream of wedding garments, and had spent the better part of today engaged in preparations for the arrival of the king and bridegroom.

"Mistress Picot did not protest?" Maudelyn peered over the rim of his raised goblet. He regarded Sir Thomas with the haughty suspicion that had been known to make men betray themselves. The priest bore an uncanny, discomfiting physical resemblance to the king. Like his majesty, Maudelyn was fair of face, and had thick, curling yellow hair; verily, the fact that both men possessed the beauteous features of Richard's mother, Fair Joan of Kent, had provided much sustenance for court gossips. Beyond the physical, Maudelyn's mien was educated, mannered, crafty, and suspicious. He trusted no one, and no one trusted him, especially since it was rumored that priest and monarch had on more than one occasion changed places.

"Nay, I heard not a hint of complaint," Sir Thomas proclaimed the boldfaced lie in the belief that such a falsehood could not be a sin. "My niece is aware of the honor his majesty bestows upon her. So, too, does she esteem such a distinguished match, and independent though she may be in some ways, Annora has never been one to prattle on about love. She is a most sensible female in that respect. But I should not be speaking in her behalf. You will have the chance to discuss these matters with her yourself. I have asked her to join us for a privy interview at this time tomorrow."

"You discern the direction of my mind and are most considerate, Sir Thomas, in your arrangements," Maudelyn said before proceeding to another topic. By the king's order, the priest had been charged with overseeing any necessary repairs to the castle, and he wished to discuss the condition of certain buildings as well as the availability of artisans and lumber. There was not much time, and all things must needs be perfect for Richard's arrival and the wedding celebration.

Even under the best of circumstances, Sir Thomas had no patience for such a discourse, but it was especially wearisome when a far more urgent matter demanded his attention. There was not a minute to waste, not when Annora's scheme to evade the king's matrimonial plans allowed for only three nights—yesterday, today, and tomorrow—in which to effect her flight from Dublin. One day had already slipped away, and if she did not leave tonight or tomorrow, it would be too late, for it was not good enough simply to escape Dublin. Annora had no choice except to leave Ireland, and to do that, she must travel south to meet the *Hera* when it moored at the mouth of the Vartrey five days henceforth. Under ideal circumstances, a journey by land to Wicklow required four days, usually five; a bad trip, beset by raiders or delayed by rain and winds, could take much longer.

Since agreeing to help Annora, Sir Thomas had conveyed the change in the *Hera's* itinerary to James Buttevant, he'd ridden to Our Lady of Victory to tell Abbess Thomasin to expect unidentified travelers at any time over the course of the next three consecutive nights, and he'd made passable the old tunnel that ran from Annora's tower to the other side of the town wall.

Those tasks had been simple, but it was not as easy to find a prisoner willing and able to kidnap the niece of Sir Thomas Picot. There were, as Annora had assumed, many desperate men imprisoned in the castle towers and donjon holes, but there were none whom Sir Thomas considered reckless, intelligent, or strong enough for the task. Mayhap he was being too picky, but then it was not everyday he recruited a rapist or murderer to escort a wealthy gentlewoman on a perilous journey.

Through the open windows drifted the peal of Vespers bells. The sun was setting, mass for St. Petronilla had been said at midday, the revels would soon be at an end, and time was running out. In all likelihood, Annora was doing what was needed to abet the entrance of a stranger into her chamber, while Sir Thomas—who needed to be searching for her escort—was debating the best mortar for the Irish climate. In an effort to bring closure to this tedious conversation, he remarked, ''The town gates will be locked earlier than usual this night.''

''That is wise. A spy was captured yesterday, and there are certain to be more of them sneaking into Dublin once the news of the king's advance spreads into native-held territories. No sense in making it easy for them.''

''A spy?'' Sir Thomas asked casually.

''One of the wild Irish.''

''I know nothing of this. Only yesternight did I inspect the prisoners, and again this morning. We had a death, but I was not told there was anyone to be added to the rolls.''

''This prisoner is not in your custody. My men hold him in their quarters.''

''And why is that?''

''It has always been my practice to keep the men under my command satisfied. The prisoner murdered one of their comrades, and as I understand it, they wished to exact their own retribution. To have naysayed their purpose would have produced a most malcontented mood in the ranks, and soon after malcontent comes disloyalty. The loyalty of one's men is not something with which to trifle, don't you agree, Sir Thomas? Their request was not unreasonable. I merely asked that his face not be disfigured. That task will be left to the ravens.''

Sir Thomas repressed a shudder. He didn't know which was worse: the ruthless, uncompromising manner in which the priest spoke, or his own mind's picture of the abuse that the prisoner would certainly be suffering at the mercy of Maudelyn's soldiers. It was unlikely the Irishman would be capable of holding up his head, let alone be a suitable candidate to effect Annora's flight from Dublin. "What do you intend for the prisoner?"

"He is to be executed at first light."

"I would like to question him before then," Sir Thomas said. "You have no objection?"

"None, sir. You would know best what intelligence is required from these people; so, too, would you have a greater sense as to whether he lies or speaks true." The priest rose from his seat before the trestle, expressed thanks for the fine meal, and the two men descended to the castle yard.

Dublin Castle, built into the southeastern corner of the town wall, boasted eight towers. Sir Thomas's lodgings were located on the upper two levels of Store Tower at the most northeastern corner, and from there, the knight walked with Maudelyn in the direction of guest apartments adjacent to the great hall. Upon reaching Castle Gate in the north curtain, Sir Thomas instructed one of his officers to bring the Irish spy to the chamber in which he conducted interrogations. On either side of Castle Gate were twin towers used for the confinement of prisoners, and on the upper level of one of these towers was a room set aside for Sir Thomas. He bid farewell to the priest and went to await the prisoner.

In the privacy of his official chamber, the misgivings Sir Thomas had contained in Maudelyn's presence began to unravel, and he set to pacing between the narrow windows that looked down upon the drawbridge over which all traffic passed between castle and town. He had little expectation this new prisoner would be suitable, and he regretted ever having agreed to Annora's scheme, for he had given her false hope. It laid a burden of sadness upon his heart to know that when he next saw her, whether it be a year henceforth in Lubbeck or here in Dublin, she would be much changed. Annora's heretofore unshakable confidence, and her faith in the basic goodness of man, had been already undermined. Shortly her spirit would be sullied, and it seemed to Sir Thomas one of the greatest strokes of injustice that the only choices she had were equally abhorrent: she could obey the king, marry a lad and surrender her assets, or she could retain her dignity and independence by fleeing her home. Either way she lost.

A knock came at the door. The officer entered.

"You have the prisoner?" Sir Thomas went to stand behind a table that served as a writing surface and upon which were stacked numerous rolls, annals, and toll records incumbent to his administrative duties.

"Aye, my lord, the Irish spy is here." The officer stepped aside and a shackled man, who had to duck his head beneath the lintel, entered the chamber.

The prisoner, whose hands were manacled before him, presented a savage sight. A mass of snarled hair hid his face, yet much of his huge frame was revealed through a tattered coarse tunic. Sir Thomas knew a rush of trepidation at assigning Annora into such a creature's custody. Silent curses rose in his throat, an impotent denial that it had come to this. Sir Thomas scrutinized the prisoner, taking inventory of the bruises and welts across his chest and along his limbs that attested to his having been flogged and beaten. Fresh rivulets of blood, bright red and thin as threads, hinted that perhaps a flogging had been interrupted. The sickening, acrid odor of confinement and decay clung to his body. He seemed more beast than human, and if Sir Thomas hoped to glimpse the nature of the Irishman's character and state of mind, he must needs look into his eyes.

"Raise your head, man," Sir Thomas ordered. The prisoner did not move, and Sir Thomas knew a moment of panic that the fellow was deaf or otherwise touched. "You, prisoner, raise your head, if you please. Can you not hear me?" This time the man obeyed. "You have been brought here in order . . ."

There was a catch in Sir Thomas's voice, and unable to draw a breath, the knight leaned against the table, his regard locked upon the prisoner who returned his stare with a dull, blank gaze. There was no hint of what he might be thinking, if he was still capable of thought. Rugged, handsome features were twisted with pain, his mouth was hardened to a thin line, his skin had an odd grayish hue. A few moments elapsed, then the man lowered his eyes. Sir Thomas exhaled, and spoke to the officer, "That will be all for now. I will call for an escort when I am done."

"An extra guard has been posted outside, my lord," said the officer.

Sir Thomas gave a nod, the officer closed the door behind him, and the sound of the latch falling in place was the loudest noise in the chamber. Sir Thomas moved from behind the table and went to the center of the room to stand no more than a forearm's distance from the prisoner. In a hushed voice, he said, "It looks to me as if you should sit down, O'Byrne. Please, won't you come over this way." He pointed to a bench near one of the windows.

The prisoner looked up. Gone was the vacant stare, and for the space of a heartbeat, his emotions were painfully, piercingly visible. Gratitude flickered in his eyes, an instant of hope softened the lines about his mouth, and there was poignant uncertainty in his voice. "I was not certain whether ye knew who I was. It's been many years."

Sir Thomas forced a smile. "Not so long that I've forgotten such a fine traveling companion as yourself, nor could I ever forget the man who saved my niece's life." Of all the men in Ireland, indeed, in the whole of Christendom, how could it be that this man would be the one to walk into his chamber this night? For the first time, since Annora had concocted this scheme, Sir Thomas dared to think it might succeed. He slipped a hand beneath the younger man's arm as if to guide him to the bench. "They've been harsh with you."

"Not bad for a condemned man," Rian replied. He reached the bench and sat before the window, conscious of the evening breeze against his battered flesh.

"I may be able to change that," Sir Thomas whispered.

Rian regarded him with a narrow, inquiring look.

"That's right," he whispered again, turning slightly to pour some wine into a drinking horn. "I may be able to keep you alive." He set the drinking horn in the Irishman's manacled hands, noting they were steady, his grip was firm. The English had flogged and beaten Rian O'Byrne, but they had not robbed him of his strength. Sir Thomas watched him drink. "This need not be your final night."

Having drained the wine to the last drop, Rian wiped his mouth with this back of his hand. His muted voice matched Sir Thomas's whisper. "Why do I think 'tis not as easy as ye make it sound?"

"Nothing ever is. Verily, to even speak of this poses a great risk to the parties involved."

Rian nodded for Sir Thomas to continue.

Sir Thomas pulled up another bench. He sat facing O'Byrne, and tilted forward. "You, of course, remember my niece."

"Aye, I remember her," Rian said, revealing none of the emotions that were stirred by this quiet admission. For an instant, the pain that permeated his body was not nearly as immediate as was a vision of changeable blue eyes. He had a glimpse of a scowling angel, and he heard a woman's voice as if she were beside him. *You're an impenitent rogue.* He heard a ripple of laughter. *Yours for all time. I won't forget.* How strange it was that since he'd been dragged from the brothel house, he'd contemplated her more in that short time than he had over the course of years. He was fully expecting her voice—not his dead wife's or his father's, not the executioner's, or the fair English priest's—to be the last thing he heard before drawing his final breath.

"Once before, you saved her life," said Sir Thomas. "Now I ask that you do the same again. She is in grave jeopardy and must needs leave Dublin this night, and while I could not adequately repay you before, this time I can offer your life in exchange for taking her out of harm's way."

Rian wondered what the *grave jeopardy* could be. An ill-tempered husband was the worst he could conceive; it was impossible to imagine the Annora Picot he had known having any enemies. But he didn't ask Sir Thomas to elaborate. The precise nature of the trouble wouldn't matter. Any chance to save himself was better than none, and the prospect of deliverance from death sent a thrumming sensation through his body. It started in his head, then spread to the muscles of his legs, and down his arms to his hands, the tips of his fingers. It was a good feeling. Hopeful, energetic, positive, and stronger than the pain. "Ye'll be releasing me to escort yer niece out of town?"

"Nay, I cannot release you, but I can allow your

escape, following which you must kidnap her, or at least create the appearance that she was taken against her will, and was injured, mayhap fatally, in the process.''

"That is all?'' Blood was surging through him, restoring his endurance and vitality. He would accept any proposition, if it offered the possibility of living beyond tomorrow.

"Nay, there is more. My niece must needs be on the other side of the town wall by midnight, out of the fringes by dawn, and at Wicklow harbor within five days.''

Rian responded with a low whistle of disbelief at this nearly impossible task. Inside him, the thrumming intensified. "And if she's not there in five days?''

"The entire exercise will have been for naught. If you fail, you'll be pursued, hunted down, and upon your apprehension, I'll deny any knowledge of this discussion. Get my niece to Wicklow, and your freedom is guaranteed. Plus there will be silver waiting for you at the harbor.''

"Why do ye do this?''

For an instant, Sir Thomas wondered if he should divulge Catherine's secret to Rian O'Byrne. The truth might secure the Irishman's commitment to Annora's safety. So, too, might it increase the danger. It was not worth the risk. The secret would stay with him. Forever. "It is as I told you, my niece faces grave jeopardy. I had intended this night to find a man desperate enough to do my bidding, and it would appear Fate and Fortune look down upon the both of us with Favor. It is nothing less than a miracle that the moon and stars align to cross our paths at this particular moment in time. As for the unusual, if not drastic, measures I employ, if there were any other solution, it would already have been pursued. This, however, is the only way to save my niece.''

And the only way for me. "I will do it, Sir Thomas,'' Rian said, and for one awful moment, he feared the knight was going to shed tears. He attempted to reassure the older man. ''And 'tis a pledge on my very life I give to ye that I'll be seeing yer niece safely to her journey's end.''

''Full well said, Rian O'Byrne. Full well said.'' The older man's face trembled, he gave a sigh in relief. ''It is an unholy bargain we strike, but you should know it is a good and right thing you do. Until I had charge of my niece, there was little I feared, but as the years have passed I've come to dread one thing above all else. I could imagine no greater pain than to outlive her, no greater failure than to be unable to intervene at the time of her greatest need. It would have been impossible to endure her death that long ago winter just as it is impossible for me to watch her suffer now, and I thank you for saving me from such anguish, for preventing my failure. Tomorrow was not meant to be your judgment, but when that day comes, there will be a place in heaven for you, of that I'm certain.''

Rian said nothing. Two or three days before he would have laughed to hear such a thing. *A place in heaven*. Now Rian took pause to wonder. Perhaps even the forsaken were given second chances.

Sir Thomas went to fetch a miniature chest with iron hinges from its resting place on a shelf. Setting it on the trestle, he lifted the lid and reached inside. The chest held the master keys to numerous gates, locks, and doors throughout the castle. ''Come, let me unlock your hands. There is not much time, and the plan is a detailed one. You have your wits about you, and are ready to hear the whole of it?''

''As ready as I'll ever be.'' Rian extended the manacles to Sir Thomas. His injuries from Maudelyn's men were not bad. He'd had worse. A few bruises, a rack of sore ribs, and the sting of a flogging were nothing that freedom, time, and the prospect of cheating the English king out of his severed head would not cure.

Chapter 14

❧ ❦ ❧

Bells shattered the mild May evening. The first to sound was the public bell at the High Cross, its prolonged, leaden peal commanding the attention of anyone within range. Before long the silvery bells of Christ Church and St. Thomas's Abbey chimed in, then those in the steeples of St. Audoen's, Trinity, and St. Patrick's joined until the growing clamor reverberated through every lane and into every corner of Dublin— within and without the wall. This was not, however, the solemn striking of the canonical hours, but a frantic, continual clang, the sort of discordant racket meant to alert the populace to spreading fire or some other matter of public disaster.

Annora rushed to a window. She opened the shutters that had been secured against the night air, and rested upon the sill to look out at the lane. Up and down the quayside heads poked through windows and doorways of smaller dwellings, people called for answers, and several young men came out of the nearby tavern to investigate. They pointed up Fishamble Street, but Annora could not see beyond a hodgepodge of close-constructed dwellings, tilting to each other at odd angles with their jettied second and third stories leaning over the street until they nearly touched the dwellings on the opposite side.

"To the castle! Men-at-arms! Make haste! To the castle," a crier shouted. His voice growing clearer as he strode down Fishamble, calling to muster any of the garrison who were not at their posts. Another cry went forth to secure the town gates—there were five of them—and to lower the portcullis and double the watch at each entry.

"Blessed Heaven," Annora whispered, her heart soaring, somersaulting, then plunging. This call to arms meant her uncle had either been discovered in a heap or had regained consciousness to spread the alarm. *Escape. A prisoner is escaped.* It meant she was about to be *kidnapped.* She made the sign of the cross as she went to a different window, "Bless to me, Oh God, the path whereon I go this night."

The sun had set, twilight had almost given way to blackness, and she saw nothing out of the ordinary in the rear garden. From the other side of the garden wall came the thud of running feet. It was not one person but several hurrying through the alley in the direction of Dame's Gate—probably soldiers, by the accompanying metallic clatter. Annora's stomach tumbled once more, and her mouth went dry as she stared into the shadows for some sign of movement, a shadow too short to be a tree, too narrow to be a bush. There was nothing to indicate anyone was in the garden, and the terrible possibility that her escape had already failed brought on a sickening combination of doubt and guilt.

Perhaps staging a kidnapping was a mistake. What if her determination to save herself had caused her uncle to be injured? Or worse. What if his role in her deception were discovered? It was not merely his good health or the soundness of an arm or leg that she put at risk. Not even his career was the worst of it. Verily, his life was at stake. She should not have involved him, nor Master Buttevant, nor Nicholas nor Abbess Thomasin. She should not have been so quick to decide; she should have thought harder, with more clarity and less focus upon her needs. If only she had taken adequate time to devise an alternative that involved neither her uncle nor anyone else, and most certainly not a complete stranger, who was, by the by, a condemned felon.

It was her idea down to the last detail, and she'd been more than satisfied with her ingenuity, yet now—only in afterthought—did she see the recklessness of it. She had not given this the advisement it merited. By the saints, what of the man whom her uncle had recruited and allowed to escape this night? Until now she had considered him naught beyond his desperation to save his life; she had not considered whether, having achieved freedom, he was someone who could be relied upon to do as he'd agreed. He might already be out of town and headed into the west, or mayhap his intention was to rob her once they were away from Dublin. He was, after all, a criminal, and there would be no one to check him. She would be at his mercy. And what of pestilence? She had not considered the consequences of spending several days with someone of low company and poor habits; and picturing a wretched creature afflicted with warble fly or another hideous malady, her hands grew clammy. There was a churning in the pit of her stomach.

Or perhaps this night would be nothing more than a repetition of the last, when no one had entered the tower to take her away. Perhaps she would never reach Wicklow before the *Hera* made for the open sea. How heedless she was to have denied the possibility that she might be here when the king arrived.

Annora tried to envision some unaccustomed youth taking up residence in her tower, dining at her table, sleeping in her bed; she tried to imagine calling husband an Englishman of an age to be her son. She tried, but could not envision such things coming to pass any more than she was able to feel the smallest grain of compassion for Harry of Monmouth, being held hostage while his father was in exile, forced to wed a woman nearly past her fruitful years. She felt nothing akin to sympathy when she bethought herself of Monmouth. The only reactions she experienced were the same nausea and defiance as when she had sat in the garden and read the king's missive.

Her intention now was as then: she had always been in charge of her future, and that was not going to change.

"Curfew!" From the alley two criers shouted in unison. The proclamation went forth. All persons were to return to their dwellings, secure their doors, and remain inside until sunrise. "Curfew!" The faint glow of a swinging lantern marked the crier's progress. "Curfew!"

From the chamber in the tower below Annora there came an abrupt crash. Her body jerked in startled reaction. Someone was in the solar. Someone who did not know their way without a rushlight and had stumbled against the cupboard in which her mother's plates and goblets were stored. The clatter continued as another batch of pewter, steel, and silver landed on top of each other. It was a good thing Annora had encouraged the maid to visit her sister for several days, else Devasse would certainly have summoned the watch by now, if she had not yet pummeled the fellow herself with a heavy cook pot.

At last came a measure of silence. Annora held her breath, and moving not a single muscle, she strained to hear what she might. She imagined the rustle of dried rushes as someone trod upon them, the creak of a floorboard in need of repair, the scrape of boot-leather against stone.

There were footsteps on the stairs. Slow, cautious. Someone was coming.

Annora trembled. This was what she wanted, what she had been waiting for, yet her trembling worsened. She held fast to the cool window ledge, her fingers tensed, and she stared at the shrouded garden, searching for the rose arbor, the table and benches beneath the chestnut tree, and the winding path of seashells that led past the dovecote and sun dial. She saw none of those familiar things, and it only made the trembling worse. In another moment, when the chamber door opened, she would turn away from this window for the last time.

After tonight the garden, this chamber and beloved tower home would become things of the past. They would be nothing but memories as was a vision of her mother strolling along the iridescent path, a basket overflowing with bright flowers dangling from her arm.

No more than memories as was the voice of an Irishman standing below her window, whispering, *Even if ye can't speak Irish, I'll still love ye forever*.

She could not restrain her trembling, nor her grief.

"Curfew!" was proclaimed up and down the quay. "Curfew!"

Even inside dwellings and public houses the order was heard, and halfway up the stairs between the second and third levels of Annora's tower, Rian O'Byrne came to an abrupt halt. Quickly he pressed against the wall, his shoulders barely fitting in the space between two narrow window slits. Outside, there was the rapid patter of someone running; the pair of criers called again. Someone cursed the noise. Someone else yelled a warning.

Rian peered out the window. A band of shadowy figures was coming down the hill, and it didn't require magic to know they were soldiers. He watched half their number enter a tavern while the others fanned out to search doorways and behind a line of carts. Rian didn't need to look any longer to know they were searching for someone.

Thus far, Rian's escape had been flawless. His exit from the castle had been achieved by lowering himself down a perpendicular passage in the wall of the chamber in which he'd made his bargain with Sir Thomas. It was a chute of the sort that might have once been used as a garderobe, having nothing more than the natural clefts in the rocks upon which to gain a foot or handhold, and its existence was known only to the knight. At the bottom, Rian had landed knee-deep in foul water; from there, the passage had opened into the ditch that circled the castle, and using the shadow of the curtain wall for cover, he had moved away from the gate tower. On the other side of the ditch was a row of modest dwellings. As Sir Thomas had promised, the rear gate to one of these houses had been ajar, and inside, there had been food and drink, a basin of water for bathing, a sword, two daggers, and a coarse, brown cowl.

It had been easy to walk down Castle Street. No one gave the slightest notice to one more friar hurrying through the dark town, his hooded head bent low, arms folded before him, a crude wooden cross hanging from his neck, and hands hidden beneath the folds of a long robe. Such was a common sight. At the first crossroads, Rian turned north. He had not forgotten how best to wend through the lanes to reach the alley behind the Picot home, and soon he had arrived at the exact spot where he used to vault over the wall into the garden.

Nothing had hindered his progress until the moment he'd found himself passing the arbor. There, he'd hesitated, deterred not by any visible foe but by the workings of his mind as the sweet scent of roses had revived the past. Since the last time he'd been in this garden, Rian had allowed himself to remember nothing more than the victory of seduction. He'd forgotten that Annora Picot had affected him in any way beyond the physical.

Yet as he'd passed the arbor, the truth had come back. He'd remembered how Annora had awakened his conscience, and how he'd decided to leave Dublin not so much because the political climate had changed, but because being with Annora Picot had made him care.

Now he was returned, and with no more intention of caring about anyone or anything than before. As Sir Thomas had said, an alignment of the moon and stars had brought him to this tower garden, and self-preservation was his only motivation. His survival was the only thing that signified. At dawn on the morrow, he intended to have his head affixed to his shoulders; four days hence, he intended to be exchanging Annora for a plump purse of English silver.

"Curfew." The criers were on the move again.

Rian glanced up the stairs. A faint thread of light seeped beneath a door, and he knew Annora waited on the other side. He bent low to pass beneath the narrow windows, and upon reaching the landing, every vestige of hesitation had been vanquished. He grasped and twisted the handle, pushed open the door, and stepped into a chamber the likes of which he'd never seen. Instead of rushes an abundance of furs were strewn across the floor; wax tapers instead of tallow dips were flickering throughout; plump, colorful cushions graced the chairs and benches; and upon the bed curtains were embroidered crowned thistle heads to match the pattern carved in the legs and posts of a massive tester bed. Tansy, Our Lady's bedstraw, and lavender sweetened the air with such strength it was unlikely more than a few fleas had ever survived in this chamber. No wonder Annora Picot had been reluctant to wed.

His gaze swept over the room again, this time searching for Annora. He spotted her standing before a window. Her back was to him, and his first impression upon seeing her again was how the outline of her feminine form had not altered. Her small waist, the curve of her hips, the delicate lines of her back and shoulders were as appealing as they had been four years before. Her slender body did not proclaim a woman approaching the end of her third decade. So, too, did her bright golden hair belie her age. The thick tresses were not coiled about her ears as she had used to style it but secured with a single ribbon at the nape of her neck, from whence they flowed freely to her waist, lustrous as a girl's half her years. Out of nowhere came a sensory memory of honey mingled with cumin. If the circumstances had been different he would have crossed the chamber to slip his arms about her waist and whisper a provocative greeting. If he had been a different man, he might have smiled when she turned from the window.

"Sweet seraphim," Annora gasped at the hulking creature who dwarfed her chamber. The top of his hood was crushed by the ceiling, its cowl hid his face, but her imagination offered bulging eyes, a grotesque nose, blackened teeth, and a menacing sneer. One hand flew to her mouth to hold back another outcry when he moved toward her. She must be brave.

"Nay, mistress, do not be alarmed." Rian extended a hand to offer reassurance. It was palm-side up and open as if to symbolize he had nothing to hide.

Annora drew away. It was a huge, rough hand, bruised to purple on one side. She was frightened not only by his attempt to touch her with that awful hand but by his voice. The man's accent was Irish. His tone was low and rasping.

"Were ye not expecting me?" he asked, and when she replied, her voice was nothing more than a choked whisper. He had to step closer and ask her to repeat herself.

"You are right, sir. I was expecting someone." Annora could hardly breathe. He was so near that he towered over her, forcing her to tilt her head back to look up at him, and then his battered hand moved into her line of vision. She watched him push back the hood. *"Bene-*

dicte,'' she uttered as a pent up breath rushed out, and she felt herself swaying.

Rian was certain she was going to faint, but he dared not reach out to her. He would catch her if she fell, but would make no move otherwise.

"Do ye not recognize me?" he asked as gently as he'd ever spoken.

Chapter 15

"**A**ye, I know who you are, Rian O'Byrne."
Annora said his name on a whisper. She
took in the burnished hair, the deep-set eyes that she
knew were the color of the ocean, and the sensual mouth
that had been prone to grinning at the most inappropriate
moments. The last time they had been together they'd
been lovers, and in an instant, all the heated gazes, the
sweet kisses, and stolen caresses that she had tried to
forget hastened back to her. Annora's heart beat faster.

A thousand questions whirled through her brain. A
thousand hopes, sympathies, dreads, doubts, and mysteries. She took a step as if to reach out in greeting, and
hesitated. Was it a miracle or a curse that he was here this
night? She looked into his face, but found no answer.
Something was different, and forthwith, it came to her.
Gone was the twinkle that used to light his eyes. Gone
was the probing, wicked glint that had beckoned to her,
beguiled her, tempted her. Instead she stared into dull
eyes that did not probe or beckon, eyes that revealed
nothing, that did not speak to her in any way. She had
been prepared for the arrival of a stranger, and sooth to
say, it seemed this man was one. She did not move
toward him.

"I did not mean to frighten ye," Rian said, grateful

that he hadn't experienced any great rush of sentiment upon seeing this woman. Of course, there was his physical reaction to her beauty, but that didn't concern him; it could be controlled, and would pass once she was aboard her ship and sailing away from Ireland.

"My uncle sent you here?" It could not be otherwise, yet she asked. Her mind was still trying to convince her soul that it made no difference who her uncle had recruited this night. Any man would do, and she must not attach importance to the fact that Rian O'Byrne had returned. Ireland had not changed, and he had not come back to her, at least not of his own free will.

"That he did."

"You were in the castle?"

He nodded.

"Condemned?"

Again he nodded in reply.

"Why?"

"Murder."

She focused on his hands, bloodied and bruised. "And did you do it?"

He shrugged. "An English soldier is dead, stabbed with his own knife while we fought. I am Irish and in Dublin."

"Was it my uncle who arrested you?"

"Nay, 'twas yer king's priest, Maudelyn. Yer uncle knew nothing of it until this night."

Annora could not conceal the tender pity in her voice. While her mind told her this man was no different than any other prisoner who her uncle might have found to do her bidding, her soul knew otherwise. "I am sorry."

"Sorry, ye say. And why might that be?" he asked, but got no answer.

Outside there was a renewed hue and cry. Through the window drifted news of an escape from the castle.

The fugitive was one of the savage natives. *Take care!* The fiend had already killed once, only yesterday, and the lust for murder was on his breath. *Take care!* The Irishman was a beast. He could easily kill again.

Annora scrutinized Rian. ''You did not hurt my uncle, did you?''

''He will recover.''

There was a banging from below.

Annora glanced about in alarm.

Someone pounded on the tower door.

''Who might that be?'' Rian asked.

''I—I don't know.''

''Yer uncle spoke naught of anyone coming here before we were gone.'' He grasped the hilt of the sword Sir Thomas had left in the house on Castle Street. Beneath the brown habit, he wore an English-styled tunic, leggings, and was armed to fight. He slid the sword up and down, testing the ease with which he could pull the weapon from its sheath.

''You are correct. This is not part of the plan. I must answer and find out what happens, else I shall arouse suspicion. Come, you must hide here while I am below stairs.'' She went to the tester bed and pulled back the curtains, indicating that he should climb upon the mattress. Rian complied. ''Stay there until I return.'' She drew the curtains.

Rian was not as worried as she might have weened. True, his heart was thundering, but he liked the way his blood pumped fast and furious. He knew he was alive. He was ready to fight if soldiers entered the chamber. It was a good feeling, this energy, this thrill for danger, and it had been a long time since Rian had been this eager about anything.

The pounding continued.

'' 'Tis not necessary to demolish the door. I'm on my way,'' Annora called from somewhere on the stairs, each word growing fainter as she went lower. ''Who is there?''

A few moments of silence elapsed before Rian heard a muted reply. Annora must have opened the door, but he couldn't make out what was being said, so he moved to a better hearing place. After a while, he heard the door closing, a bolt falling into place, then quick, ascending footsteps.

Annora entered the chamber to discover Rian hovering near the window. "Move away from there." She tossed an expression of pure irritation and closed the shutters with a bang.

"And will ye be telling me what I've done to be deserving such a darkening scowl?" On impulse, he added, " 'Tis not seemly for an angel to scowl."

"No more unseemly than such a remark. You would be wise to hold your tongue on matters of the past," Annora admonished, strident. "My uncle will see you flayed alive, Rian O'Byrne, should you do anything other than fulfill your bargain. Did not I leave you in hiding and ask that you remain behind the bed-curtains until I returned?"

"Aye." Rian's expression conveyed wounded innocence. He contrived to look like a lad caught in the act of stealing tarts from the cooling shelf. "But 'twas the worst kind of torment, for I could not hear a thing ye were saying."

Annora did not smile at this attempt to beguile her. Her voice was frosty. "And what did you hear for your disobedience?"

"Nothing," he admitted.

"Ah," she said, vindicated and self-righteous. Having closed the shutters at the other window, she took her time fiddling with the latch before revealing what it was that he had not heard. "Maudelyn expresses concern for my safety and has generously assigned some of his guard to watch my residence."

"Yer plan is foiled then?"

"Nay. 'Tis possible to leave the tower without being detected. Although I'm not certain how anyone will believe I was kidnapped while the guards heard nothing."

"Mayhap ye should take them some refreshment as a token of yer appreciation. Something potent to muddle their vigilance."

"An idea most worthy," said Annora. "A flagon of my finest Portuguese wine with a platter of fried fig pastries would be an excellent complement. The pastries are fresh, for the pieman came yesterday, and delicious though they are, fried fig does bring on a ferocious, excessive thirst."

While Annora went below stairs to prepare a tray for the guards, Rian commenced the task of ransacking the chamber. He began with the cushions, slashing each one with his dagger to delve about its stuffing as if searching for treasure; the ruined cushions were tossed away in haphazard fashion to land where they might. He did the same to the bed mattress, then turned his attention to the furs upon the floor, flipping them over, and pushing them this way and that. Cautious and quiet, he moved about the room, setting chairs and tables on their sides. He damaged a few items, spilling a wooden container holding flowers, cracking a hand mirror, and crushing a basket filled with dried herbs. He was searching about for the next object to damage and did not hear Annora return.

"What are you doing!" She rushed to block his advance toward her mother's Holland lute and Psalter. "Stop."

"Nothing more than what yer uncle instructed. We must create the impression yer chamber was looted. So too must there be the appearance of a struggle. Did ye not know?"

"I knew. Of course, I knew. But I did not think . . ." Her voice faded away as she glanced at the chaos he'd created. To see the familiar chamber defiled in this way was a powerful reminder that once she left Dublin, she could not change her mind. She could not turn back, for there would be nothing to which to return. After this night everything that was dear and familiar would be lost to her forever. "Those were my mother's. Do not destroy them, please," she said softly, humbly.

Rian said nothing. He turned away from the lute and Psalter, going instead to a wooden casket ornamented with medallions. "It will go faster if ye lend yer help. We need to empty the chests and hampers," he said as he lifted the casket lid and began pulling out its contents. An assortment of bed linens and tunics floated through the air. Done with that, he moved toward the coffer at the foot of the bed when he realized she hadn't budged. "Is something amiss?"

"I—I suddenly find . . ." Annora shook her head. Her voice thickened with gathering tears. "I have . . ."

"Do ye change yer mind?"

Annora saw Rian O'Byrne through a curtain of tears, and her every fear, every disappointment and heartache was of a sudden stronger than her determination to do what she must to escape Dublin. She was frightened but not about to admit such a thing to this man, for it was not the danger of the coming journey that roused her apprehension. It was him, and the price she must pay to escape the king's greed. From the start she'd reckoned with having to leave Ireland, yet there was an even greater price. Rian O'Byrne would deliver her to the *Hera*, making his the last face she would see before leaving this land forever. Rian O'Byrne would be her final memory of Ireland, and that frightened her more than being apprehended by Maudelyn's men-at-arms or being forced to the altar with Monmouth. Over the past four years, she'd failed to forget Rian O'Byrne, and now she never would.

"If ye change yer mind, ye send me to my death, my lady," Rian said, softly. "Ye're holding my future in yer hands, and I would beg that ye consider it tenderly."

She met his gaze and was reminded of a caged wolf she'd once seen on the quay. Some settlers had brought the animal to Dublin in the hopes of getting a handsome price from a foreign merchant, perhaps one who furnished beasts for menageries. The wolf's eyes had been blue as Rian's, and like the man, the animal had exuded a grace and power that pulled her nearer to its cage. There had been something about the wolf as there was about the Irishman that fascinated Annora. While the rest of the world knew that to get too close to the beast could be fatal, she had gone to that cage, had spoken soothing words, and dared to stroke its back. The wolf had nipped at her, and she'd received naught but a row of small scars running from her thumb across her wrist, but she might not be as fortunate with Rian O'Byrne, if she got too close a second time.

"Would ye send me to my death? Ye can't back out now. I made a promise to yer uncle. Do ye force me to drag ye out of here against yer will?"

"I do not change my mind." As it had with the wolf, Rian's desire to be free flickered in his eyes as trenchant and desperate as Annora's need to save herself. Overwhelmed by a sense of helplessness, she started to cry. The prospect of relying upon a stranger had not bothered her in this way. Why could it not be as simple with Rian O'Byrne? He was too much like the wolf, and while that frightened her, quickly fear turned to frustration. Sooth, she was incensed. Angry at her tears, disgusted by her weakness, and furious at him, although she was not certain why. Using the back of her hand, she swiped at damp cheeks. "Naught has changed. I must flee Dublin and cannot do so without your aid."

"*A Thiarna Dé*," Rian swore on an underbreath. *O Lord God*. He'd been prepared for danger and stealth, but not for tears. He'd even been prepared for acrimony or bitterness when he revealed himself to her, but tears were something else altogether. "My recollection is that ye were spun of stronger fiber, Annora Picot."

"As was mine." She sniffled.

"Why then the tears?" He shifted his weight from one foot to the other and waited for her reply.

" 'Tis hard to accept that of all the men in Ireland I must depend upon you to survive," she said as if his being here were a curse.

Rian winced. "Am I such a contemptible man? So vile that ye would spurn my help and lose yer chance to escape?"

"I will not lose this chance."

For a second, Rian thought this scene was ended, and they could get on with the matter at hand.

"I cry because yours will be the last face I see at Wicklow." Annora's tears began anew. She couldn't stop them, anymore than she could prevent herself from saying, "Would that it might be anyone else but you, Rian O'Byrne. Anyone else." This last sounded more like a wail.

Rian scowled. He hadn't imagined she held any feelings for him, let alone such loathing. This tangled glimpse into Annora's memories was disturbing. He didn't like to see her cry and be told it was because of him. There must be some way to make her stop. Again he shifted his weight from one foot to the other, feeling totally inept. He was a warrior not a nursemaid.

"Go de an donas a duine!" he cursed. To see the tears on her face, and to hear her choked little sobs was more than he could stand. *What the plague!* In two swift strides, he was before her, and with the sleeve of his cowl, he reached up to wipe her cheek. "There, ye must be stopping that now."

Still she cried and gulped, and he wiped her other cheek, then set to drying her eyes, the end of her nose.

"Hush, else ye'll be rousing the guards," he said, but she did not seem to hear him. There were new tears and more noise, and fearing this might never end, Rian forced himself to pull her to him. With his arms about her shoulders, he gave her what he hoped was a reassuring pat. He'd seen others do this with some success, and while he stroked her upper back, Rian whispered in Irish,

"Tarr liomsa," and then in English, *"Come along with me.* Think not of the past nor to the future, my lady. *Na bi gul.* Think only of what must be done this night. *Do not cry."*

Annora heard his gentle words and was confused. She wanted the comfort of his tender words, but she did not want to be hurt. She wanted the solace in his touch, but she was afraid. She wanted the security of his protection and escort, but she didn't want any more memories. Her back tingled where his hands stroked her, and she was terrified by her awareness of him as a man. She sensed his warmth, smelled the salty tang that was his potent scent, and she closed her eyes against this unbidden reminder of how lonely she'd been before and after Rian O'Byrne. How lonely she would be again. The need to protect herself from him was powerful, and she held her breath to stop the tears. She must not depend upon him any more than was necessary; she must not take anything from him nor give anything to him. They could not get to Wicklow soon enough. A tiny sob escaped, and she took another breath.

Rian knew Annora was holding her breath. She was stiff as a felled oak. Even when he gently held her to his chest, she did not relax. Plainly, Annora Picot did not want him to touch her. It made sense, of course, given what she'd told him, and thus Rian said what he supposed she wanted to hear.

"Ye've nothing to be fearing from me, Annora Picot. I made a pledge to yer uncle, and 'tis my intention to be doing as I promised and nothing more than that. I mean only to be helping ye escape Dublin and get to Wicklow harbor. Nothing more." His arms fell from her shoulders, and he set her away from him. "This time there will be no sport between us. There will be no mistakes. No regrets. There will be nothing between us this time. I promise."

Sport. Mistakes. Regrets. The words hurtled at Annora,

and she held her breath, determined not to cry another tear because of Rian O'Byrne. If he'd struck her, the pain couldn't have been sharper than that which his words inflicted. Annora turned away, her insides tightening into a hard knot. The tears had stopped.

" 'Tis sorry I am not to be able to erase the past,'' he said, hoping the sentiment would in some way improve her spirits. He searched for a way to convince her of what he said. "Do ye not recall? I always keep my promises, and I will get ye to Wicklow; I will protect yer life, and see ye on board yer ship. Do ye believe that much?''

"I do,'' came her quiet reply as she knelt down to pull a wicker hamper from beneath the bed. Atop the slashed mattress she set a girdle and purse, several folded woolens, and a leather coffer about the size of a modest sack of grain. "Avert your eyes, if you please, sir.'' She hoped her voice conveyed quiet, collected dignity. "I must change, and wish a measure of privacy while I do so.''

Rian grumbled something in reply. It was obvious there was no apology or promise, no prudent little speech that would soften her opinion of him. The past—as she remembered it—could not be revised, and the cocksure Rian O'Byrne, who never failed to get what he wanted by persuasion or guile, charm or flattery, found himself reduced by Annora Picot. It was not that he was well-liked and respected, or unaccustomed to censure. Indeed, there were many people who held him in contempt, and one woman's sentiments should not matter. He had not, however, tried to be kind to those others, nor had he tried to convince them that they need not fear him, and thus it was that her rejection chaffed at him. Indeed, he would not accept it, and with a determination similar to that which had sustained many a seduction, Rian resolved that by the time they reached Wicklow he would have influenced her opinion of him for the better. By the time she sailed out of Ireland she would be smiling at him.

"This will not take long." There was almost no inflection in Annora's tone. She had removed her kirtle and tunic, and as was her custom, hung them on the clothes perch. Over a fresh undertunic, she secured a girdle about her waist to which a plump, oblong purse was attached. Inside the purse were some two dozen parchment credits, having a total value of more than twenty-seven thousand silver marks. Since Catherine's death, Annora had often accepted parchment credits in lieu of silver from foreign merchants; they would be negotiable in Lubbeck, and eliminated the need to carry a large amount of cash. Verily, it would have been impossible to transport such a vast sum in actual coin.

Having double-knotted the purse, she donned a kirtle suitable for the journey ahead of her. It was unadorned, with a skirt that allowed freedom of movement and loose sleeves that could be rolled up in warmer weather; but for this simplicity, it was remarkable for the extraordinary quality of its wool. The fabric had been washed and bleached, carded, boiled, and woven with such expertise that it was the color of new straw, and as soft as velvet, as light as silk. She adjusted the plain bodice, then twisted her hair into a coil and secured it with thin sticks of polished bone. She unlaced her shoes, and as she did each night, set them side by side beneath the clothes perch. Next, she unfolded another garment from the hamper. It was a habit similar to Rian's. She put on the cowl and pulled the hood over her head. Finally she took a pair of slippers and tunic from the hamper; she draped the tunic over one arm and carried the slippers, in which there were coins in the toe of one and a necklace in the toe of the other.

"Are ye done with it?" he asked when she stepped into view. "Ye've got everything ye'll be needing?"

"That must come with us." She pointed to the leather coffer on the mattress. "If you would please carry it for me."

Rian picked it up, and finding it was heavier than it appeared, mumbled an oath as he hoisted it to one shoulder. No doubt, it was laden with silver. Indeed, it was more than likely that this jeopardy which Annora Picot must evade had not so much to do with herself as with her money.

As if this night was no different from any other, Annora extinguished the lights in her chamber, then she and Rian descended to the ground floor. They went slowly in single file, for Annora had warned him to stay behind her else he stumble upon a rat trap. On the last flight of stairs, Annora set out a few coins from the slipper as if they'd been dropped by someone in a great hurry. Upon reaching the front room, Rian glanced to Annora for guidance, and she motioned toward a door at the farside. In silence, they crossed and went into the rear workroom. At the garden door, Annora reached down to pick up an earthenware pitcher and dagger she'd left there before retiring for the night; and having opened the door, she dipped the end of the dagger into the pitcher, and made a single incision on the bodice of the tunic she'd been carrying. Then she tossed the dagger into the garden along with the slipper and coins, and wadded up the ruined garment with the necklace and slipper to carry with her. She sloshed some of the contents of the pitcher on the doorjamb, and the smell of chicken blood rose about them; she drizzled a little blood here, a little there.

"Nay," she said when Rian moved as if to go into the garden. It was barely a word, more of a quick breath as she put out a hand to stop him. "There is another way," she whispered, not daring to say more even though the walls were the thickness of two cubits. Leaving the garden door ajar, and carrying the pitcher with her, Annora went to the southeast corner of the workroom. With her free hand, she lifted a tapestry away from the wall to reveal a low door that opened outward.

Two large tapers in wall sconces illuminated a ceiling

of rotting wood, dirt walls that were oozing water. A great iron key was hanging from the back of the door. The air was heavy with the scent of wet earth, the acrid odor of rat droppings, and the stench of sewage. Crude steps had been hacked out of the ground, and at Annora's indication, Rian entered first. She followed, set the empty pitcher on the top step, and having assured herself that the tapestry had dropped back into its proper place, she pulled the door shut and locked it from inside.

Without further ado, they made their way into the tunnel. The first portion of their journey was commenced. Praise be to all the company of heaven, they would soon be on the other side of the town wall.

Chapter 16

 ⁓⚬⚬⁓

"**H**asten!" Abbess Thomasin pulled Annora inside the postern gate. Rian slid behind her.

For an instant, they sagged against the interior convent wall, trying to catch their breath. Horsemen were close behind them, advancing at a gallop, and there was not a moment to spare. Rian barred the door with a heavy timber. Only soldiers—or raiders—would dare travel the Dublin road without the light of day, and both were an equal threat to Rian. The pounding of hooves grew louder. It was the sound of many horses, and that their riders drove them at such speed indicated purpose.

"We must needs hie ourselves to the library," the abbess said. She began to edge her way along the wall. "'Tis the greatest security I can provide you."

Rian and Annora followed but got no farther than the kitchen compound when the bell at the main entrance began to ring. The riders had arrived at the convent and desired entrance. The thundering of hooves was replaced by the jangle of bridles, the snorting of warhorses, and above this racket rose English voices demanding that the gates be opened.

"We are trapped," Annora exclaimed. One could not reach the chapel without passing before the main entrance, and already Matthew, a rushlight held high above him, was on his way to answer the bell. He would ask who wished entrance and for what purpose, and soon soldiers would swarm through the gates.

"You're not found yet. Do not despair," said the abbess. "Go instead to the loft above the schoolroom, and may the blessed Virgin protect your souls. Lead the way, Annora, while I receive our guests."

Annora and Rian darted from the shadows, their cowls billowing like wild geese winging through the half-light before dawn, dashing across the open space to the shelter of a mud and wicker cottage. Once again, they blended into shadows; the abbess saw the low door close, and proceeded toward the main entrance.

The schoolroom was a round cottage with shuttered windows to keep out wind and rain, and a wall hearth for warmth. Here, seated before one of two trestles, the boys and girls of Our Lady of Victory learned the Gospels; scribing was taught, as was counting numbers and using tally sticks. Annora located a ladder in the dark and scrambled up to the loft. Rian ascended with three great steps, set down her coffer, then pulled up the ladder. Together they scooted away from the edge into a low space beneath the eaves, Rian pulling the coffer with him.

Outside, the convent yard erupted with confusion. The thud of running feet and the clang of swords came closer to the school cottage Men were yelling orders, doors were being kicked open, buckets and barrels sounded as if they were flying.

Annora started to tremble and pressed closer beneath the eaves. The trembling turned to shuddering, and wrapping her arms about her knees, she held tight but could not control her body. As the soldiers searched outside the cottage, the shaking worsened until she was certain the loft, if not the whole building, must be quaking along with her. She held her breath. For a few seconds, her body stilled, then she shivered anew.

Rian watched her silhouette shaking, and despite the stinging memory of how she hadn't accepted his comfort in the tower, he moved closer to Annora. Nothing mattered more than his survival, and right now it appeared Annora's quivering could expose their hiding place. Rian had no choice except to put an arm about her shoulder.

In the dark he didn't know her hood had fallen back, nor that her hair had come unpinned. Soft as silk, it brushed across his hand, his wrist, and along his arm to where the sleeve of the monk's robe was pushed to his elbow. It was a lovely, unexpected sensation, reminding him of things gentle and unsullied, and of the pain and degradation he'd suffered at the hands of the Maudelyn's men. Rian pulled Annora closer, and to his surprise, she relaxed against his chest, still trembling but not as badly as a few moments before. He had intended to comfort her, but unexpectedly found his own solace, and in doing so, forgot about safety.

It seemed to Rian that this moment was too perfect for a man condemned to die. Too perfect to waste. Too perfect to ignore. He bent his head, and before his intentions were apparent even to himself, he buried his face against the soft mass of hair at the nape of her neck.

Attar of roses. Sweet and fresh, the perfume affected Rian as had the softness of her hair. His free hand moved upward, and he didn't stop it. Indeed, to do so would have been impossible. He threaded his fingers through her hair, feeling an inner tremble of his own at this reminder of how elusive, how unattainable was perfect grace. His palm spread wide, and he pressed her head to his chest to further steady her. Again Annora didn't resist, and Rian couldn't stop wondering what was in her heart, in her soul at this moment. He didn't know why she fled Dublin, nor if her immediate terror was born from fear of being returned should he be apprehended by the soldiers, or from something greater. Was it possible that inner demons haunted Annora Picot? His head dipped forward, and he dared to set his lips against her forehead. He did this for himself, not for her; he needed to offer something of himself to her, he needed to be as near to forbearance as fate would allow, and he was pleased that she didn't protest his touch.

The cottage door burst open, and Annora's heart did something that was bound to shorten her life. Her breath caught, her stomach clenched into a knot. Part of her focused on the soldiers entering the room below, while another part of her focused upon her forehead, where Rian's lips continued to linger. He hadn't moved. His breath was warm, the featherlight touch of his lips was soothing, and in the midst of chaos, she had an overwhelming sense of everything she'd given up this night. Tears pooled in her eyes. Time was passing too fast. Everything she'd known was already in the past, and she was terrified there was no future for her.

Another man entered the cottage. "Open the shutters," he ordered.

The sharp crack of wood against wattle resounded through the cottage as the shutters were thrown wide. Silver light flooded into the space below but did not reach the loft.

"Take a good look behind that chest, under the trestles," was followed by the bang and crash of the simple furnishings being overturned. "And inside that chest yonder. It could be filled with vermin."

"Even the two-legged sort," the first man quipped. Both soldiers laughed.

"'Tis said these barbarians know magic and perform feats no God-fearing soul would try."

In the loft above, Rian held Annora. His lips hovered at her brow, and his arm was hooked over her shoulder and across her chest like a baldric. A drop of moisture fell upon his forearm. She was crying, and even Rian knew that softly whispered, kind words were needed. But speech not being possible, he did the next best thing. Firmly, purposely, he pressed his lips to her brow, then he held his breath in anticipation of her response. While the rest of her was immovable as granite, Annora's hand slid across her lap, then brushed up his thigh as it sought his. He didn't exhale until her fingers had closed about his wrist.

Outside the cottage a man called to the soldiers. They must not tarry. There was yet a dormitory and stables to search, and the soldiers left to hunt elsewhere. Still Annora and Rian didn't move. A cock crowed in the yard, and the soldier's voices faded away. Time passed, and the schoolroom lightened, but Annora and Rian remained as they were, her head resting against his chest, her fingers holding his while his other hand gently combed through the loops of her hair.

At length, Rian whispered, "A new day is upon us, and there are two things I should celebrate."

She tilted her head to look up at him in silent query, *What might they be?*

"Firstly, 'tis a great joy to find my head remains affixed to my shoulders. And secondly, I'm thinking ye don't find me as disagreeable as I'd thought. Mayhap, Annora Picot, 'tis no longer a curse that my face shall be in yer memories when ye sail away." His hand slid from her hair and down to her chin to tilt her face higher. The light was dim beneath the eaves, but not so faint that he didn't see her eyes widening as he lowered his mouth to hers.

It was a quick kiss, ethereal and careful, and over—she was troubled to admit—too soon. Her lips were tingling, her heart was racing. Yet in that moment it seemed that whatever might happen at the Wicklow quay and beyond were too faraway to consider. For the moment, the future didn't concern her. In faith, it seemed to Annora there was nothing more she could ever need. Unless it was another, longer kiss. Of a sudden, it was four years before, and it mattered not what she had promised herself these past years.

There was a noise below. Someone entered. "They mount their horses and ride out. 'Tis safe to come down." It was Abbess Thomasin.

Rian was glad to be able to move away from Annora. Kissing her wasn't the wisest thing to have done, especially if he hoped to improve her opinion of him. He hadn't planned to kiss her, and it was as much a surprise to him as it must have been to her. Indeed, he had no idea what he'd intended beyond that kiss. He slid the ladder back into place and moved aside for Annora to climb down from the loft.

" 'Twas the archbishop's men," the abbess said. "Eight knights, heavily armed."

"What business had they?"

"Merely to warn us of an escaped prisoner. He is a stark naught, murderous savage, they say." She looked at Rian as if expecting him to deny this, but the Irishman didn't speak, and she invoked the Holy Trinity, making the sign of the cross as she sought Divine intercession for this man. "You must take shelter in the library before the Prime bells."

Soon the holy sisters would file into the chapel stalls to sing their morning devotions, and without delay, the abbess led Annora and Rian to the chapel wicket. Once inside, they proceeded to the sacristy in which sacred vessels, altar cloths, and candlesticks were stored; and there, constructed into the far wall, was a closet that housed not shelves of chalices and censers, nor a supply of beeswax tapers, but opened to a passage into the convent's most ancient chamber.

In this chamber, where the aroma of ink mingled with incense, there was always a brazier burning, and into this chamber, morning light poured through nine tall windows on the eastern wall. Rounds of pale green glass sealed the room against the elements and tinted the light that spilled across the rush-covered floor. Food had been set on a trestle. There were several benches draped with tapestries and a straight-backed chair set before a smaller table with a sloping desk, goose quills, and horn inkwells.

"Here is the key." Abbess Thomasin handed it to Rian. "I must needs be about my normal duties and will be back at nightfall."

"Nightfall," exclaimed Annora. "Could we not leave ere?"

"Dawn is come, and the archbishop's men are on the move," the abbess reminded.

"But a whole day. 'Tis too long." She must not idle when she should be getting closer to Wicklow. Nor should she be alone with Rian O'Byrne. It was not a wise idea. He might protect her from soldiers, might allay her fears and trembling. Truth to tell, he might not be disagreeable, but who would protect her from him? Sooth to say, who would protect her from herself? Too well did she recall what had happened the last time she'd mused about Rian O'Byrne and kissing. It was not as if she did not know such thoughts were both wrong and foolish. It was not as if she failed to appreciate the gravity of her situation and the need for discretion, speed, and self-possession. "Please, can you not check the countryside from the tower, and we will depart only when the road in both directions is clear."

" 'Tis not wise," Rian spoke for the first time. "The good abbess is correct. We must needs wait for the cover of darkness."

Abbess Thomasin bestowed a grateful smile upon the Irishman. "I see now that God must have had a hand in sending you to Sir Thomas and our Annora. It was no accident that you were in Dublin, nor that you knew Sir Thomas already. The way of the Lord is oft mysterious, yet his miracles are many." She made the sign of the cross, then addressed Annora, "You must heed him well, my child. 'Tis God's will."

Chapter 17

"**G**od's will," Rian scoffed after the abbess departed. He faced Annora. "Ye need not be heeding me for the sake of God. Indeed, to think the hand of God guided me to yer uncle is ridiculous. Isn't it now?"

"You speak as if you do not believe."

"Indeed, never in all my days would I believe such a thing."

"Never. But why not? His grace is everywhere. Why should it not be in this? Not be with us? With you?"

"Why not, ye wonder?" Rian helped himself to the wine on the table. After a long drink, he gazed into the empty cup, then at Annora. He knew the truth would horrify her. It might even offend her, but he was willing to tell the truth, for he knew she valued honesty. "Why not? Because, in truth, I do not hold faith in God."

"'Tis impossible." Shock was evident in her voice. "Everyone believes in one god or another."

"Not everyone."

"Of course, they do. Why, it's the common thread between the Irish and English, between Christians and Hebrews and Moors. I have always believed that. And I trow with equal certitude that such a verity is God's confirmation that all races are his children, that all people possess the same humanity, that despite external differences in appearance or language or customs and behavior, we are the same within our hearts and souls. I cannot imagine the world otherwise.''

Rian stared at Annora and experienced the impression of standing at the edge of his universe, standing in isolation and trying to make sense of things he did not understand. He should be in control of this conversation, not her. He spoke as mindful as he knew how: ''Ye're a noble woman, Annora Picot, and blessed with a kind, pure heart. But I am afraid it is not always that way. Verily, there are darkened souls roaming this earth who know not of any god or goodness, nor of light or salvation. Stark naughts. Good for nothings, who know not the difference between decency and evil—worthless, wretched creatures that they are.''

''You're wrong,'' she protested. ''Even the most heinous felons, who have sinned against His every commandment, beseech the Lord for mercy and forgiveness at the hour of their executions.''

''They act out of fear,'' said Rian. Neither his voice nor expression gave any sign of emotion. ''Fear of eternal damnation.''

''Were you not afraid when you bethought this morn was to be your last?''

''Nay, I am already forsaken. Already damned. There is nothing more for me to be fearing.''

She wondered if this accounted for his brazen, almost heedless fearlessness, and why it was he seemed unaffected by many things. It was hard to consider, harder to accept, for a man who knew not fear and claimed to be damned could have no heart, not even the little bit of hers that she'd been so foolish to let go. ''Damned?'' She refused to accept what he said, what he believed. ''Nothing to fear? How can you utter such a thing?''

''Och, trust me in this, noble lady. I know 'tis true.''

'Twas why it was so easy to seduce ye, so easy to take from ye without giving. Why it's been easy to place value on nothing but the pleasure of each moment as it comes and goes. "I've known ever since I was a lad when a priest told me there was a reason for my wickedness."

"And what was that reason, pray tell?"

"He said the angels and the devils had fought over my soul, and the devils had won."

"I cannot imagine telling such a horrible thing to a child. What was your sin?" *No child's transgression could be deserving of eternal condemnation.*

"It does signify, for I believed he spoke true. Indeed, I still believe, for there has been nothing in the intervening years to convince me otherwise." His young wife's death had affirmed the priest's condemnation, and Rian was thankful Annora didn't know that sad story. To know about his betrayal of sweet, innocent Muiríol, or why the priest had been prompted to utter such a remark, would confirm there were wretched, worthless creatures who counted Rian among their legion.

"Nothing?" she asked. Surely there was some small act of kindness toward a stranger that had made him doubt.

"Not a thing."

Having no response to such a confession, Annora turned away from him, finding strange comfort in leaning against the wall, in surrendering the whole of her weight to it and pressing her cheek against the rough stone. She sighed.

"Perhaps ye should sleep," said Rian.

"I cannot." She swiveled her cheek away from the wall. "Though I am tired, something spins through me."

"Och, my lady, 'tis the boundary between life and death ye've encountered, and well I know it. 'Tis the terrible, overwhelming fascination one meets while skimming at the extreme of the ocean where the sea falls off into oblivion and there be dragons. 'Tis the powerful rush of exhilaration one gets staring at a field of knights, full-armored and glinting in the sun. 'Tis the tremor that ripples through a warrior upon hearing the long, fierce cry to join the fray; the excitement that makes ye fearless when ye charge into the midst of yer enemy. And glorious, indeed, it is now.''

"Glorious, you say? Can it be that you take pleasure from such—such . . .'' She stared at him, incredulous. "From such recklessness. Can it be you appreciate such uncertainty?''

"Aye, ye might be saying I'm fond of such, for 'tis the finest, sharpest way of knowing I'm alive.''

"You sense nothing else otherwise?''

He raised and dropped his shoulders, playing at indifference.

"What of your family?'' she asked, wondering if he was truly as alone and hard, as callous and disinterested as he wanted her to suppose. He was different from before. Granted he had not cared for politics then, and he'd espoused pleasure as his greatest ambition, but four years before, such an attitude had not seemed bleak, or desolate. Verily, it had been intriguing, for Annora had never known anyone as bold as Rian O'Byrne. What could have happened to him?

"I was not hatched in a bog hollow, if that's what ye're wondering. There is no forked tail beneath this robe. My mam and da live in the mountains still, and I've brothers and sisters, and nieces and nephews by the score.''

"And a wife? Have you a wife?'' she asked, and did not take another breath.

"Long ago.''

This response pleased Annora. She was not usually gladdened by another's misfortune, yet it pleased her to discover Rian O'Byrne had no wife, especially not one who had failed to nourish his soul. "How did she die?''

Annora's question was neither unexpected nor disrespectful, merely dreaded by Rian. Anyone else would have asked the same. It was the next logical query. How else would one have had a wife who was no more? And to wonder how a particular woman had perished was not intrusive. Death was part of the cycle of seasons. To talk of death was as ordinary as inquiring if a harvest had been plentiful or a growing season over-wet, or why a stream was of a sudden too low for salmon—and for Rian to avoid answering would make a puzzle out of a subject he did not wish to belabor.

"There was an accident," he said. "She was injured and infection set in. There was no herb or charm to help."

That was the simple answer. It did not hint that everyone blamed him. It said nothing of the fact that while more than ten years had passed, folk still whispered, *Rian O'Byrne could not have slain his wife more surely himself than if he'd been the one to wield the dagger.*

The simple answer was tidy. Uncomplicated. It did not mention the settler who had come after Rian, nor the girl who had protected her faithless husband with her own frail body. Rian had always been ashamed of that. Even before that awful day, he'd known he was unworthy. Hadn't the priest told him so? And when Muiríol died, he'd been willing to accept the blame heaped upon him just as he had when the devils had won his soul. So, too, after Muiríol had been washed and dressed and buried, had he been willing to distance himself from kith and kin in a form of self-exile. Better that than to be forever sent out of the thick forests of *Uí Briúin Cualann*, than to be sent out of Leinster, out of Ireland.

Everyone in the hills knew the truth of Muiríol's death, but not Annora Picot. She knew none of it, and Rian could not endure the animus that would score her features if the debased nature of his character were revealed to her. It had been easy to tell her he didn't hold faith in God, but to confess responsibility for his wife's death would destroy any chance of changing her attitude within the next two or three days.

"Do you still mourn her?" Annora wondered if this accounted for why he'd never married another.

"Not in the way ye may be asking. Muiríol was young, and protested the betrothal, claiming my uncommon height and overgrown size—not to mention my rogue's reputation—were offensive to her; and I, having five winters more experience, should have been sympathetic. She was fourteen on the night I took her to our marriage bed, and had only celebrated her fifteenth summer when she died. I did not love her when we wed, but came to prize her gentle, agreeable ways. She was a niceling, tender and delicate, and endeared herself to my heart. Indeed, now will ye be telling me, what man could not cherish the woman willing to receive fatal blows in his stead?"

Tears clouded Annora's eyes. Rian O'Byrne spoke of his young wife's death as if it were a curse haunting him, a penance he must needs bear in this life and beyond. "I would like to have known your Muiríol. She must have been courageous."

Courageous. Rian had never thought of Muiríol as *courageous* nor as *his,* and something within the fastness of his soul warmed to hear Annora speak in this way. He had always accepted the burden of Muiríol's sacrifice. He had always been bitterly, vividly, aware of how he'd let her down, but he had never seen her courage, and it was not merely the bravery of throwing herself before the dagger, but the fortitude she'd maintained to her last breath. Never once had she blamed him, nor had she uttered a single unkind or accusatory word. "Ye did not know her, yet ye're right. Yer eyes are not blinded by the selfishness that obscures mine, Annora Picot, and 'tis a good thing yer making me know the sad result of my neglect."

"That was not my intention," she said as unwanted tenderness for this man swept through her. "I am sorry."

"Do not apologize." He turned away before she might see his anger. He poured more wine and began to pick over the food.

Annora stood on the other side of the table and nibbled at some fruit, some cheese, a pickled egg, but as she could not sleep, she could not eat. Nor could she stand the silence. "Do you read?" she asked, having no intention of passing the day pretending she were alone.

"Irish, Latin, and English well. But only a little French. Though I can speak the Norman tongue with a notable degree of competence."

She was not surprised by this fluency. Although the English liked to act as if the Irishry were illiterate heathens, in truth it was the Irish who had brought Christianity to England. Six hundred years before Strongbow came ashore at Waterford, it was Irish monks who had founded the great missionaries at Iona and Lindisfarne. Indeed, the whole of England north of the Thames was indebted to Ireland for its conversion as was much of the world east to the Baghdad Caliphate. For those monks who were not missionaries, there had been the great schools at Clonfert, Derry, Clonard, and Clonmacnois in which to study and teach.

Centuries before Normans ever thought to conquer England, Irish monks could read and write, not only Irish, but Latin, Greek, and Hebrew. They were linguists, poets, lawyers, philosophers, astronomers, mathematicians, and historians, and trained in the arts of illumination and scribing, the scope of their labor over centuries was enormous. Indeed, were it not for the Irish, numerous ecclesiastical works, not to mention the writings of Cicero, Virgil, and Aristotle might have been lost to mankind. Of a certainty, the Irish were far from ignorant, although the English worked hard to make the world believe otherwise.

On the wall opposite there were two rows of wooden pegs with a leather satchel hanging from each. Some of the satchels were large and heavy in appearance; a few were not much bigger than a man's palm. There were plain satchels, while there were others that had been ornamented in much detail. Annora unhooked the strap of one of the larger ones and set it on the trestle. "You will perhaps appreciate this." From out of the pouch came a vellum text bound within a bejeweled cover. She handed it to Rian.

He turned it over to admire the red and green gems that studded the leather. They were impressive stones, but in no way did they compare to the magnificence of the gold-leaf trumpets interlaced with animals and flowers that flowed across the top and down the sides of the cover. "The convent enjoys abundance to own such a work as this. 'Tis owing to yer generosity, I'm suspecting, that this library has prospered."

"None of this is my doing." She swept a hand round the chamber. "This library and its contents are what remain of the original, ancient structures built on this site. It has been here for centuries and was part of a scriptorium in the age before the Anglo-Normans, even before Ostmen. These beauties are but the handful to have escaped the greedy snatching of those raiders from the north. These few have been kept safe here, a few more survive mayhap in Derry or Clonard. Why, there may be Irish treasures buried in the fields of Limerick. Who will ever know?"

Rian knew well of what she spoke, and it surprised him to hear one of the English of Dublin—even the singular Annora Picot—speak of Irish scholarship with understanding or appreciation. "When I was a lad my grand-da took me to Glendalough, where one of his kinsmen was a monk. There were three monks responsible for maintaining the annals, and our kinsman was the one who recorded the entries. My grand-da was the O'Byrne *sencha*, the keeper of the clan genealogies and history; and four times each year, he would recite the news of births and deaths, of great battles and plagues, marriages and alliances for the annalists to record at Glendalough, and I was allowed to watch while the words were being made.''

''It was my grand-da's kinsman who taught me to scribe, and there was one time when I was allowed to make an entry. Such a privilege, it was, that I've never forgotten. Indeed, the words are as clear to me as they were twenty-two years past: *Art MacMurrough, son of Art Kavanagh, deceased warrior King of Leinster, now in his twentieth year, sat in the chair of coronation at Cnoc-an-Bhogha, and being nominated by O'Nolan, he was invested with the title the MacMurrough, King of Leinster.*''

''My grand-da's cousin died in the next pestilence, and his job passed on to a younger monk as it had once been passed on to him. *The Annals of Glenn da Locha* they were called, and it was a miracle of sorts to read about the men and women who had once ruled the hills and ridden the plains, and whose blood ran through me. It made me laugh to know my great-grandfather's grandmother had been called the port and haven of three enemies because she was married to three husbands that were professed enemies of one another. And upon my death, I wanted the annals to be written as they had been for Broen of the Uí Faelain: *warrior and benefactor of poetry and music, who fought his enemies fiercely, died a good death*. Och, I was thinking those annals were a wonder, indeed, and certain to last another six hundred years, yet they're gone now. The English rode out of Dublin last summer and destroyed Glendalough. 'Twas the whole of it burnt to the ground, and those who tried to save its contents were put to the sword.''

Annora gasped. She tried to hold back tears at this example of English cruelty and wanton disregard for God and man, art and knowledge. She had always admired these illuminations; verily, she had been touched by a certain jealous awe, but never had she succumbed to the rotting, morbid invidiousness that consumed many English and drove them to destroy evidence of talent in anyone who was not of their race.

''I have never seen anything as glorious as this. 'Tis a rare privilege.'' Rian set the book on the trestle and opened the leather cover. Slowly he turned the pages, not reading so much as devouring the astonishing illustrations in shades of blue, from vibrant to sky pale, crimsons, verdant greens, and shimmering gold. It was the epic *Táin* in Irish. ''Ye went to this one straight away. Ye've read it?''

''Nay, I have not, for I have no Irish, and there was no one who would teach me. But I have gazed upon those pages more times than I can recall. As a child, I spent hours in this chamber, and having an unhealthy curiosity for those things about which grown-ups would not talk, I had a particular fondness for this and other Irish stories. I have examined every aspect of those pictures, pondered every detail, and while I did not know the meaning of the text, I created my own stories from the illustrations.''

''Tell me, what were ye seeing here?'' He indicated the page before him.

Annora stood beside Rian. She looked at the familiar picture and smiled. ''I see a queen, beautiful and proud. She is as brave as a warrior, but mayhap is too much concerned with the material world.''

''How right ye are,'' he said. Annora's insights delighted him, and the hint of a smile softened his expression. ''Her name was Méabh, Queen of Connaught, and indeed, she was a covetous creature, for when she accounted her worldly goods to those of her husband and discovered the king possessed one more bull than she, Méabh waged war upon Ulster to acquire the famed brown bull of Cuailgne. The story is the *Táin Bó Cuailgne*."

She repeated the Irish, wondering as she did if that momentary trace of a smile upon his harsh features had been a trick of her imagination. There was no hint of it now, but it had been there, she was certain of it, and she could not help wishing that she might see his eyes glow as they'd used to when he'd focused that lopsided grin upon her. "What does it mean?"

"The Cattle Raid of Cooley." He moved close to her. "And would ye like to be hearing it now?"

The airy rustle of his words fell upon Annora's neck, and she sat upon the bench as if to compose herself. "I would like that, aye." Her voice cracked in reaction to his nearness, and she wished her reply had not been hieful, wished that she had remained standing, for he slid onto the bench beside her, and she was not thinking about Queen Méabh but remembering those moments in the loft when he had kissed her all too quickly.

"I shall be pointing to the words as I read. First in Irish, and then I'll be translating into English," he said, and began.

Annora tried to listen as if it made no difference how close they might sit. Rian, for his part, appeared to be entirely unaffected by this proximity. His voice was unwavering, his hand as it moved from word to word was steady. If he had any memory of kissing her in the loft, it counted for naught. Evidently it was to be as he'd pledged in the tower. *There will be no sport between us. No mistakes. No regrets. There will be nothing,* he'd promised, and Annora—much to her dismay—found this wrought more wretchedness than gratitude. Thankfully the *Táin* was a dramatic tale, the illustrations were enthralling, and the rise and fall of the Irish text tumbling from Rian's rough, masculine voice was mesmerizing.

The hours passed, ere the morning was gone. Annora and Rian were hardly aware of the shuffling entrance of nuns for devotional prayers, first at Tierce, then at Sext, and again at None. When they'd finished the *Táin,* Rian selected a quire of Irish poems, and after that, Annora showed him *The Lives of the Saints* in Latin.

"Have ye never wished to paint such images as these yerself?" Rian asked at the end of *Lives*. He returned to a particular page. It was a depiction of Saint Kevin receiving salmon from an otter. The details were minute, each strand of fur on the wet otter clearly defined, each iridescent scale of the salmon's skin illuminated with gold and silver leaf. With the tip of one finger, Rian traced the mauve outline of a blackbird observing this scene from the intricate border of ripe haws.

Annora did not answer. Instead she rose from the bench and went to the writing table, where she checked the contents of several inkwells for freshness. She gathered up a few items, selected a piece of powdered vellum and, returning to the trestle, set vellum, quills, a sharp little knife, and inkwells before Rian.

"Aye, as a girl I tried many times to create such splendors. But my saints had grotesque heads, and it was impossible to discern my hounds from boars or my cranes from peacocks." She dipped one of the quills into a well and handed it to Rian. "Perhaps you will do better."

Rian stared at the bright red tempera at the tip of the quill. He knew how to scribe, although there was little necessity for it in his life. But he had never penned letters in a color such as this, nor had he drawn a picture of anything unless one counted the lines for forest paths or humps for mountains made in the dirt with a pointed stick. He hesitated to put quill to vellum, hesitated because it seemed a task reserved for the holy, hesitated because there was nothing brilliant in his head.

"What will you draw?" she asked.

"Have ye any suggestions to be offering?"

"It would not be right. Each of us must needs find our own subjects from within ourselves."

"Then it's serious reflection I'm needing here." He said not another word as his mind sorted through the pageants and battles, fairs and feasts, and easy, willing women he had known. Moments passed, perhaps minutes, until an idea came to him, and then he began.

Hand and quill moved about the vellum's edge. A series of red flourishes were the beginnings of a border, and having gone around once, he switched to yellow as he varied the design, then added more flourishes in green and finished with a daub of yellow here and there. Next he focused on the middle of the vellum, this time working in green and blue and a pale rose that resembled the skin of a newborn. His strokes were precise and balanced, and when he was done, there was before him a remarkable picture of a school of minnows. They were swimming through a forest of water-lily roots, and in their midst was a human child who had tiny, frilled gills and fins. The border was a pattern of yellow waterlilies and four-winged waterflies.

"How charming and fanciful," said Annora, thinking it was also odd and frightening, and remarkable. Astonishing. Intriguing. She regarded Rian—taking in his size and strength, the enormous, scarred hands, and the gone-to-gaunt face with features that spoke of a man who had fought hard—but for no reason beyond the moment; a man both blessed and cursed; a man without past or future, who believed God had forsaken him. Rian O'Byrne was as intriguing as was this painting. "In good faith, sir, have you never done this before?"

"Never." Rian did not look at her when he answered. His gaze was fixed upon the child in the water.

"Your detail and form, the sense of proportion and style are a revelation of talent. 'Tis not devils that claimed yer soul, Rian O'Byrne, for only angels could grant a mortal so rare an ability.''

Rian did not hear Annora's words. He was stunned by the scene beneath the water's surface, transfixed by the sight of what his hand had created.

''What does it mean?'' asked Annora, at once wondering and frightened by the swell of emotion she experienced in anticipation of his reply. For a moment, it was as if she'd reconnected with that bit of her heart she'd given to him four years before.

He heard this quiet question and glanced upward to see kindness in her eyes, gentle concern in the little lines across her forehead. That she did not disguise her thoughts made answering her question harder, for there was no way Rian could prevent himself from being drawn closer to her. He didn't want to tell the truth and reveal himself to her as a moth self-immolates. The meaning of the painting lay in a memory that had been reduced to dark secret. It's meaning lay in something that was never discussed, something that had changed him forever, and he wondered if she would understand the weight of such a secret. Of course she would. Didn't she hide memories that had changed her forever? And out of nowhere, Rian conceived the idea of an exchange of secrets. He would tell Annora about the fish child, if she would tell why she'd chosen him that winter.

That was something about the past that he'd never understood. Seduction and the powers of poetry aside, Rian had never been able to make sense of why the daughter of Catherine Picot had given her maidenhead to an Irish warrior. There had been no promises between them, no affection of the sort that flourished as a friendship deepened. Once he'd wondered if her intimacy with him had been some sort of rebellious, defiant act— an explanation which he found entirely displeasing. Although Rian didn't speculate about *why* as much as he'd used to, he knew it would not go away altogether, and if he ever hoped to have an answer, this was in all likelihood his best chance.

A knock came from the sacristy. Abbess Thomasin whispered, "I am returned."

"At last!" Annora exclaimed, having utterly no notion of the incredible direction in which Rian's mind had meandered.

As for Rian, he silently thanked fate for thwarting such an ill-conceived notion as exchanging secrets. He shook his head to free it of anything else that might be witless, unsound, or sentimental. Quickly he moved to unlock the cabinet.

The abbess entered and set a roasted hen on the trestle. "You must not be in such haste to depart," she said to Annora. "First, you must needs eat."

"Ye will join us?" asked Rian before he'd forgotten the dignity of a courteous guest. Steam was rising from the hen, its delicious aroma filled the chamber, and he was already tearing off a leg for himself.

"I am fasting but will sit with you." The abbess welcomed this opportunity to be with the daughter who had never been hers, yet for whom her hopes and expectations had been no less. Her heart was heavy this night, but there would be no teary good-byes. These moments would suffice as farewell. "Come, Annora, 'tis your favorite, with a touch of garlic beneath a smothering of honey. I did not dare ask Sister Winefride to prepare it, for she would have been a wellspring of many questions; but twice I slipped inside the roasting shed, and added the flavorings myself. You should sit at my side, and let me see you eat your fill."

Annora complied. She understood their parting was nigh.

While they ate, Abbess Thomasin told Rian about the library. Few souls had knowledge of the manuscripts, even fewer had actually seen them, yet each who knew guarded their existence. Their security was threatened not only by common thieves but by the English who would destroy or plunder anything that was Irish. To learn that the sisters of Our Lady of Victory risked their lives for these treasures wrought a most unexpected affect upon Rian. As the vision of the fish child had appeared to him, so too did he arrive at the certain conclusion that he must accept some measure of responsibility for this chamber and its priceless contents.

Rian made a vow of silence and pledged his service to Abbess Thomasin. "My home is in the mountains, south of Glendalough. 'Tis called Aghavannagh and can be found on the lower slope of Carrickashane, above the Ow water. If the convent faces danger, ye must send someone to Aghavannagh, and my brothers and I will be coming to yer aid."

"Such a promise is neither offered nor accepted lightly," said the abbess. "I thank you, Rian O'Byrne."

He waved a dismissive hand, not wanting thanks. Rian had never done such a thing as that before, never committed himself to support anyone or anything without getting something in return. He'd always been willing to face peril alongside the other warriors of Leinster, but he had never acted because of any conviction of his own. God wasn't the only entity in which he placed little credit. Politics and the fight for Innisfail were too burdensome, too depressing—they got in the way of pleasure—and yet he'd committed himself to something that offered no pleasure, no reward. In silence, he walked around the trestle, stashing food into a sack for their journey. It was a curious turn of behavior. He couldn't help wondering if it might have influenced Annora's opinion of him for the better. He'd rather she didn't loathe him when they parted at Wicklow.

When the sack was full, Rian knotted the end and handed it to Annora before lifting her coffer to his shoulder. Before going through the cabinet, Rian indulged in a last glimpse at the child swimming between the reeds. He had thought that part of his childhood was long forgotten, and he was glad to be leaving the picture behind, gratified to hear the cabinet door close. Mayhap the memory would be locked away for good this time.

They slipped out of the chapel. The sun had set, dusk was rapidly giving way to the black of night. Quickly they moved across the yard, and had almost reached the gate when the abbess paused. Taking hold of Annora's hand, then Rian's, she joined them together; and molding her hands over theirs, she invoked a blessing.

"O Thou Father in Heaven, to whom to love and to be are one, hear my faith-cry for your children who are more thine than ours. Give each of them what is best for each. I cannot tell what it is, nor do they themselves know. But Thou knowest, and I only ask Thou protect them, love them, and guide them to the true path as Thou didst Mary's Son and Thine."

The abbess gave a brusque hug to each, then sent them on their way. Rian and Annora hurried to the gate, where Nicholas waited in the shadows with horses from the convent stable.

"Godspeed," Nicholas whispered to Annora. There was nothing more to be said.

The bell atop the chapel tolled for evensong, and while the good sisters, mothers with babes, orphans, widows, and harlots of Our Lady of Victory filed toward the chapel, Rian and Annora began their journey into the night and out of the fringes.

Chapter 18

❧ ⌒◯◯⌒

The king's highway meandered through fertile lands. A thin veil of clouds shrouded the moon, but Annora had often traveled this route over the plain from Dalkey to the Holy Trinity holdings at Killiney. This was the road to Shankill. So, too, did Rian know the hillocks and bends, the orchards and vills in these southern fringes, for he had been this way before, and usually without the benefit of daylight. Holding their mounts to a walk, they kept on the grassy roadside to muffle their passing. At Killiney, Annora waited in the shelter of a copse while Rian walked downhill to where the land dropped away to the sea. There, in a stunted tree, he entangled the tunic Annora had sliced with the bloodied dagger, and onto the cliff below, he dropped her slipper with the necklace in its toe. The slipper matched the one Annora had left in the walled garden; the tunic was meant to be evidence of a fatal wound; and the necklace was known to have been Catherine Picot's. These were the evidence of Annora's demise, intended to stop any search or rescue efforts at the very spot of their discovery.

"'Tis done," Rian told Annora, having retraced his way uphill.

She acknowledged with a nod, and they continued toward the archbishop's manor, where young Annora had picked cherries and quince, and where her daydreams about the mountains wherein the Irish dwelled had been kindled. Shankill was, however, the farthest she'd ever been, its castle and walled vill being the last significant English settlement in the Dublin vale. *The little place* it was being called these days, for in the territory beyond nearly every homestead had been abandoned, and over the past fifty or sixty years, the colonial presence had been reduced to a military one. The old de Ridelesford castle at Bré was a royal garrison, standing as the main defense between the vale and the Irish, intent upon reclaiming their lands.

Past the manor and outlying tenant cottages at Shankill, Rian headed off the main roadway. "It would be a fool's excursion to continue down the coast," he explained. There were some twenty horsemen and forty archers at Bré, and with the return of King Richard, the number of English soldiers on the road ahead would increase. "Past Bré there is almost no natural shelter in the marshy lowlands. 'Tis safer to travel the high ground."

They pressed onward through the night, slowly, cautiously, riding foot-sure palfries; and upon reaching a river, they made their way westward to its natural ford. The water ran high and fast, rushing cold over their bare feet as they crossed. On the other side, they veered to the south as the mist of early dawn wafted across the landscape. Between alder, rowan, and hazel, slender fingers of vapor twisted up from the earth, a reminder that even if the ancient race of the Tuatha De Danann were millennia gone, their spirits had not left these hills. In single file, the horses waded through furze and bracken. Black sky gave way to gray. A rook cried from the uppermost branches of a tree. A second bird gave a similar caw, and from the birch wood came the trill of linnets, chatter of magpies, and high warble of larks.

"Do you know I've never greeted a new day without the clangor of a portcullis being raised," Annora said, and Rian slowed his horse to ride at her side as the sky went from gray to palest rose. "In Dublin 'twas not the call of birds, but the final cry of the watch, followed by the slosh of the contents from Mistress Reese's chamber pots, and the thud and bump of buckets on their way to the well that told me daybreak was nigh. 'Tis no wonder the English of Dublin want more than their walled town."

"And what of ye, Annora Picot? Did ye ever want anything beyond those walls? Beyond the wealth ye've accumulated with such dedication?"

Annora reacted as if she hadn't heard, and said nothing. The sun was coming over the horizon, and she raised a hand to shield her eyes. It would not do to let Rian O'Byrne see the tears his question had wrought. She was afraid of revealing the misery hidden within her soul. Mayhap she had been wrong to refuse so many suitors. Perhaps she had been misguided to believe that a man might love her first, and always more than wealth. Thankfully, Rian didn't press for a reply, and Annora's tears faded away as the horses ambled between fields that had not been cultivated for several seasons. Bracken colored by purple trefoils had reclaimed the countryside. A rotted and splintered footbridge spanned a stream, and here and there, stones had been pilfered from walls. Eventually she turned her attention from their surroundings and broke the silence between them. "We are out of the fringes?"

"For some time."

His answer surprised her. "This place not quite alive, but not yet claimed by ghosts, is *terra guerre*?"

" 'Tis what the English call it."

"And the Irish?"

"Cuala are the mountains into which we are headed, and that odd-shaped hill before us is *Óe Cualann.* The Ear of Cuala.'' From the hill, his arm swung round to point west, where wilderness marched headlong over blanket bog to mountains black with forest and gray-peaked with schist and granite. *"Gigais. Malainn.* Do ye see the cleft above which the mountain rises abruptly? Along the ridge of that long hill is where we will rest. 'Tis uncommon for the English to dare go into those woods and hills, and it will be safer for us up there.''

The bridle path led into a thickening wilderness, and as they went deeper, closer did the forest encroach upon the narrow trail, dimmer did the light sifting through the leafy canopy become. Annora had heard of such forests where the sun did not shine, nor did rain reach the ground; forests where men were forced to hack their way through the underwood. The dense foliage had been cut away by a recent traveler, allowing Rian and Annora passage between prickly whitethorn and holly without having to flatten themselves to their horse's neck.

Moist earth, ripe berries, pine, old wood, and moss scented the air. The wilderness was a dominion unto itself. The dwelling place of dragons. *Impenetrable to the weak. Fatal to the lost.* Annora had heard her uncles warn soldiers about this realm inhabited by wolves, cattle thieves, rebels, faeries that lured men to sin, and timber devils that ate the toes and fingers of children, especially English children. None of that had dissuaded Annora from imagining, yet nothing had prepared her for the actual glory of its beauty. This splendor, Annora bethought herself, must be much like Eden had been, for surely it was not by choice that man lived in crowded, fetid towns, or upon land depleted of such richness.

It was no wonder the Irish had vowed to drive the English out of their land. Who could blame them for wanting to hold on to such a garden? God had set the Irish upon this land, and it was not for any man to drive them out. That the Irish fought to protect these mountains from being cleared for pasture and field, and to prevent these mighty woods from being felled for English castles and warships, was honorable.

The path became steeper, up ahead light seeped through the verdant tangle of branches and leaves, and they dismounted to walk the final distance to the ridge. Emerging from the forest, the first thing of which Annora was aware was the sun. The second thing was the wind that rushed against her, buffeting her cowl and lifting the hair off her back.

"Soon we'll rest," was the only thing Rian said, and they continued to make their way along the ridge on foot. It was littered with loose stones and gravel as if it were a dried stream bed, or the leavings scooped out of the earth by the whimsical hand of a giant in the age before the De Danann, a time even before the Firbolgs, Ireland's earliest inhabitants. The path widened into a clearing. On one side the mountains rose above the ridge, and on the other side was the forest through which they had passed. Rian stopped. There were several patches of moss upon which to sit, and a frothy stream beside which Rian hobbled the horses.

In a spot shielded from both sun and wind, Annora spread her monk's robe on the ground and set out the food. Rian joined her, carrying the coffer, upon which he propped his head, having stretched out upon the ground. She passed him cheese and fruit, a boiled egg, and some roasted hen. They ate in silence.

At length, Rian wiped his mouth, crossed his elbows over his chest, and closed his eyes. Annora rinsed her hands and face in the stream, and then poked through the nearby underbrush in search of a stick to hold her hair in a coil. She found nothing to suit her purpose, and returning to the monk's robe, she knelt and tied back her hair with the cord that had belted the robe. Unaware that Rian was watching her, she began to put away the remains of their meal.

She was no longer hidden beneath the monk's robe, and Rian needed no imagination to appreciate the fullness of her breasts, the curve of slender hips, and creamy expanse of skin. It was all before him, or, at least, almost all of it, and he found himself wishing that she might face him and lean forward. Oh, to see those rounded swells straining at the bodice of her kirtle, while in that same movement, her hair might float over her shoulders, shimmering in the sunlight as spun gold. In her tower chamber, he'd thought she looked much as she had four years before, and now in the revealing light of a summer morn, he saw this was true. He thought of his sisters near to her age, and how the winters had marked them, how their sorrows and losses had tired them, draining them of the glow that was Annora's. Like his sisters, she was not a young woman, yet her beauty was as remarkable as ever.

Blessed by faeries. Rian recalled having heard that said about her, but if true, where had those faeries been when she'd needed them? What, he wondered once more, had caused her to flee Dublin? He could not imagine why anyone might wish her ill, nor why she had been forced to resort to such dire means to escape. "Yer mother is dead?" he asked.

"You are rested." Annora had heard him speak but wasn't certain what he'd said. She looked at him and noticed the darkening bruises on his upper arms. He had been beaten.

"I am." He stood.

"You are injured?" She, too, rose, and raised a hand to touch him.

He stepped out of her reach. "I've had worse floggings. 'Tis nothing that will not mend itself in proper time."

"Of—of course," she said, wondering why his reaction bothered her. She set about folding the robe. "Did you ask me something?"

"That I did. Is Mistress Catherine dead?"

"She is." Annora went to her horse and wedged the folded robe behind her saddle.

" 'Tis sorry I am to be hearing such news." Rian came up beside her.

"Do not be. She was at peace, and the end was not painful."

A guarded quality in Annora's voice made Rian think she'd given that same answer many a time before. *But are ye at peace, Annora Picot?* he wondered, staring down at her and seeing that while she might restrain her speech, she could not keep the sorrow from her eyes. "Ye're missing her dreadfully, are ye now," he said softly. It wasn't a question, but a statement of fact spoken with uncommon sympathy.

She sighed. "I miss her more than ever did I expect could be possible."

Annora's loneliness flashed before Rian with such intensity it seemed he felt rather than discerned that privy emptiness. As had happened that Epiphany Eve at Hoggin Green, Rian knew this was more than a glimpse into her soul. He was seeing something of himself. Wary, he wanted to turn away from Annora, but instead he found himself searching for answers. "Will ye be telling me something?"

She stared at Rian, not so much seeing him as absorbing a tangy, salty aroma that seemed to be everywhere. She tried not to tremble at this unbidden awareness of him as a man.

"Will ye?"

"If I can," she whispered, breathless.

"For all yer kindness and generosity, who has been there for ye, Annora Picot?" he asked, for he did not believe in faeries.

"My mother and Uncle Thomas. Abbess Thomasin and . . ."

Rian frowned. "That was not my meaning." He'd meant a man, a lover, someone to guard and protect her, to spoil and cherish her, but he could not bring himself to speak those words. He bit his lower lip and instead he asked, "Ye've never wed, have ye?"

Her head was spinning, her senses were swimming with the scent of Rian O'Byrne. He was standing much too close, and she could hardly draw enough breath to speak. "Nothing has changed."

Ridiculous gladness rushed through Rian that she'd not wed some English ass, or any other man for that matter. "The English are more clowns than men to be persisting in their passion for other people's money. It cannot have been easy to hold them at bay, for a gluttonous Englishman is a beast, indeed. Ye're to be commended for yer strength and wisdom."

"I give you thanks, Rian O'Byrne. You're right. It was not easy, and 'tis a fine thing to hear someone speak with such understanding." She repeated in Irish, *"Taim buideac duitse."*

"Ye remembered," he said. He was flattered to hear her speak so gently of the past.

"Verily, there is little I forgot. *Is fírithir ad-fíadar,"* she whispered. *This is as true as anything told.* "And while I did not forget the Irish you taught me, there was one thing I never understood, for you never told me it's meaning."

"What was that?"

"Follamnaig mo chridesea corop tú mo dilisea."

"Did I say that?" Rian asked with the right touch of bafflement. In truth, he knew he'd spoken those exact words, and he couldn't stop the desire that coiled through him as he remembered the exact moment in the flint cottage when he'd been swept away by the sweetness of her surrender, when the ardency of her response had drawn forth those words from the fastness of his soul. "It does not make sense," he lied.

"Perhaps I've disordered it," she said in disappointment.

"That must be," he lied again.

To the contrary, she'd remembered perfectly, and Rian was as incapable now as he'd been four years before of reckoning with their meaning. Never before had his soul gained control of his actions, nor had his emotions instead of his mind controlled what he said. Such a thing had never happened with any other woman before or after Annora, and to hear her repeat those words was as stunning as when he'd heard them fall from between his own lips.

In English they meant, *Rule this heart of mine that thou mayst be my love*.

That was one of the things he'd needed to pretend had never happened, that he'd struggled to forget, and for a moment it seemed nothing had changed. Indeed, they could have been back at the flint cottage. She was a beautiful woman, they were alone, and he wanted her more than he'd imagined a man could want a woman.

"Ye must not be letting it distress ye. Do not be sad, now," Rian murmured. He set his hands about her waist. "Will ye not be giving me a smile before I put ye up on yer horse?"

Annora gave a shy smile, but he didn't put her on the horse. She held her breath. Even through the fabric of her kirtle she was acutely aware of his hands at her waist, and she waited. His fingers were long and firm and thick. She remembered their heat and the things they had done to her, the places they had caressed, the pleasures they had inspired. She sensed his eyes examining her, ocean eyes washing over her, yet they didn't make her cold as the sea would. Her skin was warming beneath his gaze.

Rian watched a delightful flush fan across Annora's brow. It bloomed upon her cheeks, and those lovely blue eyes darkened to a deep, rich clarie. His blood quickened at this proof that he could still affect her. His voice dropped. It became huskier. "There is one thing that does remain clear to me."

"What is that?" She wondered if he heard the throaty catch in her voice, if he saw that her cheeks were brighter. If he would not let go of her waist, Annora knew she must look away from him. But she did not, she could not. God and Saint Mary, save her!

" 'Tis very clear to me what it was like to kiss you."

A little quiver rippled through Annora. Her lips parted in a small, soundless, "Oh," and she could but stare at Rian while time seemed to stop. The wind stilled in the trees, the stream ceased its bubbling, and there was nothing except the over-loud pounding of her heart. Annora remembered the tawny-haired giant who'd stood beneath the tower window, and she felt his hands at her waist. She remembered a bold man who had promised to teach her the ways of love, and she was aware of an intense male heat. She bethought an Irishman whose rugged features bespoke strength and boldness, and she saw his lips lowering to hers.

Rian slanted his mouth across Annora's, firm and hard and commanding. It was the kind of kiss intended to yield an immediate response; and when her lips relaxed, his tongue flickered along the slightly parted seam, opening them further to him. The kiss deepened, and he curled his fingers tighter at her waist as he pulled her against his chest, her softness arousing him, her sweet scent exciting him. He heard an inarticulate little noise somewhere in her throat, and thought of the whores at Drake's; they had been willing and eager, but had not inflamed him as was happening with Annora Picot. He thought of the lonely wife in Carlow; she had been satisfying, but there had been none of this intoxication.

Pleasure coursed through Annora. No man—except Rian O'Byrne—had ever kissed her this way. His tongue was plundering between her lips, exploring, probing, and no other man filled her with this aching need. Wantonly she kissed him back, meeting his tongue with her own, and with each stroke, each twist, each taste, the need became sharper. Annora leaned into Rian, wanting more of this kiss, more of his touch. Her arms went about him, reaching as far around his massive shoulders as she could, but it wasn't far enough, and in frustration she rubbed her hands up and down the prominent muscles of his upper arms. This evidence of bold, male strength weakened her legs. The friction of his hard torso against her breasts made her breathing shallow. Her hands gripped his arms, and her head fell back as Rian ravaged her with his mouth.

Passion was rising in Annora like flames engulfing a wicker hut. Rian sensed her need and liked it. Over the years he'd discovered each woman's response was unique. Some were slower and must needs be coaxed, while others were seized by a wild desperation that had them clawing at a man. Rian had not forgotten how Annora had responded to him in the flint cottage. She'd needed no extraordinary coaxing that first time, nor any time thereafter. At his kiss, she'd relaxed and accepted his tongue as she did now. At his caress, she'd softened and held tight to him, making unmistakable—as she did now—that she wanted more. Rian had not forgotten how quickly she'd been ready for him, and recalling the honeyed juices that had flowed from her, the length of his manhood became hot and hard. He let out a low growl as his erection pressed against her inner thigh, and his hands moved from her waist over the curve of her hips to knead the flesh of her buttocks.

Annora's breasts throbbed to have his bare skin against hers. Shamelessly her hands moved across his tunic and between the fabric, where the upper laces were not tied. Her fingertips brushed across warm skin as his mouth lifted to whisper something in the space between their lips, but she understood not what he said, and her lips tried to reclaim his. "Oh, please," she almost begged for the kiss, her fingers tensing, raking at his chest. "Please."

"O, leannán, ni gebaid frim athaig," he murmured, hardly believing the raw passion that trembled in her voice. His groin cramped, his hands cupped her buttocks, and he squeezed her as he set his desire to her woman's cradle. It had been perfect before between them, and it would be that way again this very day. *"Sweetheart,* that ye whisper with such sweet urgency is more than I can bear. To know that *ye shall not resist me for one moment* will be making yer nectar the sweeter. Och, how everything changes for me. That final image at Wicklow will indeed be a difficult one for the both of us. Ye'll not be alone with yer memories."

With a sound that might have been a gasp or a sob, Annora jerked away from him. Reality returned with cruel clarity.

"No!" She thrust her hands between them when he tried to pull her back to him. One thing had saved her. *Wicklow.* That was the only reminder she'd needed to put a stop to this folly. "No!"

"No?" He was confused.

"Do not touch me!" She needed a gulp of air to say the rest. "Nor come near me again."

The muscles in Rian's face went taut, and his eyes changed color, not to deep blue, but to the green of ice that has come from the frozen depths of a forgotten cave. A chill tore through her. She bethought herself of the caged wolf, and wondered if Rian was going to murder her. He looked that angry, and he was still that hungry.

"What made ye change yer mind?" he asked. His mouth moved to speak, but there was no change in his expression.

She could not bear to look at him, and glanced downward. "I didn't."

"What are ye saying? That ye were only toying with me, was it now?"

His voice was taunting, demanding, and it forced Annora to look at him. There was a terrible pain in her heart. "I beg your understanding."

"Prettily spoken, but ye'll not be getting a dram of it." He started toward his horse, then abruptly turned back. "Do not be toying with me, Annora Picot, else ye'll be sorry for having done it." She sniffled as if trying to hold back tears, and Rian clenched his hands into fists, his anger rising anew. "Ye've no reason to be crying, for I'll see ye to Wicklow as I promised yer uncle. But if ye trifle with me again, I'll not stop from having what I desire from ye, Annora Picot. I'll be sheathing myself between yer thighs, and riding ye hard. That I promise ye."

Annora's heart jumped into her throat. Her eyes went wide as rounds of window glass. She heard the fury, the lust, and the brazen determination in his voice. A terrible trembling seized her, and she forced herself to stand tall and stare at him as if she cared not what he might promise.

In two strides, Rian was standing before her. He grabbed her chin, forced her mouth to his, and seared her lips with his own. "Let me guess the sudden source of yer bravery. Could it be ye're telling yerself 'tis not so far a distance to Wicklow that ye need be concerned any more mischief might be happening between us?" He laughed, harsh and short. "'Tis a naive, unwise judgment, and ye'd better take caution, Annora Picot. I'm thinking ye never dreamt of this particular mischief coming to pass. Am I right? But it did. And quite quickly, I might be adding. 'Tis a natural thing, it would appear, this attraction between us. And a powerful thing, too, which is why ye'll be heeding me. As ye well know, I've never been a man to be forgetting my promises. Not a one of them."

Rian went to his horse. He sensed her gaze upon him,

but did not look around. The clarie blue would be gone from her eyes, her cheeks would be ashen, and he didn't want to see the evidence of his cruelty.

In the next twelve hours, they covered a remarkable distance.

By eventide, the path started to slope downward. From the forest came the rush of water over rocks. They were headed to the lower hills, and toward the sea.

Rian and Annora rode through a village, a patch of gray and brown and yellow in the midst of lush green. Women stood before stone or wicker huts to greet Rian with a word and offer a nod to Annora. Dogs barked. Somewhere a cow lowed, and leggy hounds and children ran in the mud alongside his horse. Such beautiful, flourishing children they were, with clear eyes and pink cheeks, sweet, lilting voices, and merry laughter. They babbled at once, lads puffing out their chests as they spoke with much excitement while Rian listened intently, but Annora didn't ask what it was they said. She merely followed in silence as she'd been doing for the past eight or more miles. Beyond the village, the path turned away from the high mountains, going once again into a dense forest before opening to a large clearing dominated by a massive motte-and-bailey fortification.

They dismounted, and Annora waited while Rian climbed to the top of an earthwork bank that circled the castle. He presented himself to the view of a warrior on the rampart.

"*A bfuaras an caora seac ran?*" the warrior called to Rian. Three other warriors appeared alongside him. They were Irish, for none but natives wielded such distinctive javelins as those lethal, long darts they aimed at Rian.

"*A bfuaras an caora seac ran?*" The words that meant nothing to Annora were repeated with the intonation of a question.

Rian cupped his hands to his mouth. "*Taim annso a*

maigistir,'' he called back. *Here I am, master.* In these hills and glens, the Irish had an almost playful method of identifying friend from foe. The warrior on the rampart had asked, *Was the stray sheep found*? and Rian had given the correct answer. Two more questions were put forth. Neither making any more sense than the one before, but Rian's responses satisfied the warriors, who lowered their darts.

A triumphant war cry pierced the air. Rian offered one in return. The whoops were each warrior's salutation for one of his own. More warriors joined in, each trying to attain a more bloodcurdling, more fiercesome pitch than the other. Over this din, Annora heard the familiar creak of a portcullis, and she sent up a silent prayer that their day's journey might be at an end. The sun was setting, and the wilderness that had earlier offered such spectacular beauty began to assume an ominous character as daylight dimmed and the night chill rose. Rian motioned Annora to join him on the earthwork ridge.

'' 'Tis Castlekevin, built by O'Tooles,'' he said. They walked along the bank to a footbridge that led over the water-filled fosse to a gatehouse. ''And while the Anglo-Normans were loud to boast when it was theirs, there has not been an English garrison at Castlekevin for many years. 'Tis again occupied by O'Tooles, and we will be safe from English patrols within its walls this night.''

Annora now understood why Rian had pushed a relentless pace this day. They crossed the wooden bridge, where a warrior greeted them with a flaming rushlight in his hand.

Darkness had fallen, and as they passed through the gatehouse and into the bailey, Annora found comfort in being surrounded by high, gray walls and a throng of Irish warriors. This was not a place the archbishop's men could enter and search at will, and casting a sideways glance at Rian, Annora knew there was only one danger against which she must guard herself.

Chapter 19

❧❧

"**W**ho interrupts my meal, this night?" Fínán O'Toole stood on the threshold of his great hall. He surveyed the outburst of activity in the bailey.

Usually by nightfall, a certain calm settled over the fortress. Mothers would gather their wee ones close, warriors set aside their darts for carving knives, and the unmarried women of the clan would pinch a little color into their cheeks. But this night, children dashed between piglets and chickens, mothers chased children, and every male above the age of seven—when an Irishman was admitted to the dignity of knighthood—was armed, alert, and curious to see the travelers who had been admitted to Castlekevin. Young women appeared in doorways. They drifted into the bailey from the kitchens or bathhouse, or their dormitory in the house of the women. They whispered behind raised hands and rose on tiptoe for a glimpse of who was being admitted to the castle. Someone said it was Rian O'Byrne who'd been spotted from the rampart, and a fine thing it would be to catch that handsome rogue's eye, if only for a night. Lips were moistened, hair smoothed, and bodices were adjusted over heaving bosoms.

Fínán O'Toole grinned. He liked excitement, and there was always place at his table for a traveler, always safe harbor within these walls when the night creatures roamed the woods and hills beyond the fosse. By the blood of kinship and the blood of might, this was his fortress, defended and held secure against the English and always a refuge to Irish—even those who interrupted his evening meal. O'Toole was a descendent of the Uí Dunlaigne, first of the overlords of the Leinster hills, who had ruled from Imail, where the chieftain of the Leinster O'Tooles lived to this day. Fínán O'Toole was an imposing man, with thick auburn hair, a square jaw, a nose that was prominent and strong, and a fondness for roast boar that was evident by the dimensions of his torso. He headed toward the gatehouse. A man and a woman were entering the bailey on foot; the man led two English-looking palfreys. "Do my eyes deceive me?" He raised his arms in readiness to greet his visitor. "Can it be ye, Rian O'Byrne?"

The two men embraced.

"Dia isteach anseo, Fínán O'Toole," Rian responded with the traditional Irish salutation given by one arriving into the midst of company already gathered. *God save all here.*

Despite the relief of being within strong walls, and amid the familiar bustle of too many people in one place, Annora was ill at ease. She had no connection to this particular setting, and heedless of keeping a safe distance from Rian O'Byrne, she moved closer to him. Perhaps her unease was because she heard not a word of English, or because she saw not a single gentleman or merchant swathed in a velvet houppeland as she was used to seeing in any ordinary crowd. There were no ladies wearing shaped linen caps, no lordlings with pointed shoes or popinjay leggings, no gentlemen whose hair had been bobbed, and most notable, there were no lepers, no beggars, no hungry faces. She looked at the man who greeted Rian, and wondered what he was saying.

"We'd heard a woeful tale the English had put a stop to

yer sorry ways, Rian O'Byrne. 'Twas many a fair heart that's been weeping at the notion of yer manly head giving roost to rooks and ravens.''

"Ye heard true." Rian chuckled. "The English were, indeed, hoping to have done the deed by now, but I was too busy to be lingering about Dublin for their pleasure.''

"Busy, *an ndeir tú liom é?*" O'Toole cast an admiring eye upon the woman at Rian's side. *Do ye tell me?* "Aye, 'tis easy to see what's been keeping ye busy. She's a beauty, she is, with that plenitude of golden hair. Almost fair enough to be an O'Toole. Indeed, if she were one of my sisters, I'd not be letting her idle with the likes of ye.''

"Rian!" a woman called from the swarming bailey. "Rian! Is it ye?"

He turned toward the voice. Annora did, too, and saw a beautiful woman holding her kirtle above bare ankles as she rushed toward Rian.

"Órla told me ye were here, but I did not believe it could be true no matter what the child claimed to have seen." She was tall and slender with glossy hair the color of ripe bilberries, and by the expression upon her face, she adored Rian.

"Isobel!" Rian pulled her into an embrace, kissed her on the lips, then swung her in a lively circle. "And who else would it be, I'm asking? Has yer Órla ever been wrong?"

Annora watched Rian and the beautiful woman, but she heard not their laughter. Instead it was the question he'd asked her this afternoon that echoed through her mind.

Who has been there for ye?

Loneliness washed over her. *No one.*

Who has been there for ye?

How painful it was to admit that she'd been lonely for a long time, even while her mother lived. How discouraging to accept that when all was said and done she would still be alone. She tried to convince herself that great things lay ahead for her once she'd boarded the *Hera*, but she could not deny what was true. Of a sudden, the accomplishments, and praise, the wealth, and independence withered in value. It was no wonder Rian asked if she'd ever wanted anything more than the riches she accumulated with such dedication. No wonder there had never been a man to want her more than her fortune. That was all there was.

Which had come first? Did her isolation from scenes such as this result from devotion to work? Or had she dedicated herself to the wool trade and the convent in order to compensate for the emptiness within her? She could not remember where it had started, and loneliness turned to bleakness as she wished she might flee from this place, that she might find a quiet corner into which to take herself in her desolation.

"*Buíochas le Dia,*" exclaimed the beautiful woman when Rian stopped spinning her. "Yer mam will be crying tears of joy. *Thank God.* Ye live to return to the hills."

"Och, Isobel, ye should not be making such a fuss," Rian scolded in affection.

"Else yer head will be swelling to an even larger, more offensive size, do ye say? I do not think that is possible, Rian O'Byrne." She gave a merry laugh as she hooked her right arm through Rian's, the left through one of Fínán's, and only when she turned to lead them to the great hall did she notice the slender, flaxen-haired woman hovering like a shadow behind Rian. "Och, I am sorry not to have been greeting ye properly. *Gabh mo leith-scéal. I beg yer pardon.* Ye must be thinking I left my manners in the cow byre, but 'twas not my intention to be rude. Will ye forgive me and accept my welcome to Castlekevin?"

The woman spoke in Irish. Annora looked to Rian for a translation.

"Ye must reassure my cousin ye're not thinking she's ill-mannered as a cow," Rian told Annora as he put a hand beneath her elbow to coax her within their circle.

She stepped from behind Rian and smiled in response to the woman's amiable and somewhat contrite expression.

"This lady before ye is yer hostess, Isobel O'Toole, wife to Fínán, who holds his ancestral fortress against the enemies of Innisfail," said Rian. He motioned with a large hand from the woman to the man. Isobel appeared curious. Fínán grinned. "Isobel is kin, she and my mother both having been O'Connors before they wed. Her mother is the wife of the O'Connor chieftain, who is my mother's brother. Indeed, Isobel is my favorite cousin. And this lady beside me is Mistress Annora Picot."

"A thousand welcomes to our home, Annora Picot." Fínán spoke English with the same lilting accent as did Rian, rolling over the sound of the *r* in Annora. He winked at her. "'Tis a pleasure to be having such a fair-lovely guest within our walls this night. I would be giving ye a great embrace, if I did not think it would be winning me the ire of both my wife and Rian."

"Listen not to him. He is a wretched jester." Isobel smiled. "Welcome to Castlekevin, Annora Picot." Unlike the men's English, her accent was slight, and the words flowed with natural rhythm from her tongue. "How careless I am to leave ye standing about the bailey when there is a fire and food in the hall." This time, Isobel didn't slip her arm through Rian's or her husband's, but through Annora's in a way that conveyed more genuine cordiality than words could have done. "Ye must be coming along with me."

"I thank you," Annora murmured, exhausted, grateful. Her uneasiness was almost gone. She took a tentative step alongside Isobel, then hesitated to glance over her

shoulder at Rian. He encouraged her with a nod. The men
followed a few paces behind, and Annora was reminded
of the couples she had seen strolling across the commons
in fine weather; always the men walked a distance from
the women, who whispered between themselves. Always
it had seemed a ritual she would never know.

Isobel set her head close to Annora. ''And have ye
known my cousin long?'' she asked as only one woman
can ask of another.

''I heard that question, Isobel, and there's to be none
of that now,'' Rian said. ''I'll not be letting ye take
Mistress Annora away from my side unless ye promise
not to be bothering her with such meddling.''

His tone made Annora blush. It was as proprietary as it
was reproachful. Fínán broke into laughter.

''Och, Rian, ye know better than to be telling my wife
how to conduct herself. Ye'll only be rousing her curiosity to extreme heights with such admonitions.''

Rian did not respond to Fínán's remark, but took two
steps to set himself before Isobel. He frowned. ''There's
naught here of which to be curious.''

Isobel cocked her head to one side, her glance darting
between Annora and Rian. She was not blind to the way
the woman had hovered close to him, nor to the blush that
flared upon her cheeks and brow, and as for Rian, Isobel
knew him mayhap better than anyone else. No matter
what he said, there was, indeed, something most curious
to consider here. As often as Rian O'Byrne had passed a
pleasurable hour or two in the company of a woman,
Isobel knew he hadn't been in any single woman's
company for more than a few hours in many years, and he
certainly hadn't taken any woman under his protection as
it appeared he had this one. Nothing curious, indeed.

''And don't ye be giving me such a grin as if ye'd
uncovered a rare secret,'' Rian told his cousin. He slipped
into Irish. One didn't need to understand his words to

recognize the stern, unbending tone in his voice. " 'Tis not what ye may be thinking between myself and Mistress Picot. Ye're not to be plaguing her, and make certain yer Órla does not either." He switched back to English. His tenor remained firm. "We're traveling companions—no more—and having come a long way this day; we are tired and hungry. While I know Annora will appreciate yer excellent hospitality, ye're not to be quizzing her on matters that don't concern ye."

"We will be fine, I am certain," said Annora, motivated by the urge to reassure Rian, and her own need to get away from him. That his kinswoman questioned their relationship seemed natural, but that Rian would have such an adamant reaction put her ill at ease.

On the rampart, one of the watch let out a war cry. Again the fortress erupted with heathen howls fiercesome enough to keep wolves at bay.

"Let the women proceed without us. Do not be worrying about Mistress Picot. She does not appear witless, and I am sure she does not need yer constant protection, especially not from my wife or daughter," Fínán said to Rian. From the gatehouse came the clank and groan of a rising portcullis. "Let them go ahead. 'Tis too soon for me to return to the hall. I wish to know what further excitement arrives at my fortress." He gave his wife a pat on the backside, then went toward the gatehouse with Rian as Annora and Isobel went to the hall.

The hall at Castlekevin would have pleased even the most discriminating Dublin housewife or lady of the manor, even those to England born. It was clean, well-aired, and appointed with handsome furnishings. Ornate iron sconces held blazing torches, the floor was covered with fresh rushes that smelled of sunshine and woodroof beneath Annora's feet. The rafters arching above were painted carmine, and angels robed in blue were carved into the crossbeams; one held a harp, another a lute, another a horn, and the last a cluster of bells, each instrument being gilt with gold from the rivers that cascaded through nearby hills. Hounds slept throughout the hall, there was a fire in a center hearth, and several long trestles draped with woolens were set with food.

Isobel led Annora near the fire and pulled out not a bench but a chair with arms and a high back. ''Sit up to the table now while I attend to matters in my kitchen. If more visitors have arrived, there must be additional wine and food, and Fínán will be asking for *uisce beatha* tempered with fennel seeds and honey. 'Tis his favorite libation when the hall overflows with warriors. There will be much drinking this night while they talk of driving the English into the sea, and Fínán will ask for the harper, and there will be dancing.''

Annora sank into the offered seat. She sighed. It was good to be off her feet. She was content with the crackling fire, the sound of liquid trickling from flagons to drinking vessels, the gentle whispering of women, and the singsong of a nursery rhyme recited by voices so young they seemed neither male nor female. At length, Annora realized a lass of about twelve or thirteen summers was standing a few paces away and staring at her with an intensity of focus. It made Annora shiver.

It was almost as if the girl was studying her, perhaps discovering something, and to see her made Annora think of an old woman who had once stood at the gates of Dublin Castle demanding an audience with the king's lieutenant. She had claimed to know King Richard's fate, and was determined that his majesty be warned. Annora had been dining with her uncle when the guards brought her in, and she hadn't forgotten what the woman had said, *''The head shall be cut off; the head shall be lift up aloft; the feet shall lift up above the head.''* The poor old thing had insisted her words were true, had pleaded they be conveyed to the king himself, and for her troubles she'd been escorted to a religious house, where she might spend the remainder of her days in quiet solitude, and none other might hear her prophesy. Annora wrapped her arms about herself and wondered if this girl had seen her aboard a ship sailing away from Ireland.

"I am Órla, eldest daughter of Fínán and Isobel." The girl spoke English, and her ephemeral voice was a marked contrast to the concentration that scored her features. Her hair was the same iridescent black as her mother's, her eyes were serious and intelligent, and there was about her the awkwardness that came to many girls as they made the transition from child to woman. "Who are ye, woman, who travels with Rian O'Byrne?"

"I am Annora Picot," she replied, drawn to the girl. She knew what it was like to be different, and she admired the bold way Órla addressed a stranger.

A serving girl set a wooden cup and trencher before Annora, then indicated she should help herself from the platters arrayed on the table. There was cheese, jellied eel, fruit, swine, goose, and some kind of soup. Órla slid onto the bench beside Annora. A woman with a babe balanced on one hip took the seat beside her.

"That is my baby sister and her nurse, but they have no English," Órla stated, dismissive but not unkind. "Over there are more sisters with our twin brothers not yet old enough to join the warriors. There are nine of us from our father's loins. And that small, pale woman who hovers by the shuttered window is my father's great-aunt, who likes to boast she is the oldest living O'Toole in Leinster, although there is an old warrior at Imail who claims the same right. 'Tis a good thing, my mother says, the aunt can no longer be going over the hills to Imail, for the arguing between the two of them was loud enough to be raising the old kings from their graves beneath Dún Ailinne."

Annora filled her trencher with soup and considered asking the girl if she knew which of the two was the older, but instead she asked, "And how did you learn English?"

"From my grandmother, the chieftain's wife at Baravore. 'Tis where Rian learned as well when he fostered with the O'Connors."

"Your grandmother?" Annora pulled off a piece of soup-drenched bread and took a bite, tasting leeks and a touch of thyme.

"She was the Lady Aislinn Clare, daughter of an English knight and raised in the castle called Killoughter."

"I did not think such matches were allowed."

"A knight's daughter wed to a warrior in these hills? Why, I know of many such happy marriages. 'Tis said there are more unions between Anglo and Irish than the English in Dublin and Kilkenny will ever admit."

"But what of the statute? Is it not feared?"

Órla seemed perplexed. "Feared? It is an English law, not ours. Designed by the English to control their own people who do not behave as they believe they should; the Irish do not seek to dictate anyone's behavior. Why should they be afraid?" Her gaze narrowed. She tilted her head as Isobel had done and added in a voice that was almost a whisper, "Besides ye're not afraid now to be with Rian O'Byrne. Nor were ye afraid before, were ye?"

"You misunderstand," Annora demurred. While it was true that she had not been afraid, at least not for herself, that meant nothing now. "'Tis not what you imagine between myself and Rian O'Byrne. We travel together. Nothing more. I needed an escort to Wicklow, and he agreed to help me."

"I do not misunderstand, nor do I imagine," the girl said with calm assurance. "*I see.* I have always seen, and sometimes I hear. But whether the sights and sounds are of past or present or future, that I know not."

Annora studied the guileless young face before her. Some people believed such power as this girl possessed was a sign of evil, but Annora discerned naught but an aura of innocence and goodness. There was nothing dark nor frightening about Órla O'Toole. "Will you tell me, if you please, what it is you see?"

"Nothing clear. Flashes. Warriors, a man in prayer, dancing, and a great bonfire. Blue clarie in snow. A rising tide swirling about a woman's ankles. You are there, Annora Picot, with Rian O'Byrne in a place so thick with mist, so hot and loud with howling it could be hell. And over the horrible shrieks I can hear Muiríol's voice. Mind ye now, I'm not old enough to have known Muiríol, but it is her, for she has spoken to me before, and this time, she whispers of how someone among us will be returning from the living dead."

Chapter 20

❦❦

"**T**hat must be Rian of whom Muiríol speaks, for he escaped the executioner in Dublin." Annora was fascinated.

"Nay, 'tis another."

"Who then?"

"I do not know." Órla lapsed into silence. She picked at a bit of salmon, and after awhile glanced again at Annora. "Rian would never ask to know what I have seen, for he does not believe and gets angry when I speak of the things that crowd my thoughts."

"And what have you seen of Rian? Can you tell me?"

"I have seen him as a babe with tiny gills like a fish and swimming in a forest of water-lily roots."

A gust of wind roared through Annora's head. There was no draft in the hall, yet the sound and sensation were real. Harsh, cold air pierced her, and she grabbed hold of the trestle to prevent herself from bending to its force. Her gaze locked with Órla's.

"Ye've seen this?" The girl was amazed at what she read in Annora's expression. "The fish-babe?"

"I . . ." Annora's eyes closed. She was back in the library at Our Lady of Victory when Rian had stared in horrified fascination at what his hand had wrought. She thought of devils fighting for a child's soul, of a man who believed God had forsaken him, and her heart twisted. "I, too, have seen such a child. Drawn by his own hand. Can you explain its meaning?"

"Only that it is a fragment of his past, yet somehow a part of his future."

Annora wanted to know more, but Isobel interrupted. She came toward them with a great flagon in each hand, and set one at each end of the table.

"I trust my daughter is not disturbing ye, Annora Picot."

"Órla does not disturb me. I enjoy her conversation."

"Och, I know not what she may be telling ye, but do not take it to heart." The hall was filling with the household, the wolfhounds were being displaced from their sleeping places, and Fínán, who was the last to enter with Rian and several other warriors, called out for music. A *bodhrán* commenced a rousing cadence while harp and pipes played the melody. Isobel leaned close to Annora to be heard above the growing racket. "Would ye like Órla to show ye to the guest tower? It will be quiet there."

"I am fine," she replied, looking not at Isobel but at Rian on the other side of the hall. He stood with Fínán among a group of men who had the appearance of travelers. They were fully armed with darts and long swords, and were swathed in saffron-colored, shaggy woolen *brats*, the distinctive mantles that were unique among the Irish.

Isobel saw where she glanced. "The talk among the men is serious and may go long into this night. Rian O'Byrne tells of having seen the king's soldiers in Dublin, and the other warriors have news from the western foothills."

"They are from Baravore," said Órla of the men in the saffron *brats*. "O'Connor kinsmen all of them, whether by birth or marriage or ancient bloodline."

Someone gave a short cough as if to attract their

notice, and Annora turned to discover one of the *brat* enveloped warriors standing behind her. He was tall and lanky with hair as black as midnight, and a handsome face darkened by the sun. He was a man who smiled easily, for when he grinned at the three women, the corners of his eyes crinkled into a familiar pattern.

"Calum Kirkpatrick, how good it is to be seeing ye." Isobel gave him an embrace, then maneuvered him onto the bench. "If ye wish to be eating instead of talking of war, ye should be sitting beside Mistress Picot. Try some of the eel and boar. It is fresh yesterday." She pushed a platter before him, and leaning forward to fill his cup, said to Annora, "This is one of the cousins from Baravore. He is named Calum Kirkpatrick, born in Scotland at a place called Loch Awe, and he has crossed the sea to be joining our battle against the English."

The Highlander nodded at the truth in her words, but spoke not. His mouth was full of roasted pig, and he continued to nod, giving yes or no replies as Isobel asked about Baravore and her parents. A young warrior took Órla away to join the dancing.

"I must be seeing to our other guests," said Isobel. She looked between Annora and Calum. "Is there anything else either of ye would be needing?"

"A dancing partner," said Calum. He grinned at Annora. His expression was playful. "I'm needing a dancing partner with fair hair and blue eyes, I'm thinking. A golden flower of the O'Toole's."

Annora's cheeks grew warm. "But I am not an O'Toole."

"Och, but ye're a golden flower nonetheless, aren't ye now?"

Isobel and Annora laughed. On the other side of the hall, Rian glanced over his shoulder in time to see delicate pink staining Annora's face. He heard a woman's laughter, observed the way the O'Connor kinsman from the Highlands was regarding Annora with too much appreciation, too much interest. Rian lifted the drinking horn to his mouth and took a long draught of Fínán's potent *uisce beatha*. The intoxicating beverage was distilled from grain, and burned a fiery path down his throat. Rian looked away. He did not like the look of that dark, handsome Scotsman when he grinned at Annora.

"Can ye be telling me, Isobel, will this golden flower dance with a humble warrior such as myself?" Calum's regard did not move from Annora.

"Ye must be asking her yerself."

"Will ye, golden flower? Will ye dance with me?"

Annora did not answer right away, instead she savored an unhurried look at the animated faces throughout the hall, at the trestle heaped with bounty, and the proud chieftain with his warriors. She smiled at the sight of flirting lovers, an ancient aunt asleep in her chair by a window, shy girls and bold boys. There were wolfhounds searching the rushes for table scraps, a wee lad trying to wield his father's sword, a mother prompting her children to eat, couples holding hands as they joined the dancers, and she realized this was her last night among company in Ireland. Tomorrow eve, she and Rian would camp in solitude near Wicklow town, and ere the next sunset, she would be gone from this land. It was not a new experience for Annora to be surrounded yet to feel detached, and this night she didn't want that. She didn't want to be alone. Her glance sought Rian. He was drinking from an elaborate horn with silver fittings that the warriors were passing from one to the other, and he appeared to have forgotten all else save his immediate companions.

"If ye're tired, ye need not dance," said Calum Kirkpatrick. "Are ye tired, golden flower?"

"Nay, I am not too tired to dance with you," she replied, having no intention of sitting quietly and watching the others enjoy themselves. She extended a hand to the warrior, he let out a short, carefree whoop of satisfaction, and Annora couldn't keep from laughing.

Rian turned toward the warrior's jubilant outburst. No one else seemed to have been distracted. Everyone appeared to be focused upon their own affairs, everyone except Rian. Calum Kirkpatrick was sweeping Annora away from the trestle, his arm was wrapped about her waist, and Rian heard not a word of what Áed O'Connor was saying about the English king as Calum and Annora joined the line of couples.

"The English are already marching north from Waterford. MacMurrough has sent the cattle, corn, women, and helpless into the interior fastnesses, and he waits with his warriors at Idrone for the fighting men of Leinster to be joining him," Áed O'Connor told Fínán. Art MacMurrough and all the clans of Leinster had sworn never to rest, by day or by night, as long as the English strangers remained in Ireland. "'Tis time, MacMurrough proclaims, for all Leinstermen to fulfill their pledge, says he. This time, the Irish will be driving the English into the sea."

"*Tiocfaidh ar lá!*" Battle cries burst forth from the warriors. *Our day will come!*

"*Bás no Beatha!*" Before God they vowed victory in blood, swift death to the invaders of Innisfail, and they called upon their saints to bear witness to this oath. "*Death or Life!*"

The musicians quickened their tempo. The *bodhrán* measured an untamed heartbeat, and the line of dancers coiled about the hall in imitation of circling a bonfire. Faster and faster.

"*Gach an cathair!*" The hall seemed to shake. "*To each of us a fortress!*"

The Highlander was whispering to Annora. She was smiling, her flaxen hair streamed behind her, it wisped about her face like a ring of sunlight. Her cheeks were glowing, her chest was heaving, and her kirtle spun out and upward to reveal pretty ankles, a glimpse of shapely leg.

"Rian, are ye listening, man?" asked Áed when the war cries had subsided.

"Aye, what is it?" Rian scowled, trying to recall when he had made Annora smile as easily as another man, indeed, as easily as a man she'd known for only a few moments was doing before his very eyes.

" 'Tis said they have brought gunnes."

"Can it be true?" Rian had heard tales of a fire-breathing war engine from which missiles were thrown by the wizardry of an alchemist's brew called gunne-powder.

"There are more rumors in these hills than gray crows," cautioned Fínán. "We have yet to hear from an Irishman who has seen for himself this funnel that is said to belch flames whilst exhaling plumes of smoke and roaring like thunder."

" 'Tis the work of witches, it is," an O'Toole declared, and all agreed, while the more devoted among them whispered an Ave Maria. If dark forces had been unleashed upon the shores of Ireland, then only Faith in Jesus would protect them, and they crossed themselves in the sign of the Holy Trinity as a token of their faith and an invocation of God's blessing.

Again Rian was distracted. Even the work of witches could not keep his gaze from straying to Annora. The line of dancers broke apart, each couple standing alone as partners faced one another to link their arms and spin in circles. Calum Kirkpatrick and Annora twirled in a tight circle, for he held her closer than was necessary to whisper into her ear, and seeing this, Rian took another deep gulp of *uisce beatha*.

"Indeed, witches most foul," agreed an O'Connor of Baravore. "Only the minions of evil could harness such destructive force."

"Which is reason enough to conclude the English possess such weapons," remarked Rian. His belligerent tone matched his foul humor. He was feeling decidedly surly as he stared at the dancers and raised the drinking horn again. The young man dancing with Órla gave her a quick kiss, the other dancers cheered and began to kiss one another. Rian's gaze didn't waver from Annora. Would she allow Calum Kirkpatrick a kiss if he sought one?

"If ye don't want her dancing with him then ye ought to be dancing with her yerself," Fínán said in a voice meant for Rian alone.

" 'Tis none of yer affair," Rian mumbled. What did Fínán know to be offering advice? Besides, Rian didn't want mere dancing. He wanted her smile, and her laughter, and much more. He wanted her in his arms, her flesh against his, their warmth fusing as her cries of passion mingled with his. Unbidden, the past came to him, *"Follamnaig mo chridesea corop tú mo dilisea."* He drained the last of the *uisce beatha*.

Rule this heart of mine that thou mayst be my love. Rian knew that whatever contrary spirit had taken control of his voice all those years before still gripped his soul. Four years of denial had not changed a thing. He was no different from any other man; his loneliness needed easing, and there was but one woman who might reach him, help him. Beyond that, however, he was nothing like other men. Rian was forsaken, damned, haunted, and denied. There would be no easing for him, no end to the emptiness. It would always be that way. Or would it?

He didn't bother to excuse himself when he walked away from Fínán. He strode past the center hearth, past Isobel, who gaped at his expression, past the farthest trestle, and past the musicians. He pushed his way between the dancers and pulled Annora away from the Highlander. Rian swayed. He'd moved too quickly, had imbibed too much *uisce beatha*, and his fingers tightened about Annora's upper arm in part to steady himself, in part to prevent her from escaping.

Forsaken, damned, haunted, and denied.

It would always be that way for Rian O'Byrne, but not tonight.

Tonight he would not be alone. Tonight he would do what he must to banish the emptiness for a few hours.

Chapter 21

❦❦**I** have no wish to be fighting ye, Rian O'Byrne,"
Calum Kirkpatrick said with exceptional restraint. He didn't like the way O'Byrne was gripping
Annora Picot's arm. It had to be painful, and Calum,
who was wont to brawl, knew that one whimper out of the
woman and he'd gladly deliver the Irishman an introduction to his closed fist.

"If ye've no wish to be fighting, move aside," Rian
said. He neither smiled nor frowned.

"Let go of her first, O'Byrne."

"We've a problem then, for I've no wish to be doing
that. I've no wish to be letting her go, you see."

Calum Kirkpatrick looked to Annora for a cue. He
didn't know the woman other than what one of the
O'Tooles had whispered in his ear, which included
nothing about any relationship with O'Byrne, and he had
no intention of walking away if she needed assistance.
Indeed, he hardly knew O'Byrne except by reputation,
and according to that he claimed no woman as his own. If
this lovely golden flower needed him, Calum would be
more than happy to oblige.

"My thanks to you for the dance, Calum Kirkpatrick," Annora said with unwavering dignity. She noted
the way he regarded her in concern and appreciation, and

241

it fortified her to know she had an ally, if she needed one. She chose her words with care. "I will be in secure custody with Rian O'Byrne." *I think, I hope, I pray.*

"Ye heard her speak the words herself," said Rian. "She is in secure custody."

Calum raised his hands in capitulation, and stepped backward to stand at the edge of the growing crowd of onlookers.

Rian grunted in satisfaction, then directed his glower toward Annora. Och, by the crozier of Saint Ciarán, she was, indeed, a woman worth fighting over, if needs be, he thought as he swayed slightly. He tightened his hold about her upper arm. Aye, she was an enchanting vision with masses of hair tumbling about slender shoulders, cascading down her proud little back. It twisted round her like a gossamer cloak, holding the glint of flames from the torchlight. She looked nothing like the dutiful daughter of Dublin's wealthiest merchant he had once known. To the contrary, she was the epitome of every man's most carnal desire, a wild, disheveled creature who gave the impression she cared not how the English lawmakers and bishops might judge her. The crimson glow upon her cheeks spoke of exhilaration as did the light in her blue eyes. She was undaunted, challenging, spirited, and Rian O'Byrne wanted this Annora Picot more than he'd wanted the other one, more than he'd wanted any woman. He closed the distance between them. "Do ye know what's in my mind?" he asked on a whisper.

A shiver rippled through Annora. His low voice was as suggestive as the way he loomed over her, staring at her mouth. His blue eyes were flecked with the green of the sea before a violent storm, and her thoughts drifted to kissing. It was wrong, oh, so wrong, but she couldn't stop herself from thinking about the kiss in the loft, and how quick it had been. *Oh, Rian O'Byrne, that you might be wishing to kiss me again.* Her tongue darted out to moisten her lips. She remembered the first time he'd kissed her that winter afternoon on the road to the convent, and she remembered his warning this very day in the clearing on the long hill. "Nay, I know not what ye think."

"I'm thinking ye'd be well worth fighting for, Annora Picot. Well worth a fight, if the prize was spending another night with ye, *leannán*."

She tore her gaze away from his, and fastened it on the ground, where she had a view of his full-large feet and her toes peeping from beneath her kirtle hem. They were almost touching, and her mind drifted from kisses and toes to bare legs and muscled thighs. She stifled an inward groan and scrunched her eyes closed in an effort to purge herself of such wayward meanderings. It was urgent that she get back to her seat and away from him. Annora heard Rian chuckle, low and quiet. A warm flush spread over the whole of her body. *He knew! By the bones of Saint Mary Magdalene, and every maiden seduced by fleshly temptations, he knew!*

"Ye can hide yer eyes from me," Rian murmured, knowing and beguiling. "But don't be thinking ye've hidden yer thoughts as easily. Don't be forgetting how well I know ye, Annora Picot. I've tasted what ye conceal so carefully beneath yer dignity and grace." He tucked a finger beneath her chin, forcing her to look upward.

Annora trembled beneath his smoldering gaze. He was standing too close, she was too warm, and her senses reeled with the scent of him. Rian smelled of sunbaked skin and the saltiness of sweat when it evaporates, of the whiskey Isobel called *uisce beatha* and of the tangy male aroma Annora associated with no one but this Irishman. Her mouth went dry.

"Ye should know better than to be hiding from me." Rian's hand replaced the single finger at her chin, and firmly, gently he held her to receive his kiss.

It was more than Annora could bear. His firm lips seared hers. Such a heady kiss, slow and tender, that she could not repress a sigh, could not keep herself unyielding and indifferent, and when his arms pulled her against his hard chest, she had no defenses against this sensual assault. Her arms coiled about his neck, her fingers threading through burnished curls as the kiss deepened. She met his tongue with hers.

The collective gasp that rose from the crowd was followed by a rousing cheer. *A noble conquest,* someone called. There came another cheer. To the Irish, romance was always noble, and as for this particular scene, it was especially gratifying to observe, since it appeared both parties were to be winners this night.

Annora leaned against Rian, she tasted whiskey and heard bawdy acclamations. Ribald comments, it would appear, that were directed at her. Aghast, Annora turned her face to break their kiss, giving him her cheek.

"You may unhand me now, sir." Annora pushed at him when he didn't free her. "You have succeeded in taking me away from the dance and making me the center of attention. Now let go of my arm, if you please," she said, but Rian didn't acknowledge her request in word or deed.

Let go of her? Is that how she imagined this would end? Rian continued to grip her upper arm as he made his way toward the other end of the hall, giving her no choice but to follow. Dancers and onlookers scattered to make a path.

Isobel moved toward them. Annora Picot was a guest in her home, and she couldn't allow a guest to be treated in such a manner by any man—even if that man was her adored cousin. Nor could she remain silent while another woman was treated harshly. Isobel had heard that English women did not marry for love, being treated for the most part like chattel at their family's disposal. Indeed, her own mother had been expected to wed to a stranger before she fled her father's English castle for the hills. Even an occasional Irishman had been known to ill-use a daughter—hadn't Diarmait MacMurrough pawned his Éva to Strongbow? But, as a rule, the Irish were a more sensitive and generous race when it came to matters of the heart, and Isobel did not suppose the hearts of English women could be indifferent to tenderness or affection. Surely Annora Picot yearned for gentleness from the man who'd made her blush. Thus Isobel decided that her cousin, who was wont to boast of how he didn't care about anyone or anything, needed guidance, and she opened her mouth to speak.

"Nay," Rian growled.

"But—" Isobel was not easily deterred.

"Say not a word," he warned.

" 'Tis merely—"

"Nay, 'tis none of yer affair."

Rian's expression was more defiant, more shameless than she'd ever seen. Isobel backed off. Indeed, there was an almost jealous aspect to Rian's behavior, and she didn't know whether to be pleased or alarmed.

"Over there. That is where I was sitting. Near the fire. You may leave me at the trestle, if you please," Annora whispered to Rian beneath her breath, wishing that she'd never agreed to dance with the Highlander in the first place. "I do not like being made a spectacle of before so many eyes."

"Do ye not? Well, 'tis something ye should have considered before ye began twirling about the hall with Calum Kirkpatrick." Rian did not mention the way she had beguiled him into kissing her, nor the way she had responded to him, neither of which became the conduct of a woman who wished to remain unseen. When they reached the trestle where she'd been sitting, Rian did not free her or stop at her seat. They continued. Rian led the way, knowing precisely what he intended, and at the great oak door, they went into the empty bailey.

"Where are you taking me?" Annora's question was

breathless, and she was forced to gulp her next breath as she hurried to keep pace with Rian's longer, rapid strides. She was not frightened but indignant. "Where are we going?"

She got no reply. Rian stared straight ahead. Uncompromising lines scored his rugged features as he cut a diagonal path across the bailey.

At the far corner was one of Castlekevin's four towers. It was primarily a defensive edifice distinguished by the crenellated battlement around the top and access to the wooden ramparts built along the castle walls. There were arrow loops on two upper level walls, and at the base there was a simple wicker door. As Rian kicked it open, the wicker creaked, the door bobbled on its leather hinges, and rodents scuttled in the shadows.

Inside the tower, the air was ripe with salted meat and dried apples. Rian guided them across a tamped dirt floor, up spiral stairs, and into a chamber. Annora heard the door close and its latch fall into place; ahead of her coals hissed, but she saw very little, the chamber being illuminated by nothing more than a brazier's glow and threads of silver light filtering through a closed shutter. It was warm, compared to the lower level, and quiet after the merrymaking in the hall. Annora inhaled the smells of beeswax, tansy, and lavender, and of washed linens dried in the sun. At least he had not delivered her to the byre or falcon shed.

Rian let go of her and moved away.

Rubbing at her upper arm, Annora watched him put a rush to the brazier. It ignited, orange light circled Rian, and he secured the flaming torch in a wall bracket. Annora saw her coffer at the foot of a tester bed hung with white curtains, the monk's robe lay atop the plump mattress. How comfortable the bed looked, how inviting, and she started toward it when Rian blocked her way. He was scowling as if he had some grievance, as if he were the one who'd been dragged out of the hall before gaping onlookers and deserved some sort of recompense. It was more than she could tolerate.

"You had no right to humiliate me like that," Annora berated.

"No right, ye say?" Rian cursed. "Ye'd be wise to reconsider what ye say to me. Do ye not remember my warning?"

"How could I forget?" She heard the husky tenor in Rian's voice and recognized desire in his eyes. His meaning was clear. She took a step away, and whispered, "No," as if one word might erase everything that had happened this day. Her breasts heaved with no thought of enticement. "No, you wouldn't."

"Och, but I would, for I own not a shred of conscience, my soul being depraved and damned. A stark naught," he said without a shade of emotion. His gaze dropped to her breasts; they were high and full, such a startling contrast to her angelic face and tiny waist. His loins tightened in anticipation of how he could fill his hands with her softness, and beyond that, of how tightly he could be held within her. "Nor am I in the habit of denying myself something I've decided to take."

"No!" The word was nothing more than a gasp. Annora moved farther away, and Rian lengthened his stride to narrow the distance between them. She stepped backward again, he followed, and little by little, he stalked her to the wall until her back was pressed against cool, uneven granite. "No," she cried in denial. There was nowhere to go except forward. To him.

"*Tá cinnte,*" he murmured in Irish. *Aye.* He set his hands against the wall, one on either side of her neck, and slowly he leaned into her. His whisper was a warm caress against her ear, "*Aye,* and do not bother to waste yer voice with more denials or calls for help. Yer pleas would be for naught, *leannán.*"

Her stomach dropped. There was nothing she might do, if a man as strong and large as Rian O'Byrne wished to have his way with her. In sooth, there was nothing she might do, if Rian O'Byrne touched her, for she wouldn't be able to resist him. "Please, it isn't too late. Why can't you turn around and leave me?" Her voice was no more than a whisper. "Lock me in ere morning comes, if you wish. But please let me alone for the night before—"

"Before what? Before it is too late?" He slid one hand down the wall as if he were outlining her body. It moved along the curve of her shoulders, it edged as close to her torso as possible without actually touching her, and when it was level with her waist, he stopped. For a moment he didn't move, then his fingers fluttered out to brush at her.

Annora's heart raced. Had he touched her? Or had she merely imagined it? She stared into his deep blue eyes, searching, wondering. He grinned at her, roguish and knowing, and this time, she didn't wonder what was happening when the flat of his hand skimmed across her stomach, then swiftly upward to her breast.

Annora gasped.

" 'Tis already too late," Rian murmured.

"But I did not toy with ye—"

"Did ye not?" Gently, his enormous hand closed about her breast, his fingers kneading the soft flesh. "With yer flirting and flaunting before me with Calum Kirkpatrick?"

"We were dancing," she forced herself to speak. "There is nothing wrong in that."

"Isn't there now? And what of the way ye kissed me?"

" 'Twas you who kissed me!"

"Aye, and ye responded most hungrily I might remind ye."

"I could not help myself," Annora confessed. Even now she was awakening to his touch, and she imagined the pull of waves about her ankles.

"And why was that, I'm asking?"

"Mayhap you should tell me." She met his eyes with a glint of challenge and tried to ignore how thick and firm and long were his fingers. "It would seem you have more than enough answers."

" 'Tis true. I have the answer. Ye could not help yerself because yers is the soul of a wanton." His other hand joined the first. Both continued to caress her breasts, both hands full. He felt her trembling. "Because one touch from a man and ye come alive."

One touch from a man. Her voice was thin, disbelief mingled with heartache when she asked, "Is that what you believe?" *Did he believe any man could produce that affect upon her? Didn't he understand?*

" 'Tis what I remember." He took in every detail of her upturned face, enthralled by the flash of color in her eyes, the quiver in her lips; and as he massaged her breasts through her kirtle, his hands also twisted the fabric upward. It skimmed past her knees, leaving nothing between her bare legs and his. Higher went the fabric, and when it was halfway up her thighs, he positioned his legs, one on each side of her slender leg. Her eyes widened, and he grinned. He closed his legs about her thigh, and she quivered, smooth and soft and warm. " 'Tis what I remember," he murmured in that seductive voice. "Just as I remember how ye rubbed yer private parts against me. Tell me, would ye have opened wide for Calum Kirkpatrick? Would ye have let him taste yer readiness?" He leaned closer until his chest rested against her, until his muscled legs clamped about her, and he buried his face beneath her mantle of curls to whisper softly against her ear. "Or is there something else ye learned from yer other lovers? In four years time, ye must have acquired a wealth of knowledge about pleasuring a man. Would ye be showing me what ye know, *leannán?*"

They were the cruelest words he could have uttered,

and Annora was astonished at her calm, amazed there were no tears streaming down her cheeks. "It has not been like that," she said in a steady voice.

"How many were there?"

"How many what?"

"Other men." Rian was tormented by a vision of Calum Kirkpatrick wrapped in a swirl of golden hair. His voice hardened. "Four? Five? Did ye let any other Irishman between yer thighs?"

"No," the denial was torn from her. *Why didn't he understand? He was the one man who did this to her. The only man who'd ever had this power over her. Was he going to make her speak the words aloud? Hadn't he guessed at the truth?*

"No Irish, was it? Only English lovers ye were swyving then. How many of their randy cocks did ye sheath in yer velvet queynt?"

Annora had overheard such vulgar words on the quays, but no one had ever used them in conversation with her, and certainly not with reference to herself. She raised her hand to slap him for such an odious insult, but he was quick and dropping the gown, he caught her wrist. The skirt drifted back to her ankles, around his legs, where he straddled her.

"How many, Annora?" Rian squeezed her wrist. Her eyes were wide with hurt, but that did not stop him. "How many other lovers? How many?"

She saw Rian's dark, brooding expression, and hesitated, finding herself saddened by the harsh lines that appeared across his brow and at the corners of his mouth. Sorrow pressed heavily about her. What an odd, unaccountable reaction, yet stranger still was her consideration of what had caused that expression to appear upon his face. Was it possible that he, too, was suffering? Could it be as agonizing for him to ask such questions as it was for her to hear them?

Mayhap Rian needed to hear the truth. Mayhap she needed to stop hiding.

Annora forced herself to speak. ''There was no one else.''

Chapter 22

No one else, she'd said.

Rian could but stare at Annora as her words sank in.

No one else.

In all this time there had been no other man. Horrifying joy soared within him. "If I was a different man, I would feel shame at what I so carelessly allowed to pass between us." He stared at the woman who had allowed him to be the man to release the carefully guarded passion within her soul—and the enormity of what this meant stunned him. Indeed, it thrilled him, excited him. Something twisted inside Rian. It was intense and stark, and it made him ache with yearning. Annora Picot had been his alone from the beginning; and now at the end, she was still his—a fact that Rian ached to reaffirm one final time. "If I were different, I would feel shame at what is going to happen this night."

She knew of what he spoke. "It cannot happen."

"Why not?" The velvet-soft quality of her voice drifted along his spine. He heard its desperation, poignant and melancholy. He heard her distress as clearly as he heard her desire. Rian stared into her eyes, holding her gaze for several heartbeats, and listening to her shallow

252

breathing before murmuring, "Ye're mine by yer own admission."

"But—"

"But what?"

"That was before, long ago. It was different then."

"Nay. It is not so different, I'm thinking." Splaying wide his hands, Rian brushed the palms across her breasts. The nipples puckered to his light touch, encouraging him to more. He grazed over them a second time, then a third. "I can have ye wanting me, begging for me like ye did before."

She looked away in disgrace. He was right. It was impossible for her body to resist even though her mind remained lucid. Already her breasts ached at his touch. "No, you must not."

"Again, I ask ye, why not?"

There were a million reasons, Annora bethought herself, and there were none. *Because I'm leaving. Because I don't want to be hurt. Because I want more than memories.* He tucked a finger beneath her chin as before; though she knew better, Annora didn't resist when he angled her face upward. Again he set the weight of his body against hers, and even though her face was raised to his, even though his smell filled her senses and she felt his heart beating, sensed his mouth coming closer to hers, she kept her eyes diverted.

"Tell me," came his whisper. His lips were atop hers. "Tell me why."

"Because," she began softly, her eyes downcast, her heart beating a frantic tattoo. "Because I want more in return for what I might give of myself. Because I want the same as any other woman. Because I need more."

"And what is that?"

"I want a beginning, not an end."

"Fiafraig sin do duine éigin eile," Rian murmured. There was genuine remorse in his voice when he said,

"*Ask that of some other man*. A beginning? Ye know 'tis not possible, *leannán*. At least, not from me, and I'm sorry for that, *sweetheart*. I truly am, but not sorry enough to be letting ye spend this night alone." There was a little pulse at the base of her throat, and he put his lips on it. "Do ye deny how good it was between us?"

She moaned a breathless, hopeless sound. A terrible longing coursed through her.

"Do ye deny how sweet? Do ye deny how right?"

"Right?" Annora's eyelids flew open. She stared at him. Her lips had become cold in a face that must be leached of any color. He was the one man who'd dismissed the importance of her money. The only man. That was why she'd given it all to him with no promise of anything beyond what they might take from each other. "Nay, there was nothing *right* about what I did." She gave a mirthless laugh. Could he possibly understand how she'd been hurt by her own self-deception? "I bethought myself worldly and mature, but 'twas a grand lie I foisted upon myself, and I won't do that again. I can't."

Rian frowned. A flash of nothingness tried to wrap itself around him, a bleak eternity of emptiness that would eventually sap the life from him. "If I asked like a proper suitor, would ye be mine?" he said in a stilted voice.

"You're not a proper suitor, and never will be one."

Of a sudden, Rian's loneliness loomed before him, and he was afraid. This time, he wouldn't win. He couldn't bear it, and the awful prospect of having nothing, of being further detached from life and light exerted a mighty force upon him. Indeed, it turned his world inside out. Upside down. "Not a proper suitor, ye charge," he said humbly, and went down on one knee before her. "'Tis something we should have to remedy, isn't it now?"

"Get up, Rian. You must not do that." Her throat was choked with tears. Annora sensed the need in him, the desperation. Misery twisted around her heart. His pain was hers. She didn't want him to do this. "Get up. Please."

Still kneeling, Rian fumbled for the pouch at his waist, and finding it, pulled open the cords to reach inside. He glanced at her. She was watching, waiting. "Put out yer hand," he said, and when she did as he asked, he withdrew a cluster of dried petals. The remnants of a red rose. He looked at it now, and sensed not shame but gladness. For a man who'd tried to forget about his seduction of Annora Picot, Rian never understood what could have compelled him to keep the rose any more than why he'd failed to discard it over the years. He'd loathed himself for such a weakness, now he was glad. He set it on her open palm.

Annora's heart leapt. How well she remembered walking with this Irishman in her mother's garden, and how he'd stood in the entryway and helped himself to a crimson rose from her basket. She remembered how he'd kissed the flower and touched it to her lips. How he'd tucked it behind his ear and walked away. Her hand rose to her mouth, but a gasp escaped nonetheless. So, too, a tear rolled down her cheek to know that he'd kept it all these years.

"Would ye be mine tonight?" His voice, deep and smooth, repeated in lilting Irish, *"Croidheag, in rega lim i tír n-ingnad hi fil rind?"*

She hadn't forgotten. *Mistress of my desires, will ye go with me to a wondrous land where there are stars?* Her trembling hand closed about the petals, and Annora went down on her knees. She faced him and knew what was going to happen in this chamber. It was as inevitable as the sun rising and setting, as certain as the tides that swept in from the sea, and to resist was futile.

"What say ye, Annora?" He framed her face with his hands, tenderly brushing a thumb over her lips. "Would ye? Will ye? Be mine this night?"

Unable to tell him with words, Annora turned her lips into his hand and kissed his palm.

Rian groaned at the sweet evidence of her assent. He shifted his weight to kneel on both legs, and reaching round to the back of her kirtle, he unlaced the top closure. "Raise yer arms," he whispered, and pulled the loosened garment over her head. Underneath she wore a sheer tunic with a belt about her waist. He untied the belt. It dropped onto the rushes. Then he slid the tunic down her shoulders. She raised her arms to help him undress her, and the garment slid past her hips and thighs to pool about her knees. Annora didn't flinch at his touch or try to move away, nor did she cover her nakedness from his admiring gaze.

In the torchlight, her skin was as luminescent as the finest Muscat pearls, her hair was vibrant as sunshine, floating downward to an incredibly tiny waist, and the fair triangle that marked the location of her sex shimmered as a treasure. Her hips were narrow yet rounded, and slender, shapely legs hinted of strength. But it was her bounteous breasts that most excited him, full as ripe fruits and tipped with oversized, dark nipples. Rian throbbed. Fierce, burning desire engorged him, his mouth watered, and he leaned closer for a taste. His lips trailed down her throat, across her chest, and when he reached her breast, his tongue drew a moist circle about the areola. He inhaled her body's essence, tasted her flesh, soft as silk, and absorbed her rising warmth. His tongue went to her nipple, and finding it taut and tempting, his lips took root upon the inviting crest.

Little noises emanated from Annora. A wave rolled in from the sea. She heard its approach as she arched her back, offering her breast to his suckling. There was another wave, another, and she tilted her female parts to him.

A tremor ripped through Rian when Annora brushed against his groin. He abandoned her breast. His hand moved down her belly toward the apex between her legs, lower until the tip of his middle finger reached the nether lips of her sex. Slowly the finger slid along the outer seam, opening her ever so slightly, and when the whole of his thick finger entered, her body vibrated in reaction. She was nicely damp but tight as a maid. Aye, there had been no other man. Gently Rian inserted a second finger to ready her for him.

Desire hot and wet burst within Annora. She cried out. The crash of waves roared in her ears. Swirling eddies rose about her, holding her in the shallow water. A flush spread across her exposed skin, the wetness within her increased. It had never been like this before. She did not remember this hunger, this urgency, and possessed by shameless yearning, she tore at his tunic, the leggings.

"Easy, *leannán*. Easy." Rian laughed as he released his erection, and the hard, wildly aroused shaft rubbed against her inner thigh. He pulled her into his embrace, her breasts against his flesh, his legs against hers, and she quivered so violently that he wondered if she might swoon. "Are ye light-headed, *sweetheart?*" She nodded in reply. Her eyes were heavy-lidded, and he recognized the effects of passion. How quickly, how urgently they had come to this. Rian stood and scooped her into his arms. He carried her to the bed and laid her on her stomach.

"What do you do?" she asked when he pulled her to the edge of the mattress.

"I intend to fill ye as never before. Do not fear. 'Tis only pleasure I intend for ye." He trailed a finger down her spine. "Be folding yer knees up beneath ye."

She did. Her pretty little bottom rose, and the dewy cleft between her legs was exposed to him. Rian stood between her legs and moved close behind her to set his arousal at the petals of her opening. Annora wiggled against him, a terrible shudder ripped through Rian, and he pressed forward. Like delving into butter, he slid inside, and her sheath encased his massive girth, her inner muscles pulling him deeper. Inch by inch, he entered her velvet warmth. She made another little sound as she rocked back and forth on her knees.

Blood surged through Rian. To have her so eager and slick, so wild and free was as much pleasure as pain. She was ravaging him, taking him deeper and tighter, and for a moment, he feared his climax would come too soon. Beads of moisture dotted his face, his upper back, and he held her hips to stop their rocking. Neither of them moved, the sound of heavy breathing filled the chamber, and Rian looked at his man's sex joined into her. He wondered if she could feel his shaft pulsing within her for release, throbbing with the need for more pleasure. He ached to move, but did not want to climax too soon, and forced himself as still as he could.

Slowly, slowly, he descended from the brink of culmination. Only when he was certain of his control, did he begin to plumb her, quickly gaining speed until the tempo was as hard and fast, as frenzied as hers had been.

Annora answered his movements with a long, sweet keen, and raised herself higher to him. She whimpered at the friction of his immense manhood caressing her highly receptive inner flesh. "I want more," she said in a voice made uneven by craving, and in response, Rian grasped her upper thighs. His large hands girded her. He held tight.

He was opening her to him. It was exquisite to feel him spread her wider, rapture to have more of him within her. Her senses were heightened beyond all knowing. Annora cried out at the ecstasy of being filled. Her bottom rocked against his groin, meeting his thrusts, matching his accelerating tempo.

There was an almost reckless quality to their movements as if their bodies were engaged in some frantic attempt to hold on to what would pass with the coming of dawn. A wave was pulling Annora to the edge of its crest.

Her skin was tingling, blood thrummed through her, and a surge of pleasure seized her. She whispered his name, and Rian roared something in Irish.

There was a burst of light. Both of them experienced the same sensation.

A shower of heat raining across arms and legs, backs, shoulders, thighs, necks.

Warmth again. Undulating through them. Lifting them up as a frothy wave carries flotsam on its foam.

And finally, an explosion that took them soaring past the stars and across the universe in an inferno of fulfillment that left them drenched with the dew of lovemaking.

Like petals washed upon the lakeshore after a storm, Annora's senses floated back to normalcy. Rian collapsed on the bed beside her and pulled her into his arms. She lay on her side, fitting securely in the shelter of his body.

There was no him. No her. Two hearts beat as one. A tangle of arms and legs, bellies, chests, thighs.

Rian held her close, the fingers of one hand threaded through golden loops of damp hair. God had played a cruel trick; indeed, mayhap this was Rian's ultimate proof that He did not exist, for surely no merciful God would create a woman such as this for any man only to deny him.

On a hush, he whispered, "Sleep now. Yer journey is not over, and morning will arrive too soon." Rian's last thought before surrendering to sleep was a wish. If only she had no farther to travel; if only this was where she risked everything to be.

Annora nestled deeper, deeper into the cradle of his arms. This night, she would dream of the crimson rose. She fell to sleep, listening to his heartbeat, and in her dreams, she mourned the sorrowful beauty of this night, wishing that it might never end.

INTERLUDE
SECOND

Interlude

*I*n the schist and granite mountains on the lower slope of a height called Keadeen, a woman lay upon her straw mattress, wide awake and staring through the dark toward a shuttered window. She had been bedrid since the first snowfall. Winter had come early this season, and her fever had started when her grandsons left to bring the cattle down from the summer pasture, snow swirling around them as they set off for the high meadow. The blood had commenced flowing after the lads returned to the fortress. More than once these past months, her family had thought she'd breathed her last, so weak and blue and cold did she become. But with the arrival of spring and the warming in the glens and passes, she had revived. She was not well enough to leave the sleeping chamber to help with chores or to join the clan for meals in the hall, but she was recovered enough to sit up to the window to watch the eagles gliding above Imail. She was well enough to converse with visitors, and well enough to begin hoping anew.

She was Íde, named after the sainted Irish nun upon whose feast day she had been born some forty-five years before. She was an O'Toole of Ballinaclash by birth, an O'Toole of Imail by marriage, and her life had not been easy. Wed to her first husband at the age of twelve, she had suffered the loss of six children, had raised eight others to adulthood, had endured war and kidnapping, famine, pestilence, and had thrice been widowed before her thirtieth year, all three of her husbands having been beheaded by the English.

Most others would have already surrendered to death, but not Íde. She had unfinished business on this earth. There were questions she needed answered, and Íde intended to cling to life no matter how weary or weak she might become. Dying did not frighten her, she believed in the miracles of the Resurrection and Redemption, yet her heart twisted with anguish to think of departing this world without those answers.

The door opened. A slender woman entered the sleeping chamber.

Íde turned her head. A rushlight in the corridor silhouetted the woman. Her face was not visible.

"Is that ye, Éva?" Íde asked in a frail voice.

"Aye, mam." Of the eight children Íde had raised, Éva was the oldest, the only one born of her first marriage to have survived to womanhood, and like her mother Éva had lost her husband to the English before the last of her children had learned to walk.

"Ye were taking very long with yer time," said Íde, more fretful than complaining. A prudent Irishwoman did not grumble, for those who sniped usually lagged behind and perished. Íde had learned from her mother to look for solutions, and she had learned from the Gospel that it was possible to feed a multitude with less than a full basket of eels and only half a loaf. No one had ever found fault in Íde, not even when the choices she'd made were the sort no mother should ever have to decide. "Where were ye, Éva?"

"It was not so long," said Éva in a comforting tone. "I was in the hall picking out the rushes after dinner and would have come sooner, but Áedan brought in his new babe to be showing off the wee one. Four days old he is now, and with as powerful a set of lungs as his da was ever having.'' She did not tell her mother that her daughter-in-law had not survived the birthing, that her youngest son had no wife, and his brood of wee ones were without their mother.

"How many is that now?" asked Íde, feeling the same tug of sadness she'd experienced each time an infant of her womb had been set to her breast, each time one of her children had added one of their own to the family.

"Twenty-one grandbabes."

Íde frowned. That could not be the proper count. She wanted to sit up and look beyond Éva but did not have the strength. *"Agus Ona, céard fúithi sin?"* she asked. *And Ona, what about her?*

In the past, as many as two or three years might go by between such questions, but since the snow had melted on Keadeen, Íde had been asking similar questions with alarming frequency. Éva had been eleven when Íde first spoke to her in this way, and then Éva had pretended not to hear. That had been the easiest way to respond, and she wished that she might continue to ignore her mother at times like this. It had, however, become impossible. To disregard Íde would be wicked, and detrimental not only to her health but to the well-being of her heart and soul; and Éva had no desire to hurt her mother, especially when the end might come at any hour.

Éva was a good daughter, and would never let her mother die with a burdened heart. If the questions continued, there was only one answer she might give. This was part of Éva's debt. Íde had done more than most mothers ever dreamed to keep Éva safe, and this was one way Éva might ease her mother's anguish.

"Did ye get any news of her since?" Íde persisted as had become her habit.

Tears welled in Éva's eyes, and as she had done many times before, she answered with the same lie, *"Beidh sí ag teacht abhaile aon lá anois."* She spoke with tender reassurance, taking her mother's cold, thin hand and raising it to her own warm lips. *"She'll be coming home any day now."*

"Buíochas le Dia," Íde whispered, relaxing against her straw pillow and letting her eyes close for the first time that night. *Thank God.* "Wasn't I often telling ye that? Coming home, she is, just like I always said she would be doing one day. Thank ye, Éva, for bringing yer mam the good news. I'll be sleeping well this night, certainly I will. Ye're a comfort, ye are, indeed, and 'tis no doubting the power of God's hand is what's kept ye by my side."

There were other wishes that night.

To the southeast, Rian's parents sat before the open hearth at Aghavannagh. They, too, had a new grandchild born that night to one of their daughters. The babe had been cleaned and swaddled and brought to his grandmother, who smiled and clucked as only grandmothers can do, and then she sang a lullaby to the sleeping newborn.

"The babe reminds me of Rian," remarked Rónán O'Byrne. He would be leaving at first light to join MacMurrough at Idrone, and his thoughts were teeming, not of imminent departure from his wife and home but of his eldest child. He was not usually wont to such melancholy, and his mood made him feel very old, indeed. "Do ye see the slant of the brows and that wisp of hair? There's only one other O'Byrne with that ginger-brown coloring."

"Aye, I was noticing," said his wife. "And I was thinking how the wee one should be our Rian's babe."

"Och, Grella, 'tis a soft heart ye have, my love. Ye say that each time ye take another grandchild into yer waiting arms."

"And each time there is virtue to my words. 'Tis true: our Rian should have been having a wife and family long before. There should be more for him than the emptiness he endures. As long as I live and breathe that will be my wish, for I'll be his mother always no matter what else comes to pass, and I'll always be wishing the next babe to be his.''

''And breaking yer heart is where such a yearning will be leading, to be sure.'' Rónán could not meet his wife's eyes, and he looked into the fire. He knew it was too late for Rian but couldn't bear to talk of it. They had not spoken to one another of the rumor, but surely Grella had heard in the women's bower the same he'd heard in the armory. Rian, their first born, was dead. No one had seen his head atop the gates of Dublin town for themselves, but the news of his capture had not surprised Rónán. He'd never expected any different end for his Rian. Of course, he had hoped for Grella's sake as well as for Rian's that his son might one day find the strength to believe in himself; Rónán had even prayed once or twice that his son might care for someone or something before he died. Now it was too late. Too late for Grella to know a mother's ultimate happiness for her firstborn; too late for Rian to experience the fullness of life a warrior might only know when he had a wife and children; too late for Rónán's own dream. The Leinster Irish were about to fight the English, but Rian would not be fighting at his side, would not be there to rejoice in their victory.

Rónán cursed in silence. If it had been possible to shelter the lad from unjust punishment, he would have done so. Mayhap their lives would have been different. But Rónán hadn't known what had happened in the hills that summer until it was too late, nor had he realized there had been some who blamed an innocent child for the loss of another.

Grella looked at her husband and knew what he was thinking. She always did. It was Rian who occupied her husband's sorrowful thoughts, and she knew his grief was different from hers. A warrior needed his eldest son standing at his side, a father needed to know he hadn't failed, and as tears began to roll down her cheeks, Grella rocked the infant.

That she had not been able to help her son or husband heal was her greatest failure as a wife and mother. Softly, she began another lullaby.

To the north, Sir Thomas was returning to his castle lodgings from a late audience with the archbishop and the king's priest, Maudelyn. Matins bells tolled across the Liffey. The outcome of the meeting had not been good, and upon entering his private chamber, Sir Thomas began pacing in uncharacteristic agitation. He had been commanded to ride out on the morrow at the head of a company of men-at-arms, pikemen, and mounted archers. His orders were to lead this battle-ready force in pursuit of his niece.

Although neither the archbishop nor Maudelyn appeared to suspect Sir Thomas in Annora's disappearance, their judgment of his niece was not as favorable. It was widely known that in spite of abundant virtues, Annora Picot had on occasion been influenced by a most unpredictable and unbecoming independence. Faith, she had been known to be *defiant*. Even Maudelyn had heard the tale of how she'd doused an impassioned suitor with a pitcher of claret, and of the Fair Week when she'd *accidentally* kicked over several cages of valuable fighting cocks that flew their coops and escaped into the throng. Mistress Annora loathed cockfighting, and it was whispered the accident had occurred after the owner had refused to sell them to her.

The priest had informed Sir Thomas that he considered those incidents most telling. He'd had been suspicious of Annora since her absence was reported by a hysterical maid, and had offered his condolences to Sir Thomas for having been duped by his niece. Had not Sir Thomas been in the least skeptical of his niece's reaction upon learning the king had betrothed her to Monmouth? Or had her charade been flawless?

"You are correct, my lord, to inquire. In truth, I did wonder, but only for a moment, as her manner was naught but genuine. Truth to tell, it was that seeming ingenuousness to which I was susceptible." Sir Thomas had felt the blood drain from his face, but he'd remained steady and had done nothing to betray himself or Annora. He had lied with uncommon naturalness. "There was nothing remarkable about her reaction save the ease with which she accepted the news. There were no tears, no ranting, no silence or sulking, nor anything unusual in her subsequent behavior. I was most satisfied when she sent her maid for the dressmaker and appeared to be undertaking preparations with efficient enthusiasm."

Maudelyn had accepted this from Sir Thomas. Of course, the archbishop had never doubted the loyal knight's devotion to his king, nor his faith in English ascendancy over Ireland. Nor did either of them suspect any connection between the escaped Irish spy and the missing bride.

In the morning, Sir Thomas would ride out of Dublin at the head of a search party, and it was of no comfort that his orders were to ride toward Maynooth, where there would be no trail to follow. Although his party might not apprehend Annora, there were others already searching to the north and south. Surely someone must have discovered the blood-stained tunic on the Killiney cliff. How could it be that the search for Annora continued with such zealousness? Earlier this day, a carrack of troops had sailed from Dalkey to Wicklow harbor. No doubt those soldiers were already ashore and fanning into the countryside, and at the prospect of English patrolling the approaches to Wicklow, Sir Thomas fell to his knees in fervent prayer to the Almighty Father that Annora would not be punished for his treason.

Through the night he invoked the Lord's mercy and divine guidance. He prayed that His grace would sustain Rian O'Byrne, and that the Irishman was the bold, swift, and quick-witted warrior Sir Thomas believed him to be. He prayed there would be no trail to follow beyond the fringes, and he petitioned the Blessed Virgin for her intercession.

If the English came near Annora, Sir Thomas beseeched Our Lady to make certain Rian O'Byrne would protect his niece from harm, and most important, that he would be able to evade capture.

Beyond the western slope of the Wicklow wilderness, and a full two days march south, King Richard II was feasting at the earl of Ormond's high table in Kilkenny Castle. The great hall—in which Lionel, duke of Clarence, had celebrated the Kilkenny Statute with his parliament—was gay with banners, flutes, and tambours. His majesty's immediate coterie counted the lord steward of England, Sir Thomas Percy; John Holland, duke of Exeter; Thomas le De Spenser, the young duke of Gloucester; the bishop of London, and the abbot of Westminster; a French chronicler, Jean Creton, and an interpreter, Henry Cristall; and the two hostages, Harry of Monmouth and Humphrey of Gloucester.

The fourteen-hour journey from Waterford had been uneventful. The king had sailed up the Nore past New Ross to the monastery of Inis Tiog, where he had disembarked to continue by the right bank to ancient *Cell Cainnig*, as the Irish had called the town for centuries, *Wooded Head Near the River*, and the great stone castle built by Strongbow on the site of the old court of King Donnchadh. In summer, the woods of the Nore valley were in their glory. The forest was rich in mast, swine rooted under blackthorn and birch, hawk and falcon nested in oak, yew, and fir, and Richard granted the bachelors-in-arms permission to hunt.

It was a grand day, and the English vanguard rode
boldly into Kilkenny before dusk. The army had encountered no hostile Irishry, the gunnes had been transported
overland without incident, and in another two or three
hours the last of the 24,000 troops would have arrived.
Without the walled town, a vast encampment sprawled to
the north and south, the warm, dusk-tide air was heavy
with the smoke from hundreds of cookfires, pale purple
mist hovered over the river, and the bell of St. Canice's
tolled Compline as grumbles and whispers, laughter,
snores and the grunts of love-jousting issued from every
slip and alley.

"A message arrives, my lord king," the earl of
Ormond informed his guest.

Richard, once considered by many to be the handsom-
est monarch since the Conquest, had changed little since
his last expedition to Ireland. He was still fine of face, his
hair was still thick and yellow, and although he had
grown heavier in form, he was arrayed in his usual degree
of magnificence. He looked at Ormond in expectation.
"'Tis a report of the duke of Aumerle's arrival at
Waterford with reinforcements?"

"Nay, not news from the coast yet, but from Kildare."

"It is favorable?"

"Indeed, sire, most auspicious. The Gascon knight,
Jenico d'Artois, who serves your majesty in Kildare, has
fought and triumphed over the enemy. Several hundred
wild Irishry are dead."

The king lifted his chalice. "Honor to the noble
Gascon." His commanding voice reverberated through
the grand chamber. "To a valiant warrior, who again
proves himself bold and loyal, and equal only to thine
host in his conquests. To all the English of Ireland that
they might follow in such worthy efforts."

The toast was echoed by the assembled noblemen, and
knights, abbots, courtiers, and priests, and when their
cheers subsided, Ormond was the first to speak.

"That your will might be further implemented in Ireland, my lord king, what is your wish?"

"We wish to teach a stern lesson, and to do so We wish to seek out MacMurrough," Richard declared.

"Seek out, my lord king? Or draw out to engage in battle?" Ormond ventured to clarify.

"Seek out!" The king went white with rage about the rim of his glowering mouth. Was he being questioned? *By Saint John the Baptist, did the earl imagine the king of England and France would wait for anyone?* Richard glared at his host while motioning two pages to step forward. Someone cleared the space on the table before the king, and the lads unrolled a large piece of vellum in the middle of which was a pile of wooden shapes. It might have been some sort of a game.

Richard rose. He stood over the vellum and pushed the wooden pieces to one side. Taking a charcoal stick from a page, he pointed to the nobleman at each end of the high table. "Come closer. And you, Ormond, take heed."

First, the king sketched a crown in the lower left-hand corner of the vellum, then he picked up the largest piece of wood from the pile. It was the figure of an important personage as evidenced by an excess of carved plumes in his helm, a sword that was more ornamental than practical, and by the magnificent horse he rode. The king held this figure over the crown he'd drawn on the vellum.

"This is Kilkenny, and here We are." He placed the figure on the crown and made a sweeping motion in the air above the vellum. "None among you forgets, We trust, how familiar this territory is to Us. The route to Dublin has not changed in centuries. 'Tis the same valleys and waters we traveled on Our last expedition to this island. Leighlin Bridge, Carlow, Ballygory, Naas," he said whilst drawing a gently winding line from the middle of the bottom to the top. "There is the Barrow, and to its east the wilderness wherein my enemies and the foul murderer of Mortimer hides."

A short distance to the right of the Barrow he depicted mountains with a series of triangles, after which he commenced setting the rest of the wooden pieces within and around those mountains. As each little square or rectangle went down, the king uttered an identifying phrase, "His people. His wife. His sons. Villages. Strongholds. Churches. And his allies, and their holdings. Their wives. Their sons. Their fortresses. Their villages and farms. Oh, how this land is infested."

The king spent a few silent moments arranging the little pieces as if designing a small world. He grinned at his handiwork, but his voice was callous. "Outlaws all of them. Rebels and savages. By the blood of Saint John the Baptist, why is it that such felons are allowed to thrive? That they are permitted to flaunt their old ways and laws before the might of England?"

From the assembly came a throaty noise as if someone were readying a reply.

"Silence!" the king roared.

Silence, indeed, prevailed. Instant, thick, terrible silence. His majesty's furies were dreaded. Every face lost color. Many eyes focused on the floor. The blow that Richard had dealt his uncle, the earl of Arundel, at his beloved Queen Anne's funeral was well-remembered. Although the collective memory had forgotten that Arundel, having failed to march in the queen's cortege, and having arrived at Westminster after the service was underway, had asked for the king's permission to leave before the ritual was concluded, no one had forgotten Richard's response. Using a baton, Richard had struck his uncle's head with such force that Arundel had collapsed to the abbey floor. A pool of blood had flowed over the paving stones so that the floor had to be washed before the queen's funeral could resume.

The fearful silence was awful. Everyone waited for the king to speak.

"We will not leave Ireland until We have Mac-

Murrough in Our power," stammered Richard as he'd use to in his earlier years, and with one arm he swept the little blocks away from the foothills and mountains and the winding charcoal line of the Barrow. Villages, farms, women and children flew off the vellum. Richard grabbed the mounted nobleman from its place at Kilkenny, and with a resounding plunk set it down again, this time, at the top right of the makeshift map. "And there! There is Dublin from which all of Ireland will be Ours! *Terra pacis* shall endure over the whole of Our domain."

Someone coughed as if gathering courage to speak.

"If it please, my lord king, we hasten to recommend that an envoy be dispatched to MacMurrough."

"Do you suggest we negotiate with these barbarians? With th-th-this upstart king who dresses and mounts for battle in the same manner as his ancestors did two hundred years before?"

"Nay, merely that your majesty dictate the terms of your ascendancy. Being wiser and more powerful, more civilized and humane, 'tis only right to offer them mercy before extirpation."

Richard gave a satisfied nod. He had never been able to discern flattery from integrity. "Attend to it without delay."

A messenger was dispatched, the vellum was cleared away, and the feasting resumed while his majesty tapped a finger to his pale brow. The inventory of Richard's tribulations and heartaches haunted him. Plagued by troublesome royal uncles, overruled by a Merciless Parliament, tested by Wycliffites and Lollards, and mobbed in the streets of London; his dearest Anne taken too soon, and now young Mortimer, his heir, slain by barbarians.

Vengeance, Richard had discovered, could be a highly agreeable physick. His uncle Arundel's arrest had been gratifying, his trial most enjoyable, and his execution fulfilling.

Now it was time for the Irish to pay, and not even the Devil could have guessed what manner of evil Richard of Bordeaux was planning that night in Kilkenny.

Part Three

Chapter 23

❦ ❧

"'Tis time to awaken, *leannán*." Rian had been standing beside the bed, watching Annora for some time. He checked the impulse to brush back the yellow curls that fell across her cheek and brow.

Annora turned her face into the bedding. The wool smelled of Rian. Of sex. She remembered the night before, and sighed. A wonderful, rare contentment cloaked her. What had started in anger and pain had ended with beauty, poignant and bitter. She didn't open her eyes right away, savoring instead the gentleness in his whisper. A morning such as this would never come again.

"Ye should be dressing," he said. It was past time for them to be on the road toward the coast.

She stretched her arms overhead, and blinked twice. Rian looked as if he'd been up for hours. Sunshine flooded the chamber. It was well past the break of day, and she sat up, clutching the woolen bedcovering to her nakedness. "How could you let me lie abed and jeopardize my rendezvous with the *Hera?* Do you forget your promise to my uncle?"

Nay, I forget nothing so painful as truth. Rian didn't have the will to frown at her scolding tone, let alone to reveal what was within his soul. "Our journey from Dublin could not have been easy for ye, and I had not the

279

heart to disturb yer peaceful slumber.'' Never before had they passed a night together in a proper bed, and he'd wanted to hold on to her for as long as he might. But he didn't tell her that. ''A few hours does not portend disaster for yer plans. There is not far to go this day, nor is the terrain difficult. Ye'll be to Wicklow on time. Fear not.'' He gathered up her undertunic and kirtle and handed them to her. ''Are ye hungry?''

''A little.'' She stared at the clump of clothes, wishing that she had not sounded snappish, and that she might be happy with the time she'd had with this man.

''I will have a bite brought to ye.'' He sheathed a *skian* at his waist.

''*Go raibh maith agat.*'' She forced a smile. *I thank you.*

Today he wasn't wearing the cast-off English tunic and leggings her uncle had supplied, but the saffron-dyed *leine* of an Irish warrior. Beneath the tunic his muscular legs were bare as were his feet, and the weather being warm, he wore no mantle or brat. Rian appeared as Annora had remembered him and would remember him in the years to come. An imposing, handsome man with irresistible, beckoning eyes, and a sensual mouth. A dangerous Irishman with a wild tangle of burnished hair that hung below his shoulders in a manner that would cause all proper English gentlemen to shudder in disdain. A mental image of lying down in a field of wheat passed before Annora, and her cheeks warmed, but she didn't look away from Rian. This time, she wanted to remember.

As for Rian, it was hard to look upon Annora and know that he had already lost her. Never before had he wanted anything more from a woman other than the pleasures they'd shared together. Never before had he regretted when his time with any particular woman was coming to an end. *Ná bi a mbaile mor, no a geaislean, gan bean air do leitsgeul.* Rian had adhered to the old adage with uncommon skill. *Be not in a city or castle without a woman to befriend ye.* Would that it might be Annora Picot in every town and fortress. Would that it might be Annora always waiting for him. Always eager.

He returned her gaze, held his breath, and plowed fingers through his hair. This wasn't easy. It was complicated and frustrating, and there was no use pretending otherwise. He exhaled. A miserable, almost frantic groan rumbled forth from his soul. Last night had not been enough. He wanted more time, and Rian couldn't stop himself from pulling her into a close embrace as if doing so might change everything. *If only she had no farther to travel. If only this was where she risked everything to be.*

His lips sought hers. It wasn't an arousing kiss. His caress did not speak of passion and fire, but of tender appreciation. It was the fragile link between a man and woman who have known intimacy and fleeting joy, but for whom there will never be happiness, for whom this moment could never be anything more than an ending. A kiss that lingered as in a dream. A kiss too wise to resist the inevitable.

Alone in the chamber, Annora dressed, then she sat upon the bed to look inside her coffer. When she'd packed the small leather chest, she had filled it with those things that would enable her to start a life beyond Ireland's shores. Now she wasn't certain whether its contents would be enough. In addition to silver and gold, there were a number of objects wrapped in fabric— sentimental items for the most part. First, she unwrapped a miniature about the size of a man's palm. It was of a beautiful, young woman seated beneath a rose arbor, and upon her lap was a two- or three-year-old version of herself.

Catherine and Annora in the walled garden. Both mother and daughter wore gowns of pale blue velvet, both were smiling, the light in their blue eyes was captured with uncanny skill by the artist. So real. As was the glow upon their cheeks, and the luster of their unbound tresses. Annora brushed a fingertip across the image of Catherine's joyous, tender expression. She knew that if there were angels, her mother was among them.

Setting aside the small painting, Annora took another bundle from the coffer, and unwrapped it with care. There were two ornamental crosses. The larger one, crafted of gold filigree with a large pearl hanging from the bottom of each arm, was affixed to a slender golden chain. It was the only piece of jewelry Catherine had worn for the portrait with Annora in the rose garden. The other cross was a child's, and in contrast to her mother's, it was startling in its simplicity. The small cross had been carved from wood to appear as if it were braided from leafy vines. There were no pearls, no gold, only a tiny metallic loop imbedded in the top and through which a cord had once been threaded.

Every summer on the occasion of Annora's birth celebration, Catherine had put a new cord through the loop, enabling Annora to wear the cross as she grew. " 'Tis a mother's gift of love to her daughter and has been round your neck from the first moment I held you in my arms," Catherine had always said before extracting a promise from Annora that she would give the cross to her own daughter. Annora had always promised she would, and that one day, she would sit in the rose garden, the delicate gold cross hanging about her neck and holding a little girl upon her lap.

The memory of her mother consoled Annora. On impulse, she slipped the chain with filigreed cross over her head and beneath her bodice. A knock came to the door. Annora closed the coffer and stood to drop the painting and wooden cross into the deepest pocket of her kirtle. "Enter. Enter."

It was Isobel O'Toole carrying a tray of food. "Good day to ye, Annora Picot. Ye slept well?"

"Too well, I fear. Your cousin should not have let the day get so old before waking me."

"Och, do not be fretting yerself. Rian says ye did not sleep for two nights. There is no harm in catching up." Isobel gave a sympathetic smile. She set down the tray. "The rhubarb is fresh boiled, and sweetened with *fraughán* and honey. Órla is learning her housekeeping skills, and 'tis her first attempt in the kitchen. She wanted ye to have some." While Annora tasted the fruit pottage, Isobel added, "I was concerned yesternight when my cousin took ye away in such a temper."

"As you can see, I am fine." She took a sip of cool water and another bite of the fruit.

"Ye're certain?" Isobel's gentle concern was as much for this woman as it was for her cousin. Rian had always put himself at a distance from relationships, and it saddened her romantic heart. Indeed, there were times when she wondered if he was punishing himself, although Isobel couldn't understand why he might do that. Of all the men in her large extended family of O'Connors and O'Byrnes, Rian was her favorite. He was the one who had taught her to ride and had not made mockery of her yearning to hunt. From Isobel's earliest memories, Rian had watched over her. He had protected her from harm, both real and imagined. He had shielded her from jealousy, deceit, falseness, and other unkindnesses. He had done much for her. Indeed, it was Rian who had convinced her parents that Fínán O'Toole would be a fine husband. "Is there nothing I can be doing for ye?" she asked Annora.

"You are kind, Isobel O'Toole, but you need not be concerned for me," Annora replied. But it was a lie. *No.* She wasn't fine. She was confused and sad, joyous and heartsick. But she knew how to pretend. She knew how to maintain a bland expression when she heard the gossips whispering about her independent ways; she knew how to keep an even temper when Bristol merchants tried to cheat her, and how to sing and laugh with the sick children at the convent even though she knew they were going to die. She was not fine, yet she managed a pleasant smile. "I need nothing more than to reach Wicklow, and as your cousin has brought me safely thus far, I trust him to escort me the rest of the way as promised."

While Isobel's instinct told her Annora was hiding something, she knew better than to pursue the issue. Fate was not always kind, and if her cousin and this woman were destined to travel opposite roads, there was nothing she might do to change that. Instead, she helped Annora plait her hair, talking as she did about her girlhood at a fortress called Baravore.

Shortly, a lad came for the coffer, and the women descended to the bailey, where Rian waited. Having exchanged the convent palfrey for a sleek stallion, he secured Annora's coffer behind the pillion saddle. This day, he would ride like an Irishman without stirrups.

"Good fortune, and Godspeed to ye, Annora Picot," said Isobel.

The women embraced, the portcullis was raised, and Annora bid farewell to the O'Tooles of Castlekevin.

Chapter 24

◈

From Castlekevin the track skirted bog and mountains. As elsewhere in *Uí Briúin Cualann*, this valley had reverted to its rightful inhabitants, and the fortified farmsteads of the English had been abandoned. Here and there woodland gave way to open space that had once been tillage fields. Poppies, cockles, and pine flowers flourished, where once barley and wheat had been harvested.

The vibrancy of color struck Annora as they entered a clearing that resembled a giant's feasting hall with blue sky for ceiling, a floor of wildflowers and grasses, and an outcrop of enormous, gray boulders for trestle and benches. Schist made the stones shimmer silver, the grass was bright as a pear before it ripens, and the wildflowers were lapis lazuli and rubies, amethysts and amber. It was the same intensity of hues that appeared before a storm. Annora glanced heavenward.

There were no clouds, and her gaze shifted back to the clearing, drawn to the far end, where stalks of purple thistle swayed.

Rian reined in his horse.

Annora knew why. She stopped beside him. There was no wind. The air was heavy, still, and hot, yet the stalks continued to move.

285

"Stay on yer horse for now," Rian whispered. One hand went to the sword at his waist.

It took only an instant for the boundary between life and death to narrow. Four archers rose from the thistle patch. They were English soldiers in kettle hats and haubergeons. Two more came out of the forest at the other end of the clearing. They were hobilars, mounted and unarmored spearmen, riding abreast of each other with the look of professional fighting men, not unwilling recruits.

"They are come for me," Annora said.

Rian didn't look at her. His glance darted between the archers and hobilars. They were advancing slowly, purposefully. "And how would ye be knowing such a thing, I might be wondering now? Yer king comes to wage war upon the Irish, not to pursue runaway merchants."

"Untrue. His soldiers pursue Annora Picot as I feared he would."

"Ye did not steal the contents of yer coffer, did ye?"

"I am no thief."

The hobilars kept coming.

"Then they are after me, to be certain," he countered. "Spy, murderer, and condemned man that I am."

"My crime is greater."

"Impossible."

"I defy the king."

The mounted soldiers stopped. They were parallel to the archers some eighty yards distance from Annora and Rian.

"Explain yerself," Rian spoke low and quick. He knew there were but moments left.

"His majesty has arranged my marriage to one of his kinsmen. I flee to evade the king's will."

Rian heard Annora's reply, he saw the archers raise their bows, and a burst of exhilaration tore through him. He was alive. Every sense was heightened, every emotion was sharpened as never before, and he laughed, loud and fearless. " 'Tis, indeed, the whole English army ye'll be putting at my heels, Annora Picot.''

Savage laughter resounded through the clearing. One of the horses nickered. The line of archers became a cluster.

Rian's laughter faded away. He was grinning, yet his eyes didn't waver from the soldiers. "Only ye, Annora Picot, among all women, would dare such defiance. 'Tis a delight to consider ye naysaying an English king. Indeed, there is no other woman who would shun such a lofty match.'' A wealth of emotions twisted through Rian. They grabbed at his heart, embedded themselves within his soul. By the light of the Virgin's sweet face, this was caring. It knocked into him with the impact such as one gets falling from a horse. Rian's heart swelled. He cared for this woman, mayhap more than life itself. This rush of energy gave him the ultimate sensation of being alive, and the thrill of imminent danger took on a whole new dimension. For the first time, he would be fighting for something, for someone, and that prospect emboldened him. It gave him hope and courage.

He slid off his horse, and with a slap to the animal's rump, sent the creature cantering straight toward the English. "Perhaps they will be content with yer gold."

"You cannot . . ." Annora raised her heels as if to spur her horse in pursuit.

With an oath, Rian grabbed the bridle. He dragged her from the saddle. Annora's horse bolted, and Rian flung himself—pulling Annora as he went—into the overgrown field.

Pfst. Psft. The hiss of arrows sliced the air.

Rian rolled, again taking Annora with him. The arrows landed in dirt, and he let go of Annora to peer through the tall grass. The archers were advancing. "What do ye know of warfare?" he asked, while groping the ground as if he'd lost something of importance.

"Enough to know we are outnumbered, and I will not reach Wicklow."

"Och, *leannán*, 'tis not yet the end. Not yet," he consoled, the last two words distorting to a savage roar. The fierce cry did not let up but went on and on, shrill and fierce, as Rian stood and swung his arm. Something flew from his hand. One of the archers yelped. A stone had hit him in the face. He dropped his bow, and Rian let out a jubilant whoop, then ducked back into the grass. Cold perspiration beaded his brow. He was groping in the dirt again. "Do ye trust me?"

"I do."

"Ye must know I'll not be letting them get their hands on ye."

The day was hot, yet the way he spoke made Annora shiver.

"Och, Annora, ye must not be frightened." Rian paused, and risked a moment to look into her eyes. Time and sight and sound were racing by in a blur. He wanted to make certain she understood what he said next. "Fear not, *leannán*, I'll save my final breath to take ye with me."

Through a veil of gathering tears, Annora stared at Rian. There was no mistaking the dreadful tenderness in Rian's words. No mistaking what he'd meant. Only a man who cared would pledge himself to such an awful task. There could be nothing more telling than that. A tear slid down her cheek.

With the back of one hand, Rian caught that first tear, and an anguished moan was torn from his soul. "Nay. Do not waste yer final moments in weeping. In sorrow."

"It is no waste. No sorrow." There were more tears.

He wiped her other cheek. One of the soldiers called out to them. It was an order to surrender, but Rian did not reply. He was confronting his greatest failure. He was guilty—he admitted in this final moment—as guilty as he'd been with Muiríol. He had not kept this woman secure as he'd promised. He had failed her this day as surely as he'd failed his young wife. As surely as he'd failed Annora four years before.

In this final moment, there was naught by which to judge him save negligence and excessive self-indulgence. A stark naught. *Would that it might have been otherwise.* But he had not known, had not imagined, had not cared until it was too late. Rian swore to God that if he were given another chance he would not fail again. He beseeched the Lord to spare them, vowing not to discard Annora but to treasure and care for her, and to bestow upon her everything a woman deserved.

In that gem-bright field whilst facing certain death, Rian O'Byrne plighted his troth before God.

"Ye must take shelter in those rocks." He squeezed her hand, then let go. "Pray for us, *leannán*, and wait for me. Now, go," he hollered. "Go!" He bellowed a violent battle cry and leapt up to meet his enemies.

From the outcrop, Annora watched the scene before her.

One of the hobilars galloped toward Rian. The thunder of hooves was deafening. Overhead, the sky was darkening. The charging hobilar lowered his spear and aimed it at Rian's chest.

But Rian did nothing. Why hadn't he drawn his sword? He stood in the middle of the path as if he were a target for archery practice.

The galloping grew louder. Then Rian threw something, and as before, a soldier howled. This time, it was the charging hobilar who had been hit by a stone. He lost concentration, and it was then that Rian acted, unsheathing his enormous long sword to knock the dazed spearman from his saddle.

Dark crimson appeared across the hobilar's back. He tried to stand. Another rain of arrows shot through the storm-gray sky, and Rian raised his wicker shield to protect himself. There came the horrible sound of arrows piercing wood. Annora heard Rian curse. She saw him go down, swallowed by the tall grass.

All consideration for her own safety fled Annora. She dashed into the clearing with no thought except to help Rian.

"Get back!" Rian yelled. He wasn't injured, and didn't understand why she was running toward him. "Go back! Back!" *Before it's too late*.

The archers were pulling taut their bow strings, the wounded soldier was struggling to his feet, and the second hobilar was bearing down upon their end of the clearing.

And the storm broke.

An incredible whirlwind engulfed Annora. The fluttering of a thousand wings as if a flock of swans were taking flight drowned out Rian's warning. She heard hooves pounding earth, and the wail and flutter, howl and moan of wind bringing a storm. Great black clouds roiled above the tree tops. A flash of lightning blinded her. She stopped running and called out to Rian. She couldn't see him. Twigs and leaves, dirt and petals swirled around her. She didn't see the archers drop their bows and flee.

Panting hard, she tried to get her breath. She strained for a better view of what was happening, and through the whirly of leaves and twigs, she saw a soldier astride his horse. Her breath caught. He had only to lean down and extend an arm to touch her, but he didn't move. There was terror in his eyes. His was the face of a man who believed in the power of amulets and forest demons more than faith in Jesus Christ, the face of a man who had been visited by his own pagan nightmare. Annora watched him force the horse backward several paces before wheeling the animal around to hasten away.

"Rian? Where are you?" Annora covered her face against the swirling debris. She pressed through the screen of flying twigs and soon came upon him, not lying in the grass with an arrow through him but standing without any evidence of injury, staring at something behind her. The wind was dying down. She glanced over her shoulder but saw nothing. "We cannot tarry. Do you hear me, Rian? There is little time," She raised her voice to get his attention. "Please, *Rian!* We must hasten to find my coffer."

Slowly Rian faced Annora. He didn't need to ask if she'd seen the dazzling circle of white that had formed about her as if the stars had been swept from the sky. He had heard confusion and panic in her voice, and had seen the way she flailed at the swirling debris, but not once had she looked up at the beings in shining bright garments that hovered round her. No mortal could have ignored such a sight if it had been revealed to them. Annora had no idea what had occurred in this clearing.

It had not been the wind whistling through the wilderness, but a chorus of ageless voices in song. What the English had seen and heard had terrified them into flight, while Rian had experienced not fear but reverence. For the first time in his life, he believed in true grace, and it could mean only one thing.

Rian thought about the promise he'd made in those final moments. It was the only entreaty he'd ever made to the Lord, and Rian had seen it answered before his eyes. That was true grace. A miracle. A promise to be upheld.

In that moment, wonderment replaced the harshness that had marked his face for too long. His smile was tender. The light in his eyes reflected the serenity that comes to a man when he finally knows what it is he wants in life. Annora Picot. She was everything he wanted in a woman—beautiful, sharp-witted, spirited, sensual—and God had given her to him. "What did ye say?"

"My coffer. We must be after it."

"Nay, going after yer gold is not worth the danger."

"But I cannot leave Ireland without it."

"Ye're not leaving Ireland."

"Do you abandon me?" she gasped.

"To the contrary, sweetheart. I'm not letting ye go. *Co sirinn soirche is doirche let cach lá is gach énaidche.*"

"What are you saying?" She didn't understand the Irish any more than his smile, or the sudden hope that flooded her. Her heart skipped a beat.

"*Co sirinn soirche is doirche let cach lá is gach énaidche.* I am kidnapping ye, Annora Picot, *that I might roam through light and dark with you every day and every night.* Do ye understand me now?"

Understanding was one thing. Believing was another. Annora needed to hear it again, and when she asked him, Rian readily confirmed his intentions.

"I'm taking ye into the hills. I'm stealing ye for my own as I should have done when I left Dublin with the chieftains."

Giddiness was a rare emotion for Annora, yet she experienced it now in abundance. A joyous, almost girlish euphoria, and it was accompanied by an ephemeral vision. A host of faeries come to bless her. Wasn't that what the Dublin gossips had always claimed? *Blessed by faeries.* It must be true. What else could account for the events of this day? Against all odds, Rian O'Byrne had not only saved her, he was offering her a future, and there was no coffer of gold nor anything else she wanted more than to be with him.

"Ye'll come with me?" Rian asked. "Willingly?"

"Aye. Willingly and gladly." Annora went into his arms. It didn't matter why Rian was doing this, or that he hadn't spoken of love or marriage. She could ask for nothing more than to be with the one man who had always wanted her for no reason other than herself. That was blessing enough for her.

Rian kissed her forehead. From this moment onward, his life was never going to be the same, yet he knew not fear or apprehension, nor resentment or disappointment. Indeed, he was willing to concede that the angels might have won after all. He was willing to believe he'd never actually lost his soul, only forgotten it. Until this woman. He kissed her again, once on each cheek, then gave a rueful, apologetic smile.

"Would that I might be making love to ye in this very meadow, but 'tis not safe for us here. But, this night, *croidheag*, it will be different," he murmured in a hoarse, full-deep voice. He called her *mistress of his desires*. "This night when we are within the palisades of a strong Irish fortress, I will be making love to ye from moonrise 'til the break of day."

Chapter 25

Rian made for the O'Connor stronghold within the dark, close fastness of Glenmalur. He set a pace like that of the *éaschlaghs,* the female runners who carried news through the mountains. Annora tore off her kirtle at the knees to allow more freedom of movement and didn't complain when her feet bled, but used the remnants of her kirtle to wrap them. She showed no fear when they made their way across rivers and through swamp.

It was dark when they entered Glenmalur, descending hand over hand through a steep, wooded ravine. Rian knew the way to Baravore as well as he did to Aghavannagh. More than once he'd sought the shelter of this valley, more than once he'd returned here under the cover of night from a raid upon the English. It was a haunted place. Legend claimed there were *sidhe* in Glenmalur, living in their faerie palaces within the earth, deep inside the mountains, beneath the foaming waters of the Avonbeg, and they only came out to dance in the moonlight and tempt men to sin.

Rian and Annora were safe in this valley where the English dared not trespass. They followed the river upstream toward a point of light. The beacon at Baravore had flickered since the first hill fort had fortified the rise above the stream from whence its name had come. Every night the chieftain's wife set a torch in the tower to guide warriors home, to welcome souls in need of shelter.

By virtue of its site and construction, Baravore was an inpenetrable fortress. Situated at the most remote end of the glen, and below the towering heights of Conavalla and Lugnaquillia, the fortification was distinguished by two massive towers, and a keep, deep fosse, old wooden palisade, and inner and outer bailey walls. Within the security of its ramparts resided a sizable community that included the chieftain's wife and children, their spouses and offspring, and extended to a multitude of others, who by ties of blood or service considered Baravore their home, and Bran O'Connor the chieftain to whom they owed allegiance. Smoke from dozens of fires curled into the night sky above the fortress.

An owl hooted as a small door set inside the heavier double gate that was Baravore's main entrance opened to Rian and Annora. Within the *lios* was a jumble of dwellings, a church, stables, byres, open sheds, kitchens, and storage huts. The night was mild, and this courtyard was as crowded and lively as a fair.

Rian was no stranger here. Greetings were called to him. He nodded to one, waved to another.

There were children. Always children. And wolf-hounds, hens, a ewe bleating for its lamb, and piglets. Many piglets. There were two priests, deep in conversation. Several women scolded blushing girls. Stooped and gray men, broken warriors, loitered about. Ancient aunts, pretty cousins, and shepherdesses with faces burnt by the sun mingled with a midwife, and a healer, nursemaids, cooks. Someone was learning to play the pipes, while another danced joyfully. There was a notable absence of men, the chieftain and his warriors being two days gone for Idrone.

A woman made her way through the throng. She was

Aislinn O'Connor, the chieftain's wife, mistress of this large household, and a woman celebrated for her enduring beauty. With hair as black as midnight, she did not resemble her daughter, the fair-haired Isobel O'Toole, nor did she look anything like the offspring of an English knight. There was something tempestuous about her, and those who knew her well saw it in her quick eyes, something as enchanting and dangerous as the *sidhe* within these hills. Her youngest child and only son, not yet of an age to be a warrior, accompanied her as did a servant holding a torch to light her way.

"Rian O'Byrne, *cá as a dtainic tú?*" she asked without preface. *From whence do ye come?* Her voice was soft and welcoming, yet she spoke with the authority that was hers by marriage. "I had heard ye were bound for Wicklow with an Englishwoman."

"Plans change, aunt, do they not?" Rian scanned the yard. If Aislinn knew that much about his affairs, then the O'Connor warriors who had been at Castlekevin must have returned here earlier in the day. He hoped the Highlander was not among them. "Yer cousins are here?"

"They were impatient and did not stay, for they wish to catch up with Bran and ride alongside their clansmen to meet MacMurrough." Aislinn then faced the woman with Rian. Her years were difficult to judge. She was not young, but she was certainly not old. To the visible eye, she was lovely, but to Aislinn—who had an uncanny sixth sense—Annora's comeliness went beyond bright hair, intelligent eyes, and a pleasing female form. She possessed an aura of vitality, of daring and strength. Aislinn found it hard to believe she was not one of them. In English, she asked, "You are the Englishwoman?"

"I am Annora, aye."

"And I am Aislinn. Welcome to Baravore." Only then did Aislinn notice the sorry condition of the younger

woman's kirtle. Not only was the bottom torn away, there
were other tears, splotches of mud upon it, and briars
snagged throughout its fibers. "What has happened to
bring you to us in such disorder?"

"An ambuscade," said Rian. "The English."

"You are not injured, either of you?" At their negative
replies, Aislinn signed herself. *"Tarr liomsa,* Annora.
Come with me. Let me take you directly to a chamber,
where you can bathe and rest in privacy." In a maternal
gesture, she slipped an arm about Annora and bade her
son run ahead to instruct one of the servants to open the
guest chamber, pour a bath, and bring up refreshments.
They went toward the keep from which the beacon shown.
"I am curious. How do you come to know our Rian?"

"My uncle," replied Annora.

"Is Irish?"

"Nay, not Irish. He is—"

"Sir Thomas Picot, English, and a soldier, but a fair
and noble man. If it were not for Sir Thomas, the
executioner would have had his pleasure, and my head
would—"

Aislinn did not let Rian finish. With sudden urgency,
she asked, "Picot did you say?"

"That's correct," said Rian. They reached the keep
and he stood to one side to let the women enter first. His
aunt led the way up narrow stairs.

"Do you know the year of your birth?" Aislinn asked
Annora.

"My birth year? Why do you ask?"

"You must tell me." Again there was urgency in
Aislinn's voice. It was a strange, almost beseeching tone.

At the next level, light spilled onto the landing. The
door to the guest chamber was wide open, the inside was
aglow. Aislinn paused in the doorway to ask Annora,
"Your birth year? Do you know it?"

"It was a year or two after the statute."

The color drained from Aislinn's face. She supported her slender frame against the door frame. She looked very fragile.

"Aunt, are ye ill?"

As if shooing away some pesky fly, Aislinn waved an impatient hand at Rian. She remained focused on Annora. "Your mother was Catherine?"

"How would you know that?" Annora was on the threshold, uncertain whether to go forward or backward. It should gladden her to meet someone who had known her mother, but it didn't. Instead it was troubling. "Were you friends? In Dublin, mayhap?"

"Nay, your mother and I were not friends. Yet one long ago summer, our lives came together for a brief moment in time, and we befriended each other." Aislinn laughed. It was an unsettled, melancholy sound. " 'Tis a miserable understatement. *Befriend.* 'Twas much more than that. Much more. Catherine Picot saved my life, and that of the man who became my husband. Indeed, it was a summer of miracles."

Annora was amazed. It seemed as if Catherine were standing beside her and whispering in her ear, *"Someday I will tell you the most remarkable story of a miracle, and how a great tempest surged out of the sea to change many a life."*

How often Catherine had spoken those words. How often she had promised. Annora looked at the woman standing against the door frame, the daughter of an English knight, the wife of an Irish chieftain. She whispered her discovery, "I know who you are, Aislinn O'Connor. You were one of the hostages."

"Catherine told you?"

"Never the whole story."

"What then? How much?"

"Only that there were hostages, and that somehow she came to know them through my uncle."

"And the ending?"

"That she aided your escape one night. But she did not know what happened after."

"What else?"

"I know nothing more. Although my mother many times promised one day to explain the miracle, she never did."

"Catherine is dead?" Aislinn was visibly shaken.

"Aye."

"You have been alone since?"

"I have."

Aislinn frowned, not in anger but in deep sadness. "You must excuse me, Annora Picot. If you wish, we can talk in the morning, but for now, I would that Rian might help me to my chamber." This time, she did not shoo him away but held his forearm as if she might collapse otherwise. She kissed Annora upon the cheek. *Forgive me for being such a poor hostess this night, and forgive me on the morrow.* "Good night. You will forgive me for rushing away like this?"

"Of course. You must not concern yourself."

But Aislinn did not hear Annora. She heard naught but her own troubled thoughts.

Not in a thousand lifetimes had Aislinn dreamt to see the child again. Never had she imagined that she might come face-to-face with what she had done that summer. She had always prayed to God for His understanding. Surely He knew she'd only done what she believed was best. For nearly thirty years she'd clung to the belief that He did not hold her in disdain or disapproval.

But what of mortals? Would they be so forgiving?

Chapter 26

❦❦❦

"Stay, Rian. *Tar asteac sa tseamra,"* Aislinn
said. *Come into the room.*

They entered her chamber, and his aunt went to a
window.

"There is something I must tell ye, and there is
something ye must be doing for me." She opened the
shutters. Moon and stars cast their pale light over the
mountains, and she gazed to the northwest in the direction of the old pass to Imail. "Ye remember the summer
of the great tempest, do ye not?"

Rian's blood chilled. He'd been young, still a wean,
and going about with the women instead of the men, yet
he remembered the summer of the great tempest as it had
come to be called. He remembered one afternoon in
particular, when he'd gone into the forest with his mother
and the other women to gather mushrooms.

There had been no lads his size or age with whom to
play that day. Only a silly girl named Éva, who had been
visiting from another glen and had been scared of
everything. And Éva's baby sister, who had been even
less useful, having been brand-new and mewling in her
basket.

Still, he had played with Éva. It was better than being
alone. Indeed, what boy wished to play at Ostmen and

300

Slaves, if there was no one to enslave? They had wandered away from the others and down to the river. Later Éva had said how he'd taunted her into going. She had cried how she would have never disobeyed. It had been his fault not hers that they'd gone down to the river. Of course, she'd enjoyed playing at the water's edge as much as he had, chasing caddis flies and trying to catch minnows. But when he'd suggested they wade to the wee isle a few yards from the riverbank, Éva had been frightened.

"Don't ye know the kelpies will drag ye down and carry ye out to sea? Water witches with long green hair, they be. Living in the deepest pools and waiting for children, such as yerself, who would disturb their water." Éva had hardly been big enough to scream like a proper slave, but she'd been old enough to believe in river spirits. She'd hurried off to tell her mother about the naughty boy who was going to wade in the kelpie's pool.

Good-ridden of Éva, Rian had dashed into the water, splashing and kicking, deeper, deeper until he popped under the surface, sputtering and gasping only to discover that he could float. Like a sleek little otter, he'd swum to the isle.

"Rian, where are ye?"

He'd heard one of the women calling from the shore, and thinking it was Éva's doing, he hadn't replied.

"Show yerself, lad."

No doubt she had tattled, and having no wish for a talking-to, he'd hidden in the lily plants and rushes, sedges and reeds. He hadn't known that his mother had needed to lie upon the childbed. The women were returning to the fortress to take his mother to the hut of the women.

"Rian, will ye be answering us now!" Éva's granny had called out. She was a mean old crow and was certain to punish him. He had not answered.

From his hiding place, he'd watched Éva and her mother walking along the riverbank, calling for him.

Éva hadn't believed they could get past the kelpies. Silly Éva. She hadn't even looked toward the little isle. Rian had muffled a giggle, thinking at her fright if she knew he could swim, and he'd crouched lower in the water-lily roots. He hadn't known his mother was gone back to the fortress.

"Rian!" the old granny had called again. " 'Tis time to be leaving, lad. We're heading back after yer mam. Can ye not . . ." Her old voice had erupted into a piercing scream of terror.

Soldiers. Rian had seen them, and trembled with more fear than he might know for any water witch. Soldiers. Big men, armored like awful beasts. Talking in a strange, harsh tongue. Soldiers crushing the plants and grasses along the river beneath their great feet. The women were shrieking to the high heavens. Soldiers slapping, pulling hair, prodding, shoving. Soldiers dragging away Éva, and her granny, and her mother.

The little boy hadn't made a sound, hadn't come out of hiding.

Night had fallen, and he'd stayed in the water with the eels and minnows, the water skimmers and beetles, the salmon and great-mouthed perch. He'd shivered from cold and from fear, afraid the lampreys might feast upon his toes or a thousand leeches might affix themselves to him. Kelpies might not go abroad in daylight, but who could tell what could happen when the sun set? He hadn't moved. And at last in sleep, he'd dreamt. Odd dreams, haunted dreams, wicked dreams. Rian dreamed he'd sprouted tiny gills and never returned to land, but lived forever among the lilies and eels, minnows and efts.

Only when his father had appeared on the shore in the morning light had he come out of the water forest.

"What happened here?" one of the warriors with his father had demanded.

There had been many questions. Was it true? Were there English in the hills? Some of the women had not returned. Children had gone missing. What did the boy know of these things?

"'Tis the lad's fault!" someone had exclaimed after Rian had told them what he'd witnessed. "They would have been inside the fortress with the others if it weren't for him."

"In the water, were ye, now?" the priest had said when they'd returned to the fortress. "Have ye not been taught what evil comes of doing the unnatural? If God had wanted mankind to be swimming, He would have given out fins. But I see no fins on ye, lad. No fins. Though mayhap a forked tail."

"Hush, fool. *Tá seisean na buachaill mait,*" his father had said. *He is a good boy.*

And for the moment the priest had been silent. But as days had turned to sennights, and seasons had passed, there had been many who'd found it easy to blame a child.

That summer of the tempest, English soldiers had combed the hills, venturing higher and deeper into the wilderness than ever before. They had been taking hostages, Irish women and children to hold in exchange for the good behavior of their fathers, husbands, sons, and brothers.

The mighty tempest had ravaged the whole of *terra pacis* from Dublin to Wicklow town. What trees that had not been pulled up by their roots had been blown bare, the leaves of orchards and woodlands had been turned to brown and yellow by sea salt. Fruit had withered on limb and vine, wheat had gone moldy, grain had rotted. Fields and gardens had been flooded. Homes and livestock, even families had been swept away, and naught but mud and death left in their wake.

The English were wrought with apprehension that the savage natives, finding themselves in equal want and deprivation, would descend upon their settlements to raid their meager stores. Little did they know the tempest had not wreaked devastation upon *terra guerre*. The English could not reason beyond their fear of the Irish. And of famine. There had been other storms, other disasters, and always starvation and pestilence followed. The English were sore afraid, and brought as many hostages as they could to Dublin. It was one of the ways they'd always tried to hold off famine.

Upon learning of this, warriors had prepared to ride against the English. Although they had no designs upon their stores, they did not trust the strangers to treat their women and children with compassion or respect. A rescue party had formed. O'Connors and O'Byrnes, Kavanaghs, O'Tooles, MacMurroughs, and O'Mores, and even an English knight, the Lady Aislinn's father, had slipped into Dublin wearing a leper's shroud. And all—save one—were rescued and returned. It was the miracle of the tempest. Every Irish mother and wife came home; every father, brother, son, and husband. But not every girl child, every sister, every daughter. Éva's mewling baby sister was gone forever, and the old priest had blamed the wean, Rian O'Byrne.

"In the water! Swimming, ye dare to call it!" the priest had condemned him. "The angels and devils have fought over yer soul, Rian O'Byrne, and 'tis clear the devils have won charge over it. There is already a place amid the flames awaiting ye. There will be no heaven for a dark soul such as yers."

The boy had believed himself damned. Damned for the death of another child, one younger, more helpless, and totally innocent. Damned for eternity.

"The memories remain with me, aye," said Rian. "Do ye not remember, aunt, how they blamed me when—"

"I remember, but was hoping ye did not. *Is truag liom é,*" Aislinn said. *I am sorry for it.* "It was a callous burden for a small lad, and 'tis hoping ye'll be able to forgive me, I am.''

"There is no reason—''

"Och, but there is.'' Aislinn faced him. She saw the fearless warrior and remembered a lonely, quiet boy. "I—I knew the truth and said nothing. Mind ye, I did not know right away. But later, I still kept my silence. I always believed 'twas the best course. But how do we know? How do any of us know?''

"Ye talk of imparting my forgiveness upon ye, aunt, but I do not understand yer role in any of this. *Creud is ciall do sin?*'' Rian said. *What is the meaning?* His mind searched for an explanation. He thought of how Aislinn had been among the hostages, of how she had come to know Catherine Picot that summer, and he thought of miracles and missing babies. Could it be that Éva's mewling baby sister had not died? It could not be any more amazing than what had happened in the clearing this afternoon. Before Aislinn could reply, he asked, "Annora is Íde's babe?''

"That she is.''

"But how?''

"There were hostages taken from many glens that summer, and their captors followed different routes through the mountains and up the coast to a rendezvous point in the vale. We were gathered together in an orchard at a place called Shankill, and it was there that a young mother implored my help. She had two bairns, an infant and a little girl, and the soldiers had threatened to leave the wee ones at the side of the road if she could not keep them quiet. Thus it was that I took the babe, thinking only to carry her for a time. Her name was *Onóra,* and at Dublin Castle when I was separated from the other hostages, I tried to give Onóra back to her mother, but she would not have her. *Make sure my Onóra lives.* Those were her final words, and I—being thought a chieftain's wife—was separated from the other hostages and held in a fortified tower some distance from the castle, wherein a young and wealthy widow resided.''

"Catherine Picot."

"Aye, and from the first, I saw the longing on Catherine's face when she gazed upon the sweet babe. Living in luxury, she was, having every comfort and owning not a single need with the exception of one thing. Catherine Picot had no child, and while we were in her tower, she cared and tended, held and rocked that infant with more motherly love than I had known possible. Then came the night of our escape. Bran was there and your uncle Dallán O'Byrne, and in the streets, there were English soldiers searching for Irish. It was time to leave, the babe was in my arms, and in that final moment, I heard the young mother's voice imploring me, beseeching me, *Make sure my Onóra lives*.''

"There was no predicting if we would survive the night or be captured. I did not know how the hostages in the castle fared. So many things to consider. So little time. Mayhap the child was an orphan. I did not know, and therefore I decided the best way to fulfill the mother's plea was to leave her infant with Catherine Picot. Indeed, it seemed to me a miracle of sorts that the gentle young woman, widowed and childless, would have a babe to cherish, and the babe would have a home in which there would never be want or hardship.''

"Ye placed Íde's babe into Catherine's care, do ye say?''

Aislinn nodded, remembering the exact moment she had put Onóra into Catherine's arms.

"She was never mine, but entrusted to me. I was asked to make sure she lived, and since there is no guarantee for our safety this night, I entrust her to you, Catherine, with the same entreaty. Make sure Onóra lives.''

"Do not worry, Aislinn Clare, your trust is not misplaced. Onóra will live and flourish, this I pledge to you on my own life. No daughter of mine could be more

cherished than this child shall be. She will know love and learning, generosity, courage and kindness, and someday, I will tell her the most remarkable story of a miracle, and how the tempest changed our lives."

"Was I right? Was it a good life Catherine gave her?"

"Och, aunt, more than right." Rian told Aislinn about Annora's charmed life, and about the love and friendship and devotion between mother and child. For the first time in many years, tears pricked Rian's eyelids. Tears for Catherine's joy and for Íde's suffering. Tears for Aislinn's doubts. Tears for Annora, and for himself. "But why did ye never tell?"

"It was several years before I knew the child had been an O'Toole. Then it was too late. Or it seemed to me. Íde had other children, and I did not imagine anyone, let alone yerself, oft concerned themselves with the babe. I could only think of how Catherine would suffer. It seemed a horrible prospect to set in motion something that might visit unhappiness upon such a generous, kindhearted soul. Íde had other children, the woman Catherine, mayhap only the one. I did what I believed was right, and have always prayed the Lord would judge me kindly. But now that is of the past. She is returned to us. 'Tis another miracle, is it not?"

Again Rian chilled. An awful notion came to him. Mayhap Annora had not been saved for him. Mayhap she was not his to keep and cherish, but to return to her family. His belly tightened into a hard knot. By God's splendor, why had he not earlier seen that they had been brought together for a greater purpose than his own satisfaction? They had been saved that he might finally right the wrong he'd set in motion, and to keep her for himself would be a wanton, selfish deception. Indeed, an unholy defiance of fate, and whether one believed in God and Jesus or in the old gods, to disregard fate would lead to disaster. This was a test. His chance to redeem himself.

There was one thing he must do. He must take Annora to Imail and return her to Íde O'Toole. Only then could he think of his own future.

Rian went to the guest chamber and found Annora standing before an open window. Her skin was scrubbed, her hair was combed to her waist, and she was wearing a white tunic that touched her bare feet and had long flowing sleeves. She had the look of a maid on her wedding night. An angel.

"Do you think the soldiers will come after me?" she asked.

"Ye're safe. Do not worry about that." Rian went to her side. A pleasant breeze teased her hair. He reached out to her, and one hand wandered over the soft loops. "They'll not be bothering ye ever again."

"What is it then?" She didn't like the look in his eyes.

"Yer journey has been a long one, Annora Picot. But it has not ended. *Is iar mbarr fedha ro-sna do churchan tar inrada.*" He took her hand in his. One by one, Rian threaded his fingers between hers, deliberately, slowly, and then bringing their entwined hands close to his mouth, he whispered, *"Over ridges, along the top of a wood has yer coracle sailed,* and still there is farther to go."

"To your home?" Her voice was composed, but she was baffled inside. The ominous tone in his voice made her anxious.

"Nay, Annora, not to Aghavannagh." He kissed her fingers, and for a long moment held them against his cheek. His voice was low and deliberate. "Though ye know not of what I speak, ye must believe me. Something extraordinary accounts for why we were not killed this afternoon, and for a while I mistook the reason. We were not spared that I might take ye into the hills for myself. We were saved that I might be returning ye to where ye belong."

Where ye belong. Her anxiety turned to alarm. "Please, you must not take me back to Dublin."

"Hush, 'tis not that. *Eisd an i a deirim leat.*" He pulled her into his arms and held her close. *"Hear what I say to ye.* Ye must believe me. 'Tis nothing fearful. There is a place for ye. A place where ye're meant to be, and I'll be seeing ye safely there." Beyond that Rian could not bring himself to reveal anything more. He was a coward, and had fain accepted his aunt's offer to tell Annora about Íde and the Irish baby that had been left in Dublin. They would stay another day or two at Baravore, and by the time they left for Imail, Annora would know the truth. "I've not let any harm come to ye, have I? And I'll not be letting any come to ye now."

"A place? But I do not want *a place,*" said Annora. She wanted *someone.* She wanted Rian, and she would have him. Here among the Irish no law stood between them any longer. No bigoted English society, no parliament, no English king, or royal bridegroom. Annora would make Rian stop talking nonsense and think of her. Of them. This night, and tomorrow.

Turning within his comforting embrace, Annora molded her body along the length of his, hooked her arms about his neck, and raised her face to his. She whispered in the tiny space between their lips, "And after you take me to this place? What then, Rian?"

She let the tip of her tongue run along his bottom lip, and liking the taste, she did it again. "What then?"

Rian had no answer. His mind knew not what the future held. There was only this moment, and he let his body speak for him.

His sex quivered against her belly. He was a giant of a man, and Annora felt him expanding, hardening, straining between them. Liquid warmth seeped through her. Emboldened, hungry, she brushed her lips over his. "Will you stay with me?"

He shuddered. Lust shot though him. Sharp, raw, and

with the speed of a hawk as it dives upon its prey. It had always been like this between them. Nothing changed that.

Chapter 27

In the morning, the mistress of Baravore invited Annora to visit with her. The day was pleasant, and they sat in Aislinn's sunny, walled garden.

"I am pleased Rian has decided you will stay with us a few days."

"So am I. The break in our journey is most welcomed," said Annora, glad that Rian did not seem in a hurry to deliver her to the place of which he'd spoken so mysteriously yesternight. "It is lovely here."

"And very much like the garden in which I played with my brothers as a girl. I have always found great comfort in this place." Aislinn smiled as she looked about her. It was, indeed, a special place, bee-loud and madder-sweet. "Those medlar and quince were seeded from fruit grown in my mother's garden at Killoughter, and the holly trees yonder were grafted from those that cluster round her grave. After my father's holdings were seized by the crown, there was a new lord and knight at Killoughter, and when I wanted clippings and roots, my husband stole into the castle for them. It will ever make me smile to think upon the night he returned. I could not have loved him more than when he gave me the booty of that particular raid upon the English. Your mother had a garden, too, did she not?"

"She did, and how wonderful it was, bright with roses that bloomed from the Feast of Saint Dúnchad to the first frost."

"Ah, yes, Catherine's roses. Quite the focus of her attentions, I recall. They suffered in the tempest, and she spent every moment she might staking, pruning, and raking. There was a servant to help her, but I saw how much she enjoyed the work herself, for she had a caring nature, and needed living things to tend and nurture. Those roses were Catherine's first children, I ween. The garden filled her days before she had you."

While they talked Aislinn attended to the task of taking down the hem of her son's tunic. Although it had been new at Easter, the garment was already too short for him. He was seven years old and growing like a weed. Soon her baby would be a warrior. He was her last child, born after four daughters and more than twenty years of marriage. His name was Ciaran, and he was the image of what she imagined her husband must have been as a child, dark and handsome, and mayhap too serious. Aislinn finished with one tunic and started to remove the stitches from another. Offhand, she said, "Rian O'Byrne intends to take you to the Glen of Imail."

"Imail," Annora repeated the unfamiliar name. "He did not tell me where he would take me. Or why. You know, do you not?"

"Aye, the why of what he intends is known to me." Aislinn glanced up from pulling stitches. She stared toward the mountains. " 'Tis the miracle of the tempest coming full circle. 'Tis the tale of a child cursed, a mother heartbroken, and a gesture well-meant that brought about as much joy as pain." It was hard for Aislinn to speak of this, hard to know what to say. "Forgive me. I talk in riddles."

Annora saw how Aislinn's hands, no longer busy with their task, twisted the tunic fabric. In response, she touched the older woman's forearm in reassurance. "You need not tell me, if—"

"But I must." Aislinn closed her eyes. Her hands ceased their fidgeting and she patted Annora's wrist as if to indicate, *A moment more, and I will be fine.* "It begins with that long ago summer of the tempest when I was a hostage and came to know Catherine Picot. The why of what Rian intends is wrapped within the story of what happened to one of the hostages, a mother who made a haunting, heartbreaking choice. She was very young, being not much older than my Isobel's Órla, and the decision she made was one that no mother should ever face. But she was brave, and strong, and motivated by naught but love. She did the best she could. In order to save her children, she gave up one of them."

"And was it?" asked Annora. The sad tale tightened about her heart. She had to know what happened. "Was it the best choice?" This reminded her of the children left outside Our Lady of Victory in the dark of night. Had their mothers struggled with the decision to abandon them at the convent gate? She thought of how it would have broken Catherine's heart to give up her child. Surely Catherine would have been haunted 'til her dying day with concern and worry, guilt and hope. "Did the child survive? Did the mother ever find her?"

"Soon. Soon I will tell you. But first you must know what happened to a little boy that summer long ago. A lad, not old enough to know of malice, who trusted in those older and wiser to school and protect him, guide and foster him. He had no reason to doubt the word of a priest, and that summer, the boy came to believe he was wicked and damned, that he was to blame for the tragedy the young mother endured. His only mistake was a childish one of hiding from those who might spoil his fun. He was only a child at play, and for that his innocence was destroyed before its time. Robbed, too, was his faith. Taken not by the brutality of war or the bigotry of the English, but by those very souls a good Irish child would trust; and in the place of innocence and faith, he accepted despair and loneliness into his soul. He was condemned.''

"You speak of Rian?'' Annora's heart was heavy with anguish for the man who claimed nothing for his own beyond momentary pleasure. There were tears in her eyes for the man, who believing himself cursed, had denied himself a future. Her heart ached for the warrior who could create images upon vellum with a depth of emotion most mortals never possessed. She sent up a silent Ave Maria that whatever was to happen at this place called Imail would, at last, free him.

"Aye, the lad was Rian, only a wean when that young mother lost her baby. 'Twas horrible and mean-spirited to burden a child in that way, especially when the blame was foremost with the English, and in part with myself. Aye, me. For the mother gave the infant into my care, and I failed to bring her back to the hills when I escaped.'' Aislinn paused and forced herself to meet Annora's gaze. Slowly, precisely, she said, "The babe was a wee girl. Her name was Onóra, her mother told me, and I gave the baby Onóra to Catherine Picot.''

A sudden chill raised tiny bumps up and down the bare flesh of Annora's arms. "Onóra. That is the Irish form of my name,'' she whispered. There was a pounding in her head, for in that moment the world began to spin one way while Annora went in the opposite direction. Myriad memories rushed past her. All the times her mother had mentioned the miracle. All the times she had asked about the Irish in the hills. The festivities in the garden each summer upon the anniversary of her birth. Her mother's intense, unfailing, and generous love. And the secret. There was always the hovering secret that Catherine guarded so well.

"It is, and as the English were prohibited by the statute from using Irish names, a baby named Onóra—''

"Would become Annora," she said softly, stricken.

A strange silence settled over that corner of the universe. From the other side of the wall came children's laughter, the clang of iron on an anvil, and the sloshing, digging sounds of workers deepening the fosse. Somewhere a baby cried, a dog barked, a man swore.

"You accept this?" Aislinn asked at length. She needed to be busy and began to fold Ciarán's tunics.

"How could I not? There can be no reason to tell me such a tale were it not true." Annora fought back tears wrought by confusion and shock, and by an overwhelming sense of destiny. "You are right, Aislinn O'Connor. The miracle comes full circle." The whimsical lyrics of a nursery rhyme sang through Annora's mind, *I had a little daughter, they called her Peep-Peep.* Far away, from another time and place, she heard Catherine's sweet, musical voice on those nights when she'd been small and afraid of the dark. Then she heard herself singing the same tune to Catherine in those final months.

The first half of the circle was complete. She and Catherine had received miracles aplenty, and it was time for others to receive their blessings.

"You are full-quiet." Aislinn watched Annora, carefully. The babe had grown into a woman who appeared as forgiving as Catherine Picot and as resolute as Íde O'Toole. With two such mothers, it was no wonder Annora Picot was not screaming denials or swooning in the dirt. "Do you understand what I am trying to tell you?"

"I do," Annora said in a choked voice. She would not say aloud, *That I am not Catherine's child,* for it wasn't true. Nothing would change the face of the woman who had held her in the rose garden, who had taught her to walk and ride, to read and scribe, and to sing French rounds; the woman who had indulged her, and allowed her the independence to do as she wished in the wool trade. Though not of her flesh and blood, Catherine would always be the mother of Annora's heart and soul. That would never change, and she knew what Catherine would expect her to do. *So my little daughter, she climbed up the mountain high.* She would expect her to cross the mountains to the Glen of Imail, and seek out the mother of her flesh and blood.

"Please, what can you tell me about the woman I will meet on the other side of the mountains?" asked Annora.

Aislinn sighed at this absolute demonstration of Annora's acceptance. Catherine Picot had raised the babe to a remarkable woman. Íde's hopes had been more than fulfilled. And the decades of self-reproach for having committed a reprehensible misdeed began to lift from Aislinn.

"Her name is Íde. And although she is several winters younger than myself, you will find her a very old woman." Softly, sadly, she said, "She is dying. It is a woman's ailment that came upon her after harvest, and takes her slowly, slowly. 'Tis said she clings to life for one reason. To see her babe, grown, and returned to her. More than once they have tried to convince her the child was among the angels waiting for her, but she refused to believe. Steadfast and determined, that is Íde, who has never stopped hoping. More than once it has been whispered, *Íde is mad. Possessed.* But she laughs at those who would doubt. *'Tis in my heart,* she tells them. This I have heard her speak of myself, and can attest to the conviction in her voice. *Mine is the heart of a mother,* she says, *connected across eternity to my child, to all my children. Fourteen bairns born of my womb, and I forget not one of them. My heart and my soul, they tell me Rígán, Declán, Brion, and the wee twins, Flannán and Flannat, are with the angels, just as surely as they tell me my Onóra lives.*"

"This Íde sounds like a woman I will like," said Annora, satisfied.

" 'Tis true, the Lord works many miracles upon

Ireland, *Ar is lomlan aingel finn on chinn co n-ice ar-oile,*" Annora whispered in awe. "*For it is full of white angels from one end to the other.*"

Four days later Rian and Annora arrived at a stronghold in the hills above Imail. To Annora, this fortress called Keadeen seemed a strange place. It was enclosed by three ramparts of granite boulders and an outer ring of plashed hedge that had been made by plaiting and entwining the shoots and limbs of briar bushes. In the center of these circles was a wooden palisade, and within that was a *lios* with sundry structures of wood and wattle and daub, the walls of the largest, most significant dwelling being plastered in mud and thatch. Annora was accustomed to towered walls and keeps and castles of stone, and seeing this strange place, her confidence sagged.

"I am afraid," she whispered to Rian.

"There is no reason. Look, over there." Rian indicated a small group of women standing about a great vat. "They are yer sisters, Éva and Etan. And their daughters."

Dozens of pairs of eyes looked at the stranger in their midst. Who was she? The tale that Rian O'Byrne traveled with one of the English of Dublin had reached the O'Tooles at Keadeen. They had heard of her beauty. As lovely as any O'Toole, it was being said, for the females of their clan were celebrated through the hills for their fine features, golden hair, and proud bearing, and that any other woman might be as lovely was remarkable. Who could this English woman of Dublin be?

One of the women beside the vat spoke to the others. Annora watched and marveled as they clustered together to speak to one another without being overheard. They were fair-haired to the one, and she was astonished by their similarity of features. The women nodded in agreement, and the tallest of them moved away from the others. "*Dia dhuit, a Rian O'Byrne.*"

"Dia's Muire duit, a Éva O'Toole," he replied. *Good day to you, Éva O'Toole.* "And how are ye and yers here at Keadeen? How is yer mam? She is well, I'm trusting, for we hope to be seeing her this day."

Éva could not utter a single word in reply. She could do no more than stare at the woman with Rian while his words echoed through her mind. The closer she was to the pair of them, the more incredible was the woman's appearance, for it seemed to Éva she could be gazing upon a younger reflection of herself. A thousand emotions flickered over Éva's features. Fear and hope, disbelief, and wonder. Her eyes shimmered with tears as long-suppressed images crowded her mind. A baby in a basket, her mother trying to make her go to a strange woman, her mother giving the baby to the woman, instead. She spoke to Rian, "I'm seeing a vision of a quiet afternoon gone wicked, of the iridescent wings of caddis flies replaced by the glint of helmets, and I'm seeing ye, Rian O'Byrne, just a wee lad, ye were. There's no such creatures as kelpies, ye says to me, calling me silly Éva. There would be no harm coming to us, says ye, if we go out in the water. Och, Rian, but 'tis many a year since I've been thinking of that day."

"Ye were luckier than me, Éva, for those memories were never gone more than a day or two from my thoughts." His voice was low and solemn.

Remorse pricked at Éva. Surely Rian did not carry the burden still? Many years had passed before she'd understood the real harm that had been rendered that afternoon. By then, he'd grown to a warrior, hard and fierce, and she had never imagined such a man might ponder such things. "Will ye ever forgive us, please God?"

He nodded. If he could not, there would be no starting anew, no possibility to find a way with Annora.

Éva dared to ask, "Can it be that we three are again together as we were that day?"

"It is so, Éva. It is so."

"Ca hainm ata ort?"

Rian turned from Éva to Annora. "Your sister Éva asks, *What is yer name?"*

She squared her shoulders and stepped forward. "I am Annora," came in English, then she said the same in Irish as Rian had taught her while they were crossing the mountains from Baravore. "I am Onóra."

"Onóra," Éva whispered. Her mother's little Ona. This was the sister to whom she owed her life when the English would have killed the both of them. So many times Íde had told Éva of how the soldier had pantomimed strangling the little Irish girls. Many times Éva had been reminded that she remained with her mother because another was gone. Joy swelled within Éva. Ebullient, brilliant joy for her mother, who would have her dream, have her babe, and her vindication. And joy for herself. At last, Éva could stop lying. "Welcome, my sister," she said, for she had a little English. "Glad it is, I am, that ye're among us at last."

"And I am glad to be here."

"A gcuala tú an nuaideact," Éva called to all who had been watching this little drama unfold. Tears were streaming down her face. *"Did ye hear the news?* Look, my mother spoke true. Íde was right. Her Onóra is returned. Her babe comes back to our hills."

Cheering broke out in the yard and rippled through the stables and sheds into the chieftain's dwelling, through its hall and bower. Lads, eager to be men, tested their lungs with whoops and war cries. Everyone talked at once, and the kith and kin of Keadeen pressed forward to welcome one of their own.

In her dark chamber Íde heard the clamor. "What is that, Neassa? Have they found my Ona? My Onóra?" she asked from her bed.

"Hush, old mother, ye must not be troubling yerself," said her daughter-in-law. It was Neassa's turn to sit by

Íde's sickbed this day. She hated it when Íde talked about the dead baby, for she did not have patience to deal with such foolishness. Any noise, any commotion, and it was always the same. *Is my Ona returned?* Neassa shivered. She did not like to be around a crazy woman. Íde was possessed, of a certainty. There could be no other explanation, and Neassa didn't want to be tainted.

Íde tried to rise. "I must see." But with no help from Neassa, she was too weak, and fell back upon the bed, coughing.

In the corridor there were voices. Laughter mingling with tears drifted into the shrouded room. Two slender women appeared on the threshold.

"Éva, is that ye, girl?"

"*Tá,* mam." *Aye.*

"And have ye brought news of my Ona?"

"Aye, mam. *Ta sguela iongantac a-gam dib.*" *I have wonderful news for ye.*

"Open the shutters, Neassa," Íde said, weak but in command. "The shutters, Neassa. The shutters. Let me see who stands with Éva."

Blinding light flooded the chamber. It was the brilliant white of the clouds upon which angels descended to visit mankind. Íde saw nothing for several heartbeats.

Annora took one step into the chamber.

It was a tidy room, and fresh-smelling. There were no extravagant fur rugs, no Venetian mirrors upon the walls, no silver platters with sugared almonds to tempt an ailing woman's appetite, but it was far from a dreary setting. There was color everywhere. Astonishing, glorious color. There were vibrant blue cushions of a hue that must have come from adding insects with wood ash to woad; linens dyed a wonderful crisp yellow were draped over chests; and the walls were hung with washed wool curtains alternating madder red with a celestial purple that the dyers at Our Lady of Victory had long attempted to achieve in their vats.

A bed was positioned to allow its occupant a view both toward the window and door. While the furnishing itself was neither big nor small, and its woodworking was nothing fancy, its curtains, dyed green as the wilderness, were worthy of royalty, being overstitched with leaves and flowers and all the wild creatures of the Irish forest. And there in the middle of that woodland-glorious bed was a gray and withered woman, almost every trace of vibrancy gone from her flesh, from her hair, her lips. Íde O'Toole. The pall of death clung to her as it had to Catherine, and Annora took another step into the room. She went closer to the bed, closer to Íde, noting that as with Catherine it was in Íde's eyes that one might glimpse what remained of this woman's spirit. Faith, there was a spark in her eyes that told Annora Íde O'Toole was used to getting her own way; and certainly, there was intelligence and a glimmer of stubborn perseverance.

Éva propped her mother up against a mound of pillows. Íde blinked to adjust to the sunlight. She tilted her head to one side, and a small smile turned up at the corners of her pale mouth. Faint color rose on her sallow cheeks.

"*An tu Onóra?*" Íde asked. *Are ye Onóra?*

"*Is me,*" Annora replied, using more of her newly learned Irish. *I am.* She swallowed tears.

Íde opened her arms. "*Gab anall anaice liom,*" she said, torn between hope and doubt. Her voice trembled with decades of longing about to be fulfilled. It was hard to trust her failing eyes. "*Come over near me,*" she whispered again.

Annora moved toward the bed, knowing with each step that Catherine was at her side, urging her on, and whispering how right it was to share the bounty of her heart. Reaching the bed, she sat upon the edge and accepted Íde's embrace. Thin arms slipped round her, tentative, as if fearing she might pull away, might vanish, and when that didn't happen, she sensed the frail woman's shudder of relief.

"*Aililiu*," Íde cried in wonder, and Annora smiled.

Rian O'Byrne had, indeed, brought her where she belonged. He was a wise, good man, and Annora would make him accept that.

This was, indeed, a miracle most wondrous.

Annora returned Íde's embrace, holding the ailing woman in younger, stronger arms, as if it were possible to return some meager portion of the warmth and energy that had once flowed from this woman into her.

Chapter 28

⤳⧽⧽⤳

I t was a time to rejoice.

"I am of Ireland,
And the Holy Land of Ireland.
Come out of charity,
And dance with me in Ireland."

Amid the pounding rhythm of bodhrans, and the strain of harp, flute, and pipe, the popular lyrics rose to the rafters at Keadeen. Guests from Kilranelagh and Ballytoole came to celebrate Onóra's return, and for the first time since last harvest, Íde returned to her place in the hall. She wore a fine woolen gown dyed to match the clear blue of her O'Toole eyes; her daughters, including Onóra, wore gowns as yellow as their bright hair; and eleven granddaughters wore plum-colored tunics.

It was a time for salutations.

"Slainte agasda!" In the absence of Íde's eldest son, Éva was the first to toast Annora. *May ye have health!*

Over and over, drinking vessels were raised to the guest of honor that she might have courage, hope, and wisdom. In return, Annora invoked the blessings of posterity, manna, and dominion for the O'Tooles over their ancestral lands.

It was a time for remembering.

Annora's tragedy had never been far from the minds of mothers and children, who lived in dread of the murtherous English. Any one of them, but for the Lord's Grace, could have experienced the same, and they had not forgotten Íde's Onóra. She was a thread in the fabric of their family history.

Conall, the clan *sencha*, recited the O'Toole genealogy. He detailed the ancient glories of their ancestors as well as the feats of warriors whose wives and mothers, daughters and sisters sat before him. Lastly, he told the story of Onóra, daughter of Íde and Cassán, curly-haired, the son of slender Áedan, versifier, son of Bressal, who loved combat, and of how Rian O'Byrne, son of Rónán and Grella of Aghavannagh, had brought her back to Keadeen, having three times saved her from death: first in a blizzard, second, in an escape from Dublin, and third, from ambuscade.

It was not long ere exhaustion overtook Íde, and she fell asleep. Her fourth-born daughter, who was called Cera and spoke English, came forward to attend to her.

"Would you let me see to her this night?" asked Annora. Perhaps it was the reminder of Catherine's illness that motivated her. Or perhaps it was true that the souls of mother and child were connected for eternity in defiance of time and space. Annora didn't regard Íde as a stranger. Verily, she perceived the ailing woman's strength of spirit, and marveled how it had sustained hope and affection for nearly thirty years. Íde had loved her and prayed for her when others had abandoned hope. She had been her mother always, and the knowledge of this drew Annora close.

Cera replied yes, her help would be appreciated, and she informed Éva that Annora would take care of their mother tonight.

"*Taim buideac duitse,*" Éva replied. *I give ye thanks.*

Rian carried the sleeping woman to her chamber and

placed her on the bed as the rousing strain of pipes echoed through the stronghold. Dancing had begun. He watched Annora secure the covers about Íde.

She saw him looking at her, as if he were waiting, and said, "I will stay with her."

He hid his disappointment. Tomorrow he intended to join his father and clansmen to the south at Idrone, and it had been his wish to spend this last night with Annora. He wanted to dance with her until they were both out of breath, perhaps walk with her beneath the stars and pull her into a shadowy corner. But he would not be dancing with Annora this night. There would be no breathless moments, no intimate embraces, not if she wished to stay with Íde. Rian had brought her back to the O'Tooles, and having done so, could not interfere.

"I'd best be biding ye goodnight. *Cadal maith dhuit,*" he said. There was a small bed beneath Íde's, and he pulled it out for Annora. *"A sound sleep to ye."*

She caught his hand when he turned to leave. "Will you not, at least, kiss me good night?"

"Och, *leannán,*" he murmured, the endearment was heavy with regret. "Ye ask for a kiss, but I don't think ye realize what ye do to me. Between us, there can be no such thing as a mere kiss, God bless ye. There's only roaring Beltaine fires, and exploding stars, and whirlpools, and shifting earth, I'm thinking."

Annora blushed. His words made her warm inside. He was right. A kiss was only the beginning. Her eyelashes fluttered down.

Such a reaction was irresistible, and Rian could not but oblige—albeit with the relative safety of an arm's length between them. Holding her elbows, he bent to kiss her. First, his lips rested upon her brow, next the tip of her nose, then upon each closed eye. His mouth brushed the smooth skin below her ear. "On the morrow, *croidheag,* I will allow myself a true kiss. And much more. Much more. On the morrow, *mistress of my desires,* we shall be as one, for I'll be taking ye to a wondrous land where there are stars. That I'll be doing, *leannán*. 'Tis a promise I'm intending to keep. Indeed, it is.''

When Rian released his hold on her elbows, Annora sighed, and he was gone.

"I was dreaming, I was," Íde said in Irish. She saw Annora kneeling beside her bed to arrange linens on the trundle.

Annora glanced up. She had been awake since first light and had tried not to disturb Íde. "Good morning."

Íde lay within her great mound of pillows, a small pale face dwarfed by all the color. "Dreaming of how it must have been when ye took yer first step. Or what it might have been like if ye'd come to ask me about the mysteries between a man and a woman. Dreaming my wee babe had grown, and come home to me, but in the morn, she would be gone, for dreams are creatures of our night minds, and do not live to see the light of day."

"There is more color on your cheeks this morning, I am glad." Annora pushed the small bed into its storage space under Íde's and stood. She smiled.

Although Íde did not comprehend Annora's words, she did not mistake the kindly tone and warm expression. She returned her smile, so like that of her other daughters, so like her own. Her voice was incredulous. "I awaken to see ye before me. Can it be true, this dream?"

"Ni tigliom labairt go mait. I have not much Irish. *I cannot speak well.* But I know the word *briongloid.* You speak of a *dream,* do you not? *Nil an briongloid,''* Annora said, hoping her attempted Irish made sense. *No dream,* was what she'd intended. "I am real. I am here."

Íde nodded. She propped herself up and patted the space beside her. *"Suid go dluit le mo taob.* I want to know everything. *Sit close by my side.* You must tell me everything about yerself. And whether I understand the whole of it does not matter, for your face and voice will be revealing much to me.''

Annora knew she'd been invited to sit upon the bed and did so.

"Dublin?" Íde used the English word for the town on the Liffey.

"*Tá, bhi me mo comnaig a mBaile atha Cliath,*" Annora replied, first in stilted Irish, then in English. "*Aye, I was living in Dublin.*"

"The people who raised ye? The woman? She was a good soul? And did not mistreat ye in any way, did she?" Íde's questions came rapidly in Irish. She had heard that the English abandoned children, that a child without family might be left to wander the countryside. "Ye were not a prisoner or slave, were ye?"

Annora regarded her with a puzzled look. "I'm not certain what you are asking me."

"She asks about the woman who raised ye, and wishes to know how ye were treated," Rian clarified from the doorway. He had been standing there for a few seconds. "Forgive my intrusion."

"There is naught to forgive. Truth to tell, your arrival is welcomed, for now you can assist us in conversing. Please, will you tell Íde about Catherine, and that she was generous, kind, and wise, and much respected by all who knew her."

Rian did as Annora asked. He spoke at length about the tower and walled garden; about Catherine's adoration for the child she raised as her own, and of Sir Thomas's devotion to the young woman no one doubted was his deceased brother's only child. He described how all of Dublin believed Annora Picot must have been blessed by faeries; of how she had become a successful wool merchant; and how she had shared that good fortune through generosity and dedication to Our Lady of Victory.

At length, Annora reached into her pocket for the miniature she'd been carrying since Castlekevin. She held it out to Íde. "Look, that is me. Annora. Your Onóra. And that woman is Catherine, who raised me. She called me daughter, and I called her mother, for there was never any reason to believe otherwise."

Íde held the offered painting at an angle to catch the sunlight. "Och, how very fair she is, this Catherine Picot. Indeed, I'm gazing upon a lady, I am, and 'tis clear she loved ye, true as true can be." Rian translated this word for word. "And look at yer clothes. The pair of ye dressed in similar gowns, and such fine cloth. 'Twas a prosperous household by the look of it. Blessed by faeries, indeed," she said with a touch of amusement, and then gasped. Her hand trembled. "Can I believe my eyes? 'Tis yer little cross, I'm seeing. Ye wear the cross that was put about yer wee neck the morn of yer birth. Would ye be asking her, Rian O'Byrne, what has happened to the little wooden cross?"

But Annora didn't wait for Rian to translate. She saw the way Íde's pale, thin fingers touched the child's neck in the painting, and she knew what Íde asked. Already her hand was delving inside the pocket again.

"Íde wonders about the cross ye're wearing in the portrait."

"I know." Annora's memory stirred with Catherine's voice. *'Tis a mother's gift of love to her daughter, and has been round your neck from the first moment I held you in my arms.* Now she saw the fuller meaning of what Catherine had been saying. Carefully, she held forth the clump of fabric to fold back the corners.

Again, a small gasp came from Íde. Her frail voice quivered with emotion at what she saw. "After so many years, 'tis with her even now, it is."

"She is amazed ye keep it still," Rian explained to Annora.

"You must tell her I would never do otherwise, for I

promised to give it to my own daughter one day as my
mother had given it to me. Time and again Catherine told
me it was a mother's gift of love, that I had worn it from
the first moment I'd been placed in her arms.''

Rian nodded. He told Íde about Annora's promise,
and how Catherine Picot had called the cross a mother's
gift of love.

"Bail ó Dhia ort," Íde whispered to the woman she
had never met. A tear ran down her cheek. *God bless you.*
In truth, this Catherine had known nothing about how the
babe had come to wear the wooden talisman, but Íde
appreciated what the English woman of Dublin had been
doing. Catherine had forged an invisible bond between
the child and her true family, a link that might survive
through future generations. "My Onóra has no daughter
yet? That is why she keeps the cross herself? Only sons?"
Íde asked Rian.

"She has no children at all."

"Why not?"

"She has never married."

"How can that be?"

"Do not be thinking it is for any lack of suitors. Yer
daughter has been pursued by many, including the
English king, who wished to ally her with one of his
kinsmen. But she is a proud and independent woman and
would not consent to any of them, for they did not please
her.''

"Mo bhron, what sadness is this? *Alas, my grief,"*
Íde's lashes closed for a moment, then she looked into
Annora's eyes and took her hand, the wooden cross
between them. "Ye must tell her this for me, Rian
O'Byrne. 'Tis a strange conceit that swells within me,
daughter, to be hearing how ye've kept yer independence,
but conceit gives way to a mother's mourning to consider
ye without a man and bairns of yer own. Have ye not been
lonely?''

Although the question was Íde's, it flustered Annora to

hear the words spoken in Rian's voice. This three-way conversation had become much too awkward. She felt Rian's gaze as well as Íde's. They awaited her reply, but Annora could not say a thing.

"Were there no Englishmen to please ye? Ask her, Rian O'Byrne."

"None," Annora said. That was a simple question. Impersonal. It was not hard or embarrassing to answer.

"Och, she's a demanding one, is she?" Íde was amused. "How about an Irishman, then? Has there never been an Irishman to catch her fancy?"

Rian hesitated.

Íde gave him a sharp, probing look. She repeated, "Has there never been an Irishman to catch her fancy?"

Rian posed the question to Annora, and she blushed bright red.

That was answer enough for Íde. "Och, so that's the way of it, is it now, Rian O'Byrne? Ye, and my Onóra?" She could not suppress a laugh. "The business of getting a husband for my daughter will not be a mighty task. There's no need to be looking any farther than yerself, is there, Rian O'Byrne?"

"What does she say?" Annora asked Rian.

"Nothing of importance," Rian lied, then said to Íde in Irish, "Ye're mistaken. 'Tis not the way of it."

"Och, I think not. I think not. Do not be modest. I may be closer to the hereafter than yerself, but I'm not blind. I saw the hot color rise upon her cheeks when I asked about an Irishman as clearly as I've seen the fire she lights within ye. A woman knows the way of such things. So, too, a wife and mother, and being her mother 'tis my wish that ye wed my daughter, Rian O'Byrne. What say ye?"

"Do ye forget Muiríol? Marriage did not suit me then. I was a most dishonorable husband, 'tis well agreed. Surely ye would not entrust yer Onóra to such as man as was husband to Muiríol?"

"Ye were young, and that man is no more, bless his poor heart. Indeed, ye've proven ye can be trusted with my Onóra. More than once ye've guarded her well. Indeed, I'm thinking ye'd make her a fine, cherishing, and Christian husband. Will ye take her to wife, and exchange yer vows before me in this very chamber?"

He cleared his throat. Annora was everything he wanted, and he'd been willing to take her into the hills for himself, but Íde was right. He was changed. For too long he'd acted from desire and need, for too long he'd thought of no one but himself. But that was changed, and his answer had nothing to do with desire, nor the heart. His answer was produced of serious consideration, and what he believed to be reasonable and rational. "I cannot do it."

"Pray, why not? A match between an O'Toole and an O'Byrne is always a good thing. Do ye not want her?"

They were speaking as if Annora were not in the chamber. Her glance darted between them, bewilderment marking her features.

"I leave this day for Idrone," said Rian.

"That is no reason," came her retort.

"There is no guarantee I will return." He wanted Íde to understand and paused to collect his thoughts. He had abandoned one wife, albeit under different circumstances, and would not do so again. "As long as I can recollect, I have avoided anything beyond the moment at hand; yet now that I might consider the future, I find it fraught with too many perils to be to my liking. Would ye wish the same on yer daughter as ye've suffered? To be widowed by the English?"

"I survived. Besides, 'tis the fate of many an Irish-woman. And we do manage to survive. Indeed, mayhap, we are strengthened for it."

"Do ye forget, she is green with it? Yer Onóra has no experience with those hardships we accept, mayhap too easily."

Íde could not deny this. "Yer refusal is still naught but an excuse."

"I will not be changing my mind." *At least, not for now*. He became aware of Éva and Cera standing a few feet from the bed. How long had they been there? Had they heard everything? The thought pricked him. "I must be going," he said to no one in particular, and pushed past the women.

Annora looked at the closed door. "What has happened?" she asked Cera.

"While I do not know what led to her decision, it appears our mother has decided that Rian O'Byrne should be yer husband. She wishes the pair of ye to exchange vows before her, but . . ." Cera hesitated. "But he refuses."

An uncomfortable silence fell over the chamber.

"Oh," Annora murmured in confusion, sensing Éva's and Cera's curiosity. Íde was whispering in Irish. The words sounded comforting, encouraging.

"Go after him, our mother urges ye," said Cera. "Rian O'Byrne is thickheaded, she reminds ye, and does not understand one cannot have love without pain. He does not understand there are risks on the pathway to happiness. Go after him, she tells ye. He is leaving for Idrone."

Annora needed no more encouragement, and hastened from the chamber. Some children pointed her in the right direction. Rian had left the dwelling house for the *lios*, and Annora found him near the stable. He was coming out of a stone hut with a harness slung over his shoulder, a rolled brat tucked under one arm. He was preparing for departure from Keadeen.

"You would leave without telling me good-bye?" Annora blocked his way. The smell of leather was everywhere.

Rian frowned. He didn't know if he would have sought

her out. "I did not want to say farewell." That much was the truth.

"You would not have me as your wife, I am told."

"That is not quite true."

"Explain yourself."

"'Tis possible, but not now." His voice dropped to a whisper. "'Tis possible, if fate allows. Ye must know, Annora, that where I am bound there is to be fighting. Indeed, it may be a most hideous slaughter, I'm fearing, from the talk of gunnes." Rian took a step toward her. "'Tis possible I might have ye yet for my wife, if fate allows. I cannot offer more than that. Not for now."

He was too close, and she drew back her head to look up at him. Her nostrils flared at his male scent, and with her own, sudden anger. It infuriated Annora that while Rian was rejecting her, she couldn't keep herself from noticing how he smelled. Her voice hardened. "If you leave me with nothing more than ''*tis* possible,' if you turn on your heels to go, do not bother to come back for me."

"Are ye making threats?" His gaze narrowed. A most peculiar light simmered in his eyes. Rian let the folded *brat* fall to the ground, and taking hold of a long, thick strand of her golden hair, he began to coil that softness about one finger.

"'Tis no threat." She swallowed and wished her heart would slow its quickening pace. She met his gaze without flinching, but did not jerk away as she should have done.

"What then?" Deliberately he continued to twist the hair about his finger, shortening his rein on her with each loop. His voice went even lower. "If not a threat, what is it?"

Annora did not answer right away. Her mind was a confusion of past and present. A trove of regrets and accomplishments, confessions, secrets, and failures. Satisfactions and unrealized dreams. She considered how fiercely she'd prized her independence, and recalled the host of suitors who had not suited. There was only one man for her; the man who would want her instead of her wealth, but he had never been among that host of suitors.

This was how it had been since the night of the Epiphany Eve feast. Nothing had changed. Only her ability to reckon with the truth, and the fact that she was no longer Annora Picot of Dublin, but one of the Irishry of the wild hills. Annora wanted to pledge her heart and body, her loyalty and devotion to Rian O'Byrne in front of Íde. But she would not beg. Not even for Íde.

"If not a threat, what? Can ye not be answering? Ye will be waiting for me, will ye not?" he asked.

"Why should I make promises when you give nothing in return?" She tilted her chin upward in a sort of challenge.

"Nothing." The word was a ragged, harsh whisper. "I've given ye nothing, is it?" He closed the distance between them. "I went down on my knees before ye, *leannán.* I could not be a proper suitor, but I tried, *sweetheart.* I tried, yet ye say I've given ye nothing."

Annora inhaled. Her chest heaved. She was acutely aware of his large body, its towering height, and uncommon size. Blood thrummed through her veins, her skin flushed warm, then cool, and warm again. She stepped backward to get away from him, away from the source of her agitation.

"Ye claim I've given ye nothing." Again he moved toward her, until only an inch or two separated them. "Do ye already forget the rose?"

She sensed the scarcely controlled energy seething through him, and the rapid, building pulse within herself. Annora swallowed in a dry throat, and took another step backward.

Again he stepped toward her. Again she moved away. This pattern repeated itself several times until Rian had forced Annora behind the hut. "Nothing?" he asked. "What of my child?"

"What nonsense do you babble?"

"No nonsense, *leannán*." The hand that had never released Annora's hair pulled her to him, while his other reached out to contour her belly. "Have ye not considered ye could be carrying my bairn?"

"And mayhap not," Annora snapped in reply. She didn't know what drove her to deny him. She quivered at the thought, and at the delicious, rippling sensations being roused by his touch.

"Perhaps I should be increasing my odds, then." In seconds, he had both hands at her waist, and with a rapid, short movement he yanked her against his groin.

She gasped at his insinuation, at the startling speed of his reaction, at the bulge of his sex pressing against her, and the rush of expectancy that shot through her. "You cannot mean to make love in broad daylight!"

"Och, but I do." He rotated his lower torso, suggestive, sensual against her until he was engorged.

"We cannot do this," she tried to rebuke him, tried to sound aghast, but her voice betrayed her, for it caught with the evidence of her own arousal. His hot, hard erection throbbed against her, and she couldn't stop herself from remembering what it was like to have that rigid flesh inside her. "We cannot." The denial was little more than a wisp of air.

"And why not?"

His fingers at her waist tightened, slightly digging into her, massaging, trying to overwhelm her thoughts, coaxing, teasing her body and its hungers. Annora fought to ignore the dreamy, liquid cravings within her. "This is no place—" she protested.

"We have no need of any chamber." Rian propelled them around another corner and behind another hut, where a three-sided shed had been built against a wall. It was a quiet, hidden spot with a thatched roof and relative privacy. Harnesses and bridles, kettles and bird cages hung from the roof, creels were stacked in one corner, ladders in the other, and running along the back wall was a deep ledge, where sundry tools were lined up in tidy order. "We need nothing more than this place," he whispered.

"B-But—" she stammered.

He silenced her misgivings with an incredible kiss, full, deep, and wet. A kiss that left them gasping for air like drowning souls, holding fast to each other to prevent themselves from sinking. It was a clawing, grasping, frantic kiss.

At last, Rian came up for a breath. "Do ye not want me?"

"Aye," she admitted.

The purr of her voice sent exquisite lust surging through him. With a single sweep of his arm he cleared the tools off the ledge. They clattered to the ground.

"Raise up yer skirt."

"What if . . ." She swallowed her discomfiture. "What if someone comes?"

"What if?" he rejoined. "Then I suppose they'll be seeing my backside." Easily, he discarded his belt and *skian,* then pulled off his saffron tunic to stand before her stark naked, and shockingly aroused. He grinned at her, roguish and beckoning.

Annora was breathless. The crash of waves roared in her head. There was naught for her but to gawk at the well-defined muscles of his chest and powerful thighs. Swirls of golden brown hair covered his flat belly; and there, between powerful thighs, was his man's sex. Her heart hammered to see such a sight. It did not droop between his legs but stood forth of its own with the thickness and rigidity of a walking stick, and at the end of that walking stick had been carved a large, round knob for a handle.

Rian liked the way Annora stared at him. He watched her lips part, and her tongue dart out to moisten them. But it was her eyes that were the greatest pleasure to behold. Those clarie blue eyes darkened until she had the drowsy look of one under the influence of white briony or angelica, and he knew she must be getting moist, must be thickening, must be tingling with the beginnings of need. "Raise up yer skirt," he repeated.

This time, Annora did as he asked, and Rian groaned at the display of creamy white thighs. Quickly, before she might change her mind, he hoisted her onto the ledge.

The stone was cool and rough beneath Annora's bare bottom. Her legs dangled over the edge, slightly parted. His hand skimmed up one inner thigh to brush across her mound. There was an ache between her legs. Annora thought she would die if he tarried or teased. He did neither, and she moaned when he slipped a finger inside her.

He loved the cadence of her moan, and wanting to swallow it, Rian covered her mouth with his. He kissed her again, and while his tongue probed her sweet mouth, his fingers delved her sweeter sex. She was wet as he'd imagined, he inserted a second finger alongside the first and was rewarded by more sighs.

"Come forward," he murmured. "Can ye be putting yer legs about my waist? I want to see everything when I go into ye."

What he asked was immodest, but the words made Annora tremble with excitement. His rasping tone, the lewd suggestion, they were thrilling. Mayhap she should be ashamed, but she wasn't, and she lifted her legs to his waist, hooking her ankles at his lower back.

"Sweet God, ye're beautiful."

A different woman would have been horrified by the way her private parts were exposed, but Annora was not that woman. Desire radiated through her, and she gloried in the long, low moan rumbling forth from Rian. She watched his face gripped by the thrall of eagerness and lust, she felt his hands on her flesh, inside her, and saw his manhood straining toward her. She tried to bring herself to it, wanting that large, rounded tip to spread her netherlips for the rest of him. She squirmed.

"Only a few more seconds," Rian growled. It made him crazy the way she wanted him. Crazy to think of how the rest of the world knew naught but a woman poised and demure, but he knew this wild, wanton creature. Again his fingers were inside her. The honey flowing from her was thick and plentiful, and as he'd done that very first time, he rubbed the length of his erection along her outer petals until he glistened with her desire. She writhed. It was time. He pulled back to position his arousal, then he moved forward, slowly, smoothly, all the while watching as he slid into her.

Annora keened. He was filling her. The pleasure was sharp and vivid. He was halfway to the hilt when he slowed. Slowly, so slowly, only the very end of him was moving. And then he went no deeper.

A small urgent whimper escaped her. "What?"

"There's only one thing," he murmured. His voice was a velvety, taunting whisper.

He was still moving, but slowly, oh, how slowly. He was still moving, but he did not fill her.

"Why do you torment me?" she cried at the emptiness.

"Ye must tell me ye'll wait. Tell me."

"I'll wait." Annora tightened her ankles at his back and brought him into her. He groaned at her admission, at her passion, and shoved hard and deep. She clutched at his upper arms, certain she must be scaring him, and she called his name.

He hollered hers. Rian plunged into Annora, thrusting again and again, taking her with him, higher, higher to star-filled heavens. "Do ye see them now? The stars?"

"Aye, Rian, 'tis a wondrous land." She melded with

those stars. Their hot white light became hers. "It's happening," she gasped as the core of her, bright with the fire of a thousand stars, exploded in one of the miracles of nature.

"Follamnaig mo chridesea corop tú mo dilisea," Rian bellowed. A thin sheen of moisture spread over his naked body, his buttocks tensed, and with a mighty climax, his hot, warm seed penetrated her woman's winnowing basket. Breathing hard, he gathered her to his chest to whisper his affection.

This time, he did not try to hide. This time, Rian told her true. *"Rule this heart of mine that thou mayst be my love."*

Chapter 29

～～✦～～

From the north, from the east and the west, warriors made their way to a promontory above the Barrow. Through the mountain gaps and passes, over the Great Way and the Road of the Assemblies they came to Art MacMurrough's encampment in Idrone, the vast, rich land lying between the rivers Slaney and Barrow. In pairs or alone, the newcomers sought out their clansmen who had arrived before them. By now every O'Connor of Baravore was accounted for, as were the O'Mores of Ossory, the O'Garveys of Ballaghkeen, and the O'Tooles of Imail and Castlekevin. Only one O'Byrne had been absent, and word quickly spread through the camp that Rian O'Byrne, who had escaped Dublin Castle, was among the O'Byrnes of Aghavannagh and Gabhal Raghnaill after all.

" 'Tis a good thing to be counting ye round our fire this night.'' Rónán O'Byrne embraced his son, whom he'd thought executed by the English of Dublin. "Indeed, 'tis no little vanity to be boasting of how my firstborn has cheated our enemy. But there's more to my pride than mere gloating, says I, for 'tis a worthy thing that ye've done by coming to fight at yer own father's side. What more could I be wanting, I'll be asking ye now?''

"I would not be having it any other way, Da. Fighting

340

by his father's side is where a son is meant to be,'' said Rian. He gave a shrug and accepted a cold drink, glad to have reached his destination, but weary and wishing his father would cease calling attention to him. It was too late, a crowd was gathering.

"Bigid go subac," came the jovial proclamation from one of his kinsmen. *Sit ye merry.*

"Go ndeana se mor mait duit," replied another. There was a little laughter, a little good-natured grumbling. *Much good it may do ye.*

There followed some serious debate about the English, the size of their force, and their king's purpose. Perhaps they did not intend to fight, only to intimidate. Perhaps they would march direct for Dublin.

"No an eagla a namaid ata orta?" someone asked.

This question filtered above the din of the camp, and all who heard ceased talking. An odd silence fell over the assemblage. Art MacMurrough himself rose amidst his liege men. He repeated the query as if giving it consideration, as if encouraging each man before him to do the same, *"Are the enemies dreaded?"*

Slowly MacMurrough turned that he might regard the faces of his chieftains and their warriors. He saw Rian O'Byrne and smiled. MacMurrough had a fondness for the bold warrior, and was pleased to see for himself that he hadn't been executed. He raised his voice for everyone to hear, although he addressed but one of them, "Rian O'Byrne of Aghavannagh, I am told ye've recently been among the stranger."

"That is true, Art MacMurrough." Rian stood to answer the great chieftain.

"Tell us then, son of Rónán, is this enemy of Ireland to be dreaded?"

"Ni tuigim is ni creidim go bfuil eagla no baogal orta," Rian spoke like the daring warrior of reputation. *I neither know nor believe there is either fear or danger.* "But from

experience, I must remind myself that courage alone does not shield an Irishman. Boldness must be tempered with wisdom. 'Tis right and true that we do not fear the stranger, *gidead ni fulair a beit coimeadac, agus in fein a cuinngbeal as acara an namaid.*"

"Well-spoken, Rian O'Byrne. I could not have said better. It is befitting that an Irishman fears not the stranger, *yet it is proper to keep on the alert, and to keep ourselves out of the power of the enemy.*" MacMurrough raised his drinking horn, the Leinstermen cheered, and the chieftains and warriors drank by the light of wax candles in the ruins of the ancient royal palace at Dinn Rig.

Later when the camp quieted and warriors bedded down for a few hours sleep, Rónán remarked to Rian, "Yer mam will be full with joy to be meeting this Annora."

"If fate allows."

"Aye, if fate allows. 'Tis always the way of it," Rónán agreed. There was no telling what tomorrow might bring, and it filled him with sorrow to think of how often the Irish, especially their women, were forced to settle for something other than true joy. An awful inner rage tore at Rónán's heart to know that if the worst came to pass in the lush, green woods of the Barrow valley, his Grella's only joy would be in knowing that fate had allowed her husband and firstborn son to fight together at the end.

The next day was the Eve of the Feast of Saint John the Baptist. Shortly after sunrise, the Irish made a swift departure from Dinn Rig. They headed east into the high country. King Richard was leading his army out of Kilkenny, and MacMurrough and the Leinstermen lost no time in seeking the shelter of the slopes of Slievebawn and Croaghaun.

The English followed. More than twenty thousand of them in a line that stretched from Kilkenny to Leighlin and across the Barrow, where instead of going north toward Carlow and thence to Dublin, they continued into the heart of Idrone. Richard was eager to defeat Mac-Murrough, eager for a fight; and near day's end when he had engaged not one of the wild Irishry, the burning began. At the border of the thickening forest, cottages and byres and a wee church that comprised a small settlement called Ballylaughan were the first to be torched. Seskin-ryan, and Kilgraney, Fennagh and Ballymoon were next set aflame, and having no time to flee, the women and children, the priests, the aged and infirm were rounded up, shrieking, screaming, pleading, keening to no avail.

Some thousand feet above the valley, the Irish surveyed the smoke-shrouded landscape. Hunkered down at the edge of rocky outcrops, they heard not the clang of armor nor the clash of swords as in combat betwixt warriors, but the sounds of English soldiers terrorizing the unarmed and defenseless.

"Nay! We do nothing! Indeed, we must not!" Mac-Murrough ordered when the Leinstermen would charge down from their heights in retaliation. "We stay, for to descend these cliffs is what the English intend. 'Tis a trap most hideous, a provocation to be drawing us where they have the advantage of numbers, and can slaughter our sons and fathers, our brothers and kinsmen the moment we step forth from the forest. We must not be letting our hearts rule our minds. There is naught to be done that could reverse the English crimes against our people. But remember this: here, we hold the ground. This is our domain, and in this wilderness, there is every chance for victory, every chance that we can yet best Richard at his own strategy."

Irish warriors gathered close to hear MacMurrough, and for those who were not close enough, the chieftain's words were repeated throughout the mountains that Eve of the Feast of Saint John the Baptist, when the night sky was lit not by midsummer bonfires but by the glow of burning homes and crops, flaming meadows and woodlands.

"The English try to draw us onto their field, but we will be drawing them to ours," MacMurrough declared. "Already Richard strays from the route to Dublin, and if we do not go to him, he will be tempted closer to us. Patience brings its rewards, and there will yet be time to celebrate a bittersweet triumph over this enemy. Although this terrain is unknown to the English, their thirst for blood knows not the limitations of reason. These bogs and marshes, these precipices and ravines, gorges and crags shall be our allies. Vengeance will be ours. Indeed, the ancestral lands we defend shall be our greatest weapon against the stranger and his greed for them."

The Irish waited in the mountains. The English remained in the valley.

The first day, the English spent in celebration of their victory over Ballylaughan. The second night, spies reported to MacMurrough that Richard with much pomp and ceremony admitted to knighthood his nephew, Harry of Monmouth. And on the third afternoon news was brought of the capture and subsequent oath of allegiance to Richard by Art MacMurrough's uncle, Malachy, who unbeknownst to the English, was considered by his own race, including his nephew, to be a craven, treaty-making traitor.

From the valley, a deputation was dispatched to Art MacMurrough with the message that if he would come straightway to King Richard with a rope about his neck as his uncle had done, Richard would admit him to mercy, and elsewhere—at some distance from Leinster—give him castles and lands in abundance.

"Never! Tell yer king I am the rightful king of these lands and would never abandon them for all the treasures of the sea, but would continue to oppose him." This was the answer of Art MacMurrough, a true descendant of Cathair Mor, lord of the Free Tribes of Leinster. "Tell yer king I will never cease from war, nor from the defense of my kingdom, nor my people until God so chooses.''

There was a sharp intake of breath when King Richard learned of MacMurrough's reply. The king gasped as audibly as did his earls and advisors. In outrage and astonishment, Richard stared at the smoldering wasteland, the charred tangle of oak and willow, holly and ash, and here and there, a rare, blackened trunk, its birds gone, greenery consumed, branches withered, rising out of the shifting smoke.

''Where are the people who lived here?'' the king asked the interpreter who had translated MacMurrough's defiance. Every bit of his majesty's mounting wrath was revealed in his voice and expression. He looked up at the mountains, his expression turning even darker, even more dangerous than the scorched ground from which random flames erupted now and again. *MacMurrough was naught but an arrogant savage, yet he dared to call himself king before one who might be Holy Roman Emperor! By the blood of Saint John the Baptist, the Irish upstart and all his savages would be pleading for his mercy, wishing that they had not been so hasty to reject his generous offers of mercy and lands*. Richard clenched his jaw in ire, his hands made belligerent fists as the thoughts he'd entertained at Kilkenny returned to him. Then they had only been ideas. Now they would become reality, and he would make it happen. He would bend this arrogant Irishry and their land to his will. He would triumph.

As if sensing evil, the interpreter, an Englishman who had lived many years among the Irish, did not answer direct. ''They are but women and children, my lord king.''

''Women and children.'' Richard gave a harsh, vicious laugh. ''MacMurroughs whores and whelps more than likely.''

The interpreter hoped the king did not notice how he

winced. "Not all of them are Irishry, sire," he forced himself to speak. "Some are of English stock, and very poor, indeed."

"Bah, English. I am no fool to swallow such a fiction as you would foist upon me." Richard glared at the man. "English living in this wilderness? It is neither likely nor possible. They are all savages, to be sure, and will serve my purpose."

"Your purpose, sire?" one of the earls asked while the others avoided the king's gaze.

"I intend to pursue MacMurrough, murderous felon that he is, and those people will clear a highway through the forest for my army."

"You cannot mean—"

"Do you q-question me? D-doubt me?" Richard shouted. As his rage increased, the stutter of his youth returned.

"Nay, sire, I do not question you."

Richard grinned. *Good. So be it. My will shall be done, and then there would be no doubts here or anywhere in Ireland as to who was sovereign in this land.* He spoke to his earls and issued his orders, "Let the word go forth to bring those people to the fore. Every one of them. And any others that can be found or burned from their hovels. I desire as many as can be taken from their lairs and dens, for the forest is thick, and my army wishes to move swiftly."

Thunder echoed through the mountains, but the sky was blue. Another deafening roar rumbled across the valley and into the hills, but the only clouds were stark white plumes that rose upward. There was a thin wailing as a relentless wind might moan through treetops, and there was the smell of smoke, acrid and strange, with the sharp, sickening odors of an alchemist's chamber.

"Sweet God in Heaven," cried an Irishman who was the size and shape of a great bear. He turned away from the ledge unable to bear witness to the scene below. Tears streamed down a battle-scarred face. He signed himself and went in search of a priest.

The English were using their gunnes, those massive black machines, to blast away the forest, and they were using the women and children of Leinster to clear away the debris so their army could advance.

"It has worked," MacMurrough whispered with no jubilation. He could have never imagined the callousness, the misery. "They are coming."

"And driving those poor souls before him," a chieftain said, horrified.

"Can it truly be?" another asked, disbelieving.

"*Aig Dia ata fios sin.*" A warrior signed himself. *God knows.*

"Mayhap God knows nothing of this."

There were several priests among them. They came forward to lead the Irish in prayer, and the warriors began in unison, "*Rom-snáda mo Rí; romm-ain i cach ré; ro béo ar cach ngád ar scáth dernann Dé.*"

To a man, the warriors went down on their knees to be blessed and to pray that God might be with them. The words had been the same for almost five hundred years. *May my King guard me; may he aid me always; may I be at every need beneath the protection of God's hand.*

Not a warrior among them knelt deeper than did Rian O'Byrne, nor was there another who intended to pray with more fervor, nor fight with more daring. For the first time, Rian had something to which he might look forward with expectation, and more importantly, someone for whom to survive. For the first time he thought of the morrow, and how he intended to be bringing Annora to meet his mam at Aghavannagh. Nothing would prevent him from that.

The priests moved along the cliffs, over boulders, across cascading streams, and through high gullies to stand before every warrior and urge him to a final prayer,

"Día lim fri cach sním, triar úasal óen, Athair ocus Mac ocus Spirit Nóeb." Lastly they would make the sign of the cross, *God be with me against all troubles, noble Trinity which is one, Father, Son, and Holy Spirit,* and then bid each warrior on his way to battle.

Chapter 30

⸺⟨⟨⟨⟩⟩⟩⸺

"Look, grandmother," exclaimed a wee lad who was seated at Íde's feet.

"*Suid go socair,* Pádraig," an older child admonished. *Sit quietly.*

They were in the meadow above Keadeen, where generations of O'Toole women had gathered woad and spurge and bilberries for their dyes, and where Íde had come this day, carried upon a pallet, to watch her grandchildren play and to tell them stories of her own childhood, and how many times it was that she had climbed this hill to gaze toward that faraway place the English called Dublin, wherein her Ona had been lost. The children regarded this entire tale, and the recent arrival of Annora as something both magical and miraculous. All listened to their grandmother, all regarded the beautiful Annora—who was one of them yet spoke with the voice of a stranger—with much curiosity and awe. All except little Pádraig.

Pádraig tugged on Íde's shawl. "Look, grandmother, do ye not see? Travelers approach." He pointed downhill to where a footpath came out of the hazel wood.

"*Cia an drong so air an mbotar?*" asked Neassa. She dropped her basket of meadow flowers and hurried to Pádraig. The lad was one of hers. She pulled him close.

349

What crowd is this on the road? "It could be plague, old mother, and we should not be letting them in to Keadeen."

"Calm yerself, girl, 'tis not always the plague as took yer parents. Ye should be telling us what ye see, not what ye imagine." Íde's voice was stronger than it had been in a long time. A soft glow had returned to the ailing woman's complexion. It was nine days since Rian O'Byrne had brought her Ona home, and Íde's health was improving almost as rapidly as was her Ona's Irish. Íde turned to her second-born daughter and asked, "What think ye, Onóra?"

Annora stood for a better look. Below the meadow, beyond the plashed outer wall of Keadeen, a line of women and children were making their way over a rise. They were on foot, not a single horse to carry the weakest of them, nor were they herding any sheep or even a milk cow. It was an unusual procession. Annora considered the unfortunate souls she had witnessed over the years and said, "While they have not the look of those who might travel by choice, neither do they have the appearance of anyone I have seen fleeing plague. Many times did families arrive at the convent in search of shelter, and always they were distinguished by the caution with which they approached. They were fearful of what was behind them, aye, but they were also uncertain of what lay ahead. Had pestilence infested the convent? They surely wondered. And what manner of welcome awaited them? Would they be granted shelter? With these folk, I note no such caution in the way they proceed, hurrying headlong toward your stronghold. They do not doubt their welcome at Keadeen."

Íde nodded in satisfaction at this reply. Her Ona was a fine, wise woman. She could not have taught her better. "We must return. Whoever they may be, they are guests. I would greet them properly and learn what brings them here."

There were twenty refugees. Six women, each of them a mother and carrying a child, plus an older female, the widow of their chieftain's great-grandfather, who was herself being carried by the two strongest lads on a makeshift litter. They were O'Fierghraies from Raheena-kit, smelling of woodsmoke, and there was another more pungent odor like eggs gone bad that clung to their hair and garments. Annora had been correct. It was not pestilence from which they were fleeing, but the English army; and the Grace of God was with these O'Fierghraies, for they had escaped. Not so fortunate were the thousands of captives they had seen for them-selves being forced to clear the wilderness, and whose cries for mercy had haunted them in their flight.

In the deep of night, eleven more refugees arrived. Children on their own who had managed to escape their captors.

Conall, the *sencha*, who had fought the English in his youth, questioned them.

"*Nil aon focal breige ann,*" the children attested. *It is perfectly true*. The English army was crossing the moun-tains. True as true, English knights astride heavily armored horses were attempting passage where even the ancient kings of the Úi Cheinnselaig had not dared to take their armies. It was a fool's mission. Suicidal. *Tá*, the children told Conall, they were dying like fleas in birdlime. True as true, MacMurrough and the clans were harrying them, picking off stragglers and ambushing any who would venture forth to hunt for food. And those who did not fall beneath Irish darts were perishing in bogs. The children had seen this, indeed, they had—mounted soldiers entrapped by their English saddles and stirrups, and sinking into peaty graves from which there was no escape.

King Richard had disregarded one of the five taboos that not a single king of the Leinstermen had defied.

It was forbidden, it had always been forbidden, and

only an arrogant, vain creature would march his army
through the Wicklow Hills, widdershins, from south to
north against the sun. But that was what the man who
would rule Ireland was doing. His army was headed north
to Dublin, and east from the Barrow across the Wicklow
massif to the coast, against the passage of the sun, and the
women of Keadeen hearing of this signed themselves, and
whispered an Ave Maria. Never in a thousand years had
the taboo been broken; and while the women of Keadeen
believed in Christ and the Trinity, they did not doubt the
old gods had been angered. It would be a miracle if
Richard of Burgundy lived to celebrate All Souls.

Next came rains, hard and blinding. For three days the
heavens opened wide to drench the hills. Dried stream
beds ran swift, swollen lochs and rivers overflowed their
banks, and great blankets of sodden bog, uprooted from
lofty, mountain perches, rushed and tumbled headlong
toward gorge and valley, dragging trees and cattle, huts,
even boulders, and much of the English army in a
gruesome avalanche of devastation.

The feasts of Saint Cáelán, Máel Muire, and Cillín
passed. The skies cleared, and the wives of Keadeen
prepared to trek south. They would not wait to see if their
menfolk returned but would journey through the mountains in search of them. Laden with bandages and
medicinal supplies, leading cattle, and carrying pots for
cooking, they would tend their wounded warriors before
they might fester, and provide them food before they
might starve. They would offer what assistance they
might to any Irishry who had suffered at the hands of the
English; and may God bless the poor souls of the
departed, they would bury the dead as Christians were
meant to be interred, safe from hungry beasts and with a
proper blessing.

Íde urged Annora to accompany the women. The
mother knew the way of the daughter's heart and had
faith in tomorrow.

Annora embraced Íde. "I will find Rian O'Byrne, and I will not forget you. We will be back to Keadeen."

"Och, ye must never imagine I could be expecting any other ending to this tale. Ye'll not be gone long this time, my Onóra; and while ye're away, ye must not be worrying for me, I says. 'Tis living long I'll be doing, for I intend to watch ye place that small wooden cross about yer own daughter's neck."

Rian lay facedown in a stew of mud and peat and blood. He had not moved in three days. Or was it four? He had not eaten in as long, nor opened his eyes; and whether that owed to the grime that had dried over closed lids or to some specific injury, he knew not. He only knew it was a new day, because he felt the sun upon his back. A good sensation. It gave him a shred of hope, and he longed to turn himself over to let his face soak up that celestial warmth, but he couldn't budge himself. Indeed, he couldn't tell if he had arms or legs, for he sensed nothing where they should have been. Amazing, there was no pain, no discomfort. Not even the tiniest muscular response to his brain's command to twitch. If he'd been able, Rian would groan aloud his frustration and misery, but even that was impossible. His throat was parched, his tongue was swollen.

So he lay upon the ground trying to nourish his body and soul with fond memories. It was said that it was possible to restore one's strength in that way, or at least to make one's passing into the hereafter more tolerable. He wanted to think of Annora, to see her looking from her tower window, or as she had smiled when he'd read the *Táin*. He wanted to hear her laugh, to hear her earnest enthusiasm when she spoke of Catherine and the manuscripts at Our Lady of Victory, or of her faith in God, even to hear her gentle outrage when she called him *boorish and beyond redemption* would be a delight. And oh, to hear her sensual moans, and her throaty whispered promise to wait for him at Keadeen. But he could not focus on any of that. Instead his mind was possessed of what had brought him low.

He'd been among one of the flying parties raiding the English rear. The Irish advantage had been overwhelming, and their casualties had been negligible, while perhaps as many as half of their enemy had perished before they approached the lower slopes of Croghan. That was where Rian had seen the knight, who'd long lost his mount, walking at the fringes of a disorganized mass of spearmen. It was not, however, the reduced state of the knight that had attracted his notice, but the leather satchel slung across his chest.

Suspicion seized Rian, motivating him to creep low through the underwood for a better look. The elaborate design on the leather was Irish, confirming his suspicion that the item was stolen. He peered through gorse as the knight came close enough to discern the satchel was no mere possession of a wealthy chieftain's wife, but a holy relic, and by the shape and size, probably an illuminated Gospel or Psaltery. Rian thought of the hidden treasures of Our Lady of Victory, of the glories that had been destroyed at Glendalough, and rage did not bubble within him, it boiled.

For centuries the Irish had respected sanctuary. Even when the ancient chieftains had fought amongst themselves, they had not sacked or harmed the monasteries, they had not waged war upon the monks and holy sisters. The English, however, had proven time and again they owned no such scruples, and Rian reacted without forethought when he leapt from the brush, shrieking like a thousand devils and swinging his sword to hack and slice at everything and anyone in his path. How many English he struck down before they overcame him he would never know, but of a certainty, he'd at least defeated the knight from whom he reclaimed the stolen satchel.

The last thing Rian O'Byrne recalled was making certain that when he fell, the satchel had been hidden beneath his body.

Now Rian heard voices. What tongue they spoke, he could not tell. Looters, no doubt, competing with the rooks and crows. English deserters taking what they might from their own dead. Or mayhap, if he was lucky, they were Irish coming to fetch their dead and wounded.

Someone or something poked at his back, then prodded. He recalled the sharp kick between his shoulders blades in Dublin Castle. Rian's final effort as he slipped back into unconsciousness was to tighten his grasp about the satchel, pulling it close to his belly.

As long as Rian O'Byrne lived, this little bit of his heritage would remain in Irish hands.

Chapter 31

⤙⤚

"It holds our chronicle," Brother Énán told Annora. The monk spoke of the leather satchel still within Rian's grip. "I have been tending yer man for two days, and even in delirium his hold has not weakened. Astonishing, it is. Indeed, when I tried to unwind the straps from his fingers, he reacted with such violent thrashing I could not help fearing for my safety."

Annora soothed Rian's brow with a wet cloth. "Two days in fever, you say? And how long exposed to the elements before that?"

"Too long I fear," the monk said with a grim nod, in part an apology and partially an affirmation of the unavoidable. "I tried to return to him sooner, I did. May God be blessing his poor soul, there was a debt to be repaid for his having fought to retrieve our satchel from the English thief. 'Tis sorry I am, he was several days in the mud."

"You did your best, Brother Énán. I am grateful you reached him, and were so kind to have him brought here. I might never have found him otherwise. It might have been too late."

Too late for what? Annora wondered with a touch a despair. *Too late to be by Rian's side when he died?*

She tried not to cry at the sight of his gaunt features,

evidence he had not eaten in days. The awful, grayish tinge of his skin was almost more than she could bear, and the numerous wounds about his upper arms and chest, where English swords had sliced at him, were painful to behold. She was sitting cross-legged with his head upon her lap, spooning a mixture of boiled milk with clot bur leaves and meadow sorrel between his parched lips. She fought back gathering tears. There was no fluttering beneath his closed lids to hint of life. His breathing was so shallow as to be imperceptible. Rian was dying. Although she didn't yet detect the smell of death upon him, she was sure it was there, lurking and waiting to take him from her.

They were in the *lios* of Annacurragh. Located on Croghan Kinsella above the Aughrim, the stronghold had been not in the path of the English, but the enemy had been close. For three long nights, the Irish of Annacurragh had heard the English army passing in its death throes, mayhap not more than a furlong to the south and east; and while this particular slope had been spared the trauma of combat, it was now overwhelmed with refugees, and wounded, and relatives in search of unaccounted warriors.

From Imail the O'Toole women had gone through Rathdangan to the Ow Water, which led a clear course to the Aughrim. They had made a brief stop at Aghavannagh to assure themselves all were safe and, from there, being joined by some of Rian's kinswomen, had made their way to Annacurragh. They had arrived at the MacMurrough stronghold four hours before, and with Brother Énán's help, Annora had been tending to Rian since. The monk had left her side only to fetch more herbal ointment or nourishment. He was devoted to Rian and quickly expanded that loyalty to include Annora.

"To have witnessed yer man when he sprang from the forest, why 'tis a sight I'll be remembering until my dying breath. The enemy held me prisoner. I was being forced to march at the rear, and it was from there I saw yer giant of an Irishman. Och, but he was strong and swift, he was, and hollering a most fiendish war cry when he charged that knight, ordering him to surrender the stolen Irish treasure. The *Annals of Finnén*, they're called, being named for our sainted founder. Och, 'tis true there's a place in Heaven waiting for yer man. Do not doubt it, for he fought the enemy as if protecting his own dear mam. It passes all understanding.''

Annora smiled. She understood. That this satchel was not from the hidden library at Our Lady of Victory mattered not to Rian, who had at last come to care and had done what was honorable without being asked, or with regard for himself. It was the act of a changed man, a hero, she thought, a man who believed in and had faith. Annora applied a salve of spiked willow herb over Rian's wounds. Numerous slashes crisscrossed his upper arms, and there was a deep cut in one shoulder, another in his chest. Although the wounds were warm to the touch, they didn't smell, and there was no blackness or oozing. Perhaps it wasn't too late after all, she dared to hope.

''If only the shrine could have been saved,'' Brother Énán said on a sigh. He crossed himself. ''It was magnificent, I tell ye, with a relic of the True Cross as was sent to Ireland by Pope Calixius, and a costly silver chalice of remarkable design that Saint Finnén himself used when he said the Mass. Mayhap ye've heard of our wee church upon the site of Finnén's first monastery, or mayhap ye came to us on pilgrimage? There were many pilgrims over the years, and such a pretty spot it was at the edge of the great Shillelagh wilderness.''

''Nay, Brother Énán, I was never among them.''

Rian's head rolled upon her lap. Annora glanced down and saw his tongue lick at a dribble of boiled milk.

''Do you see, Brother Énán? He moves of his own, I think.'' Annora held the cup to Rian's mouth to see if he might take a sip. She crooned, "Rian, can you hear me? I'm here, Rian."

"That's right," the monk encouraged. "Ye should be talking to yer man."

Again Rian's head moved. Again Annora whispered and offered some of the medicinal drink.

The first thing of which Rian was aware was a frothy warm liquid being poured down his throat. He smelled honey mingling with more bitter aromas, and he imagined someone was cradling his head, murmuring to him. There were voices fading in and out, coming near, then drifting afar. Sounds of the living world, he imagined. A rook crying, metal clattering, horses neighing, children laughing. He tried to open his eyes, but the lids wouldn't budge. He heard that sweet whisper float closer again, felt the drip of cool water and gentle daubing about his eyes. This time, when he tried, his lids came loose.

"He opens his eyes. Can you move, Brother Énán, to shield him with your body against the sun? 'Tis too bright, to be sure."

The monk positioned himself to cast a shadow over Rian, and then waited to see if the man would surface to consciousness.

In increments, Rian's sense of his surroundings was restored. Someone was holding him. His eyes opened, and staring upward, the shape hovering above him came into focus. It was a woman's face. She held him upon her lap and whispered to him, soft and gentle, smiling with tears in her eyes; and her pretty mouth trembled. Slowly, slowly, the image became clearer until there before him, below skies the color of wild clarie flowers, he saw an angel fair of face with a halo of pale yellow curls, and eyes as blue as the clarie sky.

"*Mo aingeal,*" he whispered. *My angel.* His throat hurt to speak, yet he forced out the words of concern. "Were ye not supposed to be waiting for me, *leannán?* Why are ye not at Imail?"

"I came to find you, to help if I might, and if needs be to—"

"Speak no more!" He knew she had come prepared to bury him. "Nay, I would not let that happen. Not yet. Not for a very long time." His eyes closed. The strain of talking was great, but there was something more he wished. "Would ye come closer to kiss me? Would ye set yer lips to mine?"

Annora blushed.

"I would taste yer sweetness," he drawled. "I would find strength and sustenance from their promising caress."

It was impossible to resist such a request, and Annora leaned down to Rian. Her hair tumbled over her shoulders, falling forward like a curtain behind which she hid to set her lips to his and kiss him tenderly.

"Why so maidenly? I would have ye in my arms, if I might. Indeed, I will have ye beneath me as soon as I have the strength." On a hush, Rian began to sing, *"Come, my honeyed-lassie, spread yer boughs a-wide for me. Laddie-cock's awaiting . . ."*

"Hush, Rian," she said. "Behave yourself. We have an audience." Annora straightened up, but the shameless smile upon her flushed face betrayed her. Only a fool would fail to discern what sort of bold, lusty temptations Rian had been whispering behind that lustrous golden fall of tresses. Only a fool would fail to notice how it had thrilled Annora to hear him talk of such things.

The monk gazed upon them. He was neither shocked nor disapproving. The life he'd chosen for himself had not destroyed his appreciation for the happiness men and women might find with one another. Indeed, Brother Énán owned a gratifying conceit from claiming some credit in reuniting two souls who would otherwise have been lost to each other. He coughed, then raised a hand to bless Rian. "I thank ye for saving the annals. They tell the story of these hills, and 'tis where they should always be staying. Ye're a courageous and bold warrior, Rian O'Byrne, and have proven yerself worthy to be granted their keeping.''

For a moment, Rian didn't know what the monk meant, then he remembered the leather satchel and became aware of his fingers entwined about the strap. ''I was glad to do what I might. Here, ye must be taking them back.''

The monk motioned his refusal. He would not accept the satchel from Rian. ''They are not mine to be taking. 'Tis my intention to journey onward in the footsteps of our founder to Clonard, and in my absence I ask that ye, Rian O'Byrne, guard the *Annals of Finnén* in my stead.''

''Ye need not be going to Clonard,'' said Rian. ''The O'Byrnes would welcome ye at Aghavannagh, to be sure.''

''Nay, I must be joining others of my ilk, and will be satisfied to know the annals remain near their place of origin. 'Tis a fine ending all around. Do ye not have the sense of some divine plan coming together? That mayhap it was the Lord's hand guiding each of us to this one point in time and space?''

''Perhaps,'' Rian replied in a solemn voice. ''The Lord Father is everywhere, I'm told, and I would never question His part in this. 'Tis honored I am that ye would consider me a deserving trustee for such a treasure, and there is something beyond mere guardianship I would pledge, if ye would allow. With yer blessing, brother, the chronicle can continue by our hand. My lady and I would be honored to continue yer work.''

''Ye can scribe?''

''Aye, the both of us.''

Annora was not certain what touched her more deeply, whether it was hearing Rian's acceptance of faith or witnessing his generous willingness to accept responsibility for the chronicle and its future. She reached out to wrap her hand over Rian's, where he held the leather strap. Her throat burned with tears, yet she found the voice to speak, "Aye, Brother Énán, we would continue your work, and in time, train our kin to scribe with the intention of recording the events of these hills as did the monks of St. Finnén for so many centuries before us."

Rian's fingers entwined with Annora's, and he smiled at her, at Brother Énán, at Fate and God, and the future. Indeed, he might almost laugh, might almost whoop with joy, but he merely held tight to Annora and said with a lopsided grin, "There will, of course, be more of human frailty and of earthly emotions in our version, ye must be warned."

"As along as ye write the truth," replied Brother Énán. "That is all one would ask. The truth. Let yer pen, and those who would record history, always speak the truth."

Epilogue

<figure>～∽⌒○○⌒∽～</figure>

Aghavannagh
The Eve of the Feast of Saint Finnén of Clonard, 1419

Harsh winds battered the fortress. A December storm was coming, and by morning, the passes would be covered with snow and ice. But Annora worried not. Her loved ones were within the ramparts, snug and safe, even her eldest daughter had arrived from Dún Ard with her O'Toole husband and children.

The O'Byrne clan was gathered in the hall as had become their tradition this Eve of the Feast of Saint Finnén. The eldest among them was Rian's aunt, an O'Connor by birth and widow of the old chieftain. The youngest was a wee cousin named Cianán, not but two weeks of age. Of course, there was Annora's and Rian's firstborn, Liam, who was a warrior as handsome and bold as his father ever was, with his wife and three lads by his side; there was Riona, with the burnished hair of her father, come from Dún Ard, who already had a boy and a girl, and a belly swollen with a third bairn expected to come into the world during the twelve days of Christmas. Their youngest daughter, Étaín, a pretty girl of sixteen springs, who had countless warriors wishing to wed her, sat to the right of her father's place at the chieftain's table, and beside Étaín was Annora's and Rian's babe, Diarmait, a lad of twelve years.

It was a festive occasion, this gathering of the clan on this particular night. Garlands of holly and ivy decorated the rafters, clumps of mistletoe hung above the arched doorway, and a great feast of roasted boar, beeves in fruit, salmon, trout, and the finest cheese, toasted breads, and savories had been consumed. Much *uisce beatha* had been passed round in drinking horns, and now the jovial company quieted.

Rian stood beside Annora. They were as ever a handsome couple, physically vigorous, and much admired for their devotion to one another and their family. Indeed, it was many a father who admonished a wayward son to follow the path of Rian O'Byrne of Aghavannagh, and many a mother who advised a daughter to look to the chieftain's wife as an example of the ideal balance a woman might attain between admirable independence and wifely obedience.

As Rian did each Eve of the Feast of Saint Finnén, he opened a leather satchel, removed a bound vellum manuscript, and passed it to his wife.

"A.D. 1399. King Richard of England arrived in Ireland this May, of a purpose to make war upon Art MacMurrough, king of Leinster, by whom he and his army were mightily weakened and brought low in the Wicklow mountains," Annora began to read aloud from the *Annals of Finnén*. This was the first entry she and Rian had composed. *"Also this year, Onóra, daughter of Cassán of Imail, returned to the hills from living nearly three decades among the English of Dublin, and she was married to Rian O'Byrne, a warrior of Aghavannagh, who had escaped out of prison from the English, and into whose trust the care and continuation of this chronicle was passed by Brother Énán. In noble battle against the English did warriors of valor breathe their last, notably Niall O'Connor of Baravore, Áedh of Bealach Conglais,*

and the two youngest sons of Dallán O'Byrne. The reign of King Richard ended in the autumn of this year.''

"What happened to the English king?'' asked one of the children who was too young to recall the tale from the previous December. "Did he leave Ireland?''

"Whilst he was in Dublin, his rivals declared their intention to seize his throne. Aye, Richard did leave Ireland, and upon his return to England, he was arrested by order of his cousin. Shortly after the new year, he was dead,'' said Annora. "And although he lived weakly and set an example not to be followed, 'tis said he died like a king.'' She handed the chronicle to Rian. It was his turn to read in this ceremony that had evolved of its own over the years.

"*A.D. 1400,*'' began Rian. "*One of the English of Dublin, Sir Thomas Picot, a well-disposed gentleman, appeared among the Irish seeking shelter, and was given hospitality first by Fínán O'Toole at Castlekevin and then by the O'Byrnes of Aghavannagh, wherein the English knight makes a home. A.D. 1401. The lady Íde, daughter of Teige O'Toole, and three times a widow having been wife to Cassán, Phelim, and Rígán, died after good penance and having witnessed the birth of her granddaughter, Riana, about whose neck the child's mother placed a small wooden cross. The son of the new English king, Henry IV, arrived at Dublin, but no settlers returned to farmsteads in Leinster, nor did any soldiery of the English venture into these mountains.*''

As the monks had done for centuries Annora and Rian recorded each year's most notable events in *The Annals of Finnén*. It was filled with the joys and sufferings of the Irishry of the Leinster hills, their wars and victories, deaths and births, marriages and lines of succession. They had also been teaching their children to scribe, and to prepare for the day when they would assume responsibility for the annals. The O'Byrne children and their cousins could read and scribe, and each grandchild upon the occasion of his or her third birthday was allowed the opportunity to hold the chronicle, to study the lettering, and to scratch at a worn bit of vellum with a quill. For the past two years, it was the youngest daughter, Étaín, who had been maintaining the chronicle. As had become tradition, she was asked to stand this night and read aloud her first entry. It recorded the death of Art Mac-Murrough.

"*A.D. 1417. Art, King of Leinster, the son of Art, son of Murtogh, son of Maurice, lord of Leinster, who defended his province against Richard of the English, died on the 7th day after Christmas,*" said the fair Étaín. She did not have to look at the words. She knew them by heart, so proud was she to have been granted the honor of composing and scribing this passage. Étaín was a beautiful young woman, intelligent, kind, generous, and as independent as her mother ever was. Thus far, she had not found an Irishman, though all were proper suitors, to satisfy her heart and soul. Many a man watched her this night, not a one of them realizing that only a warrior as bold as her father or an Irishman as accomplished as the great king Art himself would ever capture her. Yet they dreamed as they listened to her sweet voice. "*Let it be written in every annal of our land that Art MacMurrough, who served his race from the age of sixteen to his sixtieth year was distinguished for his diplomacy, hospitality, intelligence, leadership of men, and rare success in arms; a man full of prosperity and royalty; a versifier, father, husband, and patron of the arts and religion, being the founder of churches and monasteries by his bounty and contributions.*"

When Étaín was done she handed the chronicle to her father. It was now time for one of the younger children to read a favorite passage. A cousin read a very old entry that referenced the abbot of Clonard in the time before the Anglo-Normans came to Ireland. The evening passed in this manner as boys and girls alike took turns, and with each reading did the awe and respect, the fondness and veneration for the little manuscript increase.

The rushlights were sputtering and the fire was burning low when one of Liam's lads insinuated himself onto Annora's lap. He wrapped his little boy arms about her waist and asked, "What is yer favorite passage, grandmother?"

Annora gazed into the bright face, so like her Liam's when he was a lad, and with eyes as blue as Rian's. She smiled, thinking to herself how this boy would one day be beckoning a young woman forth with those ocean blue eyes.

"What is yer favorite?" he repeated.

"I cannot pick one from the others," she replied. "There is my wedding to yer grandfather—I always love to hear of that—and each mention of my bairns when they were born. Every one of those recalls precious memories, such very precious memories, they are, and to pick a favorite would seem to me like selecting a favorite from between the loved ones in my life."

"Och, *leannán,* I have no such trouble. Indeed, 'tis knowing mine well, I do," Rian's deep voice had lost none of its rasping, sensual quality with the passage of the years. It echoed through the hall, and everyone looked to him, spellbound.

"Tell us," the lad said. "Tell us."

There followed much excitement as a flock of wee ones encircled Rian, urging their chieftain to reveal his favorite. One tiny girl with great blue eyes the color of clarie and flaxen curls looping round her face slipped through the other youngsters. She was Riona's lass, and Rian hoisted his only granddaughter onto his shoulders. She squealed in delight.

"You must tell us," said Annora.

He smiled at his wife, the love of his life, angel of his heart. Even now after all these years, he saw the pretty pink flush rising upon her cheeks, and knew why it was that she blushed. Rian knew she still thought of him and wanted him as a woman wanted a man, as he wanted her.

"My most favorite is this one, *A.D. 1407. Rian O'Byrne, son of Rónán, and grandson of Cathal, was this year affirmed as chieftain of the O'Byrnes of Aghavannagh, with his wife, Annora, sitting at his side for his solemn oath. There was much feasting and celebrating with kith and kin.*" He paused at this point to wink at Annora.

This caused quite a reaction in the hall. The children thought it amusing to see their chieftain acting like a bachelor warrior. They whispered about the possible meaning of such behavior. The little girl on Rian's shoulders giggled, and the older folk cast knowing looks between one another, for they remembered that the chieftain's youngest child, Diarmait, was born some nine months after that evening.

Annora's blush deepened, and she encouraged her husband to finish.

"Only if ye kiss me first," he whispered.

"And if I don't?"

"I may set this child down to toss ye over my shoulder and carry ye to our chamber at a running stride," Rian said on a low, teasing growl.

"You wouldn't dare," Annora gasped, but she knew he would. Quickly she rose on tiptoe to kiss her handsome, warrior husband.

With his free hand, Rian held her close to draw out the kiss. When he finished, she was breathless, and a roguish, lopsided grin marked his features.

Rian's voice carried through the hall, "*Also this year was built at Aghavannagh a stone structure to be used for schooling in the skills of scribing and illuminating, and for the storage of manuscripts such as the scribes of Aghavannagh might produce, this remarkable building being made possible through the generosity and bounty of the chieftain's wife, and being noted by visitors from afar for its three remarkable glass windows, one depicting a host of angels hovering above a summer meadow, a second depicting a child swimming with eels in a forest of lily roots, and a third with red roses and blue clarie blossoms against a background of swirling snow.''*

Author's Final Note

In the whole of some six centuries of histories, including hand-scribed chronicles as well as published works, the accounting of Richard II's campaign through the Wicklow mountains in the summer of 1399 has either been omitted altogether from texts or reduced to a footnote (literally).

No one knows the precise route taken, nor the precise numbers of women and children (somewhere between 2,500 and 5,000), or of English knights/soldiers and Irish warriors, who perished during those eleven days.

Please know that my fiction is based on accepted fact woven with meticulously measured conjecture that is intended to be as close to reality as a writer might attain in hindsight.

The one element that is mine alone is the use of the gunnes to blast at the forest. It is historically accepted that the English used guns during Richard's second expedition, but to what use is not specified.

I, however, stand by my fiction as presented herein. For what else would an enraged monarch, determined to hunt down his enemy in a dense primeval forest, and who happened to be lugging along gunpowder and blasting gunnes, have done with those weapons?

Avon Romances—
the best in exceptional authors and unforgettable novels!

Avon Romantic Treasures

*Unforgettable, enthralling love stories,
sparkling with passion and adventure
from Romance's bestselling authors*

LADY OF WINTER *by Emma Merritt*
77985-4/$5.99 US/$7.99 Can

SILVER MOON SONG *by Genell Dellin*
78602-8/$5.99 US/$7.99 Can

FIRE HAWK'S BRIDE *by Judith E. French*
78745-8/$5.99 US/$7.99 Can

WANTED ACROSS TIME *by Eugenia Riley*
78909-4/$5.99 US/$7.99 Can

EVERYTHING AND THE MOON *by Julia Quinn*
78933-7/$5.99 US/$7.99 Can

BEAST *by Judith Ivory*
78644-3/$5.99 US/$7.99 Can

HIS FORBIDDEN TOUCH *by Shelley Thacker*
78120-4/$5.99 US/$7.99 Can

LYON'S GIFT *by Tanya Anne Crosby*
78571-4/$5.99 US/$7.99 Can

Discover Contemporary Romances
at Their Sizzling Hot Best
from Avon Books

RYAN'S RETURN   *by Barbara Freethy*
78531-5/$5.99 US/$7.99 Can

CATCH ME IF YOU CAN   *by Jillian Karr*
77876-9/$5.99 US/$7.99 Can

WINNING WAYS   *by Barbara Boswell*
72743-9/$5.99 US/$7.99 Can

CARRIED AWAY   *by Sue Civil-Brown*
72774-9/$5.99 US/$7.99 Can

**LOVE IN A
SMALL TOWN**   *by Curtiss Ann Matlock*
78107-7/$5.99 US/$7.99 Can

HEAVEN KNOWS BEST   *by Nikki Holiday*
78797-0/$5.99 US/$7.99 Can

FOREVER ENCHANTED   *by Maggie Shayne*
78746-6/$5.99 US/$7.99 Can